Illidan

William King

DEL REY

NEW YORK

Published in the United States by Del Rey,
an imprint of Random House,
a division of Penguin Random House LLC, New York.

DEL REY and the HOUSE colophon are
registered trademarks of Penguin Random House LLC.

WARCRAFT, WORLD OF WARCRAFT, and BLIZZARD ENTERTAINMENT are
trademarks and/or registered trademarks of Blizzard Entertainment, Inc.,
in the US and/or other countries. All other trademark references herein
are the properties of their respective owners.

ISBN 978-0-399-17756-9
ebook ISBN 978-0-399-17758-3

Printed in the United States of America on acid-free paper

randomhousebooks.com
blizzard.com

2 4 6 8 9 7 5 3 1

First Edition

Book design by Barbara M. Bachman

For my son Dan,
who accompanied me there
and back again

BLADE'S EDGE
MOUNTAINS

ZANGARMARSH

NAGRAND

TEROKKAR
FOREST

Outland

NETHERSTORM

HELLFIRE
PENINSULA

SHADOWMOON
VALLEY

Illidan

Six Years Before the Fall

THE ANCIENT DARKNESS SURROUNDING HIM DID NOT STOP him from seeing any more than his lack of eyes did. He had been a sorcerer once, a very great one. His spectral sight revealed every inch of his cell with far more clarity than eyes of flesh ever could.

He could navigate this prison even without it. He knew every flagstone on the floor, every enchantment that bound him. He knew them by sight, by touch. He knew the way his footsteps would echo with every one of the nine steps it took him to pace across the chamber. He felt the flows of magic all around. Spell after spell, enchantment after enchantment, their soul-crushing power intended to do only one thing: make sure he stayed buried here, unremembered, unforgiven.

The ones who incarcerated him intended this place to be his tomb. They had forgotten about him over the long millennia. They should have killed him. It would have been kinder. Instead they let him live, pretending it was mercy. It let those who had bound him—such as his brother, Malfurion Stormrage, and Tyrande Whisperwind, the woman he loved—feel better about themselves.

Long centuries had dragged by when he never heard the voice

of another living thing. Only his jailors, the Watchers, spoke to him occasionally, and he had learned to hate them. Most of all he had come to abhor their leader, Warden Maiev Shadowsong. She visited him more than any other, still afraid he would escape despite all the precautions his captors had taken. Once, she had wanted him dead. Now it was her task in life to ensure he stayed imprisoned, when everyone else had forgotten him.

What was that? A faint tremor in the ring of binding spells?

Impossible. There was no escape from this place. Not even death. Spells healed any harm he might inflict on himself. Magic kept him alive without need for water or food. Those bonds had been woven by masters, drawn so tight, intertwined so deeply, that they could be undone only by those who had buried him alive. And they would never do that. They were too afraid to let him go free. Justifiably so.

He had brooded for centuries on what he would do to those who had incarcerated him. Time was the only thing he had. The span of his imprisonment dwarfed all the years he had been free. If he had not been who he was, he would have gone mad.

Perhaps he had. How many thousands of years had it been since he was imprisoned? He had lost track. That was the worst of it. Millennia spent in darkness, trapped in this cage, unable to take more than nine steps in any direction. He who had once hunted demons across the trackless wildernesses of Azeroth had been confined in a place he would not have left an animal.

They had sentenced him to this when all he had done was try to overcome their common foe. He had infiltrated the Burning Legion, his people's—no, his world's—sworn enemy. He had tried to undo the harm the demonic invaders had wreaked.

Had he been rewarded for it? No! He had been buried alive. His people had assumed him to be a traitor, a betrayer. They had hailed him as a hero once, but no one did that now. If he was remembered at all, his name would be a curse.

Was that the sound of weapons clashing? He pushed the thought aside. Refused to let hope well up within his breast. There was no one out there who wanted him free. His family and his friends had turned against him when he had tried to re-create the Well of Eternity, the night elves' ancient fount of magic, on Mount Hyjal. The only ones who might want him to escape were demons. His jailors would kill him rather than let that happen. And as long as the wards remained in place, there was nothing he could do to stop them.

But there it was again. Another tremor in the flows of magic around him. The weaves of power that had bound him all this time were weakening. He raised his hands in front of his face, flexed his fingers, reached out to draw upon the magic. For the first time in millennia, something responded, a trickle so weak that he thought he might be imagining it. He called on his twin blades, the Warglaives of Azzinoth. They had been displayed triumphantly on weapon racks outside his cell, taunting him, but now the ancient soulbindings linking them to him caused the potent weapons to materialize in his hands. Power flowed through them, illumining the runes on their blades.

His heart beat faster. His mouth felt dry. There was a chance of freedom after all. He clutched the warglaives tight. In the past, they had killed demons. Now they would kill elves. The thought did not disturb him as once it would have. He would even take pleasure in it.

Again his magical shackles flickered. The sounds of combat came closer. Some of the bindings had failed. Perhaps they were desecrated by spilled blood or ruined by the spells he sensed being unleashed in the battle. Energy poured into him as his bonds frayed. His heart pounded. His flesh tingled. He felt as if he might exhale fire. After such long abstinence, the flow of power was almost overwhelming.

He sensed a presence outside the doorway of his cell. He prepared himself to attack. A voice spoke, and it was the last one he had expected to hear.

"Illidan, is that you?" Tyrande Whisperwind asked.

All his dreams of vengeance, all his plans for retribution, faded away, as if the long years of his imprisonment had never happened. He was astonished by the feeling; he had thought himself hardened against anything and anyone—especially her.

His speech was rusty after decades of disuse. "Tyrande . . . it is you! After all these ages spent in darkness, your voice is like the pure light of the moon upon my mind."

He cursed himself for his weakness. These were not the words he had imagined saying in his dreams of freedom and escape. Yet they rose unbidden to his lips, hope welling in his chest. Perhaps she had seen the error of what she had done. Perhaps she had come to free him, to forgive him.

"The Legion has returned, Illidan. Your people have need of you once more."

His fists clenched around his weapons. "*My* people need me? My people left me to rot!" His throat constricted with rage, choking off more words. The demons had returned, as he had always known they would, and his people *wanted* his aid. Molten anger blazed through him, creating a great void in its wake, and more power flowed in to fill the emptiness.

No doubt about it—the spells binding him were weakened. By her actions, by the loosening of her will, Tyrande had helped undo them.

He concentrated all his fury and all his pent-up frustration into one mighty spell of unraveling. For a moment the weakened chains of magic held, but only for a moment. Rivers of power eroded the barriers around him. Slowly at first, but ever faster, the imprisoning spells crumbled. He smashed through the bars of his cell, tearing apart the stone.

Tyrande stood there, beautiful as ever, staring at Illidan. The years had not changed her. She was still tall, with pale-violet skin and blue hair, graceful as a temple dancer and lovely as a moonrise over Nordrassil. She reeked of blood and unleashed magic. She must have seen his rage, for she turned away, unable to meet his gaze. That hurt more than anything, to see her cringe after all the long years since last they had met.

"Because I once cared for you, Tyrande, I will hunt down the demons and topple the Legion." He bared his teeth in a snarl. "But I will never owe *our* people anything!"

She met his gaze this time. Emotions flickered over her face. Hope. Fear. Was that pity or regret? He was not sure and he despised himself for placing so much value on what she thought. What she felt meant nothing to him! Nothing!

Tyrande said, "Then let us hurry back to the surface! The demons' corruption spreads with every second we waste."

And that was it. All the greeting he was going to get after the long, wasted millennia. No apologies. No remorse. She had helped cast him into this dreadful place, and now she needed his aid. And the worst of it was that he would give it.

BODIES LAY STREWN OUTSIDE his cell. It was clear that there had been a mighty battle here and that Tyrande had fought her way in to free him. She must be desperate indeed to perform such an act. Looking down at the massive carcass of the keeper of the grove, he realized that if the Burning Legion had returned, she had reason to be. The Legion destroyed worlds the way armies destroyed cities.

"Did you slay him?" Illidan asked, pointing at the dead body of Califax.

"I did," said Tyrande. "The keeper of the grove would not let you loose."

Illidan laughed. "Maiev will be angry. He was one of her favorites."

Tyrande's face flushed. "This is not a reason for laughter," she said.

"I have had little enough cause for mirth in the thousands of years since you imprisoned me. Forgive me if my sense of humor seems a little warped."

"Ten thousand," she said.

"What?"

"It has been more than ten thousand years since you were imprisoned."

The laughter died on his lips. The weight of her words pressed down on him like the weight of the earth above their heads.

"So long," he said, his voice soft. He looked at the ancient vault of his prison, traced the weave of the spells that had held him. He lengthened his stride, determined to leave this place and never come back.

"Why did you really set me free?" he asked, still hoping that she might show some shred of remorse about what she had done.

"As I said, the Burning Legion has returned. No one knows more about them than you. No one has slain more demons."

"You do not fear my treachery, then? Remember, I am called the Betrayer."

"Betrayer you were, but in the end you chose the right side."

He gestured at his surroundings with one tattooed hand. "And look what it got me."

"You could be dead. Like so many of our people."

"Our people. You keep harping on about our people. They are not *our* people. They are your people."

"Do you hate us so?"

"Yes," he said. His lip twisted into a sneer. "But fortunately for you, I hate the demons more."

She nodded as if he had confirmed something she wanted to hear. A suspicion flickered through his mind. He had been imprisoned not from any false act of mercy, but because she had known that one day he would again be needed. He had been stored here like a weapon hung in an armory.

Ahead he sensed a being of enormous—and familiar—power, his brother. He might have known that wherever Tyrande was, her lover, Malfurion, would be close by. Illidan's whole body tensed, prepared to spring into battle.

His companion sensed it as well. She rushed forward and then halted, barred by the mighty presence of the archdruid Malfurion Stormrage. Illidan's brother was massive. Antlers protruded from his head. His handsome face held a look of dismay at seeing Illidan free. Clearly the archdruid had not come to aid Tyrande.

Four Druids of the Claw flanked Malfurion, each in the form of a bear. They flexed their taloned paws and growled at Illidan. They had been set here to guard against his escape, and they seemed determined still to prevent it.

Tyrande said, "Mal!"

Illidan fought to keep his anger in check. Here was the brother who had condemned him. His words, when he found them, were bitter. "It has been an eternity, Brother. An eternity spent in darkness!"

Malfurion met his gaze evenly. "You were sentenced to pay for your sins, nothing more."

The hypocrisy of it was breathtaking. What sort of brother could condemn his own flesh and blood to ten thousand years entombed? "And who were you to judge me? We fought the demons side by side, if you recall!"

Tension crackled in the air between them. In that moment, they were both ready to fight, to kill.

Tyrande shouted, "Enough of this, both of you! What is done is done."

She focused the full force of her attention on Malfurion. "My love, with Illidan's help, we will drive the demons back once again and save what is left of our beloved land!"

Malfurion shook his head. "Have you even considered the cost, Tyrande? This betrayer's aid may doom us all before the end. I will have nothing to do with this."

Illidan schooled his face to impassivity. His own brother obviously still thought of him as nothing but a monster, a puppet for the Legion. He would show him. He would show them all that the demons had no power over him.

"Cower in your weakness and indecision, then, Brother, but do so elsewhere," Illidan said. "I have work to do. And little time to do it in."

Illidan sent forth a burst of energy from the power he had been steadily regaining, tossing those assembled around him into the stone walls. He strode past the dazed forms and out of his prison, knowing in his heart that before this was over, he would be named Betrayer once more, and he would deserve it.

He was never going to be imprisoned again.

CHAPTER ONE

Four Years Before the Fall

GREEN METEORS RIPPED THROUGH THE DARK CLOUDS that perpetually obscured the heavens over Shadowmoon Valley. The ground shook as the monstrously ornate demonic siege engines on the walls of the Black Temple rained death down on the blood elf forces of Prince Kael'thas Sunstrider, strewing the red earth of Outland with their corpses. Despite their losses, the elves pushed forward, determined to take the citadel of Magtheridon, lord of Outland, the Burning Legion's satrap in this shattered world.

Illidan paused for a moment and studied the Black Temple. To inexperienced eyes, the defenses might look immeasurably strong, but he saw that they had been neglected. There were too few sentries for the span of the towering walls, the warding spells were starting to unravel, and the metal struts of the gates were stained with rust and verdigris. The defenders responded slowly, as if they could not quite believe they were being assaulted by a force so much smaller than their own. Perhaps they expected to be relieved by demonic allies. If so, they were doomed to disappointment. Illidan and his companions had spent the whole long, hot Outland day sealing the gates through which the demons were summoned. No aid was coming from that source.

Illidan glanced over at Prince Kael'thas. "Magtheridon has grown strong over the years, but he has had few real foes to contend with. He has become decadent and complacent. The boisterous cur cannot match our cunning or our will."

The tall, fair blood elf prince looked up at him. The fierce joy of combat blazed in his eyes. "This will be a glorious battle, master. Though Magtheridon's forces vastly outnumber ours, your soldiers are prepared to fight to the end."

Illidan hoped that would not prove necessary. He needed to seize the Black Temple and mastery of Outland quickly if he was to make himself secure against the vengeance of the demon lord Kil'jaeden. Kil'jaeden had set Illidan a task after he rejoined the Burning Legion—to destroy the Frozen Throne and hence eliminate a rebellious servant—and he had not completed it. The Deceiver did not reward failure. Illidan believed that closing the demonic portals could thwart Kil'jaeden's attempts to locate him. Winning this fortress would give him a stronger base of operations for keeping the portals closed.

An elven sorcerer raised his hand and sent a bolt of arcane energy lancing toward the walls. Badly maintained or not, the defenses were enough to prevent it from striking the siege engine. A ball of fire arced down toward the mage, gouging the blood-red earth as the defenders sought his range. A company of Kael'thas's soldiers raced past en route to the shelter of the walls.

Illidan clenched his fists as he sensed the demons within the temple. Here in the foreign world of Outland, he felt the temptation of demonic magic even more strongly than usual, especially after he had consumed the potency within the Skull of Gul'dan. The surge of evil energy from that artifact had transformed him, changing both his physical form and the depth of his power, but it had put him off balance for months. He flexed his newly gained demonic wings, earning a concerned glance from Prince Kael'thas. Illidan took a deep breath and forced himself to be calm.

It was a long, strange road that had brought him to this pass. Since Tyrande had freed him, he had seen the overthrow of the Burning Legion on his homeworld of Azeroth, made a pact with a demon lord, and fled to Outland to evade his enemies, both night elven and demonic. He had been recaptured by his old nemesis, Maiev, and then freed by his allies, the young prince Kael'thas— whose allegiance Illidan had earned by pledging to help the blood elves sate their addiction to magic—and Lady Vashj, a leader of the naga. Now he found himself scheming to overthrow the pit lord who ruled this shattered world in the name of the Burning Legion.

Kael'thas stared at him, expecting an answer to his promise of loyalty. Illidan said, "I am pleased by your people's zeal, young Kael. Their spirits and powers have been honed in this harsh wilderness. Their courage alone may be enough to—"

"Lord Illidan, new arrivals come to greet you." The voice of Lady Vashj cut him off as she slithered into view. Great bands of muscle pulsed and bulged as she moved, twisting the coils of her lower body. Her oddly beautiful face, reminiscent of a night elf's, contrasted with the horror of her serpentine form.

Illidan turned to look in the direction she indicated. A pack of monstrous figures lumbered into view. Illidan recognized them at once. They were Broken, corrupted and devolved former members of the draenei race who had inhabited Draenor before it was shattered into Outland. They, too, were part of Illidan's coalition, bound to him by promises of aid against their common enemy, Magtheridon.

The Broken were hulking, ungraceful monsters, bearing primitive weapons in their huge hands. Illidan's mystical senses detected that more of them were nearby, potent magic concealing them from those who lacked his spectral sight.

One of the Broken, even more massive and twisted of form than the rest, limped forward on hoofed feet. "We have fought the orcs and their demon masters for generations," the figure said. His voice rasped from within his chest. It seemed to pain him to speak. "Now, at last, we will end their curse forever. We are yours to command, Lord Illidan."

It was Akama, leader of the Broken. He was not a reassuring figure. Fangs jutted up from his lower jaw. Tentacles writhed out from the bottom half of his face.

"You have arrived just in time," said Illidan. "Those machines on the walls must be silenced, and the gate must be opened."

Akama nodded and gestured. The near-invisible Broken swarmed forward across the open ground and clambered up the walls of the Black Temple. A small force of blood elves and naga took shelter against the monstrous fortifications, beneath the firing arcs of the demonic engines. Illidan, Kael'thas, and Lady Vashj moved to join them, along with Akama and his bodyguards.

Once again, the so-called lord of Outland's overconfidence was revealed. A properly prepared fortress would have vats of boiling oil or alchemical fire ready to pour down on attackers. The defenders did nothing. Long minutes ticked by. This close to the walls, Illidan could hear the hum of the magical generators that powered the demonic war machines.

Suddenly the sounds of combat came from within the walls, and the great gates of the Black Temple swung open. Akama and his bodyguards raced forward to join the fray. Explosions sounded as the Broken destroyed the generators, and the war machines on the walls fell silent. The main bulk of the naga and blood elf force advanced toward the gate once more.

Akama returned, hideous face jubilant. He had waited a long time for this day. Illidan smiled and said, "As I promised, your people shall have their vengeance, Akama. By night's end, we will all be drunk with it. Vashj, Kael, give the final order to strike. The hour of wrath has come!"

Through the open gates, Illidan could see a vast courtyard stacked high with bones. Red-skinned fel orcs milled around in confusion as their leaders bellowed commands and tried to get them into some semblance of order to repel the invaders.

Within the Black Temple, there were probably ten fel orcs for every one of Illidan's troops. Each had been twisted by foul magic into something far stronger and fiercer than a normal orc. It counted for nothing now. Illidan's forces swept into the courtyard, a tight wedge that cleaved through their disorganized enemy as easily as their blades sliced orcish flesh.

Illidan plunged his talons into the chest of a fel orc. Bone crunched as he closed his fingers and ripped open a cavity to pull the heart free. The fel orc roared and lunged forward, jaws snapping in an attempt to tear out Illidan's throat even as the creature died.

Illidan raised the corpse above his head and tossed it into the onrushing squad of red-skinned defenders. Its weight bowled them over, sending them tumbling to the ground. He leapt amid them, freeing his warglaives from their sheaths. He lashed out, striking to left and right with irresistible force. His enemies fell, decapitated, limbless, mutilated. Blood covered him. He licked it from his lips and moved forward, slashing and slicing as he went.

All around, the dying screamed. Magic thundered as Prince Kael'thas and Lady Vashj unleashed their spells. Illidan was tempted to do so himself, but he wanted to preserve his strength for the final conflict with Magtheridon.

Part of him took pleasure in the clash of arms. There was nothing quite like shedding the blood of your foes with your own hands. Deep within him, the chained demon part of his nature enjoyed feeding this way.

The fel orcs fought well, but they were no match for Illidan and his comrades. The naga were much larger and more physically powerful. They wrapped their enemies within their serpentine coils and squeezed the life out of them.

The blood elves were masters of sorcery and swords. They might not be as strong as the fel orcs, but they were faster and more agile, and bonds of loyalty stronger than life itself drove them to defend their prince.

The Broken fought with the determination of a people driven to free their homeland from the grip of demons. The howls of dying fel orcs rose to the heavens in protest as they dropped before the hungry blades of their enemies. Within minutes the courtyard was cleared, the fel orcs were routed, and the way into the Black Temple's inner citadel and Magtheridon's chambers lay open.

"Victory is ours," said Akama. "The Temple of Karabor will belong to my people once again."

"The temple will be returned to your people," Illidan said. He replaced his warglaives in their sheaths. "In good time." It was true. He fully intended to give back the Black Temple to the Broken. Once he had achieved his goals.

Akama looked at him with rheumy eyes. He interlaced his stubby fingers and bobbed his head, his need to believe etched on his face. The Temple of Karabor had been the most sacred site of his people before Magtheridon's desecration turned it into the Black Temple. Illidan sensed it had a deep personal significance to the Broken himself. That was a string that could be tugged to make him dance, if the need arose. Not that what Akama wanted counted for anything. Illidan's purpose far outweighed the desires of any Broken. He had planned too long to let scruples stand in his way.

"When we overcome the pit lord, most of his fel orc lieutenants will support us," Illidan said. "They follow the strongest, and we will have shown that their faith in Magtheridon was misplaced.

Such summoned demons as remain within the temple will be bound in fealty to me, or they will die their final death."

Vashj nodded. "Cut off the head and the body falls," she said.

"You will slay Magtheridon, Lord?" Akama asked.

Illidan allowed himself a cruel smile. "We shall do much worse than that," he said.

"And what would that be?" Akama spoke slowly. Illidan heard the doubt in his voice. Clearly, Akama had reservations about what they were doing.

"You will need to wait and see," Illidan said.

"As you wish, Lord," Akama said. "So shall it be."

"Then let us be about our business," said Illidan. "We have a world to conquer."

THE DOORWAY TO THE throne room slid open. The stench of demon assaulted Illidan's nostrils. Flames leapt around Magtheridon's throne of bones. The pit lord loomed more than five times the height of a blood elf, a centaur-like creature with two arms and a quadruped lower half, as massive as a dragon. Magtheridon's legs were like the columns supporting the roof of some ancient temple. They lifted his underbelly so high that an elf could walk beneath it. In one huge hand, he held a glaive as long as the mast of an ocean-going ship, weighty as a battering ram. Flanking him were two gigantic, batwinged doomguard, each almost as tall as their master, and a force of lesser demons. Illidan sensed their power and their hostility.

The pit lord turned his burning eyes upon Illidan. When he spoke, his voice was deep and guttural. "I do not know you, stranger, but your power is vast. Are you an agent of the Legion? Have you been sent here to test me?"

Illidan laughed. "I have come to replace you. You are a relic,

Magtheridon, a ghost of a past age. The future is mine. From this moment on, Outland and all its denizens will bow to me."

The pit lord lumbered forward, raising his gigantic glaive. The earth shook beneath his tread. "I will crush you like the insect you are. I will feast upon your pulped flesh and devour your soul with it."

He spoke with the overweening self-confidence of one who thought his might was unchallengeable. His demonic bodyguards advanced. Illidan sprang, warglaives scything through the air to bite into demon flesh. His blow slashed the arm from a felguard, forcing the creature to drop his axe. A heartbeat later Illidan's left-hand warglaive sliced his opponent open from neck to groin.

Illidan's own forces advanced into the fray. The doomguard were mighty, but they were few. Buffeted by the spells of Kael'thas and Vashj and surrounded by assailants, the doomguard were slain like bears being dragged down by a pack of hounds.

Illidan bounded forward to confront Magtheridon himself. The pit lord's huge glaive crashed down, biting into the stone where Illidan had stood. He was already away, rolling between the lord of Outland's columnar legs, hamstringing each of the front ones with a double swipe of his blades. The pit lord roared with fury and struck again. Illidan tumbled forward under his foe's belly, drawing forth ichor with his strikes. He vaulted onto Magtheridon's massive tail, ran up his spine, and drove his blades into the demon's thick neck.

From Illidan's vantage point, he could see that his forces had felled the pit lord's bodyguards. The demons were finished. Illidan raised his hands high and chanted the spell of binding. A wave of unleashed magical energy hit the pit lord. Magtheridon flinched as the spell began to bite.

Illidan's heart thundered as he exerted his will. He felt as if he were engaged in a tug-of-war with a giant. Magtheridon's advance slowed. His face twisted as if he, too, felt the strain.

"You are strong—for a mortal," the pit lord said.

"I am not a mortal," said Illidan.

"Anything that can be killed is mortal."

Sweat beaded on Illidan's brow. His breath rasped from his chest. He spread his wings and rose into the air above Magtheridon, signaling the others. It was time. Lady Vashj nodded, raised her hands, and began to chant. Lines of fire blazed across Illidan's sight, forming intricate patterns around the pit lord. Magtheridon roared as he understood what was happening.

Illidan fed more power into the spell. The pit lord stood transfixed, unable to proceed. His tombstone-sized fangs glistened, reflecting the light of magical energy. He reared up, fighting against the magic as much with his huge strength as with his own sorcerous might.

Illidan strained against him and glanced at Prince Kael'thas. The blood elf licked his lips like an epicure catching sight of a feast. All this unleashed magic clearly aroused something within him.

"Kael'thas," Illidan croaked. His words carried to the elf's ears. Kael'thas spread his arms and added his voice to the spell. Colossal magical energies smashed down. The spell locked into place. The pit lord screamed his rage and defiance, but to no avail. He was held by bindings so strong, not even he could overcome them. Illidan smiled. Victory was his. The first stage of his long-dreamed plan was complete.

AKAMA LISTENED AS LORD ILLIDAN howled the final words of binding. Magtheridon stood frozen, impotent, and full of baffled rage. He flexed his mighty body, but he was held.

It was done. The pit lord was vanquished. The defeat of Akama's people had been avenged. The Temple of Karabor would be free of the demon's baleful influence.

Akama allowed himself a moment of triumph. His strength,

combined with that of the outworld sorcerers, had been enough to overcome even so potent a demon as Magtheridon.

Illidan descended to the ground. His wings snapped closed and slumped around his shoulders, and the glow faded from his magical tattoos. His arms dropped. Akama rushed to his side.

"Victory is ours, oh lord," Akama said.

"Yes, faithful Akama, it is," Illidan said. Was there a note of mockery in the way he stressed the word *faithful*? It mattered not.

"You have freed the Temple of Karabor."

"We have freed the Temple of Karabor."

"May I ask when I may begin, Lord?"

"Begin what?"

A cold hand clutched at Akama's heart. He looked up at Illidan's face. He could not read the expression there. The demon hunter's features were a mask. A strip of runecloth concealed his empty eye sockets. Perhaps it was to be as Akama had feared all along.

"We must purify the temple, Lord, and prepare it to be returned to holiness. My brethren and I will work day and night to finish the required rituals. It will be as if Magtheridon's vile touch never tainted this place."

Illidan nodded slowly. "There will be time for that afterward."

"Afterward, Lord Illidan?"

"After my business is concluded. There is much to do before Outland is freed."

"But the temple is free now, is it not, Lord?"

"Nowhere is free while the Burning Legion reaches out for conquest. We must fortify this place. It must become a beacon to all who oppose the demons."

Akama swallowed his disappointment. He had been half expecting something like this. He let none of his thoughts show on his face. Instead he cast his eyes down and said, "It is, no doubt, as you say, Lord Illidan. May I withdraw and share the glad news with my people?"

"You may," said Illidan. He paused for a moment and said, "The temple will be returned to the Broken, Akama. Just not today."

"Of course, Lord. I do not doubt it." Akama hurried out of Magtheridon's throne room. He must prepare to travel. He had business with one who might be able to help. As he departed, he noticed that Prince Kael'thas's mocking gaze followed him. The prince had known all along what was going to happen. So had Lady Vashj. Fortunately, the Broken had not entirely trusted Illidan's benevolence. Akama had laid such contingency plans as had seemed wise when entering into any agreement with one known as the Betrayer.

If the hunter of demons would not help him regain the Temple of Karabor, there were those who would. It was time to seek new allies. The holy place of Akama's people would be purified no matter what Illidan wanted.

ILLIDAN STOOD WITH KAEL'THAS and Vashj on the highest rooftop of the Black Temple, looking out over the bleak landscape of Shadowmoon Valley. The demon hunter had proclaimed his victory to the world of Outland from the battlements, but now he was restless. He did not feel as triumphant as he had expected. Instead he felt a sense of growing dread.

In the distance the sky was red as blood. Crimson clouds raced toward the Black Temple. Powerful winds plucked at Illidan's wings. Rivers of reddish dust flowed through the air. Illidan's skin tingled, and he noticed motes of fel magic all around.

Prince Kael'thas shouted, "What is this, Vashj? Where did this storm come from?"

The naga matron replied, "Keep your head down, fool! Something terrible is drawing near!"

The motes of magic grew brighter. A shimmering aura formed in the air near the roof, coalescing into a gigantic glowing figure. It hovered above them, large as a fortress tower. Something about its shape reminded Illidan of the Broken, of the draenei. It was horned. Its skin burned, and flames flickered around its hooves, illuminating its whole body. It radiated power that dwarfed even that of the pit lord. Illidan knew he was once more in the presence of Kil'jaeden, the demon lord who commanded much of the Burning Legion.

Kil'jaeden glared down at Illidan. "Foolish little mongrel. You failed to destroy the Frozen Throne as I commanded. And still you thought to hide from me in this forsaken backwater! I thought you to be more cunning, Illidan."

It was impossible to do anything but meet Kil'jaeden's gaze. The Deceiver's eyes were magnetic. They compelled adoration and awe. They held an infinity of promises and an eternity of terrors.

A link was established between them. The thrill of contact was electric. Illidan felt Kil'jaeden's cruel mind inspect his own. He caught flickers of his adversary's surface thoughts. He saw worlds laid to waste, empires become playthings, ultimate power answer to the will of this mighty being and his servants. It was all part of the Deceiver's technique of seduction. *This, too, can be yours,* those eyes promised, and they left no doubt about the truth of that pledge. Obey Kil'jaeden, and your enemies would be destroyed, your dreams of dominion fulfilled. Whatever you wished could be yours. Disobey Kil'jaeden, and . . .

A moment that Illidan had long dreaded and long planned for had finally arrived. He could not afford to let the Deceiver read his true thoughts. There were things he did not want Kil'jaeden to see, schemes the demon lord must not uncover until it was too late.

He felt the enormous force of Kil'jaeden's will being brought to bear. The demon lord's power crashed down on him like a tidal wave. He braced himself against it, held it in check, then allowed the outer walls of his mind's defenses to collapse. Illidan reinforced the second layer of protection and slowly, carefully let it crumble as if it were beyond his strength to resist. As he did so he invoked the spells he had prepared for this moment. Subtly and near imperceptibly his secrets vanished, buried deep within the vaults of his mind. At the same time, he allowed Kil'jaeden's probe to smash through the final barrier and invade what appeared to be his innermost thoughts.

He felt the colossal, intrusive presence of the demon lord. It riffled through his memories. It inspected the web of his recollections, searching, searching, searching . . .

Illidan kept parts of his mind sealed, as any sorcerer would. Everyone had dark secrets and longings that they wanted no one to see. Kil'jaeden understood such things, as he understood the weaknesses of all living beings. Illidan had left him some tempting morsels while shielding entire levels of his mind behind wards of misdirection.

The probe did not seek his hidden secrets. Instead it went directly to the memories of recent events. Images flickered through Illidan's mind, pulled to the surface by Kil'jaeden's curiosity.

Illidan once again entered the corrupted forest of Felwood, keen to prove to his brother he was no tool of the demons. He heard the ring of warglaive against ancient enchanted blade as he battled the human traitor Prince Arthas, servant of the Lich King, the being who led the undead army known as the Scourge. They fought to a standstill. Arthas tempted him with knowledge of the location of the Skull of Gul'dan. Illidan knew he had to seek it out . . .

He felt once more the surge of ecstatic power as he broke the seals on the skull and transformed into a demon. He used the artifact's unleashed might to overcome the dreadlord Tichondrius—who had taken command of the Scourge—and his host, but even in the moment of victory, Illidan knew defeat, for his brother and Tyrande saw his transformation and turned from him. He understood again there was nothing left for him but exile.

He sensed Kil'jaeden's malevolent amusement as Illidan relived his most recent meeting with the Deceiver. Kil'jaeden offered him a chance to rejoin the Legion if he would destroy the Frozen Throne and break the power of the rebellious Lich King. Malfurion thwarted Illidan's attempt, dooming him to flee Kil'jaeden's wrath. He felt Kil'jaeden pause as he assessed the sincerity of Illidan's effort.

He relived his flight to Outland, only to be recaptured by Maiev. Luckily, aid came in the form of Kael'thas and Vashj. Even the triumph of this very day and his overthrow of Magtheridon were scrutinized. He knew this time that Kil'jaeden was with him, watching the pit lord's defeat. The Deceiver did not care who ruled Outland, so long as they ruled in the Legion's name.

As suddenly as it had begun, the contact broke. The demon lord withdrew from Illidan's mind. He realized that what had felt like long hours passing had been the space between two heartbeats.

Illidan's heart pounded against his ribs. He was instants from destruction. At this moment, not even he could stand against the might of Kil'jaeden. If he was slain here, all his schemes and sacrifices would come to naught. He searched for the right words—they were the only weapons that could save him now. He put the appropriate note of pleading into his voice, knowing it would flatter the demon's vanity to think Illidan abased himself. "Kil'jaeden! I was merely set back. I am attempting to bolster my forces here. The Lich King will be destroyed, I promise you!"

The demon's gaze turned from Illidan to Vashj and then settled on Prince Kael'thas. Illidan knew that all of their lives hung in the balance. There was a moment of silence that seemed to stretch into an eternity before the demon spoke again. "Indeed? Still, these servitors you've gathered show some promise. I will give you one last chance, Illidan. Destroy the Frozen Throne, or face my eternal wrath!"

Fel energy surged. The blaze of light around Kil'jaeden intensified to the point of being unbearable, and when it faded, the demon lord was gone. Illidan exhaled a long breath. Had he done it? Had he concealed his true intentions from Kil'jaeden? Had he deceived the Deceiver? He supposed he would find out soon enough.

His fists clenched in rage at the thought of the way Kil'jaeden had treated him. *Like a puppet.* He fought his anger down. The time was coming when he would make his enemies pay for what they had done, even Kil'jaeden. Illidan just needed to wear the mask of obedience for a bit longer. To buy himself some time, he had to do what the Deceiver asked.

He glanced at his companions. They looked back at him with doubt in their eyes. Briefly he considered telling them of his plans, but he dismissed the idea. They, too, had been examined as he had been. They, too, had felt the demon lord's threats and blandishments. Who knew how they had responded in their secret hearts?

Illidan said, "Perhaps hiding here was not the most prudent decision. Still, the quest lies before us. Will you follow me into the cold heart of death itself?"

Lady Vashj coiled her serpent body beneath her and stretched her torso to its full height. "The naga are yours to command, Lord Illidan. Where you go, we follow."

Prince Kael'thas looked dazed, as was only natural after having caught the full attention of a demon lord. He pulled himself together and said, "The blood elves are yours as well, master. We will drive the Scourge before us and shatter the Frozen Throne as you command."

"We have some time yet," Illidan said. "There are things that I must do before we go. We must be prepared."

CHAPTER TWO

Four Years Before the Fall

MAIEV SHADOWSONG STUDIED THE PARCHED LAND, shielding her eyes from the blaze of the huge Outland sun with one gauntleted hand. Her gaze shifted from the dusty road to the hillside. She caught the scuttling movement of one of their alien pursuers as it ducked out of sight behind a boulder on the slope above them.

"I see our insectoid friends are still following us," Anyndra said.

Maiev glanced at her second-in-command. Like all night elves, Anyndra was tall and slender. The sweat-stained tabard of a Watcher clung to her. A red scarf held her green hair from her eyes. Anyndra would not have been Maiev's first choice as a lieutenant, but she had to work with what she had. The thirty troops strung out along the road behind her were the only survivors of the ambush that had ripped Illidan from her grasp mere weeks before. Lady Vashj and Prince Kael'thas would answer for the deaths they had caused freeing the Betrayer.

"The ravagers will not give up," Maiev said. "They are hungry."

"I have heard they take captives to feed to their hatchlings," Anyndra said. It did not surprise Maiev. Outland was a hideous place inhabited by monstrous creatures. Even her spell-woven armor could not entirely neutralize the heat. She wished she could wipe away the perspiration trickling down her brow, but her full-face helm prevented that. Instead she squinted at the ridge again. There were more of the scuttlers up there, a lot of them. Their movements reminded her of gigantic spiders.

In the distance she heard the blaring foghorn roar of a fel reaver, one of the titanic war machines that thundered across these parched wastes with earth-shaking strides. Two days ago the Watchers had barely managed to escape one. It had threatened to reduce them to a bloody pulp beneath its enormous demon-metal feet.

Maiev's nightsaber let out a fierce roar as if responding to the challenge. The other riding cats echoed the sound. Upslope, a ravager scuttled into view to investigate the source of the noise.

"I could put an arrow through that ravager's eye," said Anyndra, producing an arrow with her distinctive green-and-red fletching. She was proud of her skill with a bow and liked to display it every chance she got.

Maiev gave her a tight-lipped smile. "Why bother? There are thousands more of the creatures." She nudged her nightsaber into its long, loping stride. "Let them follow us if they wish. If they attack, we will teach them the folly of their ways. Otherwise, do not waste precious arrows."

The troops fell into line behind her, surveying their surroundings warily. Maiev knew she was going to have to keep a close watch on them. Back on Azeroth, she would never have doubted their commitment to the hunt, but here things were different. A few of her soldiers had had a wild look in their eyes ever since they had passed through the magical portal in pursuit of Illidan.

She took in another breath of the dry air. She had been places on Azeroth that were just as parched, but something about Hellfire Peninsula made her feel thirstier than she had been even in the desert of Tanaris. At least there, she had known the ocean was near. So far they had found no evidence that this place had a sea. As far as she could tell, Outland floated in a great void. Water was scarce.

"He will not escape us, Warden," said Anyndra.

Maiev shook her head, clearing it of her musings. She refocused on her lieutenant and the task at hand. "Of course he will not. I have not crossed the gap between worlds to let the Betrayer elude justice."

"He has powerful allies here." Anyndra's voice was soft and held a hint of doubt. The other members of the company had fallen silent. They were listening to hear what Maiev had to say.

"No matter how powerful his allies are, he will not get away," Maiev said. She decided to address her troops' unspoken questions head-on. "We captured Illidan once. We will capture him again."

Anyndra's face froze into a mask. She glanced toward the ridge as if seeking to hide from her leader any doubts she might feel. The scuttling ravagers still kept pace with them. Maiev looked to the right. Scores of the insect-like beasts carpeted the other slope, flanking the road. If there were more ravagers ahead, Maiev and her people were riding into a trap. It would not be the first one they had fallen into here.

"He was not with Kael'thas or Lady Vashj when we first captured him," Anyndra said. Clearly the way the two powerful sorcerers had rescued Illidan and slaughtered her fellow Watchers was on her mind.

Maiev said, "Prince Kael'thas is a treacherous renegade. Lady Vashj is a twisted abomination. If they get in our way, we will kill them."

Maiev was not entirely sure how she would make good on that threat. She pushed that thought aside as a distraction. The blood elf prince and the naga matron were not important. Illidan was. She had not spent ten thousand years of her life making sure his evil was contained just so he could take the opportunity to work his wickedness now.

"You think this Broken sage will be able to help us against them? This Akama?" Anyndra asked.

"I do not know, Anyndra," she said. "He may be of use to us. He may not. In the long run, it does not matter. We will triumph. We always have. We always will."

Anyndra looked away. Maiev let the silence hold and gave her attention to their surroundings once more. The landscape of Outland had been torn apart by magic. It was a terrible warning of what dealing with those forces could unleash. She had seen its like before.

ALTHOUGH IT HAD HAPPENED more than ten thousand years ago, Maiev remembered it as if it were yesterday. No, as if it had happened only hours ago . . . the day when she had first seen the Burning Legion. Her memories of that terrible time were as fresh as they had been when newly minted.

No one had understood what they faced back then, not really. They had thought the Legion was merely a temporary threat spawned by uncontrolled magic. They had thought Illidan was merely a misguided sorcerer. At least the others had. She had always known different.

The ozone scent in the Outland air brought back the memory of her first encounter with an infernal. She recalled the stench of the near-mindless thing as vividly as the night blossoms blooming amid the pavilions of Darnassus. It had seemed too big and too filled with magic to be opposed. The leaves shriveled as it passed, turned autumn-sere by the backwash of its blazing body. She called on the power of Elune, and the moon goddess destroyed the demon, shattering it into scorching fragments, leaving Maiev free to heal the seared flesh of its victims.

That had been only one of a thousand skirmishes. She had witnessed horrors during the War of the Ancients. Forests had burned and nations had died. It had taught her that there could be no compromise with those who sought power through the use of perverted magic. They needed to be stamped out, crushed, slain before they could unleash destruction upon the innocent, before they could corrupt all that was natural and good.

Maiev had seen that from the very beginning. It was a pity that others had not shared her clarity of vision. If only they had heeded her back then, there would be no need for this hunt now. If they had slain Illidan when his wickedness had first been revealed, countless innocent lives would have been saved.

Instead they had followed the counsel of Illidan's twin, Malfurion, and Tyrande Whisperwind. Time and again the pair had spared his life, even after his wickedness was plain for all to see. At the end of the War of the Ancients, when Maiev was set to end the Betrayer's life, had they not granted him mercy and argued for his imprisonment rather than his death?

Since then, Tyrande had gone even further, slaying the Watchers guarding Illidan's prison. She claimed she had freed him in order to gain his aid in the fight against the Burning Legion. At first it seemed that she had been right. Illidan *had* aided them, but then his true nature had revealed itself. He had absorbed the power of the Skull of Gul'dan and transformed himself into a demon, his body mutated to mirror the inner monstrousness of his soul. Even then, his brother had only banished him from the forests rather than striking him dead.

Maiev snorted. Illidan was but a tool of the Burning Legion. He always had been and always would be. Because of those fools, Maiev had spent ten thousand years guarding the wretched sorcerer.

And for what?

Maiev ground her teeth in fury. Tyrande should have spent the long centuries imprisoned beside Illidan. She had proved that when, with a folly exceeded only by her arrogance, she had freed him. She had made a mockery of all the oaths that Maiev had sworn. She had turned ten thousand years of vigilance into a cruel joke. Even if she was now the ruler of the night elves, she had no right to do that.

A sound from the right drew Maiev's attention. The ravagers were edging closer. They held their bodies low as they moved along on all fours, taking advantage of the undulations of the land to keep out of the line of fire from ranged weapons and magic. Perhaps they were more intelligent than Maiev had thought.

Given their numbers, it would not really matter. If they got close enough, they would pull down what remained of her force. She did not have enough troops left to be able to afford the loss of one. She raised her hand and gave the signal to ride at double time. With impeccable discipline, the Watchers' pace increased. Their great cat mounts stretched their long limbs and raced forward.

Anyndra rode up alongside Maiev, a questioning look on her face. She was wondering if Maiev would give the order to turn and fight. Now was not the time to senselessly throw away lives, not when the trail of the Betrayer lay before them and they had the scent of their prey in their nostrils.

Maiev thought about Illidan—he was no longer an elf. She shuddered when she recalled what he had become. Horned and hoofed and batwinged, as much a demon as the eredar he had worshipped and then betrayed.

If he really had betrayed them . . .

That was the eternal problem with trying to comprehend the mind of Illidan. No sane individual could. Who knew what that maniac truly thought? His mind was so twisted by the dark forces of the magic he lusted after that his reasoning was impossible to follow. And that was a problem, for a hunter needed to understand her prey. It was the one sure way of trapping it.

It troubled Maiev sometimes. She had heard the whispers. She knew what was said behind her back. There were those who claimed that she had become as warped as the foe she had spent so long guarding. She laughed at the bitter humor of it.

Weaklings! All of them. They were not prepared to deal with the evil that had taken root so deeply among them. They feared those who had the strength to do what needed to be done. They made compromises with the demons that would destroy them, and fooled themselves into believing it was wisdom. Well, she knew better. She would never compromise. She would not rest until Illidan was dead or once again bound within his prison. She knew her duty. She would keep her oaths. She did not care what others thought of her. She would not be distracted from her quest.

"Warden Shadowsong!" Anyndra's voice broke into her reverie.

"What is it?"

Her second-in-command flinched at the coldness in Maiev's tone. "There!"

Maiev's gaze followed Anyndra's pointing finger. A host of ravagers lined the hillsides above them. The Watchers rode over the rise and looked down the long valley through which the road wound. Ahead of them, more of the four-legged monsters blocked their path. Maiev had not noticed the trap quickly enough, lost in her musings on Illidan. She cursed the Betrayer once again.

"Prepare for battle!" Maiev shouted.

MAIEV AND HER WATCHERS drew themselves up in line abreast. The warden studied her people, noting whose glances darted around in panic and who stared at the enemy with cold, killing calm. It made her proud that far more eyes held the latter emotion. The night elves were surrounded and outnumbered. Even facing hundreds of the alien monsters, they were not afraid.

Some of them produced their bows and glaives. Responding to the mood of their riders, the nightsabers roared defiance. The druid Sarius dismounted and transformed into a monstrous bear, his fur branded with mystical markings. Maiev considered her options.

To stand and fight was to be overwhelmed by the sheer number of the ravagers. Something had clearly stirred up the creatures.

She glanced behind her, at the way she had come. The long, dusty road lay empty. They could retreat with little resistance, but that would set them back to where they had started. She needed to thrust ahead, down into the land the natives called Zangarmarsh, if she was to make contact with Akama.

She had to admit she was curious. The Broken's message hinted that he knew something of Illidan's plans, and all she had managed to find out about Akama from the draenei at the Temple of Telhamat was that he was a leader in a faction known as the Ashtongue tribe. He had access to troops, and he knew this land. He was the only one who had seen fit to contact her. How had his agents known where to find her? Why did he choose to reach out to her? Was it a trap?

Ahead of her the sky darkened, as if low hills or perhaps huge trees glowered on the horizon. The air carried a strange tang. The wind bore hints of rot and putrefaction and something else she could not quite place. There was just the faintest trace of moisture on the breeze blowing toward them.

Zangarmarsh was a monstrous place, a boggy fenland filled with alien horrors. Maiev took a deep breath and stared down at her foes. There were many of the beasts, but they lacked discipline. There were weak points in their massed ranks. If she concentrated all her forces, they could puncture the enemy line and ride like the wind down the road. She doubted the scuttling monsters would follow into the swamplands. These dry hills appeared to be their home.

"Form up in a flying wedge behind me. We will cut down these animals and smash our way clear."

The Watchers nodded their understanding. Anyndra raised her horn and sounded one long, silvery note. The night elves charged downslope.

A smile twisted Maiev's lips as she drew her umbra crescent. Just for a moment, she could lose herself in the fury of combat and let her mind rest. Her nightsaber roared. The elves crashed into the ravagers in an avalanche of fur, claw, muscle, and blade.

She slashed the nearest scuttler with her weapon, wishing it were Illidan. *What is the Betrayer up to now?* she wondered.

CHAPTER THREE

Four Years Before the Fall

MAIEV RODE TOWARD THE BROKEN VILLAGE OF OREBOR
Harborage. She licked her lips. Her tongue tingled where it had
touched the spores. They were everywhere. In her hair, in her
clothes. They settled behind the ears and in the sweat-soaked sleeves
of shirts. A phosphorescent fungus grew on the skin of her followers, and only careful cleaning and the use of healing magic could
take it off.

She had thought Hellfire Peninsula was a terrible place, but this
was worse. The entranceway to Outland was a desert hell filled with
fel orcs and hideous creatures, but Zangarmarsh was something
darker and stranger. It was hot and humid and dank. Huge mush-
room trees, larger than the towering oaks of Ashenvale, blocked
out the sun. Manta-like flyers flitted through their shadows, and
things part jellyfish, part alien monster floated through the air.

True, there were fewer orcs, but there were other menaces.
After smashing through the host of ravagers, the Watchers had been
attacked by a giant ambulatory fungus. They had been ambushed
by ogres and swarmed by huge stinging insects. She had lost Kolea
to tiny grubs that had emerged from her flesh after she had been

stung, the vermin eating her eyes and her brain. Another death that ultimately could be laid at the feet of Illidan.

Maiev longed to look upon the beauty of Darnassus once more. She would have given ten centuries of her life just to breathe its clean air and walk through its airy plazas, to listen to its bards and singers. She suppressed the feeling, despising her own weakness. There was no sense in longing for what she could not have.

Orebor Harborage looked like the ruins of what once might have passed for civilization in these parts. Now there were only tumbledown huts built on what had been the marble base of some formerly great plaza. Stagnant, stinking water surrounded the huge plinth. Jagged ridges of towering mountains loomed over it.

All around, Broken hobbled. They stared at the night elves as if they had never seen their like before. One or two of them reached out with empty palms, begging for alms, but most averted their eyes with tired, defeated gazes. Maiev felt that they would not raise their hands even to protect themselves. They were not the stuff of which suitable allies were made.

Not all of them were like that. Some carried weapons and watched her warily. She rode up to one now, looked at him, and said, "Akama! Where is he?"

The Broken studied her and then her followers. At first, she thought he was not going to answer, but then he jerked a thumb in the direction of the town center.

From some of the huts came the sound of weeping. Her nostrils dilated as she caught the scent of rotting flesh. Wounds turned bad very easily here. Sometimes the spores got into the cuts and clung to ruined flesh like mold to old bread. An ancient Broken crone hobbled past, her hooves splashing through deep puddles in the shattered stonework. She kept her eyes down and paid no attention to the strangers or her surroundings. She seemed too wrapped in her own misery to look beyond it.

"What do these people live on?" Anyndra sounded upset. The

sight of the Broken had clearly triggered some instinct for compassion within her.

"Mold and whatever insects they can catch, I have no doubt," Maiev said. It was what her people had been living on for days. The flora and fauna might be alien, but they were edible. At least they had not been poisoned so far. It was always possible that their foodstuffs contained slow toxins whose effects they had not felt yet, but Maiev's spells had found no taint in them. "There are fish in those lakes we saw on the way here, and other things."

"Yes," said Anyndra, no doubt remembering the massive reptilian hydras that had attacked them. "I suppose so. You really think this Akama will be able to help us?" She gestured at their surroundings. "It does not look as if he can even help his own people."

Maiev agreed, but she did not want to say so aloud. Her people did not need another blow to their morale. Ahead, another Broken sentry loomed.

"Akama," she said. The soldier gestured toward a small hut on the edge of the plaza. A group of guards robed in ash gray stood there, gazing in her direction. They did not look hostile, but they did not look friendly, either.

Maiev rode closer and said, "I seek Akama." For a moment, the Broken gave no sign of having heard her; then, as if at a silent signal, they stood aside and left the way into the hut's interior clear.

The warden dismounted, and Anyndra and the others stalked behind her. As they approached, the guards lowered their pikes, blocking the way.

"Just you," said the one who had the insignia of some sort of officer. "If you are the one called Maiev Shadowsong."

Tension crackled in the air. Her Watchers did not want to leave her. She might be stepping into a trap. On the other hand, if these were potential allies, she did not want to make trouble. She was capable of looking after herself, as anyone who tried to take her would find out.

"Wait here," she told the Watchers. Sarius looked directly at her, and she nodded. The druid detached himself from the group and moved into the shadow of a rubble pile. He did not reemerge in his own form, but a large bird hopped on top and looked around with bright beady eyes.

The guards stood impassive. Maiev stepped into the hut and was immediately aware of the whimpering of a small Broken child.

In the center of the chamber, beside a fire, a gnarled, oddly altered Broken leaned forward and touched the child's brow. He muttered something, and Maiev sensed the flow of energy—not the corrupt taint of fel magic, not the twisted flows of the arcane, but something else. She did not relax her guard. There were many ways of hiding the evil in magic.

The child quieted and the Broken whispered something in her ear. More power flowed. The whimpering ceased, replaced by the sound of regular breathing and tiny, inelegant snores.

The Broken rose and turned toward Maier. His voice wheezed with more than age. He seemed to have to force his words out, as if the very act of speaking was painful to him. "I thought I might be able to do some small good while I waited for you." He paused as if he needed a rest. His breathing was labored. "Rosaria had lung rot fever, but I think I have burned it from her. If she is kept warm and dry, she should make a full recovery."

"You are Akama," Maiev said.

"I am Akama, leader of the Ashtongue."

"Your message said you wanted to talk with me," she said.

"You are Maiev Shadowsong?"

"I am curious as to how you came to know my name."

"He has mentioned it."

"He?"

"The one you call the Betrayer."

Maiev reached for her crescent blade. Akama made no response. He held his hands wide, showing he had no weapon. Not that it made much difference. He had already shown he knew how to wield magic.

"What do you know of the Betrayer?" Maiev asked.

"Alas, far too much, to my cost. Walk with me. We have much to talk about, you and I." He gestured toward the rear entrance of the hut. Perhaps this was just a ruse to separate her from her troops. If so, Sarius would be watching in his shapeshifted form. And she was not without the means to defend herself.

"After you," she said, making a gracious gesture toward the door. Akama nodded and hobbled forward, putting his back to her, as if he wanted to show that he did not fear treachery from her.

They emerged behind the building. Toppled houses surrounded them. Garbage lay strewn around the half-ruined structure. Mold clung to it, as it clung to everything here. Glittering insects buzzed around it, feasting hungrily. Maiev wrinkled her nose.

Akama said, "It was not always like this. Once, Orebor Harborage was a beautiful place."

"I will need to take your word for that."

"You should. The world has changed since Ner'zhul wrought his destruction. Once, this was a center of civilization, a place of learning, a hub of trade."

"That is hard to believe."

"You should have seen this place when tens of thousands of my people walked here, admiring the statues, looking upon the gracious homes."

"I did not come here to purchase a dwelling. I came here seeking an ally."

Akama looked up at her. "You are not the first of your kind to tell me that."

"Illidan is not of my kind. He forfeited any claim to be a night elf long ago, when he first made his pact with the Burning Legion."

"And yet once he was a great hero of your people, to hear him tell it."

"To hear him tell it. I could tell you differently."

They passed the boundary posts of the village and arrived at the edge of a vast, calm-looking lake. Small islands dotted the water. Massive buzzing insects flitted over the surface. Akama came to a halt beside a small, motionless pool. The water was clearer here. Still, a faint freckling of spores floated on the surface. Shadowy shapes moved in the depths.

"And I would most probably believe you," Akama said. He gestured toward a chipped stone bench that overlooked the lake. "Please be seated."

Maiev remained standing. Pointedly she placed her hand on the hilt of her weapon.

Akama's grimace might have been intended to be a smile, but it showed his menacing fangs. "No one intends you harm here, but as you wish. Let us talk about the Betrayer."

Maiev had been waiting for this opening. "He is a being of great and cosmic evil. Long ago, more than ten thousand years as we measure time on Azeroth, he betrayed us to the Burning Legion. For ten thousand years, I stood watch over him to make him pay for his crimes. In the end, through the murderous treachery of one who should have known better, he escaped my vigilance and fled my wrath to this place. He is a terrible sorcerer, steeped in wickedness you cannot—"

Akama raised one hand, palm outward. "I know all this. I have talked with him, fought alongside him . . ."

Maiev glanced around, half expecting at any moment to see naga emerge from the water or blood elves erupt from the undergrowth. There was nothing.

Akama tilted his head to one side and watched her as if her behavior was curious. If she had not known better, she would have thought he was amused.

"Why do you serve the Betrayer?" Maiev asked. She could not

keep the anger out of her voice. The sight of her wrath had made demons tremble, but Akama merely shrugged.

"Because he offered to help my people free the Temple of Karabor. He was the enemy of my enemy."

Maiev glared into his alien eyes. Akama looked down at his interlocked fingers and let out a long sigh.

"And that is no longer the case?" Maiev said.

"He has made no move to return the temple to my people, and we took it more than a month ago. I have my doubts as to whether he ever will. I fear we have removed our former conqueror, Magtheridon, only to put something worse in the pit lord's place. Illidan has made a new pact with the demon lord Kil'jaeden. He has agreed to destroy the Frozen Throne for him. It seems the Burning Legion still holds our sacred site. It just has a new leader."

"And you feel I may be the enemy of your enemy."

Akama nodded. "You imprisoned him. He hates you and, unless I miss my guess, he fears you. You have great power. I can sense that myself."

Maiev's smile flickered, thin and cold as a waning crescent moon. "He is right to fear me. I will see him bound once more, or dead."

"I thought such might prove to be the case." The Broken turned his head and studied the waters as if he expected them to reveal some great truth. His voice was flat and emotionless.

"And would such a turn of events be acceptable to you, too?" Maiev asked. She already knew the answer. This Broken might pose as a holy sage, but he was treacherous. The fact that he had served the Betrayer and yet was here now proved that. She could find a use for him. To use his words, he was the enemy of her enemy.

"If there is no other way of regaining the sacred ground . . ." Akama took a wheezing breath, unclasped his hands, and looked back at her. "I spent my youth in the temple. It was . . . It *is* a holy place. I would not see it desecrated again."

Maiev considered this. Akama seemed to be talking as much to himself as to her. There was pain in his voice, and a real sense of loss. "So what do you plan on doing?"

"At the moment, there is nothing we can do."

"What?" Maiev could not keep the shock from her voice. Her knuckles went white on the hilt of her blade. She had come here expecting either an ambush or a potential ally. Her soul cried out for action. How could this pitiful ancient sit there with Illidan loose?

"Illidan is too strong. He is backed by Prince Kael'thas and Lady Vashj. I believe you have already met them. To your cost."

"I do not fear them."

"Perhaps you should."

"It is not for you to tell me whom I should or should not fear."

Akama made a small, apologetic gesture with his left hand. "I can see that."

"Did you come here to beg for my aid and then cringe in these ruins?" Perhaps he was unimpressed by the size of her force. Perhaps he did not believe she was capable of capturing Illidan. Perhaps he had judged her and found her wanting. "You ask for my aid and yet you offer me nothing."

"You elves—how can you live so long and learn so little of patience? There is a time for everything, and a place. The best revenge is not hurried."

"I do not seek revenge. I seek justice."

"Yes, I can see you believe that." This time she was certain there was mockery in his voice. Akama turned to look into the distance once more. Something large broke the surface and splashed back down into the water again. One of the big insects vanished with it. "They can wait for days, those snappers. Immobile. Torpid. You would never think them a threat. But let prey come within reach, and they strike. Their jaws can take an arm off."

"You plan on imitating some fish?"

"It is an eel."

"I did not come here for a lesson in piscine taxonomy."

"But you came here for something."

"How can I help you when you will not help me?"

"When the time is right, I will give you all the help you need. But I will not have my people needlessly slaughtered because of your recklessness."

Maiev unclenched her fingers from her weapon. She put her hands by her sides and then flexed them. She took a deep breath and sought inner stillness. Slowly her fury diminished. "Very well. At least tell me what he is doing now."

"He is taking Magtheridon to Hellfire Citadel."

"Why?"

Akama shrugged. "He does not tell me everything."

"Perhaps because he does not trust you."

"Perhaps he has reason." The Broken fumbled within a pouch hanging from his waist. He produced a small, rough-looking stone inscribed with strange runes. He held it out to Maiev in the flat of his palm. She looked at it but made no attempt to take it. She could sense magic in it. It did not have the foulness of fel sorcery or the wickedness of arcane magic. As far as she could tell.

"Through this I will contact you when I have something worth telling. I carry its twin." The stone still lay on his outstretched palm. "Of course, if you are afraid to take it, we can find another way . . ."

Maiev snatched the stone from his hand. The presence of magic tingled against her gauntlet. Nothing terrible happened. "As you wish."

Akama made a small bow. "I can see why he fears you. You are very much alike."

Akama walked away, leaving Maiev to stare at her reflection in the dark mirror of the lake. Her image glared back at her, a picture of frustrated fury. She stooped, picked up a pebble, and lobbed it into the water, smashing her likeness into ripples.

CHAPTER FOUR

Four Years Before the Fall

SLOWLY MAIEV AND HER WATCHERS CREPT OVER THE WARM rocks. The blazing sun of Hellfire Peninsula sent long shadows sweeping away from the large boulders. It had been a lengthy ride back from Zangarmarsh, made at great speed, but it would be worth all the saddle sores if she caught Illidan unawares. She did not need Akama. All she needed was the opportunity to strike at the Betrayer when he least expected it.

Anyndra gestured with her right hand and raised three fingers. Maiev crept forward on her belly until she reached the lieutenant's position; then she raised her head over the ridgeline and saw that her second-in-command was correct. Three fel orcs stood there, huge, muscular creatures, with red skin and glowing eyes. Their heavy bodies hunched in the crouched posture all orcs shared. Their stance spoke of fury, every muscle tensed. Each movement was quick, hard, and sullen, as if the fel orcs were looking for an excuse to strike someone.

Maiev would give them their wish. She meant to be in position overlooking the road to Hellfire Citadel when Illidan rode past.

She invoked her powers and blinked across the intervening

space. Air displaced with a near-silent puff as she reappeared behind the largest of the fel orcs. One stroke took his head. She sprang forward and drove her umbra crescent through the second fel orc's breast, then rolled onward. The third fel orc struggled to bring his axe to bear. Her foot caught him behind the knee and tumbled him to the ground. Her blade found his jugular.

Scarcely three heartbeats had passed. Anyndra had just brought her arrow to her ear. Maiev gestured for the remainder of her troops to cross the ground to her new position, and then she dragged the corpses into the shadow of a boulder out of sight of any wind riders passing overhead.

The smell of big cat in her nostrils told her that Sarius had joined her in concealment. The druid wore the form of a huge panther, oddly marked. He moved across the parched landscape in utter silence, following the curves of the brown earth, out of sight of all but the most vigilant. He growled a greeting and stalked toward the ridge's edge. Just as quietly, she followed him to the brow of the cliff and gazed out on Hellfire Citadel.

It had the brutal appearance of all orc fortifications, in this case magnified by the sheer size of the place. The citadel looked as if it had been built to accommodate an army of giants. It loomed over the surrounding lands, each tower the finger of a gigantic hand that reached out to seize the sky. It was rough-hewn but immense, built of red rock and the bones of creatures that must have been as large as mountains. Magic saturated the stones. Even from this distance, she felt its evil. But it was not the keep that held her attention. It was the procession making its way along the road that led to the citadel.

Tens of thousands of fel orcs marched in tightly packed formation, streaming across the landscape in a column leagues long. Among them marched companies of demons, bearing the banner of Illidan. In the vanguard rode a mass of blood elves, their steeds birdlike. Prince Kael'thas was at their head. His eyes were fixed upon the enormous chariot drawn by a team of twenty clefthoof. The gigantic creatures were muzzled and blinded to prevent them from panicking.

Looking at the cage mounted on the giant chariot, Maiev understood why. It contained the pit lord Magtheridon. He stood many times the height of an elf and rattled the felsteel bars with arms the size of tree trunks. Even from the clifftop, Maiev felt his power. It smashed into her senses like the stench of ten thousand burning bodies. Chains that could have anchored the biggest warships bound him to the chariot. Maiev could see they were wound by spells strong enough to halt the slow drift of continents.

Atop the chariot, wings spread, hands on his hips, his stance proclaiming his triumph and his lack of fear, stood Illidan. Such was the difference in size that he should have looked like a squirrel defying a helboar, but he did not. The aura of fel magical power blazing around him made him appear to be more than the equal of the pit lord.

She was not alone in watching. Along the ridges, clans of fel orcs had gathered, as well as other observers. All of them were there to witness the former lord of Outland being brought to Hellfire Citadel in chains. Hatred blazed bright within her.

Enjoy your moment of triumph, Betrayer, Maiev thought. *It will be your last.*

Anyndra dropped into place beside her. The lieutenant's eyes widened at the sight of the triumphal procession, and her fingers went lax around her bowstring. Sarius growled so softly it might almost have been a whimper. Overhead, fleshrippers circled, mangy wings spread wide, crucified on the hot thermals.

Maiev considered her options. The fel orcs surely did not anticipate an attack. Soon the sun would go down. Illidan had obviously timed his arrival at the gates of Hellfire Citadel for before sundown, but he had been too slow to get there. It was typical of his overconfidence and his sloppiness. She could order her force to fan out near the cage. They could cover her as she rushed the Betrayer. One swift stroke and she could take his head. He would be too filled with bloated pride to notice her approach until her umbra crescent had swept out.

Briefly she reveled in the image of holding his head high and tossing it into the assembled host of fel orcs. Her own death would be swift and certain after that, but it would be worth it to put an end to Illidan's cursed existence. She could die satisfied, knowing that she had sent her ancient enemy to oblivion before her. Her lips curled into a smile. She could almost feel Illidan's silky hair beneath her fingers as she raised his head aloft, almost feel the *drip-drip-drip* of blood from his severed neck.

It was not impossible. She could use her ability to blink through the intervening space and be upon him before that undisciplined mass had time to react. Her spells of distraction and concealment would cloak her approach. There was no one down there who could match her ability at this. Not Kael'thas, not Vashj. Not Illidan himself.

She became aware of Anyndra's hand on her arm and shrugged it off. "What?"

"Warden Shadowsong, I asked you what the Betrayer could possibly want with a captured pit lord. I thought they called him a demon hunter. Why would he want one alive?"

Slowly, Maiev let her hatred's fire damp down to a duller blaze. She stepped back from the edge of the precipice she found herself on. She had been on the verge of ordering an attack. The idea of dying in a final blaze of glory, slaying her foe, had almost lured her into an error. What if something had gone wrong? What if the Betrayer had managed to escape, leaving her to face his legions with only this small force?

Nothing would go wrong. She looked down at her hand. It was completely steady. There was not the slightest glimmer of a shake there. She focused on her lieutenant's question. It was a good one.

What did Illidan plan to do with a captured pit lord? A being of Magtheridon's power could not be bound to service like some lesser demon. Not even Illidan could be insane enough to believe himself that strong.

"What could he want with such a creature?" Anyndra repeated, as if she thought Maiev had not heard. She seemed determined to get an answer. Or perhaps she intended to distract Maiev from her target.

Maiev muttered, "A sacrifice, a warning—who knows what goes through the mind of that maniac?"

"But why would he want to sacrifice Magtheridon? What could he possibly gain from it?"

Maiev shook her head and scowled. "How should I know?"

Her second-in-command met her gaze levelly. "You always told me a hunter must understand her prey."

Sarius growled on the other side of her. It seemed he, too, was curious. Maiev took another step back from the brink. Her heart was racing. Her breathing was shallow. She risked another glance at Illidan. He stood there so confident that he was invincible. She wanted to wipe that smirk from his face, grind those proud features into the dirt.

Sarius scratched at her right arm with a claw. She realized what the druid was trying to tell her. Illidan's head had turned to look in their direction. All of his troops' gazes followed. There was no way they could see her from this distance. No way he could see her.

She rolled away from the scarp edge. Anyndra and Sarius were behind her. Her mouth felt dry. She tensed, expecting to hear the furious roar of legions of fel orcs dispatched in pursuit.

Maiev lay on her back for a moment, looking at the sky. No roar sounded. No alarm was given. Perhaps Illidan had seen them and did not think them enough of a threat to be bothered with. The idea was galling.

She rolled downslope and sprang to her feet, out of the line of sight of the enemy.

The rest of her grim-faced troops crept back from the ridgeline, slowly filtering toward her position. It was bad discipline and bad tactics. Some of them should be keeping watch lest an assailant fall upon them the way she had fallen upon the fel orcs. She wanted to say something, then noticed all eyes were upon her.

Anyndra flexed the fingers of her blade hand, the way she always did when trying to conceal the extremity of her nervousness. Sarius had reverted to his night elf form. His hawklike features were calm, but his mouth was a tight slash at the bottom of his face, and his eyes were narrowed as they focused on her. A frown scarred his otherwise smooth brow.

Maiev studied the rest of her troops. A few were pale, and she guessed the sweat on their brows was not just from the heat. Others glanced around like mice expecting an owl to drop out of a moonlit sky.

They were frightened.

It was near unbelievable. They were Watchers, chosen for their courage and their steadiness in the face of danger. They had followed her through countless perils without flinching. Now they seemed ready to break and run.

The night elves formed up in a half circle, looking up at her. One of them said, "We cannot win here."

Maiev wrestled with her anger. She wanted to shout at them, to upbraid them for their folly and cowardice, but she could not. Enemies might hear her voice. A disturbance could call the attention of that mighty army thundering along the road below them.

Slowly, she allowed the idea to seep into her mind that they might be right. She closed her eyes and offered up a prayer to Elune. When she opened them again, she realized that she was not looking at a force of Watchers. The proud, disciplined troops who had rid-

den out of the vaults of the Barrow Deeps were gone. In their place
was a small group of dusty elves, strangers in a savage land, lost, far
from home, and confronted by a foe with limitless fighters at his
disposal. Illidan had already overcome the mightiest demon in Outland and turned his legions into loyal followers. Perhaps her people
were right to doubt that they could overcome him.

They stared at her, waiting to hear what she had to say. Even
now, they retained the habit of looking to her for leadership. She
could not let them down. She took a deep breath and said, "No. We
cannot win here."

Some looked pleased at her admission. A few looked astonished,
as if they could not quite believe the words had come from her
mouth. Maiev understood how they felt, but she kept speaking, her
voice emerging in a rusty rasp. "We cannot win here. Now. That
does not mean the Betrayer is safe from us forever."

Several of them nodded as if she was saying what they had expected her to say, as if she was giving voice to their consciences.
"He cannot escape us. He cannot simply walk away from his trans-
gressions. We are the avenging hand of the kaldorei. We will be his
undoing. We had him in our grasp once and he escaped, aided by his
treacherous allies. But the Betrayer will not escape us again. Right
is on our side. Justice is on our side. The spirits of our dead cry out
for vengeance. They insist that we make him pay for his crimes.

"We have come too far, sacrificed too much, to waste our chance.
If we are to return to Darnassus with our heads held high, we must
go back with the Betrayer or his corpse. If we do not, our people
will think of us only as those who betrayed their trust. You have
seen what is happening here. You know that the Betrayer is amass-
ing an army. We must make sure that all of Azeroth knows, too,
and understands that we did our duty."

One elf swallowed and wiped her eyes. They looked watery
with unshed tears. Maiev shifted her hands slowly, her movements
as controlled as a dancer's. Her fists clenched. "There is a time for

everything, and Illidan's time is coming. You followed me here knowing that, and I swear to you that your faith was justified. I will not allow Illidan to escape the consequences of his deeds."

She paused to give her words emphasis. "I will do so even if I must go on alone."

She let her words sink in. "All of you swore an oath to follow me. Each of you knows the value of your word. The question you must ask yourself is whether you will remain true to your oaths, or whether you will be like him. Are you as faithless as the Betrayer, or are you true daughters and sons of Elune? In your heart of hearts, only you can answer that. I want you each to look within yourself and find the answer to that question. I want no one with me who will flinch when the moment of truth comes. Only you can decide whether you wish to stand beside me when I bring due punishment down upon the head of Illidan the Betrayer."

Some of the elves would not meet her eyes. A few looked away, but most of them, she was proud to see, stared up at her with renewed determination written on their faces. Their belief fed her own, and she felt her usual certainty return.

"I am with you," said Anyndra. She knelt and offered her blade.

"And I," said Sarius. He did the same. One by one, the rest of the Watchers pledged renewed loyalty, even those few who were visibly reluctant. They bowed because their friends and comrades were doing so and because they did not wish to be left alone in this alien place. Maiev nodded in satisfaction. She had won one small victory this day, at least.

"What now, Warden Shadowsong?" Anyndra asked.

Maiev responded, "We must find allies. This is a land where they are essential. We must seek out someone braver than Akama and see if they will aid us."

CHAPTER FIVE

Four Years Before the Fall

ILLIDAN STRODE INTO THE VAST CHAMBER IN WHICH Magtheridon was bound. The demon hunter seethed with frustration. His defeat at the hands of Arthas stung his pride. Reports of Maiev's presence had filtered in from across Outland, but so far she had proved elusive as a ghost. She still sought to bury him in chains. The spells restraining the pit lord reminded Illidan of his own imprisonment, and of those who had held him. Rage bubbled up within him. He paced eight steps and forced himself to stop before he could take the ninth.

"So you failed in the mission that great Kil'jaeden gave you, little Illidan," boomed Magtheridon. His words echoed off the massive stone blocks of the walls, amplified by the huge well in the center of the chamber. "Your failure to destroy the Lich King does not surprise me. You are destined always to fail."

Illidan stared at the pit lord. Even shackled deep in the great vaults below Hellfire Citadel, Magtheridon remained a potent figure. The magical chains holding him were taut. The binding spells from the Manticron cubes constantly deformed as the demon exerted his will.

Illidan muttered a word of power. Magical generators blazed, and fel energy surged. Magtheridon screamed. The smell of scorched demon flesh filled the air.

"How does it feel to be defeated utterly by such a failure?" Illidan asked. The enormous tail of the pit lord lashed, causing him more pain as he made contact with binding spells.

"You think you have defeated me?" Magtheridon's voice rasped out. His breathing sounded like muted thunder even within this vast hall.

"Apparently you are too stupid to realize when you have been vanquished. It seems you think being imprisoned is a sign of victory."

Illidan sent another surge of energy through the chains. Magtheridon's agonized bellow almost deafened him. The pit lord collapsed like a bull hit with a butcher's cleaver. He lay there gasping for a moment, then pulled himself up onto his knees.

"I am not the only one who has been defeated," Magtheridon said. There was a sardonic note in his voice. "I wonder what Lord Kil'jaeden will say when he learns of your latest failure. I believe this was your last chance."

"How do you know I have failed?" Illidan was curious. In the weeks since he had returned from Azeroth, he had been recovering from his wounds and gathering his strength for this moment. Had some of the jailors made the mistake of speaking to the pit lord? If so, he would make sure they never made another such error again.

"Come now, little Illidan. One need not be as clever as you to understand such things. I see that unpleasant scratch on your side. It does not take any great intelligence to work out what happened since you have been away. You have the stink of the walking dead on you, and the taint of that great blade, Frostmourne. You encountered Arthas, did you not? And you were defeated."

It was the truth. Illidan had gone to Azeroth, fought against the renegade death knight, and lost. With that defeat, Illidan's last chance of destroying the Lich King and appeasing the wrath of Kil'jaeden had vanished. Ultimately it did not matter. The break would have had to come sooner or later.

"Yes, yes, little Illidan. I smell spiderwebs and walking dead and the subtle tang of strange plagues. And I know you are still closing the gates the Legion has opened to Outland. Even through your binding spells, I can sense such sorceries. You will not escape great Kil'jaeden's wrath that way, nor will you spare Azeroth. His invasion of your precious homeworld may be delayed by a year or two, but it cannot be stopped."

Casually this time, Illidan lanced the pit lord with another surge of pain. Magtheridon managed to remain upright. Defiance twisted his lips. Illidan was careful not to kill him, for Magtheridon must still serve his purpose. He studied the shimmering aura of the demon. He was almost weak enough now. Almost. Illidan needed some more of Magtheridon's power to be bled away, some more of his will weakened. "Does it gall you that you will not be there, pit lord?"

Magtheridon laughed. "Yes, little Illidan, it does. I would enjoy the destruction of your pathetic world. I would enjoy burning your precious forests. The screams of a million sacrifices would give me great pleasure. I will miss the conquest of your world, but there will be others. A few more are left before the Legion's final triumph. It is a pity you have forsaken all possibility of participating in such delights. There is something in you that enjoys these things, too. We both know it. Great Kil'jaeden will not be gentle when he takes his vengeance on you. He is not known for his mercy. And to you he will show none. You have changed sides for the last time, Betrayer."

Illidan sent yet another surge of fel power through the bindings. Magtheridon screamed as agony tore at him. Illidan let the energy flow till the demon's howls threatened to shatter the stone dome above him. He kept it going until he judged the moment was right. The pit lord was weak enough now. It was time.

"Akama, come forth," Illidan said.

The door of the chamber opened and Akama entered, shoulders hunched, head down. Long tentacles dribbled from the cowl of his robe. He shuffled over to the dais upon which Illidan stood. Akama's eyes never left the bound pit lord. He clearly was afraid of Magtheridon. Just as clearly, he hated him for the desecration he had worked on the Temple of Karabor. There was malice in his gaze as well as fear.

Magtheridon gasped, "Tell me, Broken one, has the Betrayer returned your precious temple to you yet?"

"What do you wish of me, master?" Akama tilted his head so that he was facing Illidan, but it was clear he meant to keep the pit lord in his peripheral vision.

"Akama, what do you see?" Illidan asked.

"I see Magtheridon bound. I see great spells in place to hold him. I see you standing in triumph over your fallen foe."

Illidan smiled. "Are you not curious as to why I have preserved him?"

"I am, Lord."

Magtheridon's gurgling laugh boomed through the room. It was pained but there was wicked mirth in it. "He wants my blood, Broken one. But not the same way you do."

Akama frowned. The shadows of his cowl would have hidden his expression from a normal-sighted individual, but Illidan had no trouble perceiving it. "What does this creature mean, Lord?"

"He is essentially correct. Among other uses, his blood contains the secret to creating fel orcs. It can be distilled into an elixir that gives the orcs might and ferocity."

"Why would you wish to do that, master?" Akama asked.

"Because I have need of an army, loyal Akama. The Burning

Legion is coming for us, and the demons must be opposed." He slammed his fist into his open palm. "They *must* be defeated. No matter what it takes. No matter what it costs."

"But creating more of those foul creatures is . . . an abomination, Lord Illidan. Forgive me for speaking so bluntly, but it is true."

"You have outraged your pet's sensibilities, little Illidan," Magtheridon boomed. "And not for the first time, I must tell you. He is a sensitive creature. Treacherous, too. I can read his heart even if you are too blind to see it."

Illidan spoke a word of power that clamped Magtheridon's jaw shut. Only muffled groans and unintelligible gasps emerged from him. Illidan had his doubts about Akama, as he had his doubts about every one of his followers, but he would not let that show. There was no sense in allowing Magtheridon to undermine Akama's loyalty with thoughts that he might be under suspicion.

"We need a mighty army, Akama, and we need it quickly. Otherwise we will be overwhelmed by the force that the Legion can bring to bear. Now do what I tell you to do when I tell you to do it."

Akama placed his hands together and made a bow that set his facial tentacles to touching the ground. Illidan spread his arms wide, and his wings wider still, and brandished a Warglaive of Azzinoth in each fist. He chanted words, and the forces of magic bent to his will. Magtheridon struggled against his bindings, enormous muscles flexing as he tried the strength of his chains. It seemed that the pit lord was not quite as sanguine as he tried to appear at the prospect of the bloodletting.

Illidan strode forward, bounding into the air, wings flexed to hold him there for a moment. He twisted through the movements of an enormous ritual dance, circling ever closer to Magtheridon, blades spinning in his hands. All the while he crooned evil words in the ancient language of demons. Trails of fire appeared behind his blades as he spun them, weaving an intricate net of energy.

He reached Magtheridon and slashed. The blades bit chunks from the demon's flesh. Green blood dripped from the wounds, dribbled down the pit lord's columnar legs, and puddled at his feet. Illidan moved around and slashed again, drawing more blood. His blades never sank in beyond a few inches—each blow little more than a scratch on the demon's thick hide—but more and more blood came forth. A few droplets sprayed his face. The smell of it made Illidan lick his lips. The tang set his tongue to tingling.

Strength flowed into him. The demon's blood was like a drug. He fought down the urge to plunge his hands into the pool and lap it up. The strength it granted was not worth the price he would have to pay.

What does it matter? part of him asked. There was no greater pleasure than drinking the blood of his demonic enemies and imbibing their power. He needed it. It would enable him to kill ever more demons and absorb their energy until the moment he was strong enough to take on Kil'jaeden himself.

Out of the corner of his vision, he caught sight of Akama's horrified face. It reminded him that there was another purpose here than mere enjoyment. He needed this blood for other reasons. He needed it to make his army, to give the orc clans surrounding him the strength they craved to overcome their foes and his.

"Now, Akama!" he shouted. "Bind the blood. Set it flowing into the channels."

Akama cast the spell. The blood responded sluggishly. The demonic taint within it resisted Akama. The plasma swirled and split, flowing into new streams that filled the channels carved in the floor. Akama's magic grew and drew on more and more power. The spurts formed whirling patterns in the air and flowed down into the vents. The blood pulsed through a system of pipes to be gathered in alchemical tanks. Illidan smiled. He had collected the first of what he needed. The spell would be self-sustaining for hours.

It was time to get to work.

ILLIDAN STRODE THROUGH THE long gallery, gazing down at the orcs lying on gurneys there. Pipe connected each to a tank of bubbling greenish fluid, pumping it into their veins. Runes cut into their flesh guided the magic. Scuttling, bent-backed mo'arg servitors moved from orc to orc, checking the procedure. Their metallic claws clinked against the tubes. Their demonic eyes glinted with unholy glee. Akama watched with unconcealed disgust on his face.

"This is an abomination, Lord Illidan," he said.

"So you have said. But it is necessary."

"Are you absolutely sure of that, Lord?"

"Are you absolutely sure you wish to face the consequences of questioning me?" Magtheridon's blood still affected Illidan. Subtle anger twisted his mind. It was one of the dangers of what he had been attempting.

"I mean no disrespect, Lord."

An orc stirred in his sleep, grinding his teeth and flexing his fingers as he writhed in the grip of some dark nightmare. Doubtless he, too, was feeling the effects of the pit lord's blood, and he was receiving it in a distilled and magically enhanced form. His skin was blotched an angry red. The epidermis seemed thicker and had a raw look to it. Muscles bulged and nails had become claws. A faint glow was visible even through his closed eyelids.

"They grow larger and heavier as we go down the line," Akama said.

"It is the effects of the serum. It will make them stronger and faster. It will ensure they heal quicker."

"But at what price, master?"

"They will be foul and fierce, quick to anger and quick to kill. They will be filled with rage and hatred and a hunger for battle."

"Is there no way we can mitigate those side effects while preserving the changes we need?"

"We will need them all. You have seen what the Burning Legion is like. You have felt its wrath. We need to be just as fierce and just as deadly if we are to have any chance."

"You think the Legion can be defeated here, Lord?"

"I believe they can be held here."

"You seek then only to preserve your homeworld of Azeroth, and to do that you would turn this world into a battleground."

"This world is already a battleground, Akama. And, no, I do not seek only to defend Azeroth. I want to preserve us all."

"And how do you intend to do that, Lord? By turning us into that which we oppose?" Akama gestured meaningfully at the recumbent orc. His brow was lower. His fangs were larger. His eyes snapped open and he reached up to grab at Illidan, breaking the strap that held him to the gurney. The grip was strong and the clawlike nails bit deep. Illidan shrugged him off and brought his hand down on the orc's windpipe, breaking it. As the creature writhed, Illidan snapped his neck with one twist. He then looked at Akama and smiled. The fel blood still affected him. He had enjoyed the kill.

"That one was a little too fierce, I think."

"I thought there could be no such thing against those we face."

Illidan laughed. "I like you, Akama, but do not try my patience. I am not here to play games with words. I am here to win a war."

"We all are, Lord. Let us hope that we are all fighting the same one."

AKAMA WATCHED FROM THE battlements as the first of the new army emerged from the gates of Hellfire Citadel. A week had passed since Illidan had begun the creation of the new batch of fel orcs. Tens of thousands of transformed fighters strode in time, cursing and howling and grunting. They brandished their weapons in rough salute as they saw Illidan watching. He acknowledged it with a lazy wave. He seemed satisfied. His military power grew. He no longer needed to rely on the backing of Kael'thas and Vashj. He had armies now to match his sorcerous strength. He truly was the lord of Outland.

"They will establish control of all the lands of Hellfire Peninsula," Illidan said. "Then we shall close the Legion's gates and slow the demons' advance by another increment."

"I sincerely hope so, Lord," Akama said. Now more than ever he was convinced that he had made a deal with a demon. It was an insane plan to transform the orcs. Illidan was simply turning himself into a new Magtheridon. Indeed, he might prove to be something worse.

"When that happens, will you return the Temple of Karabor to my people, Lord?"

"Of course, Akama. Never doubt it."

Akama did, however. He touched the rune-carved stone he kept in his pouch, feeling the magic in it and thinking about the night elf warden who bore its twin.

"Make ready to depart," Illidan said. "Tomorrow we return to the Black Temple."

ILLIDAN STRODE INTO THE Chamber of Command, his council's meeting room at the Black Temple. Akama hobbled along behind him. Several Broken scuttled around, putting the last of the fittings into place. Great tapestries woven with Illidan's symbol hung from the wall. An enormous table showing a carved three-dimensional map of Outland dominated the space. A group of blood elves huddled around it. They turned and made obeisance as soon as they saw Illidan. Clearly his sudden appearance had taken them by surprise.

The beautiful Lady Malande raised her hand in a languid salute. "Lord Illidan, Prince Kael'thas regrets he could not be present. He has taken a force to close the Legion's gate in the Netherstorm and—"

Before she could complete her explanation, High Nethermancer Zerevor butted in. "The magical defenses of the temple have been rewoven, Lord Illidan. They were in a disgraceful state, but—"

Gathios the Shatterer, broad for a blood elf and encased in the heavy armor of a paladin, interrupted, "There is no sign of Legion activity in Shadowmoon Valley, Lord Illidan. The gates remain as closed as the day we sealed them, and there have been no indications of demonic manifestation."

Veras Darkshadow leaned back against the table and folded his scarred arms across his chest. Alone among his comrades, he apparently did not feel the urge to fight for Illidan's attention. Illidan shook his head. These blood elves seemed to have nothing better to do than plot against one another for his favor. It was no wonder that Kael'thas had left them behind. Still, they were efficient organizers and brilliant in their respective fields. They represented the absolute best of the sin'dorei forces in Outland. They had taken to calling themselves the Illidari Council, a measure perhaps of their self-importance.

Illidan raised his hand and stared at them until they fell silent. "We are at war with the Burning Legion," he said to Gathios. "Need I remind you that the demon lord Kil'jaeden is displeased with me? He will make his displeasure felt soon enough."

Silence settled on the chamber like a shroud. The only sound was Akama's wheezing breath. The sin'dorei looked afraid. That was good, Illidan thought. Fear might keep them all alive. He tilted his head so that Zerevor was aware that he had his full attention.

"Are you certain that the wards are ready? They may soon be put to the test."

Zerevor took a deep breath and considered his words carefully. "They are, Lord Illidan. I would bet my life on it."

"That is good," Illidan said. "Because you are doing that. You are betting all our lives on it."

Illidan turned to Malande. "Send a message to Prince Kael'thas apprising him of the situation. I do not want him taking any unnecessary risks. After me, he is the one Kil'jaeden is most likely to strike at."

"It shall be done, Lord Illidan. I shall see to it at once."

"Veras—you have done as I asked?"

"Of course, Lord Illidan. Our best trackers have scoured the routes to Hellfire Citadel and questioned the fel orc clan leaders. A number of night elves were sighted on the heights above the road on the day of your triumphal procession. They killed a group of fel orcs and made their escape. One of them wore burnished armor of the sort Warden Shadowsong wears."

Illidan bared his fangs, and his underlings flinched. He had been right. He *had* seen Maiev that day. He should have scoured the hills immediately, but it had taken all his power to restrain Magtheridon, and he had not been absolutely certain it was her. The need to impress the clans with his strength had outweighed his suspicions. It would not have looked strong to disrupt the triumphal march of his entire army to search for a few night elves. Still, it was galling to think that she had been so close. "You will find Maiev Shadowsong for me, Veras. You will assign agents to follow up on every rumor of her presence. I am keen to repay her for the hospitality she extended to me."

"At once, Lord Illidan." Veras padded silently from the chamber.

"And you, Gathios. I want you to ensure that our sentries are alert, and that a force is ready to respond to any threat."

"It is already done, Lord Illidan." Gathios paused for a moment. "I have taken the liberty of surveying the Black Temple's defenses for weak points. The sewer outflows represent one particularly easy point of attack. In your absence I consulted with Lady Vashj. She suggested that one of her champions, High Warlord Naj'entus, should guard the sewers, along with a picked force of her people."

"It is an unpleasant duty but a necessary one," Illidan said.

"Then you approve, Lord Illidan?"

"Of course. You have all done well. Let us hope you have done enough."

Akama, Gathios, Malande, and Zerevor filtered from the chamber to be about their duties, leaving Illidan to contemplate the map of Outland. Soon armies would be moving about it and war would ravage the land. He had better prepare. He had much to do and little time to do it in. This was the moment to move to the next phase of his plan. He must recruit others like him—those willing to hunt the Legion by becoming what they hated most.

CHAPTER SIX

Five Months Before the Fall

VANDEL STALKED THROUGH THE DARK LANDSCAPE OF Shadowmoon Valley. Behind him, the huge volcano known as the Hand of Gul'dan grumbled. The blazing contrails of enormous green meteors scratched the face of the sky as they crashed downward. The earth trembled like a frightened beast on their impact. In the distance, the gigantic walls of the Black Temple loomed.

Vandel touched the hilts of his scabbarded daggers, then rubbed his weary eyes to remove the ash and grit. He had come a long way to find Illidan's new home. He had come a long way in search of vengeance.

The image of his dead son flickered through his mind. There had been very little left of Khariel's body once the felhound was finished with it. He touched the silver leaf he had given the child for his third and last birthday to make sure it still hung from his neck.

Even after five years, the memory burned white hot. He ground his teeth and let the wave of hatred sweep through him. It would have been better for him if he had died that day along with his family and the rest of his village.

He should have been with them, but instead he was in the woods hunting when the alarm horns sounded. He had raced back through the forest, leaping over the fallen trees, the smell of burning bright in his nostrils.

He pushed the memory down. It was far too easy to give in to it. He had done so many times in the past and been driven to the edge of madness and beyond. In his lucid moments, he admitted that. No sane elf would have spent long years tracking the Betrayer, ferreting out the secrets of those who had followed him. No sane elf would have passed through that magical portal and come to this hellish land.

The wall loomed before him. He crept forward, taking advantage of every patch of shadow. There were many sentries and many warding spells. The Black Temple was a fortress girded for war, and he did not want to be cut down by its guardians before he had finished his business with its master.

Gigantic stones had been piled high to form the outer wall. Here and there clumps of moss clung to them. In places, wind and rain and meteor strikes had eroded the ancient blocks, leaving cracks that could be exploited by someone who had learned to climb amid the great trees of Ashenvale. He sprang as high as he could reach, digging his fingers into the first gap he spotted and pulling himself up.

He hung there for a moment, feeling as if his arm would be pulled out of its socket. Below, a patrol of fel orcs marched closer. He would have offered up a prayer to Elune if he had any faith that the goddess's benevolence could reach this foul place. Instead he made his mind a blank and continued scrambling up the wall, hoping that he would not be overheard by any sentry waiting above.

That did not seem likely. Shadowmoon Valley was a riot of noise. He doubted that any guard could hear him over the thunder of the volcano and the roar of the wind. Nonetheless he allowed himself a moment of stillness and strained his keen ears for any clue that he might have been observed. Beneath him, the patrol went about its rounds.

Vandel looked down into the pools of shadow, and just for a moment he felt the urge to let go. The long drop would break his neck and end his agony. He could join his family in death and end the torment. He resisted the urge. He could not rest while his son was unavenged. His hatred was stronger than his desire for endless peace.

He pulled himself over the edge of the battlements, rolled down onto the balcony behind, and lay in the shadows, catching his breath. So far no sentinels. He felt a brief moment of triumph. He had succeeded where an army would have failed. He had broken into the unholy precincts of the Black Temple.

A batwinged shadow passed across the moon. It seemed that all his wishes were to be granted tonight. Illidan, the Betrayer himself, soared aloft on the night wind. It seemed that he, too, was restless this evening. No doubt there were many things that kept him awake. Perhaps his dark deeds caused nightmares that kept him from his bed.

How long had it been since Vandel had slept without nightmares? He could not recall. All he could remember were the terrible dreams. He touched Khariel's amulet once more. *Not long, my son, not long.*

Illidan settled upon a balcony atop the highest tower of the Black Temple. He paced for nine steps, turned, and then shook his head. He leaned against the banister, surveying everything as far as the horizon. Vandel wondered whether the Betrayer could see him. His sightless eyes were known to perceive things that others could not. What would Illidan do if he knew that Vandel was there?

It would not be difficult to reach the tower upon which Illidan stood. The few sentinels scattered along the battlements did not seem completely awake. They were secure in the strength of the walls protecting them. Doubtless they did not expect someone like him. They were there to watch for armies and demons, not a solitary night elf maddened by grief and overmastered by the thirst for revenge.

He stalked forward, telling himself not to be overconfident. Perhaps there were other sentries and he had just not seen them. The long years of hunting the foes of his people had taught him stealth beyond that of most mortals, but he was far from the only one who could hide in shadows. Perhaps even now some deadly sentry watched him unseen and prepared to drive a dagger into his back.

Once more he paused to consider the fact that he might no longer be sane. His mind had shattered once, at the moment he had found his son's corpse being gnawed upon by the felhound. For a moment he could almost smell the scent of burning wood, and night elf blood. He could almost hear the crunching of small bones. He let out a whimper, then cursed silently. Anyone within earshot might have heard. He did not intend to be struck down by a guard because of his own foolishness. No more mistakes. From here on he would concentrate on the mission ahead.

He reached the foot of the tower upon which Illidan stood. Ahead, a ramp curled out of sight around the side of the tower. He prayed that luck was still with him and ran, preferring to trust in speed and stealth and his unexpected good fortune.

He reached the top. The one he had come long leagues to find stood before him.

Illidan's back was turned. His massive wings clung close to his body as if trying to warm him against the chill of the night. He held his great horned head low as he surveyed the distant lights of the great volcano. What was he looking for? What did he see with his eyeless sight?

Illidan turned as if he had known Vandel was there the whole time.

Vandel drew his daggers, checked the mystic runes etched into them, and padded forward. He knelt, and placed his blades at Illidan's hooves. "Forgive the intrusion, Lord Illidan. I did not wish to risk being cut down by your sentries before I had spoken to you."

Illidan said, "What do you wish of me, nightstalker?"

"I want to slay those who slew my family. I want to slaughter your enemies."

"There is no shortage of those."

Vandel said, "I wish to learn what you have learned. I want to hunt demons."

"Then you have much to learn, and the hour is late."

"Will you teach me?"

"You and a thousand like you. Go below. Rest. You will find what you seek. Or die in the attempt."

Illidan turned his back once more and returned to gazing at the horizon. It was clear to Vandel that he was dismissed.

UNCERTAIN AS TO WHAT he was supposed to do, Vandel strode down to the base of the tower. Two tattooed figures waited for him. It seemed as if they had been there all along. They were not surprised to see him, nor did they draw any weapons.

One was a tall female with a scarred face. She appeared to be a night elf, yet she had demonic features. Green flames flickered in her empty eye sockets. Small horns curled from her head. Her scanty clothing revealed glittering tattoos that covered her body. Some magic about them drew Vandel's eye and compelled him to try to unravel the pattern as if it were a complex puzzle.

She noticed his look, and her lips twisted to reveal small fangs. Vandel met her cold smile with one of his own, feeling as if somehow he was being tested, as if they were crossing blades in a soundless struggle.

The second figure, also night elven in form, paid no attention to him at all, and Vandel would have been surprised if he did. His eyelids were sewn shut, as were his lips. He was hunched forward, with his head held low and his shoulders high. He was stripped to the waist, revealing even more tattoos than his companion had. A broad leather belt wrapped around his waist held a selection of long, sharp needles, from the ends of which dangled strings of animal hide. Their tips were blotched, and a look at the male's body revealed the fact that he had recently pierced his skin. The crust on the needles' points was dried blood, most likely his own.

"You have spoken with Lord Illidan," the female said. There was a jealous note in her husky voice. It sounded as if something was wrong with her larynx, as if she had once screamed so loud and so long that she had done it permanent damage.

"Yes," Vandel said. He did not care for her knowing smile. He was not going to let himself be intimidated.

"You are privileged indeed."

"Am I?"

"He does not greet every supplicant personally. It seems he has some memory of you. Perhaps he has something special in mind."

The male raised a finger to his lips, as if she had said too much. A long talon extruded from its tip. The gesture was not threatening, but it was not reassuring, either. The blind male scratched his chin, drawing a bead of blood onto the claw. He put it into his mouth through a tiny aperture left by the thread.

"I would not presume to read Lord Illidan's mind," Vandel said.

"You show more wisdom than I expected."

"Do you have a name?"

"I am Elarisiel. He is Needle. If he had another name, it is long since forgotten, even by him."

Vandel bowed to them both. Elarisiel laughed, malice glittering in her voice. Needle bobbed his head without mockery. Vandel stared hard at him. Obviously the male had no more difficulty seeing than Lord Illidan. What was going on here?

"Lord Illidan told us to take you below."

Tension tightened Vandel's shoulder blades. "And how did he tell you that?"

"You will find out, eventually, if you live."

Needle produced one of his long, sharp pins and pierced it into the flesh of his own forearm. He dug around for a minute. Another droplet of blood appeared. He poked the point through the small gap between his lips and made a sucking sound. A blissful look appeared on his face. Vandel had come here doubting his own sanity. Now he doubted that of everyone around him.

THE PAIR LED HIM through a maze of corridors. They passed through a small sally port in the wall of the Black Temple and out into a vast heap of tumbledown ruins.

"This was once part of the Temple of Karabor," Elarisiel said. "The orcs and the demons did not leave a great deal of the original structure standing. What they did, Lord Illidan and his champions took. We dwell here now under the watchful gaze of Varedis and his companions."

"Varedis?" Vandel asked.

"The master tutor," Elarisiel said, but she did not seem inclined to amplify on her remark.

More green meteors scarred the face of the sky as Vandel and his guides passed through a series of terraces. Silken pavilions rose along their length. From them came the sounds of mad laughter. They passed through the camp and came eventually to a tunnel mouth in a ruined wall. Chill air surrounded them as they walked down worn, ancient steps and emerged into a huge hall.

It looked like an asylum or a battlefield hospital. Elves sprawled everywhere. Some lay in pools of greenish light cast by flickering fel lanterns. It made them look sick. Some of the males were bearded and green-haired after the fashion of night elves; some were clean-shaven like the sin'dorei. Some muttered to one another.

Some huddled in the shadows between the lanterns as if trying to conceal themselves. Most slept fitfully, talking in their sleep. A mad scream sounded, and a female rose up and raced through the chamber, shouting, "Worms, worms, worms!"

The shout roused many from sleep, but they did not seem disturbed by it. Only one tall blood elf rose from the soiled cloak in which he lay wrapped, and he chased the maniac through the chamber. They disappeared out of sight.

"As you can see, you are not the only one who has found their way here. Many have sought out Lord Illidan. Only a few will live to enter his service."

"What do you mean?"

Elarisiel's silvery laugh rang out. "You will find out soon enough, kaldorei. Pick out any place and get some rest. You will need your strength for the trials ahead."

She spun on her heel and departed. Needle raised a finger to his forehead and turned his hand through a half circle, then stepped back into a shadow and seemed to simply vanish.

"Do not pay too much attention to Elarisiel," said a friendly voice from nearby. "She just likes to scare the new recruits. I suspect someone did the same to her when she first came here, and she likes to spread the misery."

Vandel inspected the speaker. He had the ageless look of a mature night elf, which meant he could be any age from twenty years to fifteen thousand. As far as Vandel could see, he had no scars or tattoos. When he considered the matter and then looked around, he saw that none of the others in the hall did, either.

The speaker continued. "You are a thoughtful one. And I know what you are thinking . . ."

The unspoken question hung in the air.

"Vandel is my name."

"Elune shines on the moment of our meeting, Vandel. I am Ravael."

"I am pleased to make your acquaintance. You were about to tell me what I was thinking. I am curious to know, since I am unsure myself."

"You are thinking what every newcomer who has ever been led into this hall thinks. That the guides are strange. You are also wondering why none of us have tattoos and all of us have eyes."

"There are more like that pair, then."

"Oh yes, my friend. Lots more. Lord Illidan is building an army of the blind."

"Only they are not blind, are they?"

"No."

"And they have tattoos like his, only less intricate."

"Yes."

"And they are changed in ways he has changed."

"You are observant."

"I would have to be blind not to notice these things," Vandel said before realizing the ridiculousness of that statement.

"You think the blind here see less well than you?" Ravael asked, and just for a moment a note of hysteria sounded in his voice. Vandel was almost glad. Until that moment, Ravael had seemed so normal as to be out of place in this madhouse.

"I think they probably see more. They had no trouble guiding me here, or avoiding anyone in their way. It is possible to memorize routes, but I cannot imagine everyone in this hall occupies the same place the whole time."

"You have thought things through, it seems."

"What are you doing here?"

"I came to take vengeance, to learn to fight demons. The same reason you are here, I am guessing."

Vandel considered that for a moment. "Perhaps Elarisiel was right. Perhaps I am not so special."

"I am sure you are. After all, you got here without dying. How common do you think that is?"

Vandel took a deep breath and looked around again. He had assumed that everyone here was mad or an invalid, but he could see now that many of them bore scars, and all of them had weapons close at hand. There were warriors here, and magi, and hunters.

"You lost someone?" Vandel asked.

"I lost everything," said Ravael. He made no move to expand on that. Thinking of his own loss, Vandel saw no reason to prod him.

"I know what that feels like," he said.

Ravael looked around. "Somehow, though, in this place, I feel we have even more to lose."

CHAPTER SEVEN

Five Months Before the Fall

MAIEV FELT ALMOST RELAXED. CLEFTHOOF MEAT FILLED her belly. The long, sunny day had provided rare sport as she and her followers hunted the beasts. Enough hide lay nearby to make armor for a score of draenei soldiers. A few of them picked through it, sawing away with knives, flensing the skin. It reminded her of her long-gone youth, when she had hunted in the woods with her mother. They had made their own clothes then, cut from leather, sewn with needles of bone, using thread of sinew. The memory brought a brief smile to her face and then the return of horror. Her mother was dead, killed by the Burning Legion. That thought sent her mind circling back once more to Illidan.

The Betrayer was still at large, and his power was growing. The strength of his legions mocked her own efforts. She tried to blank her mind, reclaim her earlier good mood. It had been a long time since she had experienced a moment of unalloyed happiness.

She liked this Nagrand. The air was clean and the sky was blue and the wind was fresh. It was not like the forests of her homeland, but as long as you did not look too closely, it felt natural. Of course, you could still see the effects of the world-splitting magic that had been inflicted on Draenor. Huge islands floated in the sky, hovering on the wind. It seemed as if at any moment, they might crash to the earth—but they did not. According to the locals, they had been stable for years. And even here there were rumors of Illidan's war with his demonic masters. It seemed that the Burning Legion had established bases in the far west of Nagrand, and the demons were preparing some new attack.

Anyndra lay on her stomach near the fire, playing an improvised game of nexus with Sarius, using a hexagonal board slashed into the earth and stones of different colors. The lieutenant saw Maiev looking at her and raised her hand in salute. Her hair was bleached almost lime green by the Outland sun, and her skin was desiccated. Her tunic was patched in a dozen places. Like the rest of the surviving Watchers, she had refused to part with it. It was a connection with their home, and there were few enough of those left.

Sarius remained focused on the game. He was competitive in everything. He had acquired a dozen new scars. Some of them were pale and old, but two were from more recent skirmishes. They had been deep wounds. Druids healed quickly and easily from most injuries. Maybe he had left them as they were as reminders or tributes to his vanity. Males could be like that sometimes. They liked to have scars to flaunt and tell tales about.

The two had proved to be loyal and good soldiers in the years they had roamed through Outland seeking the key to Illidan's destruction. They had kept Maiev's troops alive under very trying circumstances. She cursed when she thought of all the months they had wasted scouting the grounds around Hellfire Citadel, making war with the naga in Zangarmarsh, watching the walls of the Black Temple. It felt as if they had achieved nothing. Illidan's power had increased a thousandfold during that period.

She glanced around her camp. Her force had grown but she could not yet call it an army. It numbered in the hundreds and consisted mainly of disaffected draenei youths recruited on her travels.

There were always those who saw the need to oppose evil and the threat Illidan represented. Not enough, though.

What had she really achieved here? Nothing. Over the years, Illidan had grown ever stronger. For every draenei who joined her, a hundred orcs marched into his citadel and emerged transformed into even more brutal, powerful fighters. There were fools out there who believed that he opposed the Legion, and they joined him willingly. They did not know him as well as she did. She knew that he was summoning more and more demons from the Twisting Nether and binding them to his will. There could be no good purpose to that.

Illidan played some deep game here. She could not see the logic of it, but she knew it must be there. There were those who claimed that Kil'jaeden sought his head. Perhaps the demon lord did. It would not be the first time that evildoers had fallen out with each other. Illidan had switched sides before, though, and he would do so again when it suited him. His evil nature would always win out. He had corrupted everything he ever touched. This time would be no different.

A commotion sounded at the edge of the camp. The sentries were challenging someone. Weapons sprang into her troops' hands. Every Watcher stood ready. Maiev moved to investigate. Ogres had been spotted in this area, but she doubted it was them. Fighting would already have erupted. She raced closer and saw a group of unfamiliar Broken, garbed as hunters. They exchanged words with one of the sentries. They did not look hostile. But it might be a trick.

Maiev circled behind them, scouting the area. There were no signs of any enemy infiltration. No Broken hid in the shadows. In the distance she heard the growl of a nightsaber. A wind elemental roared across the evening sky.

She stepped out of the shadows. The strangers' leader flinched at her sudden appearance, but he recovered his composure.

"Greetings," he said.

"What is going on here?" Maiev said.

"We could ask you the same thing. You are on Kurenai land, eating Kurenai beasts. It seems to me that we should be asking the questions." Maiev had heard of the Kurenai; they were another faction of Broken, one that owed no allegiance to Akama and his Ashtongue tribe.

"I saw no brand on these clefthoof; there were no herders, either."

"These are our hunting grounds. We have not given you guest rights."

Maiev considered this. With calculated insolence she ran her eyes over the newcomers, making it clear she was counting their numbers. She then looked at her own force. The strangers were outnumbered by twenty to one.

The Broken laughed. "You have an army. The people of Telaar also have an army if things come to that. Our army is bigger than yours."

"But it is not here," said Maiev. Anyndra emerged from the gathering gloom. A shriek told her that Sarius was watching from on high, changed into the shape of a bird.

"It could be. If I sounded this horn."

"I could put an arrow through your eye before it reached your lips," Anyndra said. Maiev glared at her. Now was not the time for displays of archery prowess. There was nothing to be gained by picking a fight with these Broken.

"We meant to give no offense," Maiev said. "We are strangers passing through this land, and we sought only food and shelter."

"You should have come to Telaar. Our people would have provided you with both, and perhaps other things beside." The Broken looked at her camp again. "So many young draenei led by so few strangers. There is a story here that Arechron would like to hear."

Maiev perked up at that. Perhaps there were allies to be gained—

maybe even an entire army. "I am sure we have much to tell each other. If it suits you, I will guide my people to your city and have words with your Arechron."

"I will leave some of my people to be your guides as I go ahead to give notice of your coming."

Maiev hoped he was not merely heading off to prepare a trap.

TELAAR WAS AN IMPRESSIVELY fortified place. Situated on top of a flat mountain peak that rose above a deep valley, it had no need of walls. The only approaches were over rope bridges or from the air. Unless they used magic or flyers, any foe would find it a difficult place to besiege.

The rope bridge swayed beneath the paws of Maiev's nightsaber. The great cat stalked on, but she could sense its pulse increase as it looked down. Through the slats of the bridge, Maiev could see the ground a long way below. If the Broken wanted to kill her people, all they would have to do was cut the ropes supporting the bridge. Of course, that would mean killing the Broken and draenei with them. Maiev had known enough leaders willing to sacrifice their own people to achieve their ends that she did not discount the possibility.

A crowd lined the edges of the town, trying to get a glimpse of the approaching force. They did not push or shove one another, but they did not have the lassitude she had come to associate with the Broken, either. They appeared to be armed and no doubt would fight if they had to.

It was with a sense of relief that Maiev rode off from the bridge. She paused to look over her shoulder and check on her people. She was happy to see that they were still there. Apparently Arechron planned no treachery. Not yet, anyway.

In the middle of the crowd, surrounded by spear-bearers, stood a particularly huge Broken of noble aspect. He was garbed in impressive armor of orange and purple. Four long tendrils descended from his face. His tail swished as he moved.

"*Achal hecta,* and welcome to Telaar," he said. "I am Arechron and I would give you welcome in my house."

Maiev said, "I thank you for your hospitality and look forward to speaking with you."

They rode along the mosaic-patterned road, through the open spaces of Telaar. Around them rose the odd, domed buildings so typical of draenei architecture.

Maiev studied it all with the eye of a veteran fighter. She noted the areas where ambushes might be sprung or archers could be placed. Every moment, she half expected to be attacked. She had spent so long in the field these past few years that every town felt like a trap, and every citizen a potential enemy. The knowledge saddened her, but she did not relax her vigilance.

MAIEV GLANCED ACROSS THE low table, studying Arechron. The Broken had an open, honest face and a welcoming manner, but she had long ago learned that such things could be deceptive. She was determined not to let down her guard even for a moment, although she gave no sign of her suspicions.

The chamber walls curved. Thick carpets lay strewn on the floor. A Broken boy pulled aside a beaded curtain and stared in, quite clearly fascinated by the newcomer. Maiev met his gaze.

"Corki," said Arechron, "go to sleep. It is past your bedtime and I have business to discuss with our new friend."

"Yes, Father," said Corki. He made no move to go.

"Corki!"

"Yes, Father?"

"Do as you are told, or there will be consequences."

"Yes, Father." The child's hooves clopped on the stone floor as he skipped away.

"He is a good boy, but I indulge him too much," Arechron said.

Maiev agreed, but it did not seem politic to say so. "You are his father."

"I worry about him sometimes," Arechron said.

Maiev saw her opportunity. "As a parent, you have a lot to worry about. We live in dark times, and they are getting darker."

Arechron nodded his head. "You speak the truth, but the Light will preserve us. It always has, and it always will."

"I wish I shared your faith," Maiev said.

Before she could say anything further, the Broken interrupted her. "Faith in the Light is open to all. All you need do is believe."

Maiev saw a quagmire of theological debate yawning before her. "Oh, I am sure that the Light watches over us. I am not so sure that it can protect us for very much longer. The Betrayer seeks dominion over Outland. Already he has recruited tens of thousands of fel orcs and other monstrous beings. I have seen the naga working on great magical engines amid the waters of Coilfang Reservoir. I cannot believe that they are up to anything good. I know their leader, Lady Vashj. Believe me, she is wicked."

Maiev let her sense of urgency show in her voice. It was a speech she had given many times before, and it had succeeded in convincing the draenei youths who had joined her force. But Arechron was not a youth. He was an experienced leader, albeit with a sentimental weakness for his son. That was her best line of attack. "If you wish your child to have a safe future, you must do something soon, before Illidan the Betrayer has overwhelming forces at his disposal."

Arechron raised both hands in her direction, palms out. He gave her a good-humored smile and said, "You do not need to convince me of the threat that Illidan poses."

"Then I can count upon your help in the coming struggle."

Arechron gave a small shrug. "It is not quite that simple."

Maiev forced a smile upon her face. "I find that such is nearly always the case in Outland."

"I have heard of you, Maiev the warden. I have heard of the way you go from town to town and village to village in search of soldiers for your crusade against the one you call the Betrayer. I have heard that some of the younger and more impetuous draenei follow you. I am neither young nor impetuous."

Maiev was tempted to add *nor a fighter,* but she clamped her mouth shut and kept her smile in place. She was not back on Azeroth now. She could not simply show up and expect help as she could among her own people. The Broken needed to be convinced to do the right thing. She was used to this reaction from the draenei elders. They were very conservative people and very cautious. The younger ones were braver. That seemed to be the case wherever she went.

"Believe me, I would like to aid you, Maiev. I think that you are right about how powerful Illidan is. I do not wish to draw the attention of such a being to my small town."

"You are afraid," Maiev said.

"I am not ashamed to admit it, but not in the way that you think."

"Fear is fear. If you allow it to rule you, it does not matter what you are afraid of."

"It is very easy for you, is it not? You ride from place to place, spinning your web of words, and young fighters follow you. You do not have to think of the consequences of your actions. You do not have to think about our young people dying."

Maiev stared hard at him. "Many of my people have given their lives to end Illidan's reign of terror. The night elves you see outside, my officers, are what remain of the mighty force that once followed me in pursuit of the Betrayer."

Arechron steepled his fingers and nodded. "You can fight your guerrilla war and disappear into the wastes to escape the wrath of your foe. I cannot. My people cannot. We have homes here in Telaar. We have children."

"I wondered why you introduced him into the conversation so early."

Arechron made a curt gesture with his right hand, then shrugged. "You are a cynical and wrathful night elf, but I think that you are also a righteous one. That is why I will give you whatever aid I can. I will provide you with supplies and weapons. I will allow you to recruit whoever wishes to follow you among our youths, provided only that you leave the town guards out of your efforts at persuasion. We need them here to protect us from our enemies."

Maiev considered his words. It was obvious that Arechron did not wish to be drawn into open conflict with Illidan. But it was equally obvious that he was no friend to the Betrayer, either. Under the circumstances, that would have to do.

She allowed some real warmth to show in her smile. "I appreciate the risk that you are taking. And I am grateful for any help that you can give me."

"Let us not misunderstand each other. War is coming. The day approaches when Illidan will turn his attention to Telaar. But that day has not come yet, and I would delay it for as long as possible. What you do, you do on your own."

He reached down and poured some clear water into goblets. He offered one to her and took one himself. As if he guessed what she would think, he put his to his lips before she could drink hers. Maiev sniffed it and took a small taste on the tip of her tongue. She detected no drugs in it, so she took a sip. Arechron smiled.

"Tell me, since you know Illidan so well, what do you think he is doing in Outland?"

"Fleeing the justice that pursues him from Azeroth."

"That goes without saying. I meant, specifically, what do you think he plans? Why does he build these mighty armies? Do you think he means to invade your homeworld, as the orcs did not so long ago?"

"I think that is the most likely explanation. Illidan has ever sought glory and conquest. He lusts for such things almost as much as he lusts for forbidden knowledge."

"It is said that he is a formidable sorcerer."

"One of the greatest my people ever produced." It galled Maiev to have to utter such words. She despised the sort of magical power Illidan dealt in.

"That is alarming. You can see the effect magic has had on our world. It shattered Draenor, cost the lives of millions." Arechron was afraid of the power Illidan's magic represented. It was a sensible attitude, albeit a cowardly one.

"All the more reason Illidan must be opposed."

"He has made pacts with the Burning Legion before?"

"Whenever it has suited him."

"And yet now he appears to make war on the Legion."

"It appears that way, yes, but who can tell what is really happening here? It may be merely that there is strife within the Burning Legion. Perhaps the Betrayer's attempt to supplant Magtheridon has made him more enemies than he expected. Perhaps his superiors have decided to punish him. In any case, this dissent represents an opportunity for all who would see him overthrown."

"Possibly, yes."

"You do not agree?"

"I mean no insult, but I suspect you would find an opportunity to strike against your enemy under any circumstances." He paused for a moment. "There are those who might aid you in your quest. They, too, have great magical power."

Maiev looked at him closely. "I do not seek an alliance with those who use blasphemous sorcery."

"The naaru serve the Light. They derive their power from it."

"The naaru?"

"They came to Shattrath City recently. It seems to me that you might make common cause with them. They are no friends to your Illidan."

"He is not *my* Illidan."

"I meant no offense. My tongue is clumsy sometimes."

"Tell me more of these naaru."

"They are beings of Light, enormously powerful. They arrived in Shattrath mere months ago, attracted by the rites of worship that the Aldor priesthood performed within a ruined temple there. The naaru protect the city from demons."

"They hold the Legion at bay, you say?"

"Indeed. They have made Shattrath a sanctuary for those who oppose the demons. They are recruiting those who would fight against the servants of Kil'jaeden. You might do well there. You could become a general in their armies without any doubt."

It certainly sounded promising. Maiev searched for a hidden purpose behind his words. Was he merely trying to get rid of her by directing her toward this Shattrath? Arechron's face held its usual expression of benevolence. He was hard to read.

"I do not seek a position of power," Maiev said. "I seek only to see that the Betrayer gets his well-deserved punishment."

"Of course, of course. I have once again misread the situation. Nonetheless I would advise you to seek out the naaru. Of all the forces opposing the Burning Legion in Outland, they are immeasurably the strongest."

Perhaps the Broken was right. She had been wasting her time, wandering these wastelands and recruiting tiny handfuls of fighters. There was nothing to be lost from contacting these new rulers of Shattrath, and perhaps much to be gained.

"Tell me of Shattrath."

"It was once a beautiful place, and may well become so again."

That was not the sort of knowledge she had been seeking, but she restrained her impatience. "How may I find it, and whom should I speak to there?"

Arechron smiled as if he had achieved his goal. "It is a long way northeast of here. You must seek the Terrace of Light and speak with A'dal. If you seek a place to stay, I can recommend an inn. A cousin of mine owns it. He will guide you right if you mention my name."

They spoke of matters concerning the city long into the night.

MAIEV WATCHED THE RISING sun. This was a good hour to depart. It was going to be another clear, warm day. Her forces had enjoyed their weeks of rest within Telaar. She had recruited another five score young fighters from among the Broken and the draenei. They were at the edge of her force, mounted on their elekk. The massive quadrupeds dwarfed the riding cats of her own people and exhibited only the slightest nervousness at the presence of the great carnivores.

A crowd as large as the one that greeted them on arrival had gathered to see them off. Many of its members seemed to be there to say goodbye to her new recruits. A few appeared to be attempting to discourage them from leaving. Maiev saw no point in trying to stop that. She did not want anyone with her who could be impelled to desert by the tears of family. Her troops needed to be made of sterner stuff.

Arechron himself appeared, mounted on the howdah of a huge bejeweled elekk.

He bowed to her and said, "Remember, seek out the Aldor. They are the strongest faction in Shattrath besides the naaru, and they are the ones most likely to aid you."

"I will do that," Maiev said.

Arechron nodded and said, "And if I were you, I would have nothing further to do with the Ashtongue and their leader. They are of little account."

Maiev doubted that. She had met Akama on many occasions

since their initial contact, and she knew his power. She still did not trust the Broken, but he had not lied to her yet, as far as she could tell.

Anyndra rode up beside her. Her gaze made it clear she was awaiting the order to depart. Maiev nodded. Anyndra sounded her horn. The nightsabers roared. The elekk trumpeted. The long line of soldiers departed Telaar, leaving the cheering, waving, crying throng behind them.

Maiev wondered what she would really find in Shattrath.

CHAPTER EIGHT

Four Months Before the Fall

VANDEL STOOD IN THE GREAT COURTYARD IN THE RUINS of Karabor along with all the others. Hundreds of supplicants lined the terraces. They had been waiting for weeks for Illidan to return. No one knew where he was. Not even his closest followers understood the Betrayer's comings and goings.

Vandel felt a growing sense of impatience. There had been long days of training under the guidance of tattooed fighters of the same ilk as Elarisiel and Needle.

Golden-haired Varedis, arrogant and confident as a god, had lectured them on the nature of demons. Of him it was whispered he had infiltrated the Shadow Council and stolen its *Book of Fel Names*.

Soft-spoken Alandien had laid out the tactics of infiltration. She claimed to have been trained by Illidan himself.

Netharel, the oldest night elf among them, was the one who taught them about weapons. Despite being bowed with age, when he picked up a blade, he moved with the agility of youth.

They had practiced with weapons, sparred with their fellow recruits, and gotten to know one another a little better, but Vandel had made no progress toward his goal.

It sometimes seemed to him that he would have achieved far more in the way of vengeance by simply walking out the gate and attacking any one of the tens of thousands of the Burning Legion's servants that swarmed through Outland. Of course, that would have led to a swift death, and he would have achieved nothing of any account. The Legion had limitless numbers of such soldiers.

Ravael stood beside him. They had stuck together since the night of Vandel's arrival. Compared with some of those present, Ravael seemed normal. Over the past few weeks, Vandel had encountered most of the aspirants. All of them had stories to tell, and all of those were tales of horror. The majority of the recruits were blood elves sent by Prince Kael'thas to learn how to fight demons. There were far fewer kaldorei.

Among the night elves was Seladan, who had come all the way from Eversong Woods. His body had been burned by a dozen fist blows from an infernal. The whole right side of his face had been caved in around the jawline. A night elf so burned should not have been able to move without pain, but somehow he did, as lithe as when he had been a village guard.

Beautiful Isteth had lost all three of her children when the Burning Legion struck. She carried the burned corpse of her baby in a pouch against her chest. Vandel had pieced together her story from her ravings. There were nights when she could not stop screaming about the burning. One of the blood elves had tried to silence her forcibly. She had killed him with one blow of her knife.

Mavelith smiled and smiled and smiled. He found everything funny. It was disconcerting when he laughed at nothing, or at the distress of some companion. There was something in his eyes that suggested he took pleasure from the pain of others.

There was Cyana. She seemed almost normal except for her keenness to come to grips with the Legion. She never spoke of what the demons had done to her, but she gave the impression that she, too, thirsted for vengeance with all her being.

Ravael said not to trust the blood elves. They had been twisted by their addiction to arcane magic. Vandel did not care. He did not pay any attention to the prejudices his own people had acquired since the Burning Legion's invasion. He had been too caught up in his own hate-driven quest.

He knew one thing, though. All the elves here had reasons to hate the Burning Legion that went far beyond those of most who had suffered because of the demons. They were like him, and he felt an odd sense of companionship with them all.

It was clear that he and his comrades were not the first to walk this path. There were others, who kept mostly to themselves or were sometimes seen practicing. They were a breed apart—marked by their tattoos and their scars and strange mutations.

Not all of them seemed blind, but all of them had altered eyes. It marked them as being part of a separate, elite group. The servants and soldiers around the Black Temple treated them with fear and exaggerated respect. The aspirants looked upon them with a mixture of awe and envy. They had something all of the supplicants wanted—poise and power and confidence. Mystery cloaked them. It hinted that they possessed other, unseen powers. Rumor had it that these tattooed soldiers had already slain demons.

There were times when Vandel sensed the presence of the Burning Legion. He told himself it was because the Black Temple housed Illidan's bound servants, but sometimes he had the skin-crawling feeling of being watched by demons, and he would turn to see Needle or Elarisiel looking at him. The tattooed fighters with their strange vision made him deeply uneasy. It had been a long, long time since anything had caused him such disquiet. There were other tales among the aspirants—that Illidan himself had become part demon, that their tutors emulated him in all things, and that in order to slay demons, you had to become like them.

The Black Temple itself was a profoundly disturbing place. It had been transformed from a shrine into something else by the presence of Magtheridon. Illidan's people, the so-called Illidari, had done nothing to change the atmosphere. For one who called himself a demon hunter, Illidan counted an enormous number of demons among his followers. Even amid the ruins of Karabor, gigantic batwinged doomguard stalked, polluting the stones with their hooves. Vandel had heard the bellowing of monsters echo from the Black Temple. Stories of succubi and satyrs abounded among the aspirants.

Vandel was so deep in reverie that he did not notice the first time Ravael shook his shoulder. He turned to look when he became aware of the shaking, and his gaze followed his companion's pointing finger. Illidan stooped like a hawk, dropping from the darkening sky into the courtyard, as if they were his prey.

Vandel stood his ground as the Betrayer landed in front of him, arresting his descent with a flap of his huge leathery wings. His sightless eyes seemed focused on the distance, but his taloned fingers pointed straight at the crowd.

A mocking smile twisted the Betrayer's lips. "And now we begin."

Begin what? Vandel wondered. So far it had all been weapons training and listening to his disturbed companions. Did this mean Illidan was finally ready to share his dark knowledge? Were they finally going to learn how to kill demons, rather than simply spar with one another and listen to endless lectures from Varedis and his ilk?

Illidan's cold smile vanished. "Take a look around you. There are more than five hundred of you here. By the time this is over, there will be less than a hundred."

He paused to let that sink in; then he laughed. "You all swore you were willing to give your lives to strike at the Burning Legion. You now have a chance to prove that. Who will be the first?"

At first there was no response. Everyone waited to see what the others would do. Now that the moment had come, no one wanted to break ranks and see what waited for them. Suspense and fear hung over the supplicants and paralyzed them.

Vandel took a deep breath and stepped forward. "I will have my vengeance or I will die. Whatever is needed, I will do."

Illidan nodded. Vandel thought that the Betrayer had expected this of him, or perhaps he was just imagining things. "Very well," he said. "Step into the summoning circle."

Illidan gestured. Lines of fire etched a complex geometric pattern on the stone.

Vandel passed into a vast pentacle surrounded by glowing runes. They pulsed with a meaning that he felt he could grasp if only he was given another heartbeat to contemplate them—yet somehow the meaning never came. As he watched, the symbols blurred hypnotically. His skin tingled. His mouth felt dry. Motes of greenish-yellow light swirled around him.

Illidan spoke a word of power. Fel energy surged. The temperature dropped. The air shimmered and congealed, and a felhound materialized. Perhaps it was his imagination, but it bore a startling resemblance to the one that had killed his son, Khariel.

The felhound shrieked and bounded toward him, long tentacles bobbing. Jaws gaped wide, revealing teeth like a shark's. Vandel drew his runic daggers and leapt to meet it, the similarity of the beast to his son's killer stoking his rage ever higher. His blades stabbed forward at the tentacles. He writhed to one side to avoid the snapping jaws. His blades made contact, slicing the sensory stalks. The felhound twisted, still attempting to bury its fangs into his flesh.

His arm burned where the felhound's jaws made contact. Razor teeth sliced his flesh. His thirst for vengeance had blinded him to the creature's surprising speed. He sprang backward and away. Something tingled at his back, and he found that he could not exit the circle. Magic imprisoned him, as if the very air had solidified. He flipped himself forward, and the demon's jaws snapped closed inches from his face. He smelled its brimstone breath even as he drove his blade up through the roof of its mouth, into the place where its brain ought to be.

The felhound tried to close its mouth, but the dagger was wedged between its jaws. The attempt merely drove the spell-wound point deeper into its skull. A gasping wheeze passed through the creature's lips. It keeled over and lay there, tail lashing in a death spasm.

Vandel looked over at Illidan, filled with the first faint surge of triumph. *What next?* he wondered. Illidan stepped into the circle, unhampered by any restraining spells.

Illidan reached down and with one clawed hand pulled the felhound's still-pulsing heart from within its chest. He presented it to Vandel.

"Eat it," he said.

This was not what Vandel expected. Looking at the disgusting mass of foul meat, Vandel considered refusing. But only for a moment. Something in the Betrayer's stance told him that defiance was not an option. He instead took the heart in both hands. The demon flesh was wet and sticky beneath his fingers. What might have been veins dripped greenish acidic ichor. His palms tingled and felt as if they were about to burn.

He glanced around and saw even through the shimmering air of the circle that all eyes were upon him. Everyone waited to see what he did. Vandel raised the meat to his lips. He reached out with his tongue. It tingled and burned just as his hands were doing. He suspected that the flesh was saturated with fel magic.

He bit into the moist meat and forced himself to chew. The flesh was tough, and he thought it squirmed as it came into contact with his lips. He swallowed and it seemed to expand in his throat as if the demon, even in death, was determined to choke him. He gagged and swallowed again, trying to force it down. It was like having a slug slither down his throat.

Illidan indicated the blood pooling around the corpse. "Drink it."

Vandel bent down and, with both hands cupped, scooped up some blood. The tingling in his fingers increased. Nausea and dizziness made his head spin, but he managed to gulp down the foul liquid. It burned like rotgut alcohol from a goblin still. Vandel wondered if it would poison him. His stomach rebelled. He wanted to vomit. To his horror, he felt as if something was kicking within his belly. He imagined the demon flesh coiling in his gut, trying to break free, gnawing its way out.

Illidan chanted. Great spheres of greenish light orbited him, burning like shimmering emerald suns. They blazed with heat and magical power, and Vandel felt as if his skin would crack. Bolts of lightning leapt from orb to orb, forming a cage of crackling energy; then at a word from the Betrayer, the bolts speared into Vandel. He screamed in agony as the magic saturated his body.

His legs gave way and he collapsed onto the ground, clutching his head, rolling over and over like someone whose clothes were on fire, trying to beat out flames. The pain was intense, and he knew in that moment that the Betrayer was going to kill him. He looked up and saw Illidan standing over him, transformed. He no longer looked remotely like an elf. A dark aura crackled all around him, his form distorted and shimmering. Pure malevolence blazed in his eye sockets, visible even through the cloth covering them. Vandel felt as if he were falling forward into those pools of evil light, tumbling downward into an endless void.

Strange emotions filled him. Rage burned in his heart. He reached up toward Illidan, wanting to choke the life from him. His body would not respond. His senses blended. He heard the sizzle of the green light, saw the words that Illidan chanted as perfectly formed runes. Beneath him he felt the pulse of magic flowing through the stones of the Black Temple, and he became aware that out of the void within him, something was rising, something vast and powerful and evil that had come to devour his soul.

The world shimmered and vanished.

CHAPTER NINE

Four Months Before the Fall

ALL AROUND HIM THE VILLAGE BLAZED. THE LEAVES OF the ancient trees shriveled. The gabled log houses crackled and burned. The smell of scorched pine needles filled the air. Sap bubbled within the wood, popping in the heat.

He raced through the smoke-filled streets, shouting for his wife and child. In one hand he held his long hunting knife. Demons cavorted amid the ruins. Imps lobbed firebolts into blazing buildings. Massive infernals lumbered through the streets. Masked and armored mo'arg waddled along, spraying anything they saw with magical fire from their weapons. On the roof beam of the central long house, the towering winged figure of a dreadlord loomed.

Ahead Vandel saw his home, and for a brief moment, hope filled his heart. Khariel's head thrust through the door. He seemed to be beckoning for his father.

It all seemed so real, as if the five miserable years he had spent wandering had evaporated and he had been given a second chance to save his son. And yet he knew that this was not the case. As in a nightmare, he knew what was going to happen next—and it did.

The little boy disappeared back into the house, his tiny fist the last thing to go. Vandel sprang over the threshold. Khariel lay there. His eyes were open, staring blankly at the ceiling. On his chest crouched a felhound, gnawing at his flesh. The tiny silver leaf the child had been so proud of still glittered on his throat.

The felhound looked up at Vandel. Its stalked sensors waved like the antennae of a huge cockroach. Khariel's blood stained its fangs. Seeing the little boy, only that morning so filled with life and laughter, cold and stark on the ground, sent a lance of agony through Vandel's heart.

Sweet, sweet pain. The voice came from somewhere deep within him.

His heart felt as if it were breaking, his head as if it were going to explode. He could not endure this again.

But you will, many, many times. And I will feast upon it as I devour your soul.

There was an alien presence in his mind. The voice sounded like his own, but it was not. It belonged to something that looked upon all this horror, drank it in, and loved every instant of it.

Your horror feeds me. It makes me stronger.

The felhound moved toward him, tail lashing, distracting him from the voice. Its short legs carried it at surprising speed. Its mouth yawned to reveal sharp teeth. Vandel sprang to one side, avoiding the strike, wheeled and lashed out with his blade, cutting a bloody green weal along the creature's side. Rage and hate drove the blow. The tear of flesh satisfied both.

Yes. Take your vengeance. Feed me.

Vandel paused, shocked, and the felhound almost got him. He sprang forward, tripped over the corpse of his wife, and rolled to his feet, back against the wall as the demon bounded closer. It sprang. There was no way to avoid it. Vandel leapt to meet it, chest-to-chest, grasping its armored throat with one hand, driving his blade into the spot where the felhound's heart should be. The creature's sulfurous breath stank in his nostrils. Its claws scrabbled against his chest, digging deep wounds, shredding his leather jerkin.

Such delicious agony.

The pain almost immobilized him, but he threw his weight forward. The felhound toppled onto its back. He jumped astride its chest, pinning it to the ground. Taking the hilt of his dagger in both hands, he stabbed the demon again and again until its struggles ceased and it lay still.

Smoke filled the air. Weak from his wounds, Vandel lay on the ground. His head was next to Khariel's. He reached out with long fingers and closed the little boy's eyes. Tears rolled down his cheeks. He could not move. He did not want to move. He would lie here until the flames turned his home into his pyre.

Such nutritious grief.

What are you? Vandel thought. The image of him devouring a still-pulsing demon's heart flickered through his mind.

You believed you were consuming me, but I am consuming you.

For a moment, Vandel felt the demon's flesh burrowing outward through his own, fusing with it, even as he felt the demon's spirit merge with his. The reality of the burning village wavered. He looked up and saw Illidan at the grounds of the Black Temple, gazing down upon him. He tried to shake himself free from the nightmare, but it returned, filling his mind, driving out all sense of being anywhere but in the ruins of his home, reliving the memory as if it were the present.

A massive figure filled the doorway, blocking out the light of the burning village. A demon. Vandel struggled to his feet. It was one thing to burn to death. It was another to let an enemy kill him.

He tottered forward, blade arcing down. Effortlessly the intruder caught his wrist and, with a flick of his arm, tossed Vandel out of the house and into the street. He landed rolling and rose. Glancing around, he saw the other demons were all dead. Only corpses lay on the ground.

His assailant turned, and Vandel saw that he was different. He appeared to be another night elf, albeit one taller than most, and with demonic features. Glowing tattoos covered his body. The face of a fallen god looked down on Vandel, somehow able to see despite the strip of runecloth shielding where his eyes should be. To his horror, Vandel recognized this figure. Here was a being around whom dark legends clustered.

"Illidan," he said. "Betrayer! You are behind this."

Vandel clutched his dagger tighter, gathered all his strength, and threw himself forward. It was a perfect thrust, expertly aimed. Never before had he struck a blow so pure. It had all the weight of destiny behind it. He was going to be the one who would end the Betrayer's life.

The tip of the blade touched the tattooed skin over Illidan's heart. A steely grip caught Vandel's wrist and halted it there.

"I am not the enemy here," Illidan said.

"I am going to kill you for what you have done."

A bitter laugh emerged from Illidan's lips. "You will not be the first to try. But you are wasting your hatred. The Burning Legion did this."

"You serve the Legion."

"I serve myself."

"You lie. You always lie."

"So my enemies would have you believe."

Vandel leaned all his weight forward. The blade did not move. Sweat beaded on his brow from the effort. Illidan gave no sign of feeling any strain.

"Because of you, my family is dead." Grief forced the words from Vandel's lips.

"Look around you. Do you see any demons? They are dead. I killed them."

"Liar."

"I arrived too late to save this place, which galls me, for I have fond memories of it. I was happy here once, briefly, ten thousand years ago."

Vandel formed his right hand into a fist and attempted to strike Illidan with it. "Liar!"

Illidan blocked the blow easily. "I grow tired of your petulance. I thought there was some strength in you. It is not given to just anyone to defeat a demon, armed only with a hunting knife. Are you going to lie there whimpering, or are you going to seek vengeance on those who did this? Join me, and you will have your revenge."

Vandel stared directly at the Betrayer's face. The runecloth made it impossible to read his expression. "I will never serve you."

"You have only two roads from this place. One of them leads to madness and death; the other, into my shadow."

"Never."

With casual strength, Illidan backhanded Vandel away. "The end of all things approaches, and I have no time to waste on fools. If you would have your vengeance, seek me out."

Darkness flickered across Vandel's field of vision. The updrafts of the burning village drove smoke and sparks into his face. When his sight cleared, Illidan was gone, leaving Vandel alone amid the ruins of his suddenly shattered life.

Mockery dripped from the demonic voice in his head. *He spoke the truth. You know that now. You knew it as soon as you had time to absorb your grief. You spent all the long years of your wandering trying to find him. Now you have. Too late for it to do you any good. You are mine, and I will have you.*

The scene shimmered. The village vanished. Vandel stood naked and alone in a tortured landscape. He had no weapons. In front of him stood the felhound he thought he had killed, alive and well. Only one thing was different. It possessed the eyes of a night elf. It took him only a moment to realize that they were identical to his own.

The creature stalked forward. Its movements were confident,

those of a hunter that knew its prey couldn't escape, that was going to take its time toying with it. Vandel flexed his hands. They were empty. He glanced around, seeking an edged rock, a boulder, anything he might use as a weapon. There was nothing. Claws scratched the stone in front of him. The felhound had taken the opportunity to close the distance between them. It reared up, huge mouth open wide.

Vandel caught the jaws just before they could close on his throat. Their points slashed the flesh of his fingers. He scrambled for a purchase that was not razor-edged, inserted his fingers into the flap of flesh between gum and lip. His right hand was not so fortunate. It snagged on sharp teeth. The pain was agonizing. The tingling of the flesh where demon saliva touched did nothing to ease the torment. It seemed to amplify it.

This is not real, he told himself.

It is very real, and if you die here in this spell-born dream, you die forever, and I will have your soul and your body. Already I have infected you. Already I can use your skills, your thoughts. Already I am so much more than I once was.

He tried to pull the jaws apart, but it took all his strength to keep them from closing. The teeth sawed into his fingers. He knew it was only a matter of time before he lost this struggle.

He lowered his head, trying to get it out of reach of the snapping jaws by resting it against the demon hound's short neck. The creature's claws bit into his unprotected chest, ripping strands of flesh free, tearing ribbons from muscle and rib. He knew he had only one chance. He let go of the beast's jaws, got his body underneath it, and raised it on high. It struggled frantically, trying to overbalance him. He held it above his head then brought it down, snapping its spine across his knee.

The felhound thrashed, all control of its limbs lost. Vandel brought his foot down on its throat and crushed its windpipe until it stopped moving.

Then driven by an instinct he could not understand, he kicked open its squelching stomach, reached into its chest cavity, and pulled out its heart. He held it up, squeezed green blood from the ventricles into his mouth, and then devoured the meat.

It tingled as it went down, but this time he felt he was gaining strength from it. The world shimmered and went dark. Nausea filled him. He fell forward over the body of his enemy. A wrenching, tearing sensation tugged at his bowels.

He stood above his own corpse where it sprawled atop the dead felhound. Slowly, impelled by some external force, his spirit rose and drifted out into the blackness. He saw that Outland was but a tiny speck in the infinity of the Great Dark Beyond. A tiny worldlet that floated in a void too vast for any mind to encompass. He became aware that all around him in that void were millions upon millions of worlds, teeming with life and glittering with promise.

He focused on one and saw a golden land, bright with sunshine, where a carefree people harvested. Then he saw a portal tear open in the fabric of reality. Through that rent poured the unstoppable forces of the Burning Legion, invincible armies of demons, bent only on destruction and slaughter.

All of this had happened many years ago. Long before the Legion had ever reached Azeroth, it had smashed its way across countless worlds, destroying everything that got in its path. Its sole relentless purpose was to kill.

There were times and places where the Legion was halted, but it always came back, stronger than before. Sometimes worlds were not destroyed; they were conquered and incorporated into the Legion's structure, producing more soldiers to feed its unceasing war engine.

He was not the only parent who had ever lost a child to the Legion. Every moment, somewhere, ten thousand children were killed by its unrelenting savagery.

Images of innumerable dead worlds flickered through his mind.

He saw gigantic ruins, toppled buildings that had once reached the sky, lakes of glass where proud cities had once stood, endless plains of rubble. He saw the lights of life in the universe winking slowly out until only a few remained.

He never doubted the truth of what he was seeing. The Burning Legion left behind a trail of smoldering worlds in its wake.

There was madness here on an incomprehensible scale. The Legion existed only to destroy. It would not stop until everything everywhere was dead, and then it would turn on itself with all its savagery until nothing remained. It was a vision of unspeakable horror. The worst of it was that he knew now how strong the Legion was. Nowhere in all the worlds in all existence was any force capable of defeating it.

Now you know the truth. Join us. The voice was back. This time there was a wheedling, pleading note, but he sensed the same hunger lay behind it.

Never.

Reality shifted. He stood amid the shattered heart of a tower. A carpet of blackened bones crunched beneath his feet. A felhound lurched forward, determined to kill him. He stooped, picked up a broken rib, and stabbed the demon through the heart. It was easier this time and he felt stronger, as if each time he slew the beast, he gained part of its strength. Once again, he opened its chest cavity, drank its blood, and devoured its heart.

A titanic vision smashed into his brain. This time he saw not just one universe but a near infinity of them, a complex fractal structure, where new worlds were born each minute from the decisions made a heartbeat before.

Everywhere the Burning Legion marched, destroying world after world. Every death narrowed the range of possible worlds, till eventually all the multitude of possibilities narrowed to but a few. In every one of them, the Legion marched triumphant, leaving futures stillborn and presents empty of all life. He saw countless Azeroths, countless Vandels, and countless Khariels, and to every one of them came death. He saw his child die in an infinity of different ways, and in every one of those possible worlds, he was powerless to prevent it.

In every world, in every future, the Burning Legion strode, invincible, unstoppable, dooming the universe to eternal darkness in its wake. Behind it all, he saw the looming demonic figures of its leaders: Archimonde—who was believed dead by so many—Kil'jaeden, and above all others, Sargeras the fallen titan, once sworn to guard the universe, now bent on destroying it.

On and on the visions roared, tearing through his brain, goading him to the edge of madness and beyond. And every time he saw one, part of him died, and the demon within him fed on his agony and gloated. He covered his eyes with his hands, but it did not stop the horrors from flowing in. He squeezed his eyes tight shut, but still he saw and saw and saw, until he could bear no more.

Drowning in horror, he inserted his fingers into his eye sockets, feeling the blood flow and the jelly puncture beneath his nails. He pulled and pulled and pulled, straining against muscle and optic nerve until his eyeballs came free with a hideous sucking sound.

At the last moment, before horror overwhelmed him, he realized this was what Illidan once saw. This was what had turned him into what he was. The Betrayer had walked this path before him. This whole ritual was intended to re-create his experience.

Pain seared through Vandel's skull.

Darkness.

Silence.

VANDEL WOKE IN AGONY. He had no idea where he was. He could see nothing around him, only flickers of shimmering light.

He reached up and touched his ruined face with fumbling fingers and found, as he had feared he would, that his eye sockets were empty. He had indeed torn out his eyes.

Fear flashed through him. Was he alive? He could see nothing. Perhaps he had died in the aftermath of the ritual. Perhaps his soul wandered in that cold wasteland where it had drifted during its voyage. Fragments of memory returned to haunt him, shards of the terrible vision eating the demon's heart had given him. He could recall only a tiny portion of what he had seen. He was grateful he could not remember more. The mind was not meant to hold such a tidal wave of horror.

He tried to stand upright but felt himself totter and fall. His head banged into the cold stone and sent tiny flickers through the darkness around him. He allowed himself to hope that perhaps it was his sight returning, but he knew it was not. He was blind and he was useless.

Mad laughter bubbled from his lips. He had wanted the power to kill demons. Now he could not even see. He had been filled with the desire to oppose the Burning Legion, and now he knew it was invincible.

Hopelessness flooded through his mind. Somewhere deep inside him, a demon was feeding. It took nourishment from his bleak mood and gloated over every crumb of wretchedness.

He would have wept if he still could. He covered his empty eye sockets in despair.

CHAPTER TEN

Four Months Before the Fall

GUARDS IN GLITTERING CHEST PLATES, MOUNTED ON armored elekk, watched Maiev approach impassively. Their tabards bore the sign of the naaru. She guessed they had looked upon far more imposing armies than her own. Shattrath was far and away the largest city she had seen in Outland, a rival in size for any of the great metropolises of Azeroth. The walls were so huge and thick, a procession of clefthoof-drawn wagons could have marched along behind the battlements and Maiev would not have known. A huge tower jutted skyward, visible even over the monumental ramparts. Above the city a range of mountains shielded the northern approaches.

A massive flying beast passed overhead and descended beyond the fortifications. She needed some of those huge sky-dwelling rays. Mounted on those, her troops could strike swiftly and be gone before their enemies responded.

She dismissed the thought. If she could get such mounts, so could her foes. The battle would just move to a new arena. At least on the ground, her troops could hide beneath the eaves of the forest. It was something the night elves were suited to and the draenei and the Broken were learning.

Not that these woods were much like home. Like so much else in Outland, they were alien. Huge moths fluttered loathsomely through the trees. Many of them were tainted by fel magic. The more she saw of this world, the more she realized it was saturated with evil mystical energies. Perhaps it had something to do with the presence of the Burning Legion. She was certain of one thing: Outland was the perfect place for Illidan. It had everything he craved. He was at home here in a way a natural elf would never be.

She stopped her teeth from grinding when she saw Anyndra looking at her. She smoothed the frown from her brow and gave the signal to advance upon the gate. If the draenei sentries were daunted by their approach, they gave no sign. They waited until the last moment to drop their lances across the entrance. It was a flimsy barrier. Her nightsaber could have jumped it, but that was not the point.

"State your business in the city of Shattrath," said the sentry on the right. He was the senior of the two.

"I have come seeking an audience with A'dal."

The draenei's face remained impassive. "And your retinue also?"

"Yes."

She guessed that the fact that so many of her troops were draenei worked in her favor. Or perhaps the guards were really just used to the sight of refugees. Her fighters were ragged from hard riding and hard fighting. Perhaps the sentries were just glad to see more troops enter the city.

The guards raised their lances. Pennons fluttered once more in the wind. Maiev rode through the huge stone arch. As soon as she crossed the threshold of the city, she gasped. There was power here, ancient and benevolent. It was woven into the stones, transforming them into more than just a physical barrier against the minions of the Burning Legion. She sensed the pulse of vast energies from within the huge central tower that loomed over the city.

"We are in the presence of the Light," Anyndra said. Whatever it was, she sensed it, too.

"Let us hope so," Maiev said. "Let us pray it is not some great deceit."

Too often evil wore the mask of benevolence. Wickedness cloaked itself in sanctity. It was easy to manipulate the gullible by such means. She considered that possibility long and hard. There had been times recently when she had thought that she would accept aid from Kil'jaeden himself if it meant the end of Illidan.

She decided that even if these naaru were less benevolent than they seemed, it did not matter. If they would help her against the Betrayer, she was prepared to make a pact with them.

THEY RODE THROUGH THE wide streets of Shattrath. Her draenei recruits pointed out the sights to one another and their night elf leaders. All of them had heard a great deal about the city even if they had never been here before. Maiev supposed that it was to the draenei of Outland what Darnassus was to her own people.

It was impressive enough in its own way, although it was a place of stone rather than living wood. Like so many of the draenei refugees it held, the city had a smashed look to it. She felt as if she was looking upon the patched ruins of a once mighty metropolis. The people around her fit their location. Many were ragged and hungry looking. Several approached her with hands outstretched. A few were children. She had nothing to give such beggars even if she wanted to. It was hard enough to keep her own troops fed and clothed, and every coin was needed to fund their war.

There were people from all over Outland. Broken huddled in

lean-tos by the side of the road. There were orcs here, which surprised her. She was not sure why. She was so used to fighting them, her hand itched to draw her blade. That urge was as nothing to the anger she felt when she saw a blood elf staring at her. She was not the only one who noticed.

"Blood elves," Anyndra said with a scowl. She felt the same loathing of these twisted elves as Maiev did. They had lost their fount of arcane magic when Arthas defiled the Sunwell and used its energies to reanimate the lich Kel'Thuzad. Now they craved arcane power with an unappeasable lust.

The blood elf's lips bent into an arrogant sneer, but he could not meet their gazes just the same.

"We should pity them," Sarius said. He walked along beside them in his night elf form. "Their lives are twisted by their unnatural craving for magical power."

"I do not think I could live if I became what they are," Anyndra said.

Sarius's smile was complex. "They were our kin once. Perhaps they could be again. They might be redeemed."

Maiev stared at him. She should have expected as much. Sarius was a druid. They had strange ideas.

"I do not think they want to be redeemed," Anyndra said. "I think they enjoy being what they are."

"How would you know?" Sarius asked. "Have you talked to any of them?"

"No. I was too busy trying to stop them from killing me," said Anyndra. Her tone was soft, and she smiled at the druid. "As you should remember."

"I certainly healed the wounds." Sarius was smiling as well. There was a definite fondness between the pair. As long as it did not interfere with the performance of their duties, Maiev did not mind.

As she rode she noticed that more than one set of sin'dorei eyes tracked them. There was no love in those gazes. She wondered if the blood elves were spies for Kael'thas and, through him, for Illidan.

THE SIGN OF THE Crystal Goblet hung over the street. The sound of music and revelry came from within. Maiev led her troops to the courtyard, and Broken stable hands rushed out to greet them. They seemed confident enough with the elekk, but none of them wanted anything to do with the nightsabers.

A massive Broken emerged from the building. His eyes went wide when he saw the number of riders. She could almost see him counting the profits.

"Blessings of the Light be upon you," he said. His horned head bowed. The long tendrils around his mouth drooped. He placed his hands together, fingers interlocked. "Welcome to the Crystal Goblet. You will find all to your satisfaction here."

"I hope so," Maiev said. "Arechron spoke very highly of Alexius and his hospitality."

The Broken's smile widened. "You have spoken to my cousin. You are thrice welcome. You will be wanting accommodations for your retinue?"

"Only for myself, my officers, and a dozen or so bodyguards. The rest of my force will be encamped beyond the city walls."

Alexius gave a small grimace of disappointment, then turned and bellowed instructions in Draenei. A small army of servants scurried off to prepare the best rooms in the house. "I would be honored if you would join me in my private rooms," he said. "I am sure there is much we must speak of."

Maiev thought she detected a note of urgency in his voice. Perhaps Arechron had already made contact. Messengers flew between Telaar and Shattrath on a regular basis.

"Indeed, I am grateful for your hospitality."

———

ALEXIUS'S CHAMBERS WERE LUXURIOUS, furnished with rugs and mirrors and racks and racks of wine bottles. He carefully selected one, blew dust off it, and showed it to Maiev, as if it meant something. She had no idea about the differences between draenei vintages, and she cared even less.

"This was a very fine year," Alexius said. "A century before our world was broken, this bottle was laid down. When you taste this, you will be getting a taste of the old Draenor."

She forced herself to smile as if she was interested and waited for him to uncork the bottle and pour. He sat there for long moments with the full glass under his lips, sniffing it with his eyes shut and a look of profound satisfaction on his face. "The scent always makes me think of my childhood."

"You drank wine as a child?"

"Sometimes with meals. But mostly it is just the scent. It makes me think of my father and mother sitting down to break bread with their kin."

"This was before your world was shattered?"

He nodded and his glowing eyes snapped open. "Yes. I am older than I look," he said, smiling to show that he knew how old he really looked.

"It must have been a terrible time," Maiev said. She had found that the more she reminded the draenei and the Broken of their suffering, the more likely they were to aid her against those they blamed for it.

"A world shattered?" His tone told her that he thought her words a gross understatement. "*Terrible* hardly begins to describe it. We thought the world was ending. The sky burned. The continents ripped apart. Lava flowed. Wild magic danced from mountain peak to mountain peak. Sometimes the tips of mountains rose into the air and floated away. Sometimes they crashed down and killed thousands."

"I have seen such things in Nagrand."

"That is like comparing a pebble to a boulder, I am afraid."

"You have been to Nagrand?"

He nodded. "Business sometimes takes me to Telaar. And family responsibilities."

His smile widened and he placed his hands, palms up, on the table. "But you have not come here to listen to the meanderings of an old innkeeper. Arechron's letters have told me something about your quest. You seek the undoing of this new lord of Outland, this Illidan."

He kept his voice low, as if even on his own property, he feared being overheard. If he thought it wise, Maiev decided that it was worth doing the same. "Yes."

"You have a very small army for such a large undertaking."

"Are you an expert in such things?"

"I was not always a fat old innkeeper. I have fought. But I have never set myself against such a mighty enemy as you have."

"I have bested him before."

"Yet he is free now and he has grown mighty. His agents lurk everywhere, in secret. There are always those who will tell tales for gold. I would be careful of to whom I spoke if I were you, and even more careful what I spoke of."

"I will bear that in mind. I was told there are those here who might aid me. The naaru, for example."

"They might, although I fear they have worries of their own."

"Still, it would not hurt to ask."

"That is so. She who does not ask, does not get, as they say." The Broken did not sound particularly hopeful about the success of her mission, but perhaps that was just his manner. "The Born from Light might help one they deem worthy."

"Born from Light?"

"The Sha'tar. That is what their name means. They are the naaru who were drawn to the ruins of Shattrath when they sensed the Aldor priests performing rites inside the rubble of one of their temples."

"Arechron mentioned the Aldor."

"As well he might. They are the servants of the naaru and of the Light. They are recruiting all they can find to oppose the Burning Legion. They would be grateful for any aid you could give them."

"I have no doubt that theirs is a worthy goal, but I feel I can best serve the Light by overcoming Illidan. He is the greatest champion the Burning Legion has in Outland."

"Is it not strange, then, that he seems to be at war with them?"

"It may be a deception. Or it may be a temporary disagreement. He has fallen out with his demonic overlords before, only to worm his way back into their favor."

"You know a great deal about it."

"I was his jailor for ten thousand years."

"He must hate you."

"And fear me, too, I hope."

"I do not doubt it," Alexius said.

"Can you arrange for me to see the naaru?"

"You can walk in and talk with them in the Terrace of Light. They will know you are here by now, and they will sense the power within you and give you a hearing."

"Is it that simple?"

"For you it will be, of that I have no doubt. Your war against the new lord of Outland has not gone unremarked."

"You said he has agents here. Would they be blood elves?"

"Perhaps, but I would not be too quick to rush to judgment if I were you. The sin'dorei here are sworn to protect the city. The Scryers look most unfavorably on those who aid your Betrayer. They betrayed him themselves."

"Did they?"

"They were sent by Prince Kael'thas to lay waste to our city. A mighty force they were, the best and brightest of Kael'thas's army, mighty magi and scholars. The Aldor braced themselves for defense, but the blood elves laid down their arms and asked for an audience with the naaru. It seems their leader, Voren'thal, had a vision. Only by serving the naaru would his people survive."

"It might well have been a trick."

"So many thought, but the naaru spoke with this Voren'thal and accepted his fealty. He and his people have served the city ever since."

"A deception."

"The naaru can see deep into the minds of those with whom they converse, and they are not easily deceived."

"If any could do so, it would no doubt be Kael'thas. He is wily."

"You speak with some bitterness."

"I, too, once regarded him as an ally."

"That is troubling. Nonetheless, the blood elves of the Scryer's Tier would be the next faction I would suggest you seek aid from."

Maiev felt her face redden. "I would rather seek aid from fel orcs."

The Broken's hand went to his mouth, and he stroked his drooping tendrils. "The enemy of my enemy . . ."

"You are not the first to suggest such a thing to me. But an alliance with the sin'dorei is a step too far."

"That is a pity, for the Scryers are mighty sorcerers . . ."

Maiev's fists clenched. The Broken realized his mistake. "I shall speak no more on the subject."

"Perhaps that would be wise." Maiev felt a brief sting of regret. She had nothing to gain by alienating the innkeeper. "I appreciate the aid you have given me. I am a stranger here, and a friendly guide is without price."

"We are all strangers in this world, Maiev Shadowsong. We must help one another."

"Is there anyone else who might help me?"

"There is Khadgar the archmage, a trusted ally of the naaru. I believe he is from your homeworld."

"Tell me of him."

"Tales swirl around this one, and it is difficult to get at the truth. He is a human. A few of them have found their way to Shattrath. Some say he is a hero who sacrificed himself to close the Dark Portal between Azeroth and Draenor. Others claim he was an apprentice of Medivh, the Guardian who was possessed by Sargeras."

"That hardly seems like a recommendation to trust him."

"The Sha'tar do."

"I fear I cannot."

"Then it is probably just as well that he is no longer in the city. The naaru have dispatched him to the Netherstorm—or so I have heard. To investigate some strange appearances there."

"You are uncommonly well informed, Alexius."

"I am an innkeeper. We hear things, particularly when we keep our ears to the ground."

"I am glad that you have done so. Of course, I would be displeased to discover that you had been talking about my business with anyone else."

Alexius looked wounded. "You were sent here by my cousin. It would be a betrayal of all the laws of kinship and hospitality for me to do so."

"Of course. I just wanted to make sure we understood each other."

"Now you sound like my cousin. I can see why he liked you."

So this is the terrace of light, Maiev thought. It was impressive in its odd way. The air shimmered. Crystalline notes sounded. Huge glowing blue crystals descended from the roof of the vast circular chamber. The scent of incense twitched her nostrils. At the center, over a massive stone dais, hovered a glowing entity of enormous power. *The naaru.* Its shape shifted constantly from one geometric form to another, but it returned most often to an outline that resembled that of a star.

Hundreds of petitioners came and went, along with priestly servants who no doubt belonged to the Aldor. Robed blood elves, wearing the tabard of the Scryers, stared at her. They did not look hostile, but they did not look friendly, either. They seemed to be wondering what she was going to do.

She made her way through the crowd, studying her surroundings. Above her the giant domed roof of the terrace echoed back the sounds of prayers and petitions.

It was some time before she confronted the naaru. She was grateful. It gave her a chance to become accustomed to its awesome presence. A'dal shimmered like a chained sun. Unleashed, the naaru's power might destroy cities or level mountains. The full blast of its attention focused on her when she stepped forward to greet it. It was all she could do to prevent herself from kneeling. She kept her head high and glanced straight into its light. Maiev felt as if the naaru was able to read her the way she might read an unfurled scroll. There was something about this being that made her feel like little more than a child.

"Greetings, Warden Shadowsong," A'dal said. The naaru radiated serenity. Its calm, pleasant voice seemed to come from everywhere and nowhere at once. Perhaps it was speaking inside her mind. "I am A'dal."

"Elune shines on the moment of our meeting," Maiev said.

A'dal said, "How can I aid you?"

"You know who I am?"

"Yes."

"You know what I do?"

"Yes."

"I have come to Outland in search of Illidan. I mean to return him to his place of incarceration."

"An ambitious goal. Illidan styles himself the lord of Outland now. He has the power to make good on that claim. Who are you to oppose him?"

"One who held him bound for ten times a thousand years."

"A blink in the eye of eternity."

Maiev's smile was rueful. "It seemed long enough to me."

"As you mortals measure time, it was, no doubt."

"But not as the naaru do?"

"We see these things differently from you. We have no bodies to age. We are beings of Light."

"Then you know Illidan must be opposed."

"It is a task you seem admirably suited to."

"It is the work of my life."

"I can see that, and it makes me regret all the more that we have no aid to give you at this time."

"What?" The word burst from her lips before she could stop it.

"Alas, we, too, have a mission in this place. We oppose the Burning Legion. This is a task that takes all our resources."

"But Illidan serves the Legion. Opposing him can only aid you."

"At this moment Illidan opposes the Legion. He is its enemy. We take advantage of this to gather our strength."

"At this moment he opposes the demons. While it suits him. When it no longer does so, he will crawl back to his masters on his belly, as he always has."

"Your hatred blinds you."

"It is not hatred. I seek justice for those he has killed, for those he has betrayed, for those he will murder. You cannot tell me that you believe that Illidan is any better than the Burning Legion."

"You have no concept of the true nature of the Burning Legion, Warden Shadowsong."

"And you do?"

"We have opposed it for a thousand times your lifetime. We shall oppose it until the end of all that is."

"I need more than fine words if I am to bring Illidan to justice."

"Unfortunately, words are all I have for you now. You must find your own path. You are not without allies here, even if you cannot see that. You can find more if you make the attempt. The chief magister of the Scryers waits to speak with you."

"A blood elf?"

"One of your people."

"The blood elves are not my people. They turned their back on my people long ago. We have nothing in common."

"Save perhaps an enemy."

"I will have nothing to do with those heretics."

"That would be your choice."

Maiev reined in her fury. She bowed and turned on her heel without waiting for A'dal to terminate the audience. She heard gasps from nearby blood elves, which gave her some satisfaction. A tall blood elf in the tabard of a Scryer moved toward her. He was most likely the one A'dal had mentioned. She swept by him without giving him the opportunity to speak.

It seemed that she still had some principles. There were those with whom she would not consider a pact. Even to bring down the Betrayer.

CHAPTER ELEVEN

Four Months Before the Fall

VANDEL MOANED AND TRIED TO SIT UP. HIS HEAD SPUN. He stretched out his hands, trying to maintain his balance, but that just made things worse. He crashed back to the hard floor, smacking his head. His forehead felt wet beneath his questing fingers. He had cut himself again. Blood matted his hair from his previous attempts at rising.

He dry heaved. The demon meat in his stomach was fighting its way free. The thought sickened him, and yet it also made his mouth water.

All around, he could hear screams and groans and babbling. Sometimes he recognized the voices of his fellow aspirants. Sometimes, he thought it was all his imagination, that he was trapped in a private hell of his own making. The air stank of rotting flesh, gangrene, pus, and excrement.

At regular intervals, the hooves of Broken servants clattered on the stone floor as they cleaned the chambers and washed the sick. Twice they had swabbed him with sponges, and he had tried to force them away. All he wanted was to be left alone.

Glowworms of color writhed across his field of vision. At first they had given him hope that he might be starting to see again, but now he thought his mind was playing tricks on him, pretending to see things whenever he heard others near.

"Broken moon, demon moon, blood moon!" He knew that shouting voice from somewhere, but he was not sure from where. "Demons approach. A demon approaches."

Leathery wings snapped. Displaced air swirled around his face.

"On your feet," Illidan's voice said. "You have rested long enough."

It was the first time Vandel had heard the Betrayer's voice since the ritual. He felt his lips tighten into a sneer. "What is the point? I cannot see."

"I thought the same thing once. But now I can see to the end of the universe. It is closer than most think."

Remembering the march of the Burning Legion through countless devastated worlds, Vandel understood the bitter humor of the Betrayer's words. "I know."

"Then you also know what we fight. And why." There was an arrogant certainty in Illidan's tone that Vandel resented. There was a challenge, too.

The demonic thing within him stirred, responding to Illidan's presence with something like hunger. It lent Vandel strength and goaded him to speak. "How can you fight against what I saw? It is impossible."

Impossible, impossible, impossible, whispered the voice in the back of his head. It still sounded like his own, only clotted with hatred. The felhound had grafted itself to his soul, and its spirit seemed able to use his mind and his memories now.

"Be quiet," Vandel told it.

He heard the creak of wings as Illidan moved. The Betrayer ignored his words as if he sensed to whom Vandel was speaking. "We must fight. Countless worlds have fallen to the Legion, and ours will be next unless we stop it."

Fragments of apocalyptic visions swirled through Vandel's mind. He saw worlds burning and nations dying, and through it all he saw the Legion marching, its victory as inevitable as death. The thing at the back of his mind snickered. "Be quiet," he repeated, but it ignored him.

"Stand up," Illidan commanded, and there was no disobeying that voice. Even the thing in Vandel's mind quailed. He lurched to his feet and stood there, swaying. His stomach heaved. The world spun once more. A clawed hand dug into his shoulder and held him upright. Writhing worms of light shimmered beside him, slithering away from the point of contact.

"I cannot see," Vandel said.

"You can see everything."

Vandel's head spun faster. Lights flickered all around him.

He lashed out with his hand, seeking to strike at the lights. They moved away. Rage surged within him. The worms of light were everywhere, covering everything. They filled the space surrounding him. He heard a whimpering sound from a mass of sickly green, knew it was a feverish elf.

He twisted to where Illidan stood, and he saw a blaze of light. If he looked closely, it appeared to be a winged shape.

"You tricked me, Betrayer. You told me you would give me the power to fight demons, to avenge my family." His anger was a bonfire as bright as Illidan's aura. It gave him strength. Hatred tasted like bile in his mouth. He wanted to smash his fists into Illidan's face and beat him till the bones broke. He wanted to drink his blood and eat his heart and be filled with the power that burned before him.

The dizziness was gone now. He had no trouble moving. He wished he had his blades.

"I have given you all that and more." The blaze of Illidan's aura moved. Vandel turned his head, tracking it, and he realized that he was also tracking the source of the voice. This did not make him less angry. Frustration built up in him. He wanted to rend and tear.

He bit his lip until blood flowed. He was going to kill the Betrayer. He was going to supplant him.

He sprang forward. He heard a rustling sound. His fist smashed into something leathery but lined with bone. A wing. Illidan's wing. A moment later it buffeted him from his feet. He hit the ground and rolled toward another swirling mass of light. He felt the contact of flesh when he reached it, heard a feverish voice groan.

No doubt about it—in some way, he was perceiving where things were.

He sniffed the air, smelled soiled bandages, unwashed flesh, and beneath that the tainted odor of demon, repulsing him and arousing his hunger at the same time. He wanted to feast upon it. He dived forward, jaws clamping on the sick elf's arm. A powerful hand caught him by the neck and lifted him like an elf might lift a nightsaber cub.

Illidan said, "Enough. You must learn to control that which lies within you, or it will control you."

Rage goaded Vandel to aim an elbow backward. Once again he felt himself cast across the room. Air rushed by. He sensed the cold presence of the wall before he hit it, and he let himself go limp. The impact hurt but not as much as it ought to. He rolled once again to his feet.

The Betrayer was keeping him from his prey. Vandel coiled his muscles to leap. Illidan's aura became sharper, its greenish-yellow light blazing. Motes of it swirled in the air around him, shifting into new patterns as the Betrayer moved his fingers and arms. Vandel realized he was seeing fel magic being bound to Illidan's will as he drew upon its power. A moment later a bolt of it leapt from Illidan's finger and impacted on Vandel's chest. Strength drained from his body like wine from an upended goblet. The dizziness returned, multiplied a thousandfold. He crashed into the stone at Illidan's hooves, rage departing in proportion to his strength.

He felt like himself once more, but he understood now what he was seeing, what had happened to him. "The demon I devoured. It is still within me, is it not?"

"Yes," said Illidan, "and it wants to be free."

"How can I control it?"

"You take the first step along that road today. Walk with me."

"Why?"

"Why what?"

"Why are you here? Why are you helping me?"

"Because you know who the true enemy is, and you have the potential to be a great hunter of demons. I saw that the day your village burned. I see it now. I will have need of fighters like you before the end."

Still dizzy and weak, Vandel forced himself to his feet. His true foes were the innumerable forces of the Burning Legion, which even now prepared to strike at his homeworld.

He stood for a moment, calming his mind, listening for any internal voice that was not his own. He heard nothing, but he knew that didn't mean anything. He did not doubt that the demon was still in there, waiting for the opportunity to break free once more.

He was aware now of the ebb and flow of energies all around. The lights were auras of living things, some bright, some filled with energy. The brightest of all came from the being who stood beside him.

"Is this how you see the world?" Vandel asked.

"It is one way. Your mind becomes accustomed to it eventually. It maps its new way of seeing onto its old way of understanding reality. There will come a time when you will be able to perceive the world as once you did. It is a much narrower way of seeing, but our minds crave familiarity."

"You are saying you can shift from seeing the world like this to seeing it as if you had eyes?"

"Indeed, and many gradations between."

He tried to imagine Illidan as he had previously seen him, and slowly a very rough image of the Betrayer stood before him, like a child's illustration drawn in mud. Its mud mouth moved as Illidan spoke. "In a way it is like working magic. You get a feel for the flows of power. You get a sense of the souls of the living and the unliving."

They walked toward a doorway. Vandel sensed its lack of density in the air and the solid matter around it. He was not sure how. He also sensed there were living things beyond it. There was power in them, too. They were waiting for something.

Illidan pushed him forward. He collided with something at about waist height. It felt like the edge of a table. "Lie down on it."

"Why?" Vandel asked.

"You are about to receive your first tattoos."

Vandel fumbled at the table with his hands, feeling the rough texture of the wood. It came to him then how much he had taken his sense of touch for granted, and how inaccurate it used to be. Now he could feel every grain of the wood, every knot, every splinter. He felt areas that were slightly rougher, as if the carpenter had been sloppy with his planing. It seemed like his various senses were now many times magnified.

He lay down on the board. Leather straps snapped into place around him. Momentary panic filled him as he was restrained. It increased as power blossomed in one of the nearby figures.

"You will learn to do these for yourself one day, but for now, you must accept them from others. Be still," said Illidan. "This will hurt."

The inker leaned forward, and something so hot it was cold, or perhaps so cold it was hot, touched Vandel's flesh. He fought down the urge to scream. When the needle withdrew, he felt as if a dagger were being pulled from a wound and twisted.

No. No. No. The voice in his head gibbered in panic. The fear communicated itself to him.

This was a trap. Evil magic was being worked here.

The needle stabbed in once more. Pain blasted his body, worse than anything he had felt since he had pulled out his own eyes. He thrashed around, trying to free himself. The restraining bands drew tight. Hard hands pushed down on him.

The needle stabbed again and again, and every touch of its point sent blazing agony searing through him. With every stitch, strength leached out of him. The voice in his head grew weaker and weaker.

He was dying. This magic was going to kill him.

He snarled threats and whimpered pleas, but the pain went on and on and on, until he could struggle no more and could only lie there while the inker went about his work.

Eventually the straps were undone. He could barely rise from the table. His anger and his fear had subsided. For the first time in days, he truly felt like himself. He could barely see the glow of auras around him. His enhanced senses had returned to normal levels. It was as if he had been drugged and the potency had worn off.

"I am glad that is over," Vandel said.

"The worst is just beginning," Illidan replied.

THE CELL WALLS CLOSED in all around Vandel. Down below in the courtyards, he could hear fighting and practicing. Were they like him, he wondered, a new intake of fools who had been seduced by Illidan's promises of power?

It was a relief to be away from the sick house, to have his own chamber. He had been brought here immediately after gaining his first tattoos. It had taken him the whole day to recover from that. It was pleasant not to be surrounded by the auras of living things. The quiet was relaxing. He lay on his bed and touched his empty sockets.

His eyes were gone forever. In the absence of living things, it was easy to convince himself that he had hallucinated the whole experience of seeing auras. Perhaps it was a dream.

The feel of rough sheets beneath his fingers told him that it was not. He was blind. He had blinded himself so he wouldn't see the terrible truth, that the whole universe was doomed, like his wife and child had been. There was nothing he or anyone else could do to stop the Burning Legion. Anyone who thought otherwise was as deluded as the Betrayer.

Such delusions were easy to have, sitting in a fortress like the Black Temple, surrounded by troops. The truth was that no one was safe. No place was safe. When the Burning Legion exerted its strength, the Black Temple would fall like a child's sand castle kicked by a giant. All those fighters practicing arms outside would die when the dreadlords came to claim the Legion's possession. Great Sargeras, the titan who would topple the universe, would ultimately triumph. He had been the first to see the truth.

Vandel stopped. Where had that come from? He had seen the fallen titan in his vision. That must be it. Some part of Illidan's original vision had been transferred to him during the ritual. He knew that. But sometimes it felt as if Vandel wasn't in control of his thoughts.

The tattoos bound the demon within him. It could not escape now. He traced the ink with his fingers, feeling the lines of power that scarred his body. His hand touched something else, something cold and hard.

At first he thought it was a piece of metal, but then he realized that it was set in his skin. He fumbled at his face and found it was there, too. He paused, chilled by the realization that his flesh had been transformed. He felt one hand with the other, and it slowly dawned on him what had happened. Every place on his skin that had been touched by demon blood had been altered. He had acquired scales of some sort.

This might just be the start of the process. He was certain that while he lay in the hospital, his skin had been normal. Perhaps this was only the first stage of the transformation. Perhaps he was turning into a demon.

It seemed entirely possible. After all, he had no idea what had really been done to him. Illidan might well be lying. He certainly would if it suited his purposes. The change had begun after the demon had been chained by the mystical tattoos. It must have. He had not been changed when he got up this morning. He was certain of that. Perhaps since the demon was unable to affect his mind, it was starting to affect his body.

He rubbed his fingers against his palms. He felt the fingertips of his left hand with those of his right. The nails were long and sharp and dense, like the claws of a hunting cat.

His gums hurt, and he fumbled at his mouth. Yes. His canines jutted out, large and sharp. He had acquired fangs.

Black depression settled on him. He had sought the power to fight demons. Instead he was being transformed into one. He was turning into the thing he hated. How long would it be before he was out there, killing other elves' children? He had felt the unnatural rage the demon had given him. He understood its strength. Who was he to try to contain that?

Perhaps the best thing he could do was to kill himself before that happened. He sat up and reached out to the small table beside his bed. His rune-woven knife lay there, along with the charm he had made for Khariel. He picked that up and thought about his dead son. How would Khariel feel if he saw his father now? He would see only a monster, a creature on its way to becoming the thing that had murdered him.

He told himself he was not thinking clearly, that something was affecting his mind. Perhaps it was the aftereffects from the tattoo sorcery.

No. You are seeing clearly, for the first time in a long while. You are seeing yourself as you are. A hollow thing that has allowed itself to be changed into that which it hates, in search of a vengeance impossible to get. Illidan is mad. You are mad.

The truth of that thought was incontestable. He was insane, and had been for a very long time. He had always suspected it, and now all his suspicions were confirmed.

Hatred filled him, turned this time on himself. He took the knife, tested its blade on his thumb. It was still magically sharp. He took the point and inserted it under the edge of one of the scales. He pulled it free. It hurt, but the pain lent him energy. If he could cut out all the scales, he could stop the transformation, like a surgeon cutting out a patch of gangrene.

The thought drove him to cut again and again until he was covered in his own blood and patches of his skin lay on the floor. He felt weak and dizzy. It occurred to him that he was losing blood and that he might die here in this cell.

Something in his head laughed at that, and it came to him that the demon was not as trapped as he had believed, and certainly not as weak. It had just turned to a new form of attack, twisting his thoughts, toying with his emotions. It had tapped into all of his dark thoughts and self-hatred. It had access to all of his feelings and all of his shame. In a way, it *was* him.

He pulled himself upright, and the demon went silent as if it had realized its mistake. He reeled toward the door. Blood stuck to his bare feet and made them sticky. He prayed that the cell door was not locked as he threw his strength against it. The door opened and he fumbled his way out into the corridor, staggering from side to side so that he grazed the walls.

He heard someone shout, "Another one. Get Akama!"

Then he passed out.

VANDEL WOKE TO THE awareness of power all around him. It was soothing. The areas he had cut felt numb. They tingled, but the sensation was almost pleasant. Someone stood over him. He smelled like a Broken. His aura blazed with magic.

"You are Akama?" Vandel's voice was weak and his throat felt parched.

"Yes. You are Vandel." It was not a question. "You clearly impressed Lord Illidan. He asked me to look after you personally."

"You are a healer?"

"I am. I do what I can to help the sick and the wounded."

"Which am I?"

"A bit of both, I would say, and something else as well. There is a taint in you that I mislike."

"Whatever it is, I thank you for your help."

"You are welcome, and you are also lucky the guards found you in time. You are the fifth of the new recruits to have attempted suicide in the past two days. You are the only one who has lived."

"I did not attempt suicide."

"What else would you call it? You hacked at your own flesh until you almost bled to death. You would have, if you had hit an artery. What has been done to you?"

There was a note below the natural curiosity in Akama's voice that made Vandel wary. "You do not know?"

"I know only that Lord Illidan takes many of your people into that courtyard, and only a few come out, and those altered almost beyond recognition. If he is trying to create an army, he has chosen a funny way of doing so. Killing recruits rarely leads to a large force."

"If you do not know what is going on, it would perhaps be better not to ask. Lord Illidan has his reasons, and if he wants you to know them, he will share them with you."

Akama made a tut-tutting sound. "As you say. There is a good deal that goes on here in the temple that it is best not to be curious about."

As if to echo this, a mighty bellow sounded from deep below-ground. The stones seemed to vibrate in time to the roaring.

"Another monster bound in the temple's defense," said Akama.

Vandel ignored the Broken. A jolt of memory passed through him. Four others had killed themselves. He recalled Illidan's words. It was possible that fewer than one in five of the recruits was going to survive the transformation. Vandel had thought the Betrayer had been talking only about the ritual, but it occurred to him now that he had also meant its aftermath.

He felt a sudden certainty that things were just beginning and that the worst still lay ahead.

CHAPTER TWELVE

Four Months Before the Fall

ILLIDAN STRODE INTO THE COUNCIL CHAMBER. AKAMA followed at his heels like a faithful dog. The Broken seemed to be doing everything possible to look like a loyal servant. Perhaps he suspected that Veras Darkshadow's agents were watching him, and had been ever since his mysterious disappearances from the Black Temple had become numerous enough to attract Veras's attention. It was possible that Darkshadow simply wanted to discredit a rival, but his claims had aroused Illidan's curiosity.

All eyes turned to look at him. There was fear in every gaze. The Burning Legion had struck hard. Prince Kael'thas had been missing for weeks, ever since he had set out in command of an expeditionary force to the Netherstorm. Everyone present knew that the war was not going well, and they expected to feel Illidan's wrath because of it. It did not matter. All was going according to plan as long as his demon hunters were coming along.

Illidan stalked over to the great map table. Massive gems carved to represent demonic transporters marred a dozen locations. They glittered like plague boils on the face of the world. They dotted

Nagrand and Hellfire Peninsula, the Netherstorm and the Blade's Edge Mountains. It seemed that almost every province of Outland held at least one, sometimes more.

"Each of these marks a new forge camp, Lord Illidan," said Gathios the Shatterer, a little too quickly. He had risen from his carved throne as soon as Illidan entered, and he stood there as if called to attention by a commanding officer. "The Burning Legion has set up bases there and fortified them. I have been putting together contingency plans to assault them and throw the demons back."

"Have you, Gathios?" Illidan kept his voice deceptively mild. "And how exactly do you intend to do that? Each of those forge camps contains a transporter. They can be reinforced by demons at a moment's notice."

"Lord Illidan, we closed Magtheridon's portals with your aid. Surely we can close these."

Illidan studied the map. "Every time we close a portal, another appears. Kil'jaeden can draw upon near-infinite forces. He toys with us."

Lady Malande gave a nervous giggle. This was obviously not what she had expected Illidan to say. "You will lead us to victory, Lord. I have every faith in you. These new soldiers you have been forging—if they are all as strong as Varedis and Netharel and Alandien—will surely be able to slaughter the demons."

Illidan stared at her. She seemed particularly well informed about the demon hunters. Had she been spying on them? Of course she had. All of his council had. They were curious about anything that shifted the balance of power within the Black Temple. It might well affect their own stations. How much had Malande uncovered? The demon hunters represented the most important part of his plan to strike back at the Burning Legion. Secrecy was critical. He could not take any chances of the nathrezim finding out what he was up to until he was ready to launch his attack. He had told no one of his ultimate goal—but he might have let something slip, left some clue from which a mind as keen and suspicious as Malande's would be able to deduce his intentions.

Illidan wished that Lady Vashj were here. She was at least straightforward, easy to understand, and utterly loyal. Alas, she was in Zangarmarsh, supervising the draining of the marshland as part of the first stage of the plan to take control of all the waters of Outland and, through them, all its people. Thirst and drought were mighty weapons.

Illidan gazed at Veras Darkshadow. "Have your agents found out anything concerning Kael'thas's fate?"

Veras shook his head. "They found the last camp of his army, but then nothing."

"Nothing?"

"Nothing significant, Lord. Traces of campfires, refuse, little more."

"No sign of a struggle?"

"None, Lord. It is as if the prince simply opened a portal and vanished. It seems he does not want to be found."

Veras was implying that Kael'thas was planning some treachery. Illidan did not discount the possibility. Kil'jaeden had shown particular interest in the blood elf prince the day the Black Temple had fallen. On consideration, Illidan had decided that the Deceiver had been trying to sow seeds of dissension between him and his allies. Perhaps the demon lord had done more than that, but now was not the time to say so. If Kael'thas had turned, he might well have left spies behind. Illidan would not make them wary. "Let us not jump to any conclusions, Veras. Just find Kael'thas."

"As you wish, Lord," said Veras. "So shall it be."

He looked as if he wanted to speak more in private. His eyes flashed to Akama. Illidan said, "All of you are dismissed. Except you, Darkshadow. I want to have words with you concerning the whereabouts of Maiev Shadowsong."

The other council members filed out. Akama paused in the doorway as if he was about to say something, thought the better of it, and departed.

THE ELEVATOR CARRIED MAIEV and Anyndra up the side of Aldor Rise. It was a low, flat platform, and nothing visible supported it as it lifted itself into the sky. Powerful magic was at work here. Maiev's nightsaber growled and stayed away from the edge. The big cat had an excellent sense of balance, but it was taking no chances of a fall from this height.

Maiev had a tremendous view of the rooftops of the city and the great tower that housed the Terrace of Light. It was so tall, it threatened to touch the sky. Inside it, she felt the power of the naaru. It galled her that they had not agreed to help. With their aid, she would have had a much better chance of bringing Illidan to justice.

Sarius soared along beside the elevator, wearing the form of a storm crow. Maiev recognized him by his distinctive plumage. He was there to watch and observe. She did not expect these Aldor to prove treacherous, but she never ruled out the possibility with anyone. Traitors could be found in the most surprising places.

Anyndra said, "They say that sometimes the Broken ride this elevator just so they can throw themselves off at the top. You would think the sentries would prevent that."

"Maybe they think they are performing an act of mercy," said Maiev.

She was wondering whether she should have brought more guards. They would be outnumbered atop Aldor Rise, but at least their presence would have spoken of Maiev's importance. In the end, she had decided that it would be better to appear as a petitioner.

The platform glided to a stop. She took one last glance down at the city and thought about those sad Broken making the long drop to the stones below.

Above them, two stone islets hovered in the sky. They had been curved after the fashion of draenei architecture, and lights glowed in their sides to leave the viewer in no doubt as to their magical provenance. It was clear that visitors were meant to be overawed by this display of magic.

Great crystals studded the sides of the buildings atop the rise. At night their glow could be seen in the sky above the city, a reminder to all of the purity of the Aldor and the Light they served. Maiev sniffed at the thought.

Aldor guards, clad in heavy armor and wearing the purple tabard of their faction, greeted her. They were not hostile, but they made it very clear that she was under observation. She stated her business, and they led her to the so-called Shrine of Unending Light.

A tall, beautiful female draenei, garbed in robes of blue and white moved to greet her. Maiev inclined her head to accept her benediction.

"Blessings of the Light upon you, Warden Shadowsong," said the draenei. "I am Ishanah, high priestess of the Aldor. I have been told that you would have words with me."

Maiev detected a subtle note of hostility in the high priestess's tone. "I have come seeking the aid of those who follow the Light."

"I have been told that a number of those already follow you."

"I meant the Aldor."

"You seek to slay the one called the Betrayer?"

"Or imprison him once more."

"Why?"

Maiev's jaw fell open. "Because he is evil."

"We do not have such strength that we can afford to throw it away assaulting the Black Temple. It is all we can do to hold our ground. And we serve other functions."

Maiev let her eyes dwell on Ishanah's rich robes, then let them slide to their beautiful surroundings. "I can see that."

"We do not all have to enter the darkness to fight against it."

"Sometimes, defeating evil means getting your hands dirty."

"And sometimes, getting your hands dirty turns you to evil." Ishanah's smile seemed mocking. "In order to work with the Light, you must be pure of heart."

"And you think I am not?" Maiev's anger simmered in her voice.

"I think you do what you believe is right."

Maiev frowned at that hairsplitting distinction. "What I do *is* right."

"No doubt. No doubt."

"You will not aid me?"

"At this moment, I cannot."

"Cannot or will not?"

"There are other struggles than your own, Warden Shadowsong. Some of them are more important."

"Nothing is more important than the overthrow of Illidan."

"Perhaps to you. We Aldor have different priorities and limited resources. We need time to gather our strength."

Frustration filled the warden. Why was it so difficult to get the people of Outland to see the importance of her mission? She felt a tingling against her breast. It was from the stone Akama had given her. This was not the usual time they had set for their meetings. Something urgent must have come up. Perhaps it was just as well. She did not want to continue this fruitless circular argument with Ishanah anyway.

"I thank you for your time," Maiev said, "and ask your permission to depart."

Without waiting for it, she turned and strode back to the elevator, followed by Anyndra.

She needed a quiet place to communicate with Akama. She hoped that he would prove less useless than the Aldor.

———

THE STREETS OF SHATTRATH'S lower terrace seemed more crowded every day. More and more refugees flooded into the city, fleeing from Illidan's wars of conquest and the aftermath of his losing battles with the Legion. They seemed determined to place themselves under the protection of the Sha'tar.

Maiev glanced over her shoulder. A blood elf hurried through the street behind her, face cowled, a scarf wound over her lower jaw. There was something in her manner that was familiar. Perhaps she was spying on Maiev. It did not matter. Sarius was out there in the crowd, watching her back. Perhaps sometime, she would order him to capture one of those who dogged her steps. At the moment, she had other matters to consider.

She stepped into the courtyard of the Refuge of the Broken. The usual wretches looked up from their sour watered wine, or stared at the ceiling in a numbed stupor. The air stank of the rough tobacco they smoked. It reeked of their unwashed bodies. She made her way to the chamber in which she had previously met with Akama, and she was unsurprised to find him there. Two of the Ashtongue guards who had watched over him before minded the door and let her pass without comment.

The Broken rose and bowed to her in greeting. At least he showed her some respect. Over the last few years, they had reached an understanding of sorts. She inclined her head regally in acknowledgment.

"What news?" Maiev asked. She hoped it was better than their last meeting, which had concerned only some minor victory in Illidan's war against the Legion.

"Great news," Akama said. The excitement in his voice communicated itself to her. "Prince Kael'thas is missing, along with some of his army. It is likely that he has abandoned the Betrayer."

Maiev could not keep the smile of triumph from her face. "If

that is true, then Illidan has lost one of the great props to his power."
She let the words hang in the air. In the past, Akama had refused to
commit his people because Illidan was supported by Kael'thas and
Lady Vashj.

Akama's smile matched her own only for a moment. "Illidan
may have found a new source of power."

A chill of foreboding passed through Maiev. Perhaps the Betrayer had a trick to play yet. It would not be the first time. "What
is it?"

"I am not certain, which is why I wanted to talk to you. They
are recruited entirely from your people . . ."

"My people?"

"Elves. Desperate, ruthless elves, hardened fighters all, and all
with a grudge against the Burning Legion, as far as I can tell. He
takes them and he kills them."

"What?"

"He infuses them with fel magic. Most of them die during the
process, and those who live are changed, and not for the better."

"What do you mean?"

"Their bodies are saturated with evil power, and there is something in them that reeks of the demonic."

Horror twisted Maiev's face. "He is transforming elves into demons."

"Unless I miss my guess, he is remaking them in his own image.
He works rituals upon them. He supervises as they receive tattoos
like his. He teaches them magic, or at least so I gather from the rumors picked up by my agents. All of this takes place in sealed courtyards far from the everyday business of the temple."

What new monstrousness is Illidan planning? Maiev wondered.
Knowing him, it could not be anything good. "You must find out
more of this."

"I am doing my best, but it is difficult and dangerous. The Betrayer has taken great pains to hide his intentions for this new army.

If I ask too many questions, I may be found out. If Illidan learns of our association, I am worse than dead. I must move cautiously."

"Cautiously, cautiously, it is always cautiously with you."

"That is easy for you to say. I am the one who will face the wrath of the Betrayer if things go wrong." Akama paused and took a rasping breath. "You do not know what it is like. Every time I leave the Temple of Karabor, I must lie. I think already Illidan suspects something . . . I feel as if I am being watched."

It came to Maiev that in her impatience, she was in danger of taking the wrong tack. Akama was clearly frightened, and not without good reason.

Akama took another deep breath and spoke in a more measured tone. "It is not the first time tattooed fighters have appeared around the temple. There have been others like this before, but only seen in ones or twos, and never for long before they went on their way. This time all of them are here, and he seems bent on creating many more like them."

"The first of them could have been experiments, intended to test the magic used in creating these demon elves."

"Such was my thought. Now there seem to be many more of them. Illidan spends lives like a drunken mercenary squanders ill-gotten silver in order to create them. For every ten who go into the hidden courts, perhaps one comes out."

This news changed Maiev's mood. Her earlier good humor about Kael'thas's disappearance had evaporated. She knew in her heart of hearts that Illidan planned some new deviltry.

"I do not like this at all," Maiev said.

Akama shrugged. "These new creatures are powerful. I have been called upon to heal them, and I sense strong, dark magic within them. Perhaps Illidan feels they will tip the scales back in his favor."

"Do you think that is possible?"

"He seems determined to create hundreds of these creatures, if not thousands. If they are all as mighty as the ones I have seen, they could change the balance of power in Outland. All I know is that the Betrayer is in a frenzy to recruit as many of them as possible. I have sensed that he has a purpose in mind, and whatever it is, time is running out."

"Time is certainly running out for him," Maiev said, trying to re-create her earlier mood. "Without Kael'thas's support, there is a chance to unseat him."

"Indeed," said Akama. "I will return to the Temple of Karabor and begin preparations. If we are to move, we must move quickly, before his new army is ready."

Satisfaction filled Maiev's mind. It was the first time the Broken had expressed a definite commitment to action. It seemed that he, just as much as the Betrayer, felt time was getting short.

AKAMA PASSED THROUGH THE portal and stepped into the Temple of Karabor. Despite all the corruption about him, it still felt like coming home. He rubbed his hands together, took a deep breath, and tried to push his worries away.

Confronting Maiev was always nerve racking. She was so full of rage and hate, and she was so determined to take Illidan to task for all his wrongdoing. She really did not seem to realize that she had turned herself into the Betrayer's mirror image.

The Broken hurried through the corridors toward his chambers. One of the abominable eyeless soldiers glanced at him as he passed. It was eerie how those blind-seeming heads turned to track him as he went by.

All around, the temple buzzed with activity. Soldiers marched, magi wove spells. The defenses were being strengthened night and day.

He reached the sanctuary of his people. His bodyguard gave him a warning sign, and as he passed the entrance, he understood why.

Illidan waited within the chamber. In his hand, he had a precious crystal statue that Akama had preserved from the destruction of the temple. He held it up to the light, turning it this way and that.

He did not look around as the Broken entered. He just said, "Ah, Akama, you have been hard to find today."

There had been a time when this simple trick would have disconcerted Akama, but he was used to it now. "I went traveling to Orebor Harborage. I had much to think about, and it helps clear my head."

"You have been doing that a lot over the past few years."

Akama's stomach lurched. Did the Betrayer suspect what was going on? Had he seen through the deceptions?

Illidan walked over and placed an arm around Akama's shoulder. The tips of his talons dug gently into the cloth of the Broken's tunic. "Walk with me to the refectory. It has been some time since we talked. I would learn more of these jaunts of yours."

With irresistible strength, he guided Akama through the exit that led into the temple's Sanctuary of Shadows. Demons moved into position all around him. Akama glanced at the great chains hanging from the darkened pillars that rose so high above. They seemed like a dark omen.

Soon screams rang out as if from someone whose soul was being ripped from his body.

CHAPTER THIRTEEN

Three Months Before the Fall

VANDEL LEAPT THROUGH THE BLAZING RING, HIT THE
ground rolling, ducked under the swinging blade. It passed him by
a hair's breadth. He rose, sprang forward over the flame pit. He was
first again. He had passed through all the obstacles without taking a
scratch.

Cyana was just behind him, not even breathing hard. She smiled
at him, but he sensed that she was piqued that he had beaten her
again. She was very competitive. Ravael was next, lithe and swift.
The others filtered in one after another.

In the weeks after the ritual, there had been many losses. Mavelith and Seladan and Isteth had hurled themselves from the battlements, unable to bear what they had become. Mavelith and Seladan
had grown progressively more monstrous looking as the days
dragged into weeks, but Isteth still had the beauty that Vandel had
noticed during the first days. It was her mind that had been twisted.
He hoped she was at peace now, joined at last with her dead children.

Any hope that the ritual had winnowed out those who could
not face the consequences of their choices was gone. Over half of

those transformed had died in the process. Their hearts had stopped, or their minds had cracked and they had needed to be put down. More had gone mad in the aftermath, unable to bear the visions they witnessed or to live with the things resident inside them.

Vandel had no doubt that their demons had pushed them over the edge. The thing within him made its presence felt every day, and he was by no means certain that he would win this struggle in the long run. There were days when depression and self-loathing made his life unbearable. There were times when he was so filled with rage that he could barely restrain himself from running through the temple and slashing elves with his blades until the guards dragged him down.

Selenis had gone out that way, and Balambor and Turanis. They had taken a lot of others with them. All of the survivors of the ritual understood what they had felt. Vandel had come within a hair's breadth of doing it himself. He sometimes wondered if the difference between him and the berserkers was just that he had not quite reached the brink yet. He clutched the amulet he had made for Khariel tight in his hand, a talisman of protection against the possibility, a reminder to himself of why he fought with his demon every day. *Vengeance, Son. One day you will have vengeance.*

Something at the back of his mind mocked him, but for today, at least he could ignore it.

Things had gotten worse since the supernatural part of the training started. Their instructors, Varedis, Alandien, and Netharel, taught them how to tap the fel powers of the demons within them, how to channel the darkest energies in creation.

In a way it was thrilling. Vandel knew now how to augment his strength and speed manyfold. He could drive the blade of his dagger into a boulder and rip it free. He had cast bolts of fel energy capable of burning through the strongest of armor. He could heal himself by draining the souls of his fallen victims.

He had battled summoned demons, learning how to kill them.

At first the aspirants had fought in groups, but as the weeks passed, they had been trained how to win in single combat. Scores had died during that period, and one night a felguard had broken free and rampaged through the corridors of the ruins of Karabor until Varedis had brought him down. Vandel fingered the long scar down his right side that the demon had given him. The felguard's axe had ripped through the inking of his tattoos, distorting them and making it hard to draw on fel energies when he tried to cast certain spells.

He had learned an enormous amount in a very brief time, but it seemed no matter how much he grasped, his instructors always wanted him to try harder, master more. They were as driven as Illidan, and he could not help but feel there was some great purpose behind this, that the day was coming when all he had learned would be put to use in the Betrayer's service. There was an urgency about this process, and a desperation. Every day the great ritual was performed. Every day more and more candidates were fed into the hungry maw of the training process. A few of them survived to be threshed through a system that often seemed intended as much to kill the weak as to teach the strong.

Kill the weak. Kill the weak. Kill the weak, the demonic voice whispered. Images of Khariel's half-devoured body flickered mockingly through his mind. *Kill them all. All are weak.*

His dreams were things of horror. One night he woke to find himself standing, clutching his blade. He wondered then if the thing within him gained a measure of control during his nightmares. Tabelius had sneaked through the cells, slitting throats, until Needle ended his nocturnal adventuring forever by putting a skewer through each empty eye socket.

There were times when Vandel felt as if he were locked in a cage with murderous beasts, and he was not the least murderous of them.

He looked around him again. Illidan had been right. He could see things now as well as ever he had seen when he possessed eyes of flesh. Better. Darkness obscured nothing. Something in his mind adjusted his perceptions. He suspected the demon aided him. It wanted him to master these powers, as if the more he mastered, the more vulnerable he became to the temptations the demon put before him.

No matter. He wanted the strength. He was glad he could see. He was glad he could hear better than any elf had a right to. He was glad he was strong as an ogre and swifter than a nightsaber. His appearance reflected the changes. He could extend claws from his fingertips, and did so in moments of danger. Massive scars marked where he had gouged himself with his dagger. The mirror showed him that a fel green glow had replaced his eyes. It intensified when he used the power.

A hand descended on his shoulder. "Exhausted, are you, old one?" Cyana asked.

Vandel shook his head. "I am just getting started."

"I hope so," said Ravael. "This sparring session, I am going to beat you. Do not give in too easily. When you struggle, it only makes my victory all the sweeter."

Victory is sweet, said the voice in his head. Every day it sounded more like his own. *Flesh is sweeter still.*

THEY ENTERED THE COURTYARD. The high, crumbling walls of Karabor's ruins loomed over the aspirants, massive and imprisoning. Tattooed elves crowded the open spaces between the training rings, waiting for their chance to fight. Greenish-yellow glowing runes, chiseled into the flagstones, formed the circumference of the mystic circles. The runes' shapes suggested similarities to the tattoos inked on the aspirants' skin.

Each ring contained two combatants fighting under the supervision of one of the trainers. Spell-wrought auras surrounded their weapons and blunted the force of their blows, turning them from fatal into something merely bruising and painful.

Vandel watched a pair of fighters circle and strike until one knocked the other down. "I claim victory!" the winner shouted, while the loser lolled on the ground in defeat.

Varedis nodded and raised his hand, and the combat was over. The circle emptied. The trainer gestured for Ravael and Vandel to begin.

Ravael stepped into the circle, a scythe in each hand. Protective auras shimmered around their blades. Varedis put the spell on Vandel's runic dagger and the other blade he had taken from the temple armory. Vandel stepped into the circle.

Ravael made an obscene gesture with his right-hand weapon. "Today you will learn the meaning of defeat."

He sprang, blazingly fast, uncannily precise in his movements. The ritual had granted Ravael even more strength and speed than it had given Vandel. It had gifted him with huge claws and twisted, circular horns. Now, in the arena, as he drew upon his demonic powers, those attributes seemed even more pronounced. The scythe impacted on Vandel's biceps with numbing force.

"If this were a real fight, you would have lost your arm," Ravael taunted.

Anger surged deep within Vandel. That had not been fair. He dismissed the thought. In combat, no demon would give him a fair chance. "In a real fight, I would come and tear your heart out."

He meant the words to sound mocking, but they came out utterly serious, and he knew, even as they left his lips, that he meant them. Ravael unleashed a flurry of blows, but this time Vandel was ready. Dagger clattered against scythe. The sound of metal on metal rang around the courtyard. Every blow Ravael launched, Vandel parried.

At the end of the storm of attacks, he reached out and struck Ravael just above the heart with his dagger. If he had been a fraction quicker, he would have struck the equivalent of a killing blow, but as it was, he would merely have wounded his foe.

"A scratch," said Ravael.

A spark of berserk rage ignited within Vandel's chest. He would not be mocked. Not by one as weak and pitiful as this. Something in Ravael sensed his mood and responded. The air between them crackled with tension. Vandel threw himself forward, aiming at Ravael's head. Ravael raised both scythes, caught his blade, and twisted, but as he did so Vandel's second blade connected with his stomach.

"And now you would be dead," Vandel said, and something within him wished his foe was. "I win again."

He was about to turn away when he heard Ravael growling. A low, bestial sound emerged from deep within the other elf's chest. Spittle dripped from the corner of his mouth. His eye sockets were pools of blood in which witch fires danced. Balls of ruddy light flickered around the tips of his horns.

"I am not defeated," said Ravael. His voice was thick and guttural and full of hate.

Power clotted in the air around him. A sheen of shadow passed across his body, turning his skin first gray and then blacker than night. Great wings of shadow lifted from Ravael's back. Vandel felt the air displaced by their movement. He could smell brimstone and the aura of demon, stronger in his nostrils than at any time save when he had fought with real denizens of the Nether realms.

Ravael sprang forward, bringing his blades down. Both blows impacted painfully on Vandel's arms. This time there was no doubt he would be either crippled or dead if the fight had been a real one. It was not enough for his opponent. Ravael rained down blow after agonizing blow. Vandel brought his own blades up and managed to parry the first scythe. The second one caught him above the temple. Pain lanced his brow. The metallic tang of blood filled his nostrils.

Shadow had engulfed the scythes in Ravael's hands, drowning

out the protective spells. His power overcame the wards upon the blades. The scythes were deadly now, and Ravael was intent upon using them.

No one made any move to intervene. Spectators licked their lips. Varedis made a careless gesture, indicating that the fight should continue. He looked more interested than worried by this latest development. The scythes flicked out. More blood flowed. Ravael smiled. White fangs became visible within his shadowy outline. "This time I will win."

No one was going to intervene as long as Ravael did not leave the circle. Vandel could step outside it himself and put an end to things by admitting defeat. He was tempted to do so, but something in him responded to the smell of his own blood and the feeling of pain. Rage reddened his vision, and with it came power. He raised his hands and wove a thunderbolt of fel energy. It surged out from his pointing finger and smashed into Ravael. The ravenous green energy tore at the shadowy integument, shredding it to blackened tatters.

He fed more strength into the spell. Ravael screamed as his flesh roasted. Vandel knew that he should stop, but part of him did not want to, and it was not just the demonic part. He wanted Ravael to experience the same pain that he had. He poured more and more of his strength into the bolt. His heart sounded loud as a drumbeat. Breath emerged in ragged gasps. He changed the focus of the spell once he knew Ravael was dead, drawing shadowy globules of the defeated elf's corrupted soul into his own, channeling the stolen power and using it to heal his wounds.

Vandel knew he should feel guilty, but he did not. He felt exaltation. His only regret was that he had to restrain himself from feasting. The smell of burned demon flesh was still in the air, and it made his mouth water.

He looked around at the faces clustered at the edge of the circle. He was tempted to unleash his power on them, to strike and slay and kill, to slake the thirst for destruction that this combat had aroused. But that would be fatal, and he was not quite ready to die yet. He fought the urge down. The thunder of his heartbeat became softer in his ears. His breathing became more regular. He waited to see what his instructor would do.

Varedis just shook his head, as if he had seen things like this before and they did not trouble him.

He tried to kill you, said the voice in his head. *And if you had not drawn on my power, he would have succeeded. You owe me your life.*

It was true, Vandel realized. He had slain one of the other recruits, and no one appeared to be doing anything about it. He stepped outside the circle. "I claim victory," he said.

"You are victorious," Varedis replied.

CHAPTER FOURTEEN

Three Months Before the Fall

ILLIDAN TOOK NINE PACES ACROSS THE FLOOR OF HIS chamber, turned, and took nine paces back. He felt calmer now. His thoughts returned to Akama. That the Broken had conspired with Maiev Shadowsong had almost cost the Ashtongue leader his life. Maiev, of all elves! Illidan would have rewarded his treachery with death, but he still needed Akama and his people, so he had devised another and better punishment. That thought gave him considerable satisfaction. He had ensured the Broken would never betray him again. Not only that, but he had found a way to get Akama to deliver Maiev into his hands. And he had fit it all into his scheme to strike back against the Burning Legion. Now he had only one more problem to solve, and he was close to doing that.

Illidan looked down at the massive oaken desk. On it lay a number of maps and charts, held down by the Skull of Gul'dan. The patterns inscribed on them in demon blood were written in a notation that he had created himself and that only he understood completely. The geometric runes mapped the flows of energy between the portals of Outland and their terminus points in parts of the Twisting Nether.

He rubbed his brow and concentrated. He was on the edge of a breakthrough. It was so close he could almost taste it. He had spent years accumulating this information, plundering it from libraries and wizards' collections all over Outland. He had visited every location marked on the map and used geomantic sorcery to chart the outflows of power into the Twisting Nether.

He had interrogated thousands of demons, listened for clues in the speech of Magtheridon and a dozen of the nathrezim, the so-called dreadlords. He had used spells to follow the trace energies of a thousand summonings. He had tortured and devoured imps and overmastered succubi. He had spent years putting together clues, and finally he was ready.

He had been goaded by the half-recalled memories he had acquired from Gul'dan when he had absorbed the power of the orc warlock's skull. Gul'dan's visions had hinted at a way to achieve his wildest dreams. He had seen things that no other mortal had, and the recollections haunted Illidan.

Excitement grew within him. Finally, at long last, he saw the pattern. The old warlock had been right. There were complex weaves of power. A mesh that fed upon itself and drew energy from the land and air around it. It held the portals open against the natural inclination of reality to force them shut. It opened pathways among dozens of worlds. Some of the arcs were incomplete. He knew they must go somewhere. Given what he knew about the forces involved, he could work out their eventual termination points with complex astronomical calculations.

He could finally create the divination spell that could search through those portals and find what he was looking for.

He needed to act soon, before word leaked and one of the nathrezim worked out what he was doing. The dreadlords were too damnably clever, and if they acted to forestall him, all his years of sacrifice, all the decades of planning, would be in vain.

Wearily, but filled with growing excitement, he inscribed the syllables of the great spell. When it was done, he laid down his pen atop the sheet of parchment with a sense of profound satisfaction. He was as ready as he was ever going to be. It was time to act.

ILLIDAN WALKED DEEPER INTO the great circular chamber. On the floor, inscribed in the blood of demons and elves and draenei, pulsed a duplicate of the patterns on his charts, written a hundred times larger. Glowing runes clustered around the edges, shaping the cataracts of fel energy flowing into the chamber.

He walked around the edge, muttering spells of warding and shielding. He wanted no prying eyes witnessing what he did here, no possible intrusions to disturb his concentration. He spoke a word of power and all the doors closed. The seals were so tight that eventually the air would turn poisonous with the effusions of his own breath. If he remained lost in the ritual too long, this place would become his tomb.

He walked through a gap in the huge pattern and followed it to the middle of the chamber, careful not to step on any of the lines. The slightest break would be fatal.

At the exact center of the chamber, he spread his wings, let them beat once, and hovered in the air. He pulled his legs up underneath him into the lotus position and invoked magic that let him remain hovering above the ground. He spoke another word of power, and the braziers set at each point of the compass burst into flames, igniting the aromatic essences they contained. Clouds of hallucinogenic smoke flowed through the air. Tendrils of burning incense slithered through the pattern until they reached his nostrils.

He took three deep breaths, and each of them drove the vapor deeper into his lungs. He closed his mouth and held it in, until he felt as if he had absorbed every last fraction of the power it contained.

Long practice in alchemy let him identify the individual components. Doomguard bone, ground with a mortar and pestle carved from the skeleton of a dragon; powdered felhound blood; distilled essence of felweed; a thousand different items. All chosen to activate key sections of his sorcerer's mind and free his soul.

Ancient hungers tugged, tempting him to bathe in those evil energies. His skin tingled. The hair on his scalp rose. His tongue felt thick. Power flowed into him. So much power. He felt like a god, as if he had only to will something to happen in order to make it so.

He held the energy for a moment, just letting it stay within him, enjoying the sensation of being on the brink. Of his last moment of calm. After this, everything would change.

Slowly, delicately, as if he were taking a scalpel to a butterfly's wing, he invoked the last stages of the spell. A sensation of lightness struck him as his spirit dissociated from his body. He looked down upon his empty shell, hovering in the air below him. He felt a moment of vertigo, a sharp stab of fear.

At this moment his spirit was vulnerable. If anything happened to him here, he would die. A silver thread, so thin as to be almost invisible, connected him to the husk beneath him. If that was separated, his spirit would wander forever, unable to return to his body.

He felt the absence of so many things. No heartbeat. No blood flowing in his veins. No air rasping into his lungs. No tug of gravity on flesh and bone and muscle.

Ever since Sargeras had taken his eyes, back when Illidan had first joined the Legion, he had been able to see into the Twisting Nether. It had taken him centuries to realize what he could do with this power. For decades dreadful dreams had blasted his sanity and driven him screaming from sleep. It had been one of the worst torments of his long imprisonment.

He doubted anyone else could have endured what he had in order to harness this power to their will. Anyone who had not mastered sorcery as he had would have been incapable of the feat.

It had been necessary, though. It had given him the ability to send his soul out into the Twisting Nether and the Great Dark Beyond, to see other worlds, other universes. It had given him terrifying insight into the plans and goals of the Burning Legion. Now he needed to stretch himself farther than he had ever done before, reach deeper into the infinite abyss in search of his ultimate goal.

The fel power channeled by the great pattern roared around him. He studied it, knowing it to be both a map and a key that would open the way to where he had to go.

He molded the flows of magic slowly, lacking the physical cues he normally took for granted. Air did not caress his limbs. Words did not cause his diaphragm to vibrate. The power moved sluggishly in response to his will. He shaped it, channeling it through the pattern, aiming it toward the chink in the wards he had created. Like water flowing down a ravine, the spell surged through the tiny opening, creating a gap in the fabric of reality that opened out into somewhere else.

Illidan focused his attention on that space. If something waited on the other side, it would attack as soon as the chink was wide enough to pass through. At this moment, he was very vulnerable. His strength was not what it was when anchored by his corporeal form. He waited, hoping against hope that there was nothing there. He could ill afford the distraction or the time or the energy it would take to defend himself.

Nothing happened. He allowed his spirit to go with the flow of energy and pass through the opening between worlds and out into the Twisting Nether. It exploded into being around him.

There were a thousand ways to perceive this place. Every voyager saw it differently, depending on circumstance and form and state of mind. For him it was a black, airless void in which a billion stars twinkled. Behind and beneath him blazed the world from which he had come. Through the void trailed the snake of energy he had summoned, guiding him outward into infinity. It represented the flows of energy of the portals the Burning Legion used to get to Outland.

With an effort of will, he sent himself flashing along the trail, faster than light, quick as thought, until he found the first connecting portal. He descended from the Nether and flashed over a world. He looked upon a desert where once fields had grown, cemetery cities where unburied bodies clogged the streets. Eerie green energy flickered from disrupted portals. Amid the ruins imps frolicked and shouted obscenities. One or two sensed his proximity and peered about them as if nearsighted. In the distance an infernal lumbered, all blazing skin and burning rock for limbs.

He flashed from place to place, finding no sign of life, witnessing only destruction. He flowed past bunkers where the skeletons of creatures smaller than elves lay beside the alien weapons that had not saved them. He flashed past suits of corroded mirrored armor and the wreckage of burned-out battle machines.

War had blasted the landscape, slicing off the tops of hills, turning fertile plains to sheets of glass. The mad ghosts of a sad people keened songs of defeat and despair. Nothing lived save a few demons that had been stranded when the Burning Legion moved on to its next conquest, or had been left to stand guard over the waypoints of the Legion's march.

Mountains had been carved to resemble dreadlords. A moat of bones surrounded the corpse of a city the size of a nation. A giant animated skeleton rose from the ossuary sea and clawed its way over a mountain of ribs and skulls and thighbones, until its spark of necromantic energy faded and it tumbled back into the mass from which it had emerged.

He followed the trail of his spell through another portal and emerged onto a different world. Water had once covered its surface, but now the ocean was red as blood, filled with poisons that had killed the whale-sized inhabitants. Massive rafts woven from dead kelp rotted on the surface. The corpses of merfolk were entwined around them. The cadavers of creatures the size of cities decomposed on the ocean floor, surrounded by the skeletons of the aquatic armies that had once guarded them. Nothing lived, not even the smallest particle of plankton. The air itself was turning poisonous without plants to purify it and keep it alive. He passed through another portal.

A world of deserts and fire. Here and there he came upon the bones of wandering tribespeople and their pack animals. The wells of every oasis had been poisoned. The sun blazed down on an empty landscape of shifting dunes, to which only the wind gave animation. Sometimes they crumbled to reveal the skeletons of great armored worms or the acid-pitted ruins of brass skyscrapers.

On and on his spirit flashed, passing through dead world after dead world, monuments to the eternal malice of the Burning Legion. Everywhere lay ruin. This would be the fate of Azeroth and Outland and the few remaining living worlds once the Burning Legion attacked. He searched for traces of life and found nothing, not even a cockroach or a rat. Sargeras's army had set out to cleanse these places of every living thing and it had succeeded.

Illidan had known what to expect and still it appalled him, this senseless, monstrous violence, this hatred of all life, this wanton murder of world after world after world. He had been a fighter all his days. He had fought and killed and hated, but still he struggled to imagine what drove the Burning Legion to this.

Here and there he came upon hubs where the ways split and the paths of conquest led onward across multiple routes to multiple worlds. Always his spell guided him, his spirit questing through infinite worlds, seeking, seeking, seeking . . .

He lost all track of time. He had no idea whether a hundred seconds or a hundred years had passed back upon the world where his body waited. Perhaps he was already dead and his spirit was doomed to wander these infinite wastelands, a spectral witness to the doom of countless worlds.

He passed through another gate, despairing, hopeless, certain that he had miscalculated. This one was an odd place, a collection of rocks imbued with potent magic, floating amid the infinite void of the Twisting Nether. A tiny sun orbited it every few minutes. Dozens of miniature glowing moons followed it. Bits of rock floated in the air, held aloft by the power of magic. Potent energies saturated this place, were sunk into the very fabric of the world, and they were not the only thing here. In the distance, amid the rocks, he sensed the presence of demons of a very specific sort: nathrezim.

Was it possible he had finally found what he was looking for: Nathreza, the home of the dreadlords?

HUNDREDS OF DREADLORDS WERE certainly here, and thousands of their servants. Cautiously he advanced. The nathrezim were creatures of power, with a near-unparalleled capacity for working magic. They would have no difficulty detecting his spirit form unless he was very, very careful. Even now Illidan thought he sensed something watching. He froze. Nothing happened. The dreadlords did not respond to his presence. Perhaps it was nothing, merely his own too-wary mind.

His bodiless state prevented him from feeling any of the physical expressions of excitement. His heart did not race. His mouth did not go dry. A cold feeling of triumph filled him. He had found it. The place he had always suspected existed was here.

Do not be too certain, he cautioned himself. *You do not know that yet. You need confirmation.* He drifted closer to the presence of the dreadlords, following the lay of the land and the pattern of the rocks, weaving spells of concealment and misdirection around himself. His spirit was strong but not as strong as it was when it occupied his body. There were beings here who could end his existence if they spotted him.

He searched for any spells that might alert the inhabitants to his presence. A city of basalt towers lit by the flare of green fel lanterns stood before him. Disks of basalt rose up the sides of buildings. Huge dreadlords flapped across the skies. It was odd to see so many sentient beings after passing across so many dead worlds.

He saw palaces where nathrezim planned the destruction of worlds, the enslavement of civilizations, where the end of all existence was plotted by beings sworn to the service of Sargeras. Servitors guided odd machines on unguessable errands. In the center of it all stood one gigantic windowless tower amid a grid of energy flows. Baleful green runes lit up its sides. Legions of servitors came and went. No doubt about it; he had found what he sought. Gul'dan's visions had not lied.

He made careful calculations of the position and pattern of the gates that had carried him here, studying the astrological significance of the stars that glittered in the sky; then, when he was certain he had fixed in his mind all the information he had come here to find, he terminated the spell of spirit walking. The silver cord tightened and drew him with unimaginable speed back to his body.

Heavy flesh and dense bone imprisoned him once more. Air thundered back into his lungs. He stretched, reveling in the feel of muscles answering the commands of his will. He took a deep breath, identifying the scents. A smile flickered across his face.

Now he would take the war to the Burning Legion. Now he would make his enemies pay. All of them.

CHAPTER FIFTEEN

Three Months Before the Fall

MAIEV DUCKED THE OGRE'S BLOW AND SLICED HIS stomach open with the return stroke of her blade. The creature gave an idiotic chuckle and clutched at his intestines with one meaty hand, trying to hold them in. With his free hand, he brought his massive club swinging back. She jumped over the tree-trunk-sized weapon. There were times when she thought it was true what they said about ogres, that the creatures felt no pain.

Anyndra threw herself out of the way, but tripped over a clutching root and stumbled back into the murky water. Sarius growled. His cat form emerged from the shadows and pounced on the ogre's back. Claws raked, drawing blood. Maiev focused her power, blinked through the intervening space. She aimed a blow at the jugular. Blood sprayed. This time the ogre fell. Anyndra rolled clear of the tumbling corpse and stood. Algae-discolored water streamed from her hair and turned her tunic a muddy brown.

Maiev glanced around. Her troops were finishing off the ogres. She could not guess what foolishness had made the huge brutes ambush them. They had grown more and more aggressive toward travelers on the roads through Zangarmarsh in the past few months.

It seemed they had forged an alliance with Vashj's naga. Whatever spell engines the serpent folk were building neared completion. Maiev's efforts to sabotage them had met with failure. All she had managed to do was free some Broken slaves, useless as recruits to her forces.

She counted fallen combatants. Two draenei corpses lay in the water, heads submerged in a way that told her they would not be getting up. Sarius had already begun healing the wounded. She felt the surge of druidic power as he set an arm broken by an ogre's club.

Anyndra shook her head, sending drops of water splashing down into the murk. Maiev wiped sweat from her brow, then swatted a huge insect that had landed on the back of her hand. Its blood-bloated body burst, staining her hand crimson. By Elune, there were times when she hated those little monsters more than she hated those who abused magic.

"I think we have taught them not to attack us again," Anyndra said. She studied the body of the fallen ogre. He must have weighed as much as ten elves even though he was only half again as tall. He was so broad as to seem almost squat, and a thick layer of fat overlaid his swollen muscles. Red and brown mingled in the water around him. A water-walking insect had its feet stained red. A large fish broke the surface and took it down in one gulp.

"They are too stupid to learn that lesson," Maiev said. She squatted down and washed her hands in the water. She could not get them truly clean, but at least the blood came off. "No matter how many of them we kill, they will insist on fighting."

"What do you think the naga are up to?" Anyndra asked. Maiev shook her head. Her lieutenant persisted in questioning her as if she had an answer for everything.

"I do not know. But if Illidan wants it done, we must see that it is not."

Anyndra looked away as if the answer had disappointed her.

Maiev wished she had a better one. She wished she could think of some way of taking the war to Illidan, but the Betrayer had not stirred from his fortress in the weeks since Akama had reported Kael'thas's disappearance. No doubt Illidan felt vulnerable without the blood elf prince's aid against the Burning Legion, but Kael'thas's absence had not helped her cause any.

She pushed the thought away. It was too easy to give in to despair. She would find a way of bringing Illidan to justice. She just needed to keep trying and the way would open. She was a night elf, and she was used to thinking she had all the time in the world. Of course, since the devastation of the World Tree Nordrassil and the loss of the night elves' immortality, that was no longer true, but old habits died hard.

A tingling sensation started at her right side. She stepped into a patch of shadow. She took the stone Akama had given her out of her pouch and focused her thoughts on it. The image of the leader of the Ashtongue appeared in her mind. The Broken looked even more shriveled with age. His eyes were tiny pinpricks. There were deep lines on his face that had not been there before.

"What is it?" Maiev asked, knowing her voice would be heard by no one but Akama and herself.

"Meet me in Orebor Harborage. Things move swiftly. The time for our vengeance has arrived." Akama sounded tired and listless. His voice was feeble in a way she could not ever recall it sounding before. Perhaps something was interfering with the spell, she told herself. Perhaps it was just her imagination.

"What? How?"

"Meet me where we first met. I have much to tell you, and it is best we be prepared to move at an instant's notice. Make sure your people are ready to fight."

"What is going on?"

"I do not have time to explain. I must go, and go now. Meet me and be ready."

Abruptly the contact was cut. Maiev wondered what was going on. Had the long-awaited hour finally arrived?

She put the stone away and stepped out into the light once again. "Mount up," she said. "We are going to Orebor Harborage."

Some of the troops groaned. They had been expecting a rest after the battle. The urgency of Akama's summons was going to deny them that. Having a chance to capture the Betrayer, at long last, far outweighed their desire or any good they might do here destroying the naga's spell engines.

"We ride," Maiev said.

Her followers leapt into their saddles. They left the corpses of their foes behind them as food for the denizens of the great marsh.

MAIEV PACED IMPATIENTLY INSIDE the hut Akama maintained for their meetings in Orebor Harborage. Her troops watched her closely through the windows. They had learned to step warily when she was in this mood. Where was that damn Broken? He had communicated urgency, but now he could not even be bothered to show up.

She put her hands by her sides and smoothed the seam of her tabard. It did not do to reveal too much impatience in front of the troops. They looked to her for leadership. She slowed her stride, measured her pacing, and turned her thoughts inward.

It was not like Akama to be late. The Broken never missed a meeting. He usually turned up early for them. She hoped nothing had happened to him. It would mean the loss of a highly placed spy if the Betrayer had slain him for treason.

That would never happen. Akama had eluded Illidan's gaze for years, and that spoke of a far greater-than-average ability to hide things. He had deceived even Illidan. All he had to do was continue to do so for a bit longer.

She thought about the strangeness of it all. Her strongest ally in

Outland was a mutated aberration who served her greatest enemy. He had proved more reliable than any of the so-called leaders of the forces of Light. She told herself she should have more faith, but she struggled with that. It was not easy to let go of things, to pass control to someone else.

The air shimmered. A way opened. Akama stepped through. His shoulders were slumped and his eyes were downcast. His steps dragged even more than usual.

"Greetings," he said. "I bring grave news."

He looked up at her, and his eyes seemed sunken, their glow dimmed.

"Let us hope that it brings us a little closer to victory than your last tidings. Prince Kael'thas may be a deserter, but that has done us no good."

Akama stumbled over to a table and poured himself a goblet of wine. He seemed to have aged significantly since the last time they had met. His hand shook as he put the jug down.

"You look as if you have seen better days," Maiev said.

Akama shrugged and spread his arms wide. "The Betrayer has had me working magic day and night since last we spoke. It has drained me. His schemes come to a head. And I believe I know what he is up to."

"Tell me!"

"Give me a moment," the Broken said. He took out a small flask of magical elixir and stirred it into the wine. He raised the mixture to his lips and downed it in one gulp. Within heartbeats, he stood taller and some of the weariness faded from his frame. Maiev's eyes narrowed. She had never seen him like this before. She had never suspected he needed unnatural stimulants to maintain his strength.

"Are you all right?"

Akama's head bobbed slowly up and down. He seemed to want to reassure her but appeared incapable of it. His movements were still slow and pained. He looked as if he was very ill. Perhaps the strain of his long subterfuge was taking a toll on his health.

"The Betrayer has finally revealed his hand. He plans on opening a new gateway."

"Can you be more specific than that?"

"I know only the rumors that I have heard around the temple. And I have managed to take a look around his sanctum, and I have found clues that he plans to perform some sort of mighty ritual."

Disappointment lent anger to Maiev's tone. "None of this is of any great help to us. If he remains within the Black Temple, there is nothing we can do. He is too well guarded."

At this point Akama smiled. It was like watching a cold moon emerge from behind dark clouds. A strange glint entered his eyes. "To perform this ritual, he is going to have to leave the temple."

"What do you mean?"

"The portal can only be opened at a specific time and place. And that place is not within the Temple of Karabor."

"How can you be so certain of this?"

"I managed to get a glimpse at the scrolls he has prepared. Some of them contained maps."

Is it really possible? Maiev wondered. Was she finally about to get the opportunity she had waited so long for? "Maps of where?"

"The Hand of Gul'dan."

"The volcano in Shadowmoon Valley? Why there?"

"It is a location upon which enormous powers are focused. Gul'dan severed the orcish people's connection with the elemental spirits there."

"Illidan will be well guarded," Maiev said.

Once again Akama gave that strange, cold smile. He shook his head. "All of the signs point to the fact that he plans to move in great secrecy. He is assembling supplies for only a few."

"How do you know this?"

"One of the advantages of being a Broken is that almost all the slaves and servants in the temple speak my language, belong to my people. Few notice the lowly Broken, but we see many things. There is little that is done there that I do not have some inkling about."

"You think he is planning on performing the ritual in secret."

"He has talked to me about needing to make a trip in the utmost secrecy within the next few days."

"Why has he talked to you about this?" Maiev was suddenly suspicious.

"Since the prince of the blood elves vanished, Illidan has taken me more and more into his confidence. He needs someone to take charge within the temple while he is away, and the Illidari Council members are all blood elves. He thinks me too lacking in ambition to plot behind his back."

Bitterness tinged Akama's speech.

"Then he is definitely going," Maiev said.

"I have never seen him like this before. He is consumed with excitement. It is as if a plan that he has held for a very long time is coming to fruition. I strongly suspect that it has something to do with all the elves he has been training."

Curiosity tugged at Maiev. She had long wondered about the tattooed demonic fighters. "Is he taking them with him?"

Akama shook his head. "Their leaders have been told to stand ready to move at a moment's notice. I think the order will come if the ritual proves to be successful. I do not think he wants to risk them beyond the temple if it is not."

"He values them so highly?"

"They are the apple of his eye. He spends more time with them than he does planning the defense of his empire. It is puzzling. They represent something very important to him but I cannot work out what it is. I believe that it will be revealed within the next few days."

"Who will accompany him for the ritual?"

"I have studied the duty rosters. Small groups of sorcerers are being dispatched from the temple almost every day. All of them are wizards of considerable strength, and all of them are well practiced in ritual magic."

"He intends to assemble them on the Hand of Gul'dan?"

"It is the only thing that makes sense."

"And you believe he is doing this in secret because . . . ?"

"He is worried about spies, and not without cause." Akama gave a sour grin.

"How many of the sorcerers have been dispatched, and how many more are going to be?"

"There will be thirteen groups of thirteen assembled on the slopes of the volcano. The number has mystical significance. It ties in with the number of nodes on the pattern he is trying to create."

"Even if there is only a small force, that number of wizards could prove a significant threat."

"Not if they are involved in complex ritual magic when the attack comes." Akama's words hung in the air. The moment was finally here. It was now or never. She was never going to get a better chance to attack the Betrayer. If what Akama said was true.

"You are certain of this?" Maiev asked.

"As certain as I can be of anything, under the circumstances. I believe that the Betrayer will be on the slopes of the Hand of Gul'dan and that he will have those sorcerers with him. He intends to perform a mighty ritual and open a portal to somewhere else. Perhaps he thinks he can escape the vengeance of the Burning Legion by opening a way to some other world, where the demons have not yet established a beachhead."

"No." The word escaped from Maiev's mouth before she could stop it. She could not let the Betrayer slip from her grasp again. It would be just like him to leave the defenders of his fortress to face the consequence when the servants of Sargeras arrived. It still did not explain what he was intending to do with his elven trainees, though.

"If you will accept my advice," Akama said, "you will take your force to the slopes of the volcano and investigate. If I am wrong, you will have lost nothing. If I am right, you will get the best chance you will ever have of capturing your great foe."

"And what about you? Where will you be?"

"I will be with you. I want to be there when you overthrow the Betrayer. I will bring my people. We will aid you."

Maiev paused for a heartbeat. "Akama . . ."

"Yes?"

"I have been critical of you and your people in the past— suspicious of your motives, too—but this day you have proved that my thoughts were unworthy. Together we will bring Illidan down."

Akama took a deep, rasping breath and held her gaze. "I pray that you are right."

"I will tell my people to be ready," Maiev said. "We have far to go and very little time to do it in."

"I will open a way for you, and then I will return to the temple and prepare my people. The time has come for us to take vengeance."

Maiev shook her head. "The time has come for us to bring the Betrayer to justice."

"However you wish to portray it, this is our chance to achieve our goal. Let us overthrow Illidan. Let us free Outland from his wickedness. Let the Temple of Karabor be returned to my people."

"It shall be done," Maiev said.

CHAPTER SIXTEEN

Three Months Before the Fall

O VER EVERYTHING LAY THE EERIE GLOW OF THE HAND
of Gul'dan. The mountain shivered like a whipped dog as the trem-
ors of some yet-unborn earthquake rippled through its belly. Green
lava spouted gigantic plumes in the lakes of burning stone visible
on the lower slopes. All around, huge cables of magical power billowed.

Maiev thought the pre-shocks of this volcanic eruption were
connected with the spell being woven. Akama was correct—a ritual of immense power was being enacted here. There could be no
doubt of the awesome magnitude of the sorcery being worked.

A shower of greenly glowing meteors left a trail across the sky.
They were an ominous portent, but of what, she could not tell.

Her people, the night elves at least, were shadows among shadows. They moved from rock to rock, silent as assassins come in the
night to a king's bedchamber. The draenei and the Broken did not
move with the same stealth. They were too big, too clumsy, and
too powerful.

Akama looked alert and uneasy, as well he might. To one with his sensitivity to the moods of the world, the shaking of the mountain must be very disturbing. She herself was profoundly perturbed. Scores of Ashtongue soldiers lay hidden over the nearby mountainside. Akama had brought a strong bodyguard with him.

Everything was as Akama predicted. Groups of thirteen sorcerers stood in circles, weaving the great spell. Some were blood elves. Some were naga. All were potent magi. Lines of magical power danced among them, linking them together. They chanted and gestured, and something answered their call. A few other robed Illidari surrounded them. They might have been bodyguards or servants, but there were fewer of them than there were sorcerers.

The covens were spread out over the mountain. Each of them represented a point in a great pattern, a focus of the energy being directed toward the central altar. As she looked down at it, a smile of triumph flickered on Maiev's lips. The Betrayer himself was there, directing the operations, standing arrogantly at the altar. He wove the great spell like the master magician he was, shaping it into a swirling vortex of potency.

She paused to consider the magnitude of the gateway being opened. So much energy, all of it centered on this one spot. Either Illidan proposed summoning a being of truly awesome power, or the portal was intended to bridge a gap across an unimaginable distance.

Not that it mattered. He was not going to be given a chance to complete his spell. By now the rest of her squads should be in position. Sarius and his group were in place, ready to slay the sorcerers nearest to Illidan.

After that, justice would be done for all of the Betrayer's victims. It would be done with her own sharp blade. She ran her finger along the edge and shivered, imagining it.

She glanced over at Akama once more. The Broken licked his lips and nodded. He knew as well as she did that it was time. She raised her armored hand and gave the signal to attack.

———

A ROAR SOUNDED IN the distance. A panther-like figure emerged from the shadows and leapt at the throat of a blood elf magician. The sin'dorei screamed and fell. The other sorcerers barely noticed. They were too wrapped up in the casting of spells.

Maiev had perfectly chosen the moment to attack. Even the Betrayer did not seem to notice them for an instant. Her draenei and Broken followers emerged from the rocks and charged downslope, brandishing their weapons, invoking powerful spells of offense and defense.

The few Illidari surrounding the clumps of sorcerers were taken off guard. Some managed to pull weapons free of their sheaths and form up in small groups, back-to-back. Maiev could only respect such bravery, even if she despised the cause they fought for.

Their courage would not make any difference. The numbers favored Maiev and her troops. She did not even need Akama's followers. The Ashtongue lacked the hard competence of her own people. They had not been honed by months and years of guerrilla warfare in the wastes of Outland.

Maiev used her power to blink from her position and reappeared behind a naga sorcerer. Her blade licked out and slit the creature's throat before she could react. A swift step took her within reach of another mage. She struck off the blood elf's arm with one blow.

The air shivered. The pulse of magic briefly halted. The other magi redoubled their efforts. It was possible that the spell would run out of control if too many of them were killed. The backlash of such unleashed magic could be catastrophic.

Maiev did not care. As long as the spell destroyed Illidan, she would not consider her own death too high a price to pay. Of course, he might yet escape. He was as slippery as a serpent and had a talent for self-preservation equaled only by his talent for treachery.

She needed to make sure. Only if he died beneath her blade could she be absolutely certain that her purpose was achieved.

The altar lay ahead, and it looked as if, at last, the Betrayer was starting to pay attention to the attack. His warglaives spun in his hands, and he glanced around to see where the threat had come from.

Maiev sprinted toward him, hoping to get within range so that she could blink behind him and strike.

Illidan's head swiveled to look directly at her. He raised his warglaives as he invoked powerful magic. The spell he wove seemed to have nothing to do with the ritual taking place around them.

A magical signal blazed.

Maiev sensed the sudden opening of the portals all around her. Gaps appeared in the fabric of reality. Clouds of mist billowed forth from them as differences in temperature and air pressure between the point of origin and the point of terminus manifested. The fog provided cover for the masses of reinforcements emerging through the portals.

Hundreds upon hundreds of naga slithered forth, along with companies of fel orcs. The gates appeared between the parties of magicians. In places, the emerging fighters smashed into Maiev's own soldiers.

She saw that they needed to throw Illidan's forces back through the gates before the superior numbers could be brought to bear. The portal mouths were not huge. A small number of troops could choke the exit points.

Maiev shouted orders, telling her soldiers to strike at the emerging Illidari. It was a stopgap measure. Sooner or later greater numbers would prevail. That was not the point. All they had to do was buy her time to reach Illidan and put an end to his evil career forever.

Even as her troops reacted, she realized that the Betrayer had taken her response into account. There were too many portals for her small force to close them all. Groups of Illidari emerged on the flanks of the swirling melee.

She lengthened her stride to try to reach the Betrayer, determined that if nothing else, she would be avenged. As if he knew what she was thinking and wanted to mock her, Illidan spread his wings and leapt into the sky.

Maiev sensed more magic being woven and looked around. Amid a court of powerful naga sorcerers stood Lady Vashj. The leader of the Illidari's serpent folk lashed about her with potent spells. Maiev's troops fell as if poleaxed.

The bitter taste of defeat filled Maiev's mouth.

A massive fel orc leapt in front of her. His monstrous axe swept down. She ducked beneath it, rolled forward, and hamstrung the creature with her umbra crescent.

A phalanx of fel orc warriors charged at her. She tensed, ready to spring. A bolt of pure cold shivered through her body, shocking her to a stop. Lady Vashj had made contact with a spell. Howling maniacally, the fel orcs rushed in. Maiev tried to move her frozen muscles, but they refused to respond. She was going to die and Illidan was going to go free once more.

The fel orcs closed the distance with terrifying speed. Spittle drooped from the lips of one massive red-skinned creature as he raised his axe to take her head. Maiev refused to shut her eyes. An arrow whizzed out of nowhere and buried itself in the creature's throat. Another one hit him on the shoulder and sent him twisting to the ground. More arrows rained down, killing more fel orcs. All of them had Anyndra's green-and-red fletching. A fel orc tripped over the corpses of his comrades. A berserker leapt over the growing pile and closed the distance. Maiev managed to get her arm moving, attempted a parry. Too slow. Too slow.

The great hunting cat that was Sarius leapt in from the side, caught the berserk fel orc's arm, twisted his weight to overbalance him, and gouged him with his claws. Reddish-black rents appeared in the fel orc's neck. Blood spurted. More fel orcs piled onto the druid, determined to bring him down. Sarius rose, this time wearing the form of a bear, shifting the enormous weight of the fel orc warriors. Their blades hacked his fur, drawing blood, but magic surged around the druid to close his wounds.

Maiev felt a hand on her shoulder. She turned her head to see Anyndra's appalled face. "We have got to get out of here!" her second-in-command bellowed. Her voice was already hoarse from shouting orders above the clamor of battle.

Not many of Maiev's troops remained: a handful of her draenei and Broken fighters, and Anyndra and Sarius. The gates were fully open now. Fel orc after fel orc and naga after naga poured through. This was more than a force of bodyguards. It was an army.

For a moment she considered flight. She could order her troops to run and fight another day, but she might never get another chance like this. She must kill the Betrayer this day. Even if it meant giving up her life and the lives of all her companions, it would be a price worth paying.

A monstrous shadow fell on her. Looking up, she saw Illidan swoop overhead, his great wings spread. His eerie laughter echoed out over the battlefield, audible even over the ring of blade on blade, the war cries of the Broken, and the howls of the fel orcs.

Magical energy surged around her as the blood elf and naga spellcasters returned to their interrupted ritual. Black spheres swirled above the battlefield. Long tentacles of darkness reached down and touched the wounded and the dying. Where they did so, the victims screamed and aged years in heartbeats, as if all their life force was being drawn out of them. Black sparks emerged from their bodies and were sucked upward into the unholy spheres. Maiev realized that their very souls were being devoured.

Not even the souls of the dead were safe. When the tentacles touched a corpse, leather armor would grow tattered, chain mail and bright blades would tarnish and rust, and a spirit would come forth as black sparks to suffer the same fate as all the others.

With every soul absorbed, the spheres grew larger and darker. Bolts of black lightning danced among them, forming great chains of energy. A shimmering hole appeared in the air over the altar, feeding on the souls of the fallen.

Maiev looked around for Akama and saw him farther upslope, standing appalled as he watched the massive spell take effect. She hacked her way toward him. Had he known about this trap? Anyndra fought calmly at her side. The massive bear that was Sarius lumbered along, dragging half a dozen screaming fel orcs with him. The druid bled from a score of cuts, his magic unable to compensate for all his wounds.

Maiev looked on hundreds of corpses. Most of them were draenei; some of them were night elves or Broken. Far too few were fel orcs, naga, or blood elves. It came to Maiev that many of the dead were Ashtongue. Akama stood atop a boulder, shouting, "This slaughter was not part of the plan! You said we were supposed to capture Maiev!"

So all of this had been a scheme concocted by Illidan and the treacherous Broken. The thought filled Maiev with rage.

Magically amplified, Illidan's mad voice boomed over the battlefield. "Ah, we will capture Maiev, Akama. But there are other things that need to be done this day."

He sounded truly demonic.

Akama screamed and raised his fist. Chained lightning circled his fingers, and he looked for a moment as if he was considering hurling it at Illidan. Then he noticed how close Maiev was. He gestured. The air shimmered around him and he was gone.

"Head for that rise!" Maiev shouted. "We will make our stand there."

Anyndra nodded; then her eyes went wide with shock. An orcish blade protruded from her chest. Blood poured from her mouth. A muscular red arm went around her throat. There was a cracking sound and her neck broke. She fell forward.

Sarius's roar of grief and rage vibrated through the air. It echoed through the chasms around them and just for a moment drowned out the thunder of the volcano. He hurled himself forward, shaking off the clutching fel orcs, and caught Anyndra's killer with his jaws. He reared up on his haunches and shook the slayer like a terrier would a rat. The fel orc's neck broke in turn.

Spells burst around the huge bear. His movements slowed. Fel orc after fel orc struck him, drawing blood. More and more charged him. Even his strength had limits, and he was pulled down and hacked to pieces.

Berserk fury overcame Maiev. She sprang into the midst of the fel orcs and chopped her way through them, slashing with her blade. She beheaded one, lopped away the arm of another, and opened the guts of a third. A red haze filled the air around her. Even the fel orcs grew afraid of her fury as she built a mountain of corpses around herself. Then one of them, braver than the rest, threw himself back into the fray, and the army descended upon her. She chopped and chopped until her arm grew weary. She bled from a thousand cuts. She knew she was going to die, and if she could not get the Betrayer, she was going to drag as many of his henchmen down with her as she could.

Blinded by weariness and the blood and sweat dripping down her face, she still lashed out. Her limbs felt like jelly. All strength was gone. She found herself standing alone in a circle of the dead. The fel orcs looked upon her with awe. She had killed scores of them, and it wasn't enough. It would never be enough.

Overhead, black lightning flickered, moving from sphere to sphere as more of the souls of the dead and the dying were devoured. Maiev realized to her horror that all she had done was aid Illidan in the casting of his spell. It fed upon the souls of her victims and used the unleashed energy to crack a hole in the fabric of reality. It was growing cold now, and a wind howled in from the edge of infinity. Illidan hovered over the carnage, looking down in triumph, wings spread, an aura of evil power surrounding him. His gaze met Maiev's. He gestured. Dark energy descended from his fist like the spear of an angry god.

Agony lanced through her. She stumbled and fell.

The fel orcs advanced toward her recumbent body. She struggled to rise but strength failed her. She heard the beat of mighty wings and looked up to see Illidan staring down at her. A smile of hatred and malice twisted his narrow features.

"So, Maiev, now you are my prisoner. I will endeavor to see that your captivity is as enjoyable as mine was." He turned his head and barked an order to the fel orcs. She pushed against the ground, attempting to rise and strike him. His fist fell like a sledgehammer, battering her to the earth once more.

"I have business elsewhere," he said. "But something suitable has already been prepared for your future home. It is a cage that will hold even you, Warden."

CHAPTER SEVENTEEN

Three Months Before the Fall

A KAMA WATCHED THE PORTAL OPEN FROM AMID THE ROCKS high on the slopes of the Hand of Gul'dan. He had seen many gateways, but nothing like this one. It was not just the scale that was daunting. It was the sheer power. It had devoured the souls of hundreds, sucked in all the magical energy for leagues around. He could feel the unholy strength of it even from his vantage point on the cliffs. What was Illidan up to? He had told his council that this was all a trap for his foe. Knowing the Betrayer's hatred for Maiev, everyone had taken him at his word. Now it seemed that there were wheels within wheels, machinations within machinations. It looked as if the capture of Maiev had merely been a feint, intended to cover the unfolding of some greater scheme. Akama almost admired Illidan for it. He was capable of using even his own bitter hate as part of his plans.

Anger surged within him. The Betrayer had broken his promise to spare the lives of Akama's people. Not only that, but he had harvested their souls. He pushed his fury down. He could ill afford such feelings, not after what had been done to his spirit.

Akama wondered whether the unholy spell that had opened the

portal could even affect him. As punishment for conspiring with Maiev, Illidan had drawn part of Akama's essence from his body. In the darkened hall of the refectory, he had subjected Akama's soul to unspeakable sorcery and turned a portion of it into a shade. His spirit, his most sacred possession, had been turned into a weapon against him, the instrument by which Illidan bound his will and, through him, his people. At his whim, the Betrayer could unleash the shade, and it would devour Akama from within. It would corrupt the rest of Akama's followers through the spiritual ties that bound them to him. It had not been merely his own life that was at stake, but the lives and souls of all his people.

Akama let out a long breath. The Betrayer had not believed his claim that he had been meeting Maiev merely to lure her into a trap, that he had wanted to present Illidan's ancient enemy as a gift to him. It was a story Akama had been prepared to give from the moment he made contact with the warden. He had repeated it to himself for so long that he had believed it. He had not convinced the Betrayer. Akama had been forced to deliver Maiev into Illidan's hands, and for that he was sorry. She had trusted him, and he had placed her into the clutches of her archenemy.

Even now Illidan stood triumphant over his former captor. He did not look as if he intended to kill her. No. He had something else in mind. He had endured much at the hands of Maiev Shadowsong. She had become a focus for his rage and his hatred and his grievances. He would not grant her a quick death.

Illidan's great spell shrieked to a climax.

Akama felt the pain and the horror of the Broken and draenei souls as the portal spell devoured them. The split in reality gleamed like the surface of a lake on which oil had been thrown. The substance of the portal swirled and parted, and Akama caught glimpses of an alien landscape, of rocks floating in the sky and globules of solidified green energy moving through the air. It felt as if the land he was looking at was unimaginably far away. Judging by the amount of power used to open the portal, it connected to a world more distant than any Gul'dan had ever made contact with.

He tried to work out what Illidan was up to. The army that had ambushed Maiev's force was drawing up around the gate to stand guard over it. Why? *In case something comes through* was the obvious answer.

Even as that thought occurred to him, a new force emerged from the portals leading back to the temple. It consisted of scores of tattooed elven fighters. The army Illidan had been training was finally going to see action.

Akama watched in fascination and horror. He sensed the power in the figures down there. They were mighty and they were touched with evil. In the light of the green gate, it was even more obvious, as if something about the portal fed whatever was in them and lent it strength.

As he watched them move en masse under the Betrayer's gaze, the resemblance between these combatants and their master struck Akama as never before. They were all like Illidan. They might have been his children. They were certainly his creation. He had forged them from flesh into something new. The question was why.

THE AIR AROUND VANDEL was rife with energy. It made his skin tingle and his head spin. The enormous portal ahead tempted him like food on a banquet table might tempt a starving elf. He could tell that his companions felt the same way.

The area around the gate looked as if an ancient battle had taken place. Skeletons and desiccated bodies sprawled everywhere, encased in corroded armor, rusty weapons lying near at hand. If he had not known better, he would have thought this the site of some long-ago war.

His spectral sight gave the lie to that. Here and there the wounded and the dying lay groaning. Tendrils of dark energy licked out from the portal and drew the shimmering souls from their bodies. They flew through the air, eyes wide, mouths open in horror, and disintegrated when they reached the hovering spheres. He knew without having to be told that they were being devoured by the magic here, and their energy was being used to power the spell.

He glanced over his shoulder at the portals leading back to the Black Temple. It hardly seemed possible that barely an hour ago, he had risen from his pallet in his cell and prepared for another day of practice. He had known that something was going on. For days soldiers had been marshaled in the drill grounds of the temple, and an army had made ready for war. It had looked like another one of those vast military exercises that had been so common since he had joined the ranks of the Illidari.

He had suspected it might have something to do with the groups of sorcerers who had left the temple in the previous days. Rumors had flown thick and fast. It had all seemed distant, though. For the demon hunters, there had only been the endless rounds of training, right up until the moment the horns had sounded, and Varedis had told them to assemble in the central courtyard with their weapons prepared.

He had been surprised that there were few signs of active conflict when they emerged from the portals. The army they had seen gathering over the previous few days was there, and it had fought. It had obviously suffered a number of casualties, too.

The spell opening the gateway had not distinguished between those who had fought for Illidan and those who had fought for his enemies. It had sucked the souls out of them regardless of whose side they had been on. Perhaps it would have sucked the life out of him if he had been wounded. He had most likely stumbled on the reason why he and his comrades had been deployed last. It was clear that whatever their purpose was, it had nothing to do with the battle here. Their lives were being preserved for something else.

Looking at the yawning portal, flickering and shimmering ahead of him, he knew what that purpose was. Through the gateway, as it swirled, he caught the psychic traces of fel energy and demons. It was like standing some distance from a kitchen on a windy day and catching the scent of food cooking within it. The stench of demon buffeted his nostrils. When he licked his lips, he tasted a faint residue of fel magic. The gate was the mightiest spellwork he had ever seen. His new senses let him appreciate it as he never could have before.

The part of him that had wandered the woods of Ashenvale hated it. He knew his family and neighbors would have, too. The part that had devoured demons and followed Illidan appreciated it for what it was.

He touched the amulet he had made for Khariel and checked his rune-worked weapons. He was as ready now as he was ever going to be.

Soon. Soon, whispered the voice within him that was not his own.

ILLIDAN TURNED MAIEV'S ARMORED form over with the tip of his hoof. She was skilled and powerful, of that there was no doubt. Looking at the carnage she had wrought among his forces, he had almost been tempted to take a hand in the fight himself. He had feared that she might break free and escape once more into the tortured landscape of Shadowmoon Valley.

He was glad now he had decided to deploy an entire army to watch over the gate. It had proved necessary before the way was opened.

She had almost succeeded in distracting him at the crucial moment of the ritual, when he had needed all his concentration to finish the weaving of energies and bring the construction to fruition.

Almost.

No matter. Maiev was his prisoner now and she would never trouble him again. He allowed himself a smirk of satisfaction. It was a good omen, he thought. A portent of how this day would go. Whatever powers still watched over these ancient worlds looked favorably on his actions.

Do not be too confident, he told himself. *We make order from chaos by the force of our wills. It is foolish to read anything more into the patterns random chance throws up.* He took one last, lingering glance at Maiev and promised himself that she would suffer as he had. Ten thousand years of pain would not be too many for her to endure. She would not live for another ten millennia, so he would need to find a way to concentrate all that agony into a much shorter span. There would be time enough to consider such things later.

The portal shimmered and pulsed. Raising his hands wide, he spoke the final words of the great spell. The knots of energy tied themselves. The structure stabilized. The shimmering curtain parted, and the way to Nathreza, the homeworld of the dreadlords, was clear. A dagger of pure force sliced reality around the gate. Through it washed a torrent of fel energy. His tattoos channeled and absorbed it, filling him with ever greater power.

His satisfaction with this achievement exceeded even what he felt with Maiev's capture. He had created a gate to a world farther away than any other reached from the surface of Outland. Gul'dan himself would have struggled to invoke it and contain its energies. This portal was the greatest feat of sorcery worked in Outland since its catastrophic creation.

An eerie green light bathed the upturned faces of his followers, making them look even more monstrous than usual. They were a weapon he had spent a long time forging. He wondered whether they would survive the first battle or shatter like a flawed blade created by a neophyte smith. They had been gifted with power, trained by masters. They had been selected from the most driven individuals with the greatest thirst for vengeance against the Burning Legion. They had survived when most others would have died.

That itself meant nothing. They could still perish in the next few hours. He could still die. His whole life could be turned into an empty cosmic joke by the whims of chance.

It was too late to worry about such things now. He would need to trust that his calculations were correct and that his schemes would work out as he had planned them.

He raised his hand into the air, flexed his wings, and soared above his troops. All gazes went from the gateway to him, just as he intended. He set himself down by the open portal, felt the tingle of magic around him, caught the scent of alien air.

He gestured for his demon hunters to follow, and then he swooped through the portal to confront his onrushing destiny.

CHAPTER EIGHTEEN

Three Months Before the Fall

VANDEL BOUNDED THROUGH THE GATEWAY, FOLLOWING Illidan. He raced to the brow of the ridge and crouched down, doing his best to keep out of sight. In the distance he sensed demons, thousands upon thousands of them.

Huge islands of rock drifted like clouds across the sky of this alien world. Green light burned from every boulder and blazed from the tiny orbiting sun. Beneath him, the ridge fell away to a cratered plain over which obelisks of reflective obsidian hovered. The portal back to Outland gaped, a hole in the fabric of reality, linking two worlds.

Illidan's shadow fell upon him. The Betrayer stood on the crest of the hill, claws extended, every muscle in his tattoo-covered body tight with tension. Massive batwings cloaked his shoulders. Bestial horns curved from the sides of his head. A circlet of runecloth hid his eye sockets. A savage smile of anticipation curled his thin lips, revealing his bright fangs. He, too, sensed the approaching demons.

Part of Vandel tittered with mad mirth. He forced the demonic presence down, knowing that he could not hold it there for long. He was going to need its strength to survive the coming battle.

Illidan's leathery wings creaked as he shifted his weight. His hooves struck sparks against the rocks as he moved.

Nearby, scores of Illidari demon hunters waited in the shadows, hidden by potent magic. Vandel prayed to whatever gods might be listening that those spells were strong enough. Out there in the darkness, enemies of terrible power waited.

Within the next few hours, they would find out whether the gifts the Betrayer had lavished on them were enough to preserve their lives. They would learn whether their months of harsh training and terrible sacrifices had paid off.

And still, something in Vandel yearned to serve the forces of the Dark Titan, Sargeras, and he feared it was not just the part that was transformed by his demon's touch. A fragment of his elven soul responded to the nihilistic glory of the Burning Legion just as strongly as any infernal would.

Illidan's nostrils flared as if he scented Vandel's weakness. A growl sounded deep in his throat.

He will fail, Vandel's inner demon whispered. *He has always failed. He cannot oppose the will of Sargeras. Nothing can.*

Vandel took a deep breath and tried to empty his mind. It did not help. It just made him more aware of the magical energy surging around him. He wanted to gather it to him and use it. He wanted to unleash a volcanic tide of destruction upon the distant demonic presences. He wanted to slay them and take their essence into himself. He wanted to feed.

Yes, the demon whispered. *That will make you strong enough to challenge even Illidan.*

He concentrated on his surroundings in an effort to ignore the mad whispers. This planetoid was carved from pure magical energy congealed into pulsing, chromatic stone. Whenever he touched the surrounding rocks his flesh tingled.

His heart thundered in his chest. He tried to focus his concentration on the approaching enemy. He told himself that he was ready for this.

ILLIDAN STUDIED THE DISTANT demons. At the moment, they were merely remote shadows thrown upon his mind by their auras of power. Their numbers dwarfed those of his own force. It did not matter. Magic would decide this battle.

Fel energy swirled around him. He resisted the temptation to reach out and draw upon it. He ran his hand over the wound that Arthas had given him. It tingled as if some small part of the Lich King's evil blade, Frostmourne, were still lodged in it. He moved his fingers away to avoid being reminded of his previous defeats. Now was not the time to dwell on such things.

Illidan sensed the nervousness of his troops, felt their inner battles. His smile became a snarl. His followers were like hounds sensing prey. He had shaped them to be so. Now was the ultimate test. Now he would find out whether all the centuries of planning had paid off. If this force failed him, he would die, and all his millennia-long designs would come to naught.

That was not going to happen. They were not going to fail at this last hurdle. He had schemed too long to let that happen.

He expanded his awareness. The wave front of his magically extended senses swept over the approaching enemy. Within a heartbeat he had counted their numbers. There were scores of dreadlords, all with their own retinues of hundreds of felhounds and infernals and every other manner of demonic creature.

They are strong. Perhaps too strong.

The thought nagged at him. He shook his horned head. He flexed his wings and caught the updraft of air sweeping the cliffside.

You have miscalculated. And not for the first time.

No. He could not be wrong. He was ready. His force was ready.

The enemy was almost upon them. The demonic army flowed across the alien landscape, an unstoppable tide intent on swamping the ridge on which Illidan waited. The huge dreadlords stalked amid their companies of lesser demons. Their enormous batwings fluttered even though there was no wind. Their horned heads turned as they surveyed their surroundings for foes. The glowing runes on their armor marked their status as much as the size of their retinues did.

Evilly beautiful succubi cracked whips and flexed tails and danced lasciviously. Scuttling felhounds sniffed the air as if they sought prey, sensor stalks twitching, shark teeth gleaming. Armored felguard brandished huge axes as they awaited orders from their commanders. Towering, six-armed shivarra shimmered on the edge of Illidan's perception, near invisible even to his keen senses.

These were soldiers of the Burning Legion, the force that had devoured worlds beyond number. They were intent on reducing the entire cosmos to smoldering ashes in the name of their master, Sargeras.

Illidan stood apparently alone. His force remained concealed. It would be revealed when he was ready and not before. The gate he had opened on the surface of this barren world drew his enemies. They had come to punish whoever dared transgress upon their realm. It was not often anyone carried the fight within the borders of the Burning Legion. In all his long lifetime, Illidan could not think of more than a handful of such events.

The army came to a halt on the plain below. The greatest of the dreadlords raised a clenched fist, then pointed at Illidan and laughed. His evil mirth echoed across the landscape and was echoed from the throats of hundreds of other dreadlords. Their mockery was obvious. Some of them might have thought the joke was upon them. They had mobilized an army to confront this single figure.

Illidan crossed his arms over his chest and flexed his wings to their greatest extent. He glared down upon his enemies, mirroring their contempt. The mirth of the dreadlords guttered in their throats. It ceased to resound among the rocks. Quiet fell upon the ranks of the huge army. Only the sputtering of the molten skins of the infernals broke the silence. The leader of the dreadlords swept down his raised fist. A gigantic meteor dropped from the sky. A thunderclap boomed. The sound echoed over the site of the coming battle and made the air vibrate.

VANDEL WAS GLAD TO be in the cover of the rocks. So far none of the demons had noticed him. He felt their malice rolling toward him, a fog of unleashed hatred and evil that somehow congealed out of the magic in the air.

Join them, the demon voice whispered inside him. *Join them and you will be rewarded as no soul in the history of the cosmos has been rewarded.*

He felt the temptation. The demon was telling the truth as it understood it. He touched the hilts of his rune-encrusted blades. It would be the simplest of actions to plunge them into Illidan's back. Was he not the Betrayer? Had ever an elf in history been more deserving of death?

Slay him, his demon whispered. *Slay Illidan and achieve eternal glory. Slay the Betrayer and become a dark god.*

The sound of the thunderclap faded as the army of the nathrezim advanced. The great meteor hit the ground, shaking the earth, disgorging a gigantic blazing infernal. It pulled itself out of the impact crater and lumbered forward along with the rest of the dreadlords' army.

Vandel felt the temptation rise within him. If he slaughtered Illidan, he would be welcomed by his demonic kindred. He could put his mortality behind him forever, live untroubled by fear and regret. He could bury all traces of guilt about failing his family, all remorse, any semblance of kinship with these weak, frail creatures of flesh and blood.

He could transcend what he was, join the Burning Legion, and become a conqueror, cleansing the universe of the foul disease of life. He could help bring creation crashing down so that a new universe could be born, one shaped in his image, by his desires.

For a moment, he wavered. He listened to the voice of his inner demon and realized that it was his own. His soul had been tainted when he devoured the felhound. It had absorbed the demon's evil and been twisted. There was really no other demon than himself.

To give in to the voice of temptation would be to forswear his quest for vengeance and break faith with his dead wife and child.

He did not want to kill Illidan. He wanted to kill the things that had made Illidan into what he was. He understood now as he never had before what the Betrayer stood for, because of what he stood against. For all his gigantic flaws, Illidan was the only being who really grasped what they fought, and he was prepared to do whatever it took to end the threat. He might well be mad. His schemes might well be doomed to failure. But he was better than the alternative.

The demons of the Legion advanced toward the ridge. It was time to do battle with the real enemy.

The army of the nathrezim moved upslope. A mortal force would have been slowed by the effort, but they seemed tireless. Felhounds loped ahead, infernals lumbered in their wake, scores of gigantic winged dreadlords bellowed orders to their followers.

Now. The thunderous voice spoke within Vandel's head, and it was Illidan's. As one the demon hunters emerged from their cover and raced down toward their prey.

For a moment, the Legion's army slowed, as if unable to comprehend the fact that it was being attacked by this much smaller force of smaller beings. One or two of the dreadlords laughed again.

With a roar like the ocean throwing itself against rocks, the two armies collided. The demons wanted to reach the portal and close it. The demon hunters wanted only to slay and slay and slay.

A felhound leapt at Vandel. Sharklike teeth gaped. He invoked his power and sent a bolt of greenish-yellow energy into its maw. The demon's head exploded. Chunks of flesh fell to the ground, charred and smoking. Resisting the temptation to feast, Vandel launched himself forward, daggers clearing their sheaths. He rolled between two monstrous mo'arg servitors, hamstrung them before they could bring their weapons to bear, flipped to his feet, and smashed his dagger through the eye socket of first one, then the other.

A moment later, he confronted a dreadlord. The creature loomed over him, twice his height, broader than an ogre and even stronger. The dreadlord brought a massive spiked mace smashing into the ground as Vandel jumped aside. Rock splintered. Clouds of green dust rose glittering into the air.

Vandel picked himself up. His foe buffeted him with a batlike wing. The force of the blow made his head ring, sent him hurtling back toward a massive boulder. He flipped himself over so that his feet made contact with the rock first, and then he sprang forward, bouncing away from the impact and rolling to a stand.

The dreadlord turned with surprising quickness for a creature of his enormous bulk and lumbered toward him. Vandel raised his hand and sent a fel bolt slashing toward the demon. A wing curled around his opponent's body. The bolt ripped through the appendage, leaving it hanging like a tattered cloak from the dreadlord's side. The monster did not even seem to have slowed.

From the periphery of his vision, Vandel saw Cyana dispatch another mo'arg servitor, then leap over the corpse to engage a felguard. A blaze of light from his right warned him, and he sprang into the air just as an imp's firebolt passed beneath him. He twisted to avoid descending into the jet of flame and found himself looking up at the massive polished hoof of the wounded dreadlord.

It stamped down, missing him. He lashed out with his dagger, catching his opponent behind the knee and drawing forth what might have been a grunt of pain or contempt. The creature smashed down with his mace and caught Vandel on the shoulder.

When he had been mortal, the blow would have killed him, smashing broken ribs through heart and lung. He rolled with the impact, riding the force of the strike. As he did so, he repaid the imp who had blasted him, hitting the demon with a fel bolt that turned the cackling little monster into a pool of bubbling slime.

Vandel sprang upward, embedding his left-hand dagger in the dreadlord's breastplate, using it to pull himself up until he could drive his other weapon through the demon's eye. The creature clutched at the socket, attempting to swat him, but Vandel had already drawn the blade clear and driven it through the other eye.

He dropped to the ground and unleashed a flurry of blows on the blinded monster. Doubtless the demon could, given time, sense Vandel the way he sensed him, using magic, but for those few crucial instants the creature might as well have been blind. Vandel took advantage to stab his blades again and again into the dreadlord. The magic on the daggers cut his flesh, leaving rotting wounds that would not heal.

Blades grated on bone, sawed through tendon, parted muscle with the sound of a butcher's cleaver going into a steer's carcass.

The demon gave up trying to strike him and tried to lumber away, flapping his huge wings. Because of the earlier damage, he could only remain on the ground while Vandel carved him to pieces.

Cruelty drove Vandel's hand. Every blow that went home gave him sick satisfaction, and he knew the thing within him was feeding on the dreadlord's death. At that moment he no longer cared. The demon's desires were aligned with his own. It did not matter if he made it stronger. Right now he could use its strength, and right now, he knew that it took just as much satisfaction from the killing as he did.

When finally he had reduced the dreadlord to a pile of skinned flesh, it occurred to him that he had wasted valuable time. There was more prey to be had, and he needed to claim his share.

Needle sat nearby, astride the torso of a fallen felguard, casually punching his foot-long needles again and again into the demon's open chest plate as if he were trying to stitch it together. Elarisiel chased a felhound around a rock before putting it out of its misery.

Over by a huge boulder, a group of dreadlords made a last stand. They looked more bemused than afraid, as if they could not quite grasp what was happening around them. It was clear that the battle had not gone as they had expected.

The demon hunters had gone through their army like a sharp scythe through wheat. Everywhere the corpses of demons sprawled. There were several elf bodies, too, but far fewer than Vandel would have expected, given the sizes of the respective forces.

Illidan landed atop the rock behind the remaining dreadlords. Vandel wondered whether the lord of Outland intended to take a hand in their destruction, but he simply stood there, watching.

The demon hunters slowly rose from what they were doing and stared at their overlord and then at the dreadlords. The demons braced themselves as a tide of fighters surged forward and engulfed them.

ILLIDAN WATCHED HIS FORCES drag down the last of the nathrezim. His doubts had disappeared. The demon hunters had exceeded his expectations. Of course, they had possessed the advantage of surprise. The dreadlords had not expected to encounter such savage power so close to their home, and overconfidently had marched to meet them. Things would not always be so easy.

Nonetheless, nothing could damp the sweet feeling of triumph. Every dreadlord who fell here would be one who no longer troubled the universe. In this place, at this time, they would die permanently. How long had it taken Illidan to realize that secret? How many times had he fruitlessly thought he had slain his enemies? His visions had shown him the answer. During his millennia-long imprisonment, he could do nothing with them, but now things had changed.

He would make the lords of the Burning Legion suffer as they had made others suffer. He counted his own dead. Less than a score. At this point each was a loss he could barely afford, but soon there would be more demon hunters. The Legion had sown dragon's teeth among his people. There was no shortage of those who sought vengeance against the demons. But that was a problem for another day. Now he had to get what he had come here for.

Time was of the essence. The force they had encountered was the tiniest fraction of the tiniest fraction of what the Burning Legion could deploy. As soon as they realized what had happened, the masters of the city would summon aid. He needed to be gone from here before that occurred. No matter how powerful his individual fighters were, they could still be overcome by enough enemies.

He gave the signal to advance.

The demon hunters moved quickly through the nathrezim city. Great obsidian towers reflected the green light of fel magic all around them. Streets of shining black shimmered in their glow. More and more demons surrounded them, stragglers or those left behind by the army to hold important posts. The Illidari overwhelmed any they encountered, like hounds pulling down a rabbit. Not even the mightiest dreadlord was a match for so many.

Illidan resisted the urge to join in the fray. Opening the portal had drained a good deal of his power; he was husbanding what was left in case any unexpected threat emerged.

Ahead of him loomed the tallest tower, the great archive of the dreadlords. Within this building lay all the countless secrets the nathrezim had obtained during their service to Sargeras.

Hulking felguard flanked an entrance that shimmered and vanished, closing off the tower to intruders. Tattooed fighters dragged the demons down, then stood before where the doorway once was, baffled. What had been an empty archway mere heartbeats before was now a wall of stone.

"Blast it," Illidan ordered. There was no doubt an easier way of opening the doorway, but he did not have time to uncover the magical key. The demon hunters raised their hands and sent fel flame licking toward the barrier. Hundreds of bolts smashed, scoured, and scratched the stone, but still it withstood the assault.

"Concentrate on one area!" Illidan shouted, and all the bolts converged at the center of the stone, drilling through it until finally the rock splintered and collapsed into a heap of rubble.

Illidan sprang over it and glimpsed a long ramp leading down into the depths below the tower. So far all was as he recalled from his memories of Gul'dan's visions. He smiled to himself as a score of Illidari sprang over the stones and fanned out into the interior of the building, scouting the way ahead.

"Down," Illidan ordered them, and they took the ramp leading down. Strange lights moved in the floor, as if triggered by their steps. The air pulsed with sorcery, currents of energy woven into potent spells by the magic of the nathrezim. Power shimmered in the air and thrummed beneath his hooves. Complex engines of magic all around drew on the energy that permeated everything on this strange world.

He was close now. So close.

CHAPTER NINETEEN

Three Months Before the Fall

"DIE, DESECRATOR!" THE MO'ARG SERVITOR SHOUTED AS he sprang forward to attack. The demon raised the barrel of his odd weapon. Magical flame sputtered.

Illidan decapitated the squat, armored creature with a casual backhand stroke of his warglaive as he entered the central archive of the dreadlords. Over everything loomed glittering towers built of countless obsidian disks layered together like stacks of coins. Each one of those disks was a record. One of them was what he sought.

He turned to the demon hunters who stood in the entrance of the huge chamber, waiting his command. "Do not enter. Hold this doorway, no matter what happens in the next five minutes."

They nodded acquiescence, and Illidan turned once more to face the stacks. He crossed his arms on his chest and wove a spell. Tendrils of magic flashed from his hands to the towers of stacked disks. As they connected, he caught flashes of imagery, splinters of knowledge.

This was the monument of the dreadlords, the heart of their world. It recorded every triumph, every conquest, and every plot.

Nathrezim schemed to have their names imprinted here. It was the living memory of their race.

Here were records of innumerable campaigns fought on countless worlds. Here were the names of long-forgotten traitors who had betrayed their homes to the Legion and were in turn betrayed by the demons. Here was knowledge of every portal the Legion had ever passed through, the names and locations of every world it had ever burned.

There was a system to it. It was organized almost chronologically, the oldest disks on the bottom of each stack. The stacks closest to the center were the oldest of these.

Illidan sent tendrils of energy racing to the middle. What he wanted would be located very near the core. The images that flashed into his mind reeked of age. He was looking at things that were old even as demons reckoned time.

A sense of urgency pushed at him. Somewhere in the distance, gates were opening. The nathrezim were responding to the invasion of their homeworld.

He became aware of the sounds of fighting. They came from what seemed like a great distance, but he knew this was because of the spell linking him to the archive. His forces were engaged with enemy reinforcements flooding in from the city above. He prayed they could hold them until his work was completed. He needed to finish quickly, or this library would become a trap and his army would be overwhelmed by the massed strength of the nathrezim.

He took a deep breath and slowed his pulse. It would not do to make a mistake here, so close to the culmination of everything he had planned for. He could not afford to fail.

There—he found the first ward, a complex spell, almost undetectable. It had been set to warn of anyone tampering with these records and rewriting history. He was not concerned with any such subtlety. He just needed the specific record he was searching for, and then he would be gone. He smashed the spell aside and felt an immediate response as defensive runes flared to life. He sensed portals opening around him.

An enormous felguard shimmered into being among the stacks. A pulse of magical energy, loud as thunder and clear as a bell to anyone with the senses to hear it, rang out. From the distance came multiple responses.

The nathrezim would know exactly where he was now. He stepped forward as the felguard aimed a blow at him. His warglaive lashed out and cut the demon in half. More felguard materialized around him. Illidan cut them down, but more and more materialized with every heartbeat.

He gazed around him with his spectral sight, looking for the pattern of the defenses, finding them inscribed around the base of each pillar of disks. Each was connected to one of three master sigils around the central pillar.

He aimed one of his warglaives at the nearest and threw. His weapon whirled through the air and scoured the stone, breaking part of the spell. The blade bounced off the pillar and returned to his hand. The onrush of felguard slackened as the portals connected to the destroyed rune collapsed.

Illidan sprang forward, moving around the pillar as the demons pursued him. Ahead lay another glowing sigil in the floor. He cut down two felguard, slid forward, powering himself with his wings, and defaced the rune with his blades, then moved toward the last of the master wards.

The remaining felguard bunched around the third glowing sigil. He sprang into the air, gained height, and swooped down on them. His blades sang as he chopped through the demonic ranks, ducking their axe strokes, evading their attempts to grip him.

He drove his blade right into the center of the runic pattern, disrupting it. A massive backwash of energy pushed him into the air. The demons howled their frustration, but the gateways through which they had come collapsed. Now he had to deal with only those who had already passed through. There would be no more reinforcements.

Once more he dived amid the demons, scattering them with the force of his flying charge. His blades decapitated some and left others limbless. He came to rest beside the central pillar. He stood next to his goal for all these long centuries.

Extending one hand, he invoked his spell of seeking once more. Images flooded his mind as tendrils of force touched the disks. One in particular, the Seal of Argus, drew him. Potent images overlaid it, the aura of beings he had encountered in the past and would never forget: Archimonde and Kil'jaeden, the two mightiest lieutenants of Sargeras, true master of the Burning Legion.

Their psychic stench was so strong, it threatened to overwhelm even his prepared mind. He felt the brutal fury of Archimonde and the subtle, intricate mind of Kil'jaeden. Even though he knew they were not present, it was all he could do to keep from lashing out as if surrounded by deadly foes.

With a mighty heave of his muscles, he tore the disk from the tower. The stack tottered but did not fall. He spoke the words of another spell, and the disk floated in the air behind him, slowly orbiting his form, the runes on its surface glowing with sinister greenish-yellow light.

A grim smile twisted Illidan's lips. He would give the nathrezim something to remember him by. He drew on all his strength and scoured the tower of records with one of the Warglaives of Azzinoth. The smell of ozone and brimstone filled the air as sparks of magical energy discharged.

Rising into the air, Illidan defaced the pillars, damaging the weaving of spells, smashing the records of which the dreadlords were so proud. Demonic glee pulsed through his mind at the thought of their fury. Part of him mourned the loss of so much knowledge. Part of him believed that no record of the dreadlords should be allowed to remain. They deserved no monument.

From the entrance came the sounds of fighting as his demon hunters sought to keep their resurgent enemy at bay. He swooped down into the combat, landed on the back of one dreadlord, and parted the demon's head from his shoulders with a single blow.

"To me, my soldiers!" he shouted. "It is time to leave this foul place. We have gotten what we came for."

THEY BATTLED THEIR WAY back to the portal. All around, Illidan sensed the opening of more gateways as the hosts of the Burning Legion poured reinforcements in. It seemed they had not yet realized what was happening, and were responding piecemeal. Sometime soon a leader would take charge, and then things would become difficult. They needed to leave this world before that happened.

Vandel slashed at a demonic mo'arg servitor as the creature aimed a blast of flame from some engine he wore on his back. Companies of imps poured fire down on them from on high. They occupied the ridgelines.

"Varedis, take a company and clear those ridges," Illidan ordered.

The demon hunter nodded and gestured, and he and his forces bounded up the hillside, cartwheeling and somersaulting through the gouts of flame. The demons shrieked and gibbered foul insults in their tongue and then turned to flee.

Ahead loomed a pack of voidwalkers, floating over the battlefield, legless, armored, and gleaming black. They were tough but slow. "Go around them," Illidan ordered. "Make your way to the portal."

He paused to glance around. His force had taken casualties during the battle in the archive, and even now attrition stalked them.

He saw Elarisiel go down and hacked his way to her side. Vandel was already there, helping her to her feet.

Illidan nodded his approval. He wanted no one left behind if possible. The wounded could be healed. Those too wounded to be moved he put out of their misery.

Ahead of them the portal to Outland blazed. There were signs of conflict there. The Legion's forces had moved to secure the gate, intending to cut off their retreat. In accordance with his orders, his own army on Outland had not moved through but remained in place to guard the way out.

"Form up into a wedge," he ordered. "We are going to cut our way free."

His demon hunters shouted their approval and charged. In battle they looked every bit as demonic as their foes—lithe tattooed forms marked by scars and mutations, some surrounded by integuments of shadow, some wielding fel magic as easily as any spawn of the Twisting Nether.

For a moment, the demons held. Then they were down and the portal was ahead of Illidan's forces. He ordered them through and then turned. In the distance, the glare of gigantic gateways opening filled the darkness. Over the ridges poured demonic fighter after demonic fighter. He looked at them and laughed.

Let them come. He had found what he was looking for. They were too late to stop him.

He stepped through the portal. Already the demon hunters were racing clear of it to join the rest of his army on Outland. Illidan took one last look at the battleground in Nathreza, sensed none of his troops alive out there, and spoke the words of unbinding. The gateway unraveled in a furious discharge of energy, all the backblast directed into the nathrezim homeworld. It was his final gift to them, a surge of explosive energy that could tear apart a continent. He prayed that on the other side of the gate, the dreadlord commanders were assembled.

He had inflicted the greatest defeat that the Burning Legion had suffered in millennia, and he was pleased.

ILLIDAN WATCHED THE LAST remnants of the portal's energies collapse behind him. He looked at his army and wondered if there were any spies among it. Almost certainly it was the case. He considered the events of the day, and his mouth twisted into a wide grin.

Today had been the first unalloyed triumph he had experienced in many a long century. He had captured Maiev. He had invaded the realm of the dreadlords and acquired their most closely kept secret. He had destroyed the armies they had sent to protect their homeworld. If his calculations were correct, he had shattered Nathreza as Ner'zhul's magic had shattered Draenor.

He gazed upon the watchful, expectant faces of his troops. His magically amplified voice boomed out over the ranks of assembled fighters. "Today we have struck a blow against the Burning Legion the like of which has not been felt in ten thousand years. We have slaughtered dreadlords and ravaged their world. We have shown them that they are not immune to our vengeance. That they will be brought to justice and made to atone for their deeds."

Approval rippled through the ranks of the demon hunters as the realization of what they had done settled into their minds. They had been concentrating only on fighting and survival. Now they began to feel their triumph in their bones. Smiles appeared on faces whose owners had never expected to smile again. For a moment demonic rage vanished, to be replaced with something almost like calm.

"We have slain thousands and lured their armies into a trap that killed a hundred times that number, and we have this!" He brandished the disk he had taken from the archives, held it aloft with both hands so that it caught the light and sparkled. The demon hunters and the sorcerers present could all see the power it contained. The sensitive among them could catch a faint whiff of the auras permeating it, even at the distance they stood from him.

There might be spies present, he told himself, but glee loosened his tongue.

"We have found the key to the homeworld of Kil'jaeden and Archimonde, to a place where the Legion's commanders can be finally slain. We have uncovered the location of Argus.

"The Legion has destroyed world after world, enslaved and massacred nation after nation. Now it will reap what it has sown. Today we have slaughtered the nathrezim, and that is only the first step. Today we put our feet on the path to ultimate victory. Today we found the means to cut off the head that guides our foe. We are taking the war to Kil'jaeden. We are going to teach him the meaning of defeat."

Let there be spies present, Illidan thought. *Let them report that to the Burning Legion. Let them think about what I have done this day and tremble.*

CHAPTER TWENTY

Three Months Before the Fall

MAIEV WOKE. SHE ACHED AS SHE HAD EVERY ONE OF the days since she had found herself in this place. She was somewhere deep underground. Nearby she could hear water drip. The air held the brimstone taint of demons, and the unwashed smell of Broken.

She rose to her feet and tested the bars of her cage once more. They had not become any weaker since the previous day. They had been forged to hold something with the power of a pit lord, and then they had been reinforced with layers of runes and spells.

She inspected the runes about her. There were spells of nourishment and restoration. She could not starve herself to death. Any wounds she inflicted on her own body were healed as swiftly as she might make them. She well knew this type of spell. It was similar to the ones used to imprison Illidan. She had discovered this when she had attempted to batter her way out with her bare hands. She had struck the blows in impatient fury, the pain goading her on even as her bones healed, knitting back together as quickly as her flesh had rent.

She suspected that the spells would bring her back from death if she found some way of killing herself. Her spirit was bound here. There was no way to set it free unless her captors willed it.

At first she had expected the Betrayer to appear at any moment to begin tormenting her, but he had not done so. He was too busy to claim his vengeance, or more likely he was just allowing her horror to mount in anticipation of his arrival. He was certainly capable of such mental cruelty.

There had been no shortage of petty torments from her guards. She had been spat upon, poked with sharp sticks, and given food in which the Ashtongue had urinated. Demons had mocked her with words that flayed like knives. A spectacularly arrogant dreadlord named Vagath had explained in great detail exactly what tortures he was going to inflict on her when the order came. She had endured all the slights with calm, unwilling to give her tormentors any satisfaction. So far it seemed they had been ordered against any worse abuse by Illidan himself. He wanted no one taking vengeance before he did.

There were other torments. Hot days on which she went without water. Days when she had been given no food and her stomach had growled like an angry nightsaber. The spells kept her going, would not allow her to die, but they did not relieve her from thirst or hunger.

And she inflicted worse torments on herself. She had led those who had trusted her to their doom. In seeking her vengeance on Illidan, she had caused the deaths of Anyndra and Sarius and all the others who had placed their faith in her leadership.

She told herself they had done so voluntarily, but it did not help. When she lay awake, she could see their faces, and they gave her looks full of reproach. In her dreams she saw them die again and again. She cursed all of those who had refused to help: the naaru, the Aldor, Arechron in Telaar. If they had listened to her, none of this would have happened, and the Betrayer would be where he deserved to be, imprisoned once more or in his grave.

It gave her no relief.

She knew whose will it was that had driven the crusade against the Betrayer. She knew whom the others had put their faith in. She had let them down. She could try to blame whomever she liked, but at the end of the day, she had to take responsibility for her own failure.

Perhaps that was the worst injury of all. She had failed. Illidan was not only free but stronger than he had ever been. It galled her worse than poison, worse than hunger, worse than torture. Illidan was free and there was nothing she could do about it. She was doomed to stay in this cage, helpless, until he chose to take her life. It was being made clear to her that she lived or died entirely at his whim.

Now he was ignoring her, letting her know how insignificant she was in the great scheme of things.

There were times when she hoped that some of her force had escaped and would come free her, and there were times when she despaired of it. Even if a few had made it clear of the ambush, why would they come back for the leader who had led their comrades to their deaths? She had filled their heads with tales of victory and glory, and their reward had been defeat. She knew, though, that no one was coming. All her troops were dead. She had seen them fall.

She cursed Akama once more. She had believed in the faithless leader of the Ashtongue faction. He had convinced her that he hated Illidan as much as she did, and that he had as much reason to want the Betrayer's downfall. How he must be laughing now, at the way he had deceived her, at the way in which she had believed his lies. She cursed the memory of their every meeting.

When had the betrayal started and why had she not spotted it?

Had he planned this from the beginning, back when they first met in Orebor Harborage? Even then were he and Illidan laughing at the way she was being led to her doom? She refused to believe that she could be so easily gulled. Akama must have meant some of what he said. His resentment of what the Betrayer had done to the Temple of Karabor was real enough.

Looking back, she could see there was a moment when he had changed. At their last meeting in Orebor Harborage, he had seemed even more aged, weaker, and listless. Perhaps he had been finally unmasked, captured, tortured. Perhaps Illidan had used some powerful binding spell on him.

Or perhaps Illidan had simply made him a better offer, promised him something his venal soul could not resist. The Betrayer could be persuasive and cloak his malice in honeyed words. What could he possibly have offered the Broken?

No. Unless she was much mistaken, Akama had been as surprised as she was at what had happened during the opening of the gate. He had spoken out against the ritual destruction of the Broken's souls even at risk to his own life. Things were not quite as simple as she feared in the depths of her despair.

It took her moments to realize that her guards had gone silent. Looking up, she saw why. Limping toward her, looking older and more tired than ever, was Akama.

"Treacherous oath-breaking dog," she said as soon as the Broken was within earshot.

"I swore no oaths to you, Maiev Shadowsong," he said, his voice weary. "Nor you to me."

The guards listened intently. Akama gestured for them to stand back as he approached the cage. They did so, clearly daunted by his presence.

"So you have managed to worm your way back into the Betrayer's favor."

"I am alive."

"That is more than many of your people can claim."

Akama winced and said, "Or yours."

Maiev kept her guilt from her face. "They died for the cause of bringing Illidan to justice. As I will."

Akama gestured at the cage. His magic made the wards and spells shimmer in the air, visible. "Look at where all your passion, hatred, and anger have brought you. Do you enjoy the view?"

"At least I did not stand by and watch my own people being slaughtered."

Akama considered his words for a moment and then said, "But slaughtered they were. Because of where you led them."

It was Maiev's turn to flinch. She could not control her movements perfectly. Imprisonment was affecting her. "They gave their lives for what they believed in. Will anyone ever be able to say the same of you?"

"I was given a hard choice. I will live with it. You of all people should know how that is."

"You chose to spare your own life and give away the lives of those who trusted you." Maiev could not keep the bitterness from her voice.

"You have no idea what was done to me. Illidan ripped part of my soul from my body and bound it with magic. If he chooses to, he can unleash it, and it will devour me."

Maiev wondered if that was true. If it was, it would explain much. Perhaps it was just another lie. "I do not need to hear your self-pity."

Akama remained silent for many heartbeats. When he spoke, his voice was gentle. "It was not just my life that was at risk. All of my people's lives were as well. The Betrayer is as ruthless as he is powerful."

"So you chose to throw away our chance of overthrowing him."

"We never had a chance, not then."

"So you think you have a better chance now?"

Akama paused. His mouth opened. He seemed to be on the verge of saying something; then he licked his lips and shook his head almost imperceptibly. "You have no conception of how strong Illidan has become. I saw him work sorcery that I would not have believed possible for anyone less than a god. He opened a portal clear across the cosmos."

Maiev thought she detected an off note in Akama's voice. He was afraid of being overheard. Were they being watched? She would have to assume that they were. Was it possible he still schemed against the Betrayer and somehow believed that she had a place in those schemes?

"And why do you think he did this?"

"He has returned, having slaughtered an army of demons, perhaps killed a world full of them. So he claimed when he came back through the portal."

"And you believe him?"

"I believe that Illidan truly hates the nathrezim, that he hates all of the Burning Legion."

Did she hear doubt in his voice? Was Akama merely an actor mouthing a script in order to avoid having suspicion fall on him? "Why are you here? Did you come to gloat?"

"I am here to make sure you are well. Lord Illidan wants to be certain of that. He has plans for you."

Maiev's mouth went dry and her heart hammered within her chest. She could imagine exactly what sort of plans the Betrayer had for her. She was being kept alive and in good health for a reason, and it was not a pleasant one. Illidan intended to make her pay for his long imprisonment. She forced the thought down. She would face any torture when it came. She would not give her captors the satisfaction of seeing her afraid.

"And he is testing you," she said. This time she allowed mockery to show in her voice. "He does not trust you."

"I doubt he trusts anybody," Akama said. "If you were he, would you?"

"I would never be like him."

"You are more like him than you can possibly know. You are just as ruthless and just as obsessed. You sacrificed your friends without a second thought when it suited your purpose. You sacrificed the lives of all your followers."

Maiev wanted to strike him but the bars restrained her. She glared at his lined face and said, "I do not accept your judgments, Akama. I have learned not to trust anything you say."

"You can tell yourself that if you like, but look into your heart and you will see my words are true."

She grasped the bars as if she could somehow twist them out of shape and make her way through to him.

Akama laughed. "You are still strong. That is good. You will need that strength in the days to come."

"I am not frightened by your threats, old one."

"You think that was a threat? Consider this, Maiev Shadowsong— Lord Illidan is not the only one who has plans for you."

"What do you mean by that?"

"I, too, have plans." Once again there was an ambiguous note in Akama's voice. Was this a veiled threat, or was it meant to sound like one while communicating something else?

"I want no part of any of your schemes, treacherous one," Maiev said, hoping to draw him out.

"You may have no choice before this is over."

Akama turned and limped away. Despite herself, Maiev was sorry to watch him go. This was the closest thing she had had to a conversation since she had woken in captivity. And Akama was at least a familiar face.

She wondered if this was what she was supposed to think, if it was all part of some subtle plan of the Betrayer's to wear her down. If it was, there was nothing she could do about it now. She just had to endure, be patient, and gather her strength.

She had nothing else now but time. She swore she would find a way to make the Betrayer pay for all the deaths he had caused. Akama, too, when the moment came. She had begun to work out the composition of a spell that would help her trap Illidan. She would test it if ever she won her freedom.

CHAPTER TWENTY-ONE

Two Months Before the Fall

THE HARSH SUN BLAZED DOWN ON THE PARCHED EARTH of Hellfire Peninsula, drying the blood almost as soon as it fell. Vandel chopped down the last of the demons, then walked over to retrieve his dagger from the eye of the one he had slain with a throw.

Looking around, he could see they had achieved their objective. Lord Illidan stood beside the palanquins the demons had fought so hard to protect, arms folded across his chest, wings spread wide in triumph.

The corpses of demons lay everywhere, slaughtered by the Illidari. Vandel's demon whispered hungrily in his mind. He fought the urge to gulp down demon flesh and instead climbed up a huge boulder and studied the battleground. He nodded at one of the new crop of demon hunters who had joined the ranks since the battle with the nathrezim. In the month since, they had almost replaced the casualties of that great battle in the archive of the dreadlords.

They had lost more soldiers since that battle. It sometimes seemed that in the weeks that followed, they had never stopped fighting. That was not quite true. There had been a period when Illidan had retreated within his sanctum to consider his next move.

For days they had done nothing but train and oversee the new recruits. Then the Betrayer had emerged with a new plan, and they had spent almost all their time in lightning raids against the Burning Legion.

They must have fought a score of battles. They had attacked forge camps in Nagrand, and ambushed convoys passing through the Netherstorm. Time and again they had intercepted forces passing through Hellfire Peninsula.

Some of the fights had been to close down portals the Legion opened into Outland. The logic of that was clear. No doubt the masters of the Burning Legion thirsted for vengeance against Illidan. Their incursions had become ever more numerous. Their forces ever stronger.

That had not been all of it, though. Some new portals had been opened into places Vandel recognized in Azeroth: Winterspring and Azshara. Illidan had insisted that the demon hunters close those and claim certain magical crystals used in their creation. He said the Legion had been launching invasions into Azeroth from Outland and this needed to be stopped.

It was clear that the demons were planning another great assault. Not all of their gates could be closed. They had established mighty beachheads in the Blade's Edge Mountains and on the very edges of Nagrand. From what Vandel had overheard, there were more forge camps Illidan's forces had never seen and perhaps were never likely to.

It was equally clear that Lord Illidan was seeking materials to create something. If forced to make a guess, Vandel would have said he was collecting components for another gateway such as the one he had opened to Nathreza. Vandel had heard some of the others, the ones knowledgeable about such things, mention this, and it seemed as good a theory as any.

Vandel would not have been surprised to discover that they would find more of the crystals in the metal coffins this force had been escorting, along with other pieces of magical equipment that could be scavenged.

Since his memorable speech after the battle, Lord Illidan had not seen fit to enlighten them any further as to his ultimate plan. He had merely dispatched them hither and yon to strike at the Legion, sometimes leading them himself, sometimes letting Elarisiel or Vandel take charge. There was no rhyme or reason to Illidan accompanying them. Sometimes the battles he led them into were little more than slaughters of fel orcs still loyal to the Burning Legion. Sometimes he was not with them when they faced their toughest opposition. Rumor had it that he worked strange rituals when the stars were right, that he was creating some work of sorcery that would lead them to inevitable victory.

Below, Illidan studied the remains of the palanquins they had ambushed. Each of the coffins had been borne by half a dozen demonic servitors, and each of them now lay in the dust, their gleaming metallic sides losing their luster.

Before Illidan a fel orc hovered in the air, one of the Legion's soldiers, bound by the Betrayer's magic.

Vandel vaulted down the rocks, leaping from boulder to boulder, passing over precipices where the slightest misstep would send him plunging to his doom. He hit the ground rolling, sprang to his feet, and strode over to Lord Illidan's side.

"Anything to report, nightstalker?" the Betrayer asked. As ever he seemed to know that Vandel was there without having to look. It was less disconcerting now that Vandel knew how the trick was done and could do it himself.

"The perimeters are secure, Lord, and we do not appear to be under immediate threat."

"I would not be too sure of that if I were you," Illidan said.

"Lord?"

"I think the Burning Legion has finally worked out what I am doing."

"How would they do that, Lord?"

"Perhaps they have spies left in our ranks. Only one of these canisters contains the helstones I seek. The rest are filled with rocks."

"How can you tell?"

"Use the sight the ritual gave you."

Vandel concentrated on the metal cylinders and saw immediately what his overlord had meant. One of them blazed with contained energy as if filled to the brim with scintillant crystals. The others did not burn nearly so bright. They contained no trapped magical energy that Illidan could use for whatever it was he planned.

As if to prove his point, Illidan leaned forward and wrenched one open. Glittering gemstones rolled out, but so did a number of glassy shards. One who did not possess the spectral sight of a demon hunter might have been fooled, but one who could see the presence of magic itself was not deceived.

"You think this is a trap then?"

"Possibly, or merely a deception intended to lure us to a different place while the real cargo goes by another route. I think this highlord Kruul I have been hearing so much about is cleverer than the Legion's former field commanders."

"Who is he?" Vandel asked.

"Let us find out," Illidan said. He turned to the fel orc, who floated in the air, wrapped in chains of energy. His face twisted into a defiant sneer.

"I know you, Betrayer. You are well named."

"If I had a copper for every time I have heard that, I could build a tower of coins to the nearest moon," Illidan said. "I wish my enemies could come up with something more original."

The fel orc tried to spit at Illidan, but his saliva sizzled and evaporated when it hit an energy chain. "Tell me of Highlord Kruul," Illidan said. "I would know more of your new general."

"I will tell you nothing," said the fel orc. "I do not fear any torture you can inflict."

"As you wish." Illidan gestured. Magical energy surged from his outstretched hands to the fel orc's head. The chains pulsed brighter. The fel orc screamed. His spirit departed, leaving only a shell. Vandel could see that.

Illidan said, "Tell me of Highlord Kruul."

The corpse opened its mouth and laughed. "No need, Betrayer. No need. He approaches. Ask him yourself."

Magical energy pulsed from within the metal cylinders, visible as light to Vandel's altered vision. It swirled into the air, forming a shimmering vortex. A moment later, a portal sprang into being where the power coalesced. A blast of furnace-like heat filled the air, driving the Illidari back and incinerating the fel orc's corpse.

An enormous figure emerged, flanked by two blazing infernals.

He looked like a doomguard, Vandel thought, but larger. He had horns like a tauren, massive, bison-like. Huge wings draped his back. Yellow demonic runes glared on his bracers. In his right hand he clutched a gigantic black blade on which runes pulsed in subdued blue. The sword looked large enough to take down an Ashenvale oak with one swipe.

"So you are the one who defeated Magtheridon," the demon said. "You don't look like much."

His voice boomed brazenly over the battlefield. Flames trailed behind him when he walked, as if the very ground could not bear the touch of his hooves without combusting in fear.

It said something of Kruul's confidence that he was prepared to face an army of demon hunters only with his infernal bodyguards. Looking at him, Vandel judged his self-assurance justified. He blazed with power. Currents of potent magic swirled around him.

"And you look like just another doomguard," Illidan said. "Have you come to see if you can get vengeance for the doom of your brethren's homeworld?"

Kruul's laughter rang out. "That was well done. Destruction wreaked upon the destroyers. But, no, I have not come to seek vengeance. I have come to kill you."

Illidan unsheathed his warglaives. "Others have tried. I shall pen you beside Magtheridon and use your blood to build my armies."

"My blood would burn your little pets. You would only have charred husks to serve you."

As the gigantic doomguard spoke, more and more infernals poured through the portal. Their skin blazed with searing heat. They seemed to grow stronger in Kruul's presence.

In the hills around them, Vandel sensed the Illidari moving into position. They were ready to attack.

"I have charted the portals you have been opening," Illidan said. "You have been busy. Ironforge, Stormwind City, Orgrimmar. Silithus. The Plaguelands. You seek to invade Azeroth once more, do you not?"

Highlord Kruul merely bared his massive teeth. "And I have studied your reaving of our forces, and I see a pattern to it. You seek to build another gateway, don't you? Ah, but to where, is the question. I have heard of your boasting. Could it be you are truly mad enough to seek Argus?"

"Perhaps we will discuss this while I have you imprisoned in Hellfire Citadel."

"I fear that your time for discussion has run out." Even as Kruul spoke, a massive core hound appeared from the portal. Its red skin blazed with fire. Two heads emerged from its gigantic shoulders. Their monstrous jaws made those of a felhound look feeble. Metallic armor encased its heavy shoulders and forelimbs.

It bounded forward to attack even as Kruul sent a bolt of dark energy hurtling toward Illidan. The lord of Outland leapt into the air and avoided it. It smashed into the rocks behind where he had stood. They turned to dust, as if they had suffered a million years of erosion in a moment.

Vandel found himself face-to-face with Kruul's demonic pet. Its jaws gaped. Lava bubbled within them.

The infernals lumbered toward him. Vandel vaulted over the core hound. His feet briefly touched the hot metal of its armor. He propelled himself into the air before they had time to scorch. As he did so he sent his own bolt of fel energy blazing down into the demon. It struck one of the heads and elicited a brief scream. The thing's skin darkened at the point of contact and began to putrefy.

From the slopes, a dozen demon hunters joined in, sending a fusillade of fel energy into the core hound's skin, smashing into the infernals and sapping them of life.

Kruul swept his blade through the air and invoked his power. A hail of shadow energy lashed out. A volley of bolts hurtled at the demon hunters. Some fell wounded. Others slumped to the ground. Kruul seemed to visibly swell as he feasted on their deaths. Behind him the gigantic portal still blazed.

Vandel somersaulted at the top of his arc, pulled his blades clear of their sheaths, and dropped onto the demonic hound's back. Pain flared where his skin touched the creature's burning flesh. He aimed for a weak spot in the armor and drove his blades in. There was a satisfying crunch as points punched through scaled flesh. Molten ichor spurted, searing his skin. He vaulted clear of the beast and rolled to one side, narrowly avoiding the trampling feet of a gigantic infernal.

He dived between the demon's legs, ignoring the scorching heat. His movements took him closer to Kruul. The doomguard paid him no mind. All his attention seemed focused on Illidan.

Magical energies swirled around the lord of Outland, gathering in a thunderhead of power as he invoked them. More demon hunters emerged from the hillside, moving to engage the infernals and the core hound. Some of them dared race forward to challenge Kruul himself.

Kruul flexed his wings and there came a sound like thunder.

Those nearest the demon were thrown back. Their movements were slowed. For combatants who relied so much on mobility, this made them vulnerable. Kruul's monstrous blade swept out and chopped an attacker in half. The demon hunter's blood vanished as if the runes on the blade had absorbed it, and Kruul grew visibly stronger.

The demon inside Vandel stirred at the sight of all this death. It longed to feed as Kruul fed. Vandel channeled all his rage into another fel bolt and lashed out at Kruul. The magical energies splintered on whatever aura protected the demon lord. Kruul raised his blade, pointed it at Illidan, and sent another titanic bolt of shadowy energy blazing up at his opponent. Illidan deflected it with a counterspell.

A low growl from behind told Vandel that the core hound had returned to seek prey. He flipped himself around to face it. Half of one of its heads had been torn away. Molten ichor spilled from several wounds in its side.

Still the creature's unnatural vitality kept it moving. It bounded toward him, mouths gaping, flames leaking around its teeth. He leapt to meet it. His blades snapped home, piercing each eye of one head, and then he jumped away to the creature's blind side, scampering quickly to keep out of its line of sight. The creature turned. Its nostrils dilated as it sniffed the air, attempting to find him.

Enraged, Kruul smashed through the demon hunters. They did their best to leap clear, but his blade slew two more. Their strikes seemed to have no more effect on him than gnat bites.

The core hound put its noses to the ground and kept sniffing. It began to move in Vandel's direction. He sent a bolt of fel energy lashing at it, and kept the beam playing on the creature, draining its life away. From the air above came a titanic surge of power as Illidan finally unleashed the spell he had been weaving. The enormous bolt of hellfire smashed into Kruul and sent him sprawling.

"No! That is not possible." The highlord's booming voice

echoed across the battlefield. There was pain in it, and a massive gap in his armored chest piece where the bolt had struck home. Venomous smoke emerged from the gap, and wounded flesh pulsed within.

Kruul raised himself up and sprang toward the blazing portal. It closed behind him. Vandel stabbed the demon hound through the chest and left his blade buried in its heart. The infernal bodyguards collapsed into piles of rocks.

THE ILLIDARI GATHERED THEIR wounded and their dead and prepared to depart the battlefield.

Illidan studied the remains of the carnage. Kruul had been strong, no doubt of that, and he had been cunning. This trap had been set with care, and only the fact that Kruul had misjudged Illidan's strength had let him escape its jaws.

It was only a matter of time before a new invasion of Azeroth began. Perhaps that was to the good. It would distract the Legion while Illidan finalized his own designs. It troubled him that Kruul had mentioned his plan to seek out Argus. He should not have boasted about that before he was ready to strike. That had been a mistake. He had let the thrill of triumph overcome his reason when he had done that.

Additionally, he felt there was more going on here than met the eye. He was missing something, and the feeling of it gnawed at him.

It was time to go back to the Black Temple and complete the preparations as fast as he could. The hour was getting late, and he could not afford to have anything go wrong now.

CHAPTER TWENTY-TWO

Two Months Before the Fall

B EHIND THE BUSHES OF THE PLEASURE GARDEN, VANDEL hunched out of sight of the blood elves. They laughed and swigged ethermead from crystal beakers. One youth had a courtesan under each arm and kissed each in turn. Another flexed a small whip in imitation of the succubi in the Den of Mortal Delights below. A tall, beautiful sin'dorei girl played a seven-stringed lute and improvised verses about a fel orc chieftain and a doomguard that were not flattering to either of her subjects.

The Grand Promenade seemed a world away from the endless warfare taking place beyond the Black Temple. It was one reason why Vandel had taken to sneaking in here of an evening. The precincts of the inner temple were a complete contrast with the stern, martial aspect of the rest of the great fortress, created for Illidan's blood elf followers for their own relaxation. The promenade had remained a refuge and a reward for those blood elves who had stayed loyal to Illidan even after Kael'thas's disappearance.

The party of revelers sprawled on the manicured lawn. Silk-clad girls held tiny tidbits of devilfish at a finger's length above the lips of the males.

The demon hunters had never been forbidden from entering the Black Temple. They had never been invited, either. They kept apart from the rest of the Illidari forces, as much from their blood elf kin as from the orcs and the Broken and the demons. No one visited them in the ruins of Karabor who could help it, and they mingled with none.

There were times when Vandel wanted to be apart even from his fellow demon hunters. He liked to hone his skills by slipping past the temple sentinels and entering the unholy precincts of the place itself.

He had climbed the great chains in the Sanctuary of Shadows and gazed in wonder on the huge statues that dominated the place. The satyr guardians had flinched away from him as if they sensed he hungered for their flesh.

He had scuttled through the gloomy orc-haunted precincts of Gorefiend's Vigil and eluded the gaze of even the most alert of the Shadowmoon clan. He had inspected their magical forges, and witnessed their spellcasters animating the bones of the dead. He had looked down upon the vast training area where demons marshaled and the Dragonmaw orcs trained their dragons amid the hulls of gigantic war machines. He had clambered across the battlements and looked out across the plains toward Warden's Cage, where Maiev Shadowsong was imprisoned. But the Grand Promenade was the place he liked the best.

The fountains tinkled. It was the sound of running water that first attracted him, and the scent of plants, some of them familiar from the forests of Ashenvale. It reminded him of home, of the night elf he had once been. It was a sweet torment. It brought back memories of his family. There were times when that calmed him. He could pick a blossom and sniff it and remember the times when he had brought back bouquets for his wife when she had been pregnant with Khariel.

At other times it stirred up the demon within him and fed its vengeful fury. Tonight it made him envy the sinful laughter of the blood elves at play.

He reached out from the undergrowth and plucked a bottle of ethermead from the hamper. The revelers were too involved with one another to notice him. He uncorked it and took a sip. It tingled on his tongue, and for a moment he felt relaxed.

Briefly he wondered whether the demon had encouraged him to do it. Tonight he did not care. Tonight he wanted to remember other things than the battles of the past few weeks, the rumors that the Burning Legion was mustering for a new offensive.

His nostrils caught the musky aroma of succubus blown from the terraces below by the hot night wind. His mouth watered. The hunger to kill banked up within him. These demons might be bound. They might be sworn to serve Illidan. They might be allies but still they felt like enemies. They felt like prey.

Trudging along the path near the revelers came Akama. The Broken moved through the garden from the direction of the council chamber, heading back down into the depths of the temple. Doubtless he had come from some late-night meeting with Illidan himself. His head was down. His gaze focused on nothing. A great weight pressed down on his shoulders.

A blood elf raised his head and shouted, "Come, old Broken, join us for a drink!"

One of the girls tittered. "Oh, Luzen. He is so ugly."

"Anyone is ugly compared with you, Alesha. Hey, old Broken. Stop your hobbling for a minute and drink with us! Damn you, Alesha! Where is that bottle of ethermead? Did you gulp it down while I was not looking?"

Vandel raised it in mocking toast to the blood elf. He was so deep in shadow that no one could see him.

Akama hobbled on.

"Hey, old monster, are you too good to be seen drinking with us?" There was anger in Luzen's voice now. He sounded as if he was ready for violence.

Akama stopped. His head turned, and he gazed upon the blood elves. He did not say anything. All present could feel the power in him. He ceased to be an old, worn-out Broken and grew into something vast and powerful and terrible. Not something to be mocked by sin'dorei aesthetes.

Menace filled the night, and the blood elves froze like rabbits seeing the shadow of an owl. For a moment, all was still, and a premonition of violence hung in the air. Then Akama shrugged and smiled and made a gesture of benediction like a senile old priest blessing a group of children. He hobbled away.

The blood elves were silent for a long time after that. Vandel stole away, wondering about Akama and his secret sorrows.

AKAMA TOOK THE WALKWAY into the Sanctuary of Shadows and fought down the urge to lengthen his stride as he passed the refectory. As always, when he passed that dreadful place, he was filled with a sense of horror. He did not want to look upon the thing he knew was in there, bound by Ashtongue channelers. It was part of him. It was all the darkness from his soul and a great portion of his pride, ambition, and will. It was being fed evil magical energies, and if allowed to go free, it would devour him utterly and walk the world in his body.

The thing in the refectory would eat him from the inside and use his voice to turn his followers over to the darkness. Already many of them were a long way down that road. They owed more loyalty to Illidan than they did to the ideals of their own people.

Well were they named, the Broken. The demons had shattered their spirit almost beyond repair. They had become so used to drifting that they would follow any strong voice, and there was none stronger than the Betrayer.

Some of Akama's people responded to their master as slaves responded to the lash. They obeyed quickly, unquestioningly, with total obedience. They had lost all ability to think for themselves and would perform any dark deed required of them, passing the blame and the responsibility on to the one who gave the orders.

Akama looked upon the satyrs and the other demons profaning what had once been the most sacred spot of his people. It made him want to weep, just as the sight of those arrogant blood elves lolling around in what had once been the beautiful temple garden made him want to howl in fury.

What had happened to the Temple of Karabor was symbolic of what had happened to the draenei. Every evil thing that had ever happened to them had taken root here. And over the whole dark cavalcade, Illidan presided.

The triumphant demons strutting through the sanctuary mocked his passage. They knew what had been done to him. They looked at him and they saw only a decrepit Broken bound by the same monstrous will that had bound them.

They saw what he wanted them to see.

They could not look into the secret chambers of his mind, where his thoughts were still his own. He kept them shielded even in his sleep. Not even Illidan could look within those warded areas.

At least that was what he told himself. There were times when he wondered whether the spell that bound him also deceived him. Perhaps it allowed him these illusions of freedom, all the better to lull him into submission. Perhaps Akama was more like his people than he knew. Perhaps he was, after all, the perfect broken leader for a perfectly broken people.

No. The day was coming when he would move against Illidan, as sure as the sun rose over Outland. He had to believe that. He would use the secret network of agents he had built up under Illidan's very nose. He would find new allies and use them to oppose Illidan's will. The Betrayer would regret that he had been too wrapped up in his mad schemes to pay attention to his lowly Broken servant. Akama ground his teeth together. He would make Illidan pay for what he had done to the souls of the Broken at the Hand of Gul'dan. The lord of Outland would have cause to lament that he had spared the life of Maiev Shadowsong.

Akama paused and unclenched his fists. He let his mouth fall open. He made sure that once again he looked the part of the chastened, humble Broken.

The hollowness within his soul mocked him. Perhaps he was being allowed to do all these things. Perhaps he was just a lure to draw out those whom Illidan could not trust. Perhaps he was bait in a trap for Illidan's enemies as he had been for Maiev.

He took a deep breath through his flat nostrils, and exhaled, as he had been taught to do back when he had been a novice in the Temple of Karabor. He remembered when this place had been a haven of peace and purity, a sanctuary for the sick and the weak. The thought calmed him for a moment, but then he caught sight of his own distorted shadow cast against the wall. He was just as twisted now as the temple, and he wondered if either of them would ever find their way back to what they had once been.

Curse you, Illidan. Curse you and all your schemes. What are you up to now?

HIGH NETHERMANCER ZEREVOR HELD the Seal of Argus. He turned it over and over in his hands. The blood elf's silver crown glinted as he tilted his head to one side. An expression of interest appeared in eyes resembling pools of fel green light. "I understand why you sought this so long, Lord. It should allow you to find what you are seeking. It is a compass for locating Argus."

Illidan snapped his wings open, then settled them back around his shoulders. He allowed a note of irony to show in his voice. "Really? You are certain?"

Zerevor flinched at the mockery. "As certain as anyone can ever be when dealing with the magic of the Burning Legion."

Lady Malande's laughter tinkled around the council chamber. "And, as ever, you try to cover yourself in case of error, Zerevor."

Gathios the Shatterer, resplendent in his gleaming paladin armor, opened his mouth as if he was going to say something, then shut it again. He rarely spoke when matters were not concerned with warfare. Instead he exchanged a knowing glance with Veras Darkshadow. The lean assassin smiled in acknowledgment. Had they been plotting against their companions again?

Impatience curled Illidan's fist. "Let him finish, Malande."

The lovely priestess shot him a hurt look. Her beauty had driven many an elf to distraction. She seemed to regard his own indifference as a challenge.

A cold smile flickered across Zerevor's face. "It could be used to steer us through the Burning Legion's network of portals and gateways. It could guide us all the way back to Kil'jaeden and legendary Argus."

"I know this," Illidan said. "I have always known this. Why do you bring it up now? What is your point?"

The high nethermancer looked over at the schemata spread on the trestle table. They represented Illidan's masterwork, but clearly something about them had Zerevor worried. "We could use their own gateways to reach Argus. There is no need for this new portal of yours, Lord. It is a work of genius, but why reinvent the wheel? With but the simplest modification, you could use your spell to tap into the Legion's system of portals."

"Because if we use the Legion's network, we will need to pass through multiple portals, giving the demons an opportunity to block us every step of the way. This gateway will take us to Argus in one jump. It will let us attack by surprise. It will ensure our lines of communication are short and can be easily maintained."

The other three councilors nodded as if they agreed with every word. Zerevor persisted in his questioning. "*If* it works, Lord. You are taking a titanic risk. The expenditure of energy needed will be on a scale unlike anything we have ever used before. Would it not be simpler to take advantage of what already exists?"

"Simpler but far more dangerous. The Legion outnumbers us by a factor of thousands. Its forces are dispersed, but if we give them time to assemble, they will crush us."

Zerevor held up the seal to eye level, as if by doing so, he could conceal his expression from Illidan's perceptions. "And attempting to open this gateway could shatter the world again as Ner'zhul shattered Draenor. If the spell is not perfectly cast. If there are any mistakes in the calculations."

Illidan reached out and took the seal from his grasp. "There are no mistakes in the calculations. The spell will be perfectly cast. I will do it myself."

"And if you are wrong, Lord?"

"I am not wrong." Illidan focused his attention completely on his councilor. He loomed over him, letting him feel the breeze from his slowly moving wings.

Zerevor looked away, shoulders slumped, palms open. "As you say, Lord. As you say."

Then the high nethermancer's face went pale. Beads of sweat appeared on his forehead. He closed his eyes and frowned in concentration.

"What is it?" Illidan demanded.

"The warding spells I set over the Dark Portal have just been tripped. The gateway has become fully operational. Someone has opened a pathway between Outland and Azeroth so wide that you could bring an army through. And that appears to be exactly what is happening."

CHAPTER TWENTY-THREE

Two Months Before the Fall

FROM THE RIDGE, THEY HAD A FINE VIEW OF THE DARK PORTAL, and a demoralizing one, Vandel thought. The gateway to Azeroth glowed darkly within a mighty arch, reached by the titanic steps of the Stair of Destiny. It was not the sight of it that depressed him. It was the army surrounding it.

Since the confrontation with Highlord Kruul, the Burning Legion had rushed armies into Outland so quickly they could not be contained. Most of them seemed to be down there now, in the valley and along the road leading to the Dark Portal. Thousands of demons and tens of thousands of their worshippers camped out. They had come through scores of portals, all opened simultaneously in such numbers that not all could be closed. It seemed as if they were intent on proving to Lord Illidan how futile his plans for opposing them were.

More and more of the Legion's troops marched along the road from Zangarmarsh into Hellfire Peninsula. The Legion's forces were moving with a terrible purpose, and that could only be a new invasion of Azeroth. The way to his homeworld was open again, and for days now the Legion had poured forces through.

So many and yet so few. All those soldiers and demons and war engines down there looked imposing, but recollecting the vision he had during the ritual of transformation, Vandel knew that they were but the tiniest fraction of what the Burning Legion could bring to bear.

Every day more and more of them arrived. He tried to imagine the uncountable distance they covered to reach this place, the vast gulfs between worlds they had passed through, and he could not.

The Dark Portal itself was daunting enough. The two robed stone giants on either side of the titanic arch reminded him of similar sculpted figures within the Black Temple. They leaned on blades large enough to smash the walls of Stormwind City. Lights shimmered within the portal, glittering like trapped stars.

Another convoy moved along the road to deliver its cargo of soldiers and munitions to the vast encampment in the portal's shadow. The Illidari had tried to stop the convoys from getting through. They had set ambushes, attacked head-on, but it was pointless. Their enemies were too numerous and too powerful, and they were merely throwing away resources that would be needed to defend the Black Temple when the final attack came.

Illidan's boast that he was going to take the war to Kil'jaeden also seemed pointless now, no more threatening than a child dressing up in his father's armor and waving his father's sword would be to a veteran soldier.

Vandel looked from face to face. Illidan's wore a sneer, as if this whole vast army was beneath his contempt. Needle's face twisted in a mad grin that stretched the seams stitched in his lips. Elarisiel looked quite frankly afraid, and Vandel wondered whether her demon was taking over her mind and manipulating it.

His own inner demon radiated a sense of satisfaction. This demonstration of strength by the Burning Legion pleased it. It would be welcome down there among that mighty force. He could join its invincible ranks at any time and have worlds as his playthings until the universe fell into ruin and was reborn.

Why are we here? Vandel wondered. Had Illidan brought them here merely to depress them? Such was not his way. There must be a purpose to it.

Vandel remembered what the Betrayer had done to the portal to Nathreza. Perhaps he planned the same thing here—a suicidal charge at the gate, a spell of destruction to make it explode, and then that whole army down there would be gone.

As would the demon hunters. The Burning Legion could always find more troops. Who would be left to oppose it once Illidan's forces were in their graves?

Why should it be opposed? his inner demon whispered. *Why should you even try? You belong to it. You always have.*

Even as the thought occurred to him, the flow of power around the gate increased a thousandfold. Troops surged through the portal, coming from Azeroth. Orcs moved alongside humans, night elves beside blood elves. Gryphons soared into the sky above the gateway. Wyverns flew beside them.

Spells shimmered in the air. Magical weapons cleaved through demon hide. A squad of felguard moved to block the Stair of Destiny, but a huge orc armed with a mighty hammer smashed his way through them. Beside him a human carrying a shield watched his back.

It was astonishing to see these peoples fighting alongside one another. Clearly the threat of Kruul's forces had done much to unite them. It looked as if the Alliance and the Horde together were invading Outland.

Once the advance force of heroes was through, more and more troops emerged, marching in closely knit groups to secure the perimeter.

A massive wrathguard smashed through one human line, a

mighty axe clutched in each hand, the demon's body encased in gleaming armor.

A company of orcs rushed to intercept him. A lightning bolt crackled and the wrathguard halted for a moment. The orcs dragged him down. More and more Azerothian troops poured through the gate. Their casualties were appalling but still they fought. For every human or orc or troll dragged down, another stepped into place.

There must be a huge army assembled on the other side of the Dark Portal, Vandel thought, remembering the size of the Legion force that had passed through. All the kingdoms of the Alliance and all the realms of the Horde must have been stripped bare of combatants. The might of an entire world had been assembled to stand against the Burning Legion. Vandel could only pray that it would be enough.

In the center of the Legion camp, he could see Highlord Kruul shouting orders to his force. Did he relish the coming combat or did he regret shoving a stick into this hornet's nest?

Illidan crouched down for a moment, wings spreading wide behind him. He tilted his head to one side. A puzzled expression flickered across his face. "Did Kruul expect this? Did he want it?"

His voice was soft, as if he was speaking to himself.

"Why would he want to provoke an attack from both the Horde and the Alliance?" Vandel asked.

Illidan's gaze remained locked on the conflict. "To draw out the forces of Azeroth, perhaps. To lure them away from their home ground into a place where they can be more easily destroyed."

"You think this is a trap, Lord Illidan?"

"It has the feel of one. The question is, for whom? There is something here that I dislike."

Vandel understood. The feeling of satisfaction his own demon radiated was troubling. Was it reacting on some level to something it sensed about this situation? If that was the case for Vandel, how much greater must the disturbance be for Illidan, who was so much more powerful and experienced?

For a moment, Vandel felt something like guilt. As he watched a contingent of night elf combatants crash into the Burning Legion line, it struck him that he should be down there, fighting with them. He was a demon hunter, after all, and down there was one of the largest forces of demons ever assembled in Outland.

But what would the kaldorei say when they saw him, tattooed with the markings of Illidan, their ancient enemy? They would not greet him as a friend and companion. They were more likely to take him for one of the demons they fought.

He wondered if anyone he knew was riding with the army and if he was going to have to go out there and kill them. He was not sure what he would do if Illidan gave the order.

He was a demon hunter, loyal to the Betrayer, but his war was against the Burning Legion, not against folk who had once been his kin. He was not their enemy, even if they thought they were his.

What would he do, then?

The answer was simple. If he was ordered to, he would fight. If kaldorei attacked him, he would kill them. Otherwise he would try to avoid them.

More and more soldiers swept down the Stair of Destiny, a flood of armored flesh. A tidal wave of violence that carried all before it. Just for a moment, it looked as if the Burning Legion encampment might be overrun. Then Highlord Kruul entered the battle, and the offensive ground to a halt.

Step by step, the armies of Azeroth were driven back up the stairs. The melee was brutal and deadly. There was no space for ducking or weaving, just a quick, savage exchange of spells or blows amid the press of bodies. Eventually the two forces achieved balance, with neither able to gain or lose a step, and the combat continued with unabated fury.

Even as the battle teetered on the brink, a new threat to the armies of Azeroth emerged. A force of felguard, dreadlords, doomguard, and wrathguard had assembled on the far edge of the Legion camp and moved along the ridge below, keeping out of sight of the main conflict. Highlord Kruul himself led them, accompanied by his core hounds. His intent was clear: to crash into the Azerothian line by surprise from the flank.

Vandel was not sure how Kruul's force was going to do that. Perhaps the doomguard intended to fly up the side of the Stair of Destiny. Some of his minions could use their wings as well, although they might lose the element of surprise. Most likely they intended to keep close to the steep side and stay out of sight until they rose to the attack. They could use sorcerous portals to bring in the rest of their force.

Illidan noticed the same thing. "If those demons can turn the orc flank, then the battle will be lost and the invaders will be sent back to Azeroth. The greater part of their force will be cut off and destroyed."

There was a musing note to his voice, as if he was turning the possibilities over and over in his head, holding them up to the light to inspect them and see which was best for him.

"We cannot let that happen," Vandel was surprised to hear his own voice say.

Illidan turned in his direction. He had the Betrayer's attention. Illidan's wings clung rigidly around his body, as if he were concealing it. His head tilted to one side, and he said, "Of course, you are correct, Vandel. Take a company and intercept the demons before they reach the stairs. Stop them."

Vandel was not sure whether he was being rewarded or punished for speaking out. It had taken the power of the Betrayer himself to vanquish Kruul during their last encounter. Vandel did not have that kind of strength, nor did any of his companions. Perhaps, working together, they might overcome the Burning Legion's field commander. He had been given a direct order, and he would obey, trusting that Illidan had some plan for victory. Vandel gestured to Elarisiel and a group of the others to follow him. Needle fell in by his side. They moved down the ridge, traveling as fast as they could to intercept Kruul's force while remaining out of sight of the combatants on the Stair of Destiny above.

THE DEMON HUNTERS COVERED the ground with the agility of panthers. Kruul's troops, as Vandel had suspected they would, had taken up position in the shadow of the stairs. The winged ones were already starting to fly up the side. The demons were a small force but a powerful one, and they might turn the course of the battle if they arrived in time.

Vandel screamed a war cry. The demons turned to look in his direction. Their burning gazes fell on him. He aimed a fel bolt at the nearest, searing into the creature's monstrous armored body. Moments later he was amid the demons, cleaving and striking, ducking and rolling, evading the blasts the wrathguard unleashed from the strange weapons mounted in their chests.

Highlord Kruul looked directly at Vandel. He lashed out with one of his deadly shadow bolts. Vandel leapt over it and closed with the giant demon.

"Ah, little one, does your master fear to face me himself?" Kruul boomed.

"No. He thinks I am a match for you," said Vandel.

He stepped aside as Kruul's gigantic blade bit into the ground next to him. Chips of shattered rock drew blood from Vandel's side. He stabbed the highlord's tree-trunk-sized leg, aiming for a point behind the greave, and his blade recoiled from Kruul's protective aura. He rolled forward, hoping to put himself behind the doomguard and out of his line of sight.

A brutal melee had erupted in the shadow of the vast stairs, hid-

den from the eyes of the combatants above. Vandel's roll took him
into the middle of it. He twisted his head and saw that Kruul was
already engaged with more demon hunters. One of them fell,
cleaved in twain by that battering-ram-sized blade, and then the
doomguard sent a volley of magical bolts ripping through his other
attackers. The great core hounds snarled by his side. Vandel aimed
himself at Kruul's back, but before he could leap, demons swarmed
him.

It took all his concentration just to remain alive. He killed first
one felguard and then another, but for every one he chopped down,
another moved into place.

His limbs grew sluggish, and even his magical dagger blades
began to dull and lose their edges. He fought amid a pile of bodies,
elf and demon. Killing and killing until he had no more power left
to draw on and even the gibbering demon voice in his head was silenced.

He knew now that he was going to die, and he did not really
care. He would sell his life dearly, taking as many demons into
death with him as he could. For the first time in months, he felt like
a mortal elf, weary and slow. The demons came on relentless, unstoppable. The tide of battle carried him back toward the doomguard. Once more he found himself face-to-face with Kruul.

Vandel ducked the swing of the highlord's massive blade, and
then he stumbled. The demon's huge weapon passed through the
spot where his head had been.

He tried to pull himself to his feet but found he could not. Kruul
stood over him, sword raised, and Vandel knew his last moment
had come. The blade caught the bloody light of the Outland sun
and then began its descent.

Vandel refused to look away. He raised both daggers in a last,
desperate attempt to parry. Kruul's chest exploded, leaving only a
gaping hole through which Vandel could see Illidan, warglaives in
hand, lightning swirling around them, the backwash of his shatter-

ing bolt of energy. The doomguard toppled. Vandel rolled aside as the demon's massive form smashed into the ground beside him. Once again Illidan had used a slow-building spell of awesome power to smite the highlord. Vandel and his companions had been a distraction.

"You killed him," Vandel said.

Illidan's smile was enigmatic. "Perhaps."

All around he heard the sounds of battle. A score of demon hunters emerged to confront the demons, taking them in the flank as they had intended to do to the Azerothian forces.

Off guard, leaderless, and facing an unknown number of foes, the demons broke into small groups and were destroyed piecemeal.

VANDEL PULLED HIMSELF TO his feet. The demons of Kruul's force were all dead. Still the hunger burned in him. He could kill a thousand of the Legion's minions and it would never be enough. He could obliterate a world of them and still be barely started.

He recognized that impulse as the same one that drove the Legion itself, and at that moment he did not care. He just wanted to go on killing and killing.

His lips twisted into a snarl, and he made ready to seek out prey once more.

Illidan placed a hand on his shoulder. "No more. Now is not the time. We have work elsewhere."

For a moment Vandel considered striking the lord of Outland, but he restrained himself, and slowly the thirst for vengeance sank back to something he could control. He exhaled, and it seemed part of the rage left him with his breath.

"We have saved the Alliance and the Horde here this day, and they will never know," Vandel said at last.

"They do not need to know. It is enough that they are here." Illidan's smile showed the depth of his satisfaction. "They will keep the Burning Legion occupied while we engineer its defeat. The enemy of my enemy . . ."

The demon hunters pulled away from the battle, heading back up the slopes toward their initial vantage point. Vandel turned to gaze back at the conflict. More troops had marched through from the Azerothian side, a colossal wave of melee fighters and spellcasters. They fanned out to guard the flanks of their force, then began the work of clearing the stairs against their foes. The tide of battle had turned in their favor once more. It looked as if the forces of Azeroth had established a permanent foothold in Outland.

Illidan flexed his wings triumphantly. "Now we must seek the Throne of Kil'jaeden."

CHAPTER TWENTY-FOUR

Two Months Before the Fall

STREAMS OF MOLTEN GREEN LAVA FLOWED DOWN CLIFFS of shattered basalt. The air blazed with heat and fel magic. It tingled on Illidan's skin, filled his lungs with every breath. He glanced around and noted that on every boulder, every ledge, every shard of rock that stabbed at the sky, a demon hunter stood guard.

They had driven off the Legion guards, but there was every chance the ritual he was about to perform would draw the attention of the demons' commanders. While in his trance state, he would be vulnerable, unable to fight or flee. He was taking a terrible risk here, but it was one that needed to be endured. If one of his followers proved to be treacherous, or even overly ambitious, his life would end.

The Throne of Kil'jaeden. The name itself had power, setting up a resonance between the demon lord and this location. Huge magical energies flowed all around. Gul'dan had used the mountain as the site of the ritual that had bound the orc clans to the service of the Burning Legion before the First War. Gul'dan's absorbed memories now told Illidan this was the place to cast his spell. Here lay a great flaw in the fabric of the universe that was connected to the lair of the Deceiver himself. This night the flow of energies from the Twisting Nether would be at its strongest in years.

He walked the edge of the great pattern he had inscribed in letters of fire on the black rock. He mouthed the words of the incantation, a constant, repetitive chanting, binding forces that he could hold in place with a mere fraction of his mind. All around monstrous energies coiled, waiting to be unleashed. It had taken weeks to forge this spell. It could only be cast at this exact location, at this exact hour, when all the signs were right.

He stared at the dark clouds in the blazing sky. A massive gout of lava spurted from the tortured depths of the earth, like demon blood pouring from a titanic wound.

He took out the disk he had claimed on Nathreza and focused all his powers of perception on it. The psychic stench of the demon lords of the Burning Legion still clung to it. When he inspected it closely with his strange vision, he could picture them: Sargeras, bleak, uncompromising, a fallen titan radiating misery and despair; Archimonde, a mad warlord consumed with fury and rage, Sargeras's fist; Kil'jaeden, the schemer, so adept at corrupting so many.

Who was Illidan to set himself against the likes of that awful trio? He touched the Seal of Argus, running his claws over the indentations of the runes until the cool metal squeaked. It was odd that it could stay so cold even here amid all the fire and fury.

He passed around the edge of the sorcerous circle he had created, checking the wards, making sure that the energy flowed correctly through it, that he had made no mistakes. Now was not the time for errors.

He was wasting time and that was folly. If he waited too long, the window in which the spell could be cast would close. Another would not arise for moons. He should proceed. And yet he could not make himself take the final step just yet. Soon, if things went according to his plan, he would be gazing upon those with the power to destroy him completely, and he would face them alone. It had not been so sweet, this life, and yet he found that now that the hour was upon him, he was still reluctant to leave it.

He prowled the edge of the circle, probing it with tiny traces of magical energy. Ner'zhul's fate was a warning. The shaman had turned against his demonic masters and paid the ultimate price for his betrayal. There were times when Illidan wondered whether he was going to do the same—whether this was just a game for the demon lords, one in which the odds were all stacked in their favor and they derived amusement from the insect struggles of those who opposed them.

He took a gulp of the air, catching the brimstone taint of the green lava. It was like breathing in the smoke from a great inferno. It made the lungs tingle and burn. Time was running out.

In an instant, before he could stop himself or regret the decision, he spoke the final words of the spell, unleashing the tidal wave of power. It tore his spirit from his body and sent it tumbling headlong into the Twisting Nether.

THE WAY OPENED BEFORE him. He felt as if he were falling into the rune-covered disk, but he knew this was an illusion, a construct created by his mind to give him some sense of understanding what was going on here. Ultimately that was not possible for a brain born in natural reality, but his mind would do its best to provide him with a framework he could work with.

His spirit emerged into the Twisting Nether and gazed down on Argus. The world hovered on the brink between the Twisting Nether and the physical universe, saturated with the fel energies of the Burning Legion.

He tumbled headlong toward the surface of the world. Once it must have been beautiful, a place of crystalline mountains and shimmering seas. Now it was cold and cruel. A darkness brooded over the place, and a sense of corruption and loss.

The seal pulsed in his claws. It was no longer the real disk but a representation of it, built from the magical energies of his spell, and it drew him downward to what he sought. The tug was almost irresistible and yet he fought against it, studying the sky, noting the position of stars and constellations, fixing them in his mind. Desperately he sought familiar signs in the sky, knowing that he could use them to plot his position in the cosmos. He looked also for magical energy tides, the auroral currents flowing out of the Twisting Nether.

Was this really the place he sought? He orbited it swiftly, taking sightings, looking for signs, still fighting all the time the tug of the spell he had created. Once more he felt the cold, emotionless distance from his body. A prickling of paranoia tickled his sorcerously trained senses. For a moment, he thought he sensed a presence observing him. He glanced around but could find nothing.

A thought occurred to him. If he could sense Kil'jaeden through this link, was it not possible the demon lord could sense him? He had created his spell in such a way that it should be impossible for any sorcerer to detect him, but what did he truly know of the Deceiver's capabilities?

No sense in worrying about it now. He was committed beyond any possibility of turning back. He let his spirit swoop down over the jagged crystalline mountains, saw the corruption that festered within them and caused them to crumble. He watched dust devils born of the powdered gems rise into the air and screech down canyons of serrated rock. Light shimmered and danced as it was refracted everywhere.

Ahead of him lay a city, looming over canyons of fractured crystal. Within it were many presences, all of them capable of blasting his soul.

———

ILLIDAN FELT A SURGE of energy as his soul crossed the borders of the city. It, too, must have been beautiful once, laid out according to complex geomantic rules. Its curved structures reminded him of the draenei buildings of Outland, only these were far more intricate and beautiful. Outland's town halls were hovels compared with the fantastic structures he passed now. These were huge machines for focusing magic. Once, according to all he had been able to uncover, they had provided peace, harmony, and health to an entire world. Now they created a cloud of fear and despair visible to Illidan's spectral sight.

At the center of the great city stood a mighty palace. Within lurked a massive, ominous presence surrounded by those only slightly less monstrous. It was to here that the disk drew Illidan.

His spirit zoomed through the streets with the velocity of thought. He tried to slow himself down, to get things under control, to stop himself from being reeled in too swiftly. He forced himself to halt by the walls of the palace.

He sensed another presence. Something lurked close by, studying him. He extended all his senses to the ultimate. There was something there, but he could not quite pin it down. It was as shielded as he was. A sentinel? Or something else? He forced himself to watch and wait, but nothing happened. Time to move.

He slipped through the crystal corridors, past runes that glowed with evil significance. It was as if the core of all the spells that had once spread light and harmony across the city and the world had been rewritten to create the opposite. When he studied the runes, feelings of rage and despair filled his mind. Even shielded as he was, the spells affected him, filling him with visions of conquest, a lust for domination and destruction, a rage to end all things. Here, written in runes of fire, was the creed of the Burning Legion.

He looked on the representation of the seal. This would be the anchor for the gateway between Outland and Argus. He invoked the final phase of the spell. The disk pulsed in his hand as it absorbed energies from all around, strengthening the connection it already had with this place. Once he was done, he would no longer need to open a portal from the Throne of Kil'jaeden. He could use the link forged here with the seal instead.

Dark energies began to permeate his astral form. A heaviness flowed through him. His spirit congealed, took on a glutinous physical quality born from the power all around him. He moved closer to the core of this dark labyrinth, feeling more and more the aura of the Deceiver. His movements slowed. His astral form floated lower and lower. For all his precautions, he had become trapped in the web of some terrible energy. The maze of spells surrounding him was binding its evil energies to his spirit.

The presence he had felt earlier returned. He twisted, trying to locate it, but could not. He cursed. It had caught him, and it now only seemed a matter of time before his severed spirit floated into the presence of the Deceiver and was enslaved or destroyed.

Desperately he fought against the spell. He sloughed off some of the magical plasm, regained something of the sense of weightlessness, but still he drifted into the vast throne room where Kil'jaeden sat surrounded by his court of demons. The eredar lord loomed gigantically, all red and burning. Vast batlike wings emerged from his back and seemed to reach to the ceiling. Huge amber lights blazed on his spiked shoulder guards. Fiery eyes dominated the face of a mutated draenei. An aura of awesome, thunderous power clung to him.

There was no doubt. Illidan had found his way to the palace of Kil'jaeden on the lost world of Argus. Unfortunately, the burning gaze turned toward where he was. A twisted smile passed over that monstrous face. Massive nostrils flared as if catching the psychic scent of prey.

Illidan felt the other watching presence again. It enwrapped him. He struggled against it but could not cast it off, even as Kil'jaeden's eyes lay fully upon him.

The Deceiver's gaze rested there, pregnant with the threat of destruction; then it passed on. Something had turned it away from Illidan, and it took him a moment to realize what. The presence that enshrouded him now pushed him out of the edge of the throne room. He had a sense of it just for an instant. It was a thing of Light, so bright as almost to be painful to behold. As he became aware of it, he heard a titanic roar of rage from within the throne room of Kil'jaeden, as if the eredar lord sensed it, too.

The shackles of ectoplasm that had bound him sloughed away.

Begone from this place. You cannot survive here. Not now. The voice spoke within his head and was gone. The spell of translocation snatched him back to the Throne of Kil'jaeden.

Illidan's spirit crashed back into his physical form. He caught himself before he could fall, realized that he had been gone for only a heartbeat in this world even if it had felt like an eternity in the Twisting Nether. The Seal of Argus blazed crimson in his hands.

He had done it.

He had survived, and he had found out what he needed. He had confirmed the presence of Kil'jaeden upon Argus. He had found the beating heart of the Burning Legion. And he had found something else, a being who had aided him to escape when all seemed lost. He thought about the Light he had sensed within it and realized he did not trust the thing.

Kil'jaeden was not known as the Deceiver for nothing. Perhaps this was all part of some vast and elaborate trap.

CHAPTER TWENTY-FIVE

The Last Month Before the Fall

ILLIDAN STOOD AT THE HEAD OF THE GREAT MAP TABLE in the council chamber of the Black Temple. His advisers came and went, along with messengers bearing the latest news. The blood elves of his council argued with Akama and with Vandel and the other leaders of the demon hunters.

Illidan rubbed his temples just below the horns. He had almost recovered the strength the spirit journey to Argus had cost him, and he could not let up yet. He needed to keep pressing on, to take advantage of what he had found out. He needed to face Kil'jaeden, and soon, before the Deceiver got wind of his plans and made ready for him. He was so deep in thought that it took him some time to realize that Lady Malande was speaking to him.

"What is your command, Lord Illidan?" Malande was insistent. There was a note of urgency to her voice that demanded attention. Illidan turned his eyeless gaze on her in a way he knew to be discomfiting to those who lacked his spectral vision.

"Concerning what?" Illidan said. He allowed his irritation to show.

"About Coilfang Reservoir. The news is not good. Lady Vashj has been overthrown and the great pumps have been shut down."

Coilfang Reservoir. Images of a vast pumping station full of magical engines leapt into his mind. He pictured miles of pipes running through gigantic underground caves. He thought about Vashj's plan to gain control of all the waters in Outland. It had seemed important once, but with events racing ahead so quickly, it was hardly worth dealing with. He had more urgent things to worry about.

"What would you have us do, Lord Illidan?" Gathios the Shatterer asked. He stroked his chin with one gauntleted hand. "The Alliance and Horde have established bridgeheads in Hellfire Peninsula. They have sacked Hellfire Citadel and destroyed Magtheridon. Should we strike back?"

Illidan considered the paladin's question—what was there to do? The Azerothians had done more than engage the Burning Legion. They had taken one of the greatest Illidari fortresses. It was just the latest in a long string of setbacks. This one would cost him dearly in the long run. Without the pit lord's blood, there would be no more fel orcs for his legions.

Except the long run no longer mattered. Things would be settled soon, and they would not be settled in Outland but on Argus. He had the true location of Kil'jaeden's homeworld, but he had found it in spirit form. Now he needed to be able to transport an army there in the flesh. It would take power to open such a portal, vast amounts of power. Only one source of such was available to him. He would need to use souls, and far more of those than had been used to open the way to Nathreza.

Gathios loomed at his full height. He banged his chest plate with one mighty fist. "Lord Illidan, what should we do? The Alliance and the Horde are expanding on all fronts. They engage our forces as well as the Burning Legion's. Should we withdraw to the Black Temple? Should we stand firm and throw them back?"

It seemed that Illidan's hope that the Azerothians would focus on the Burning Legion had been a deluded one. Their hatred for him was so great they were prepared to ignore the larger threat. Kruul must have known they were as vengeance-crazed as Maiev Shadowsong when he lured them into invading Outland. Well, Illidan had made the doomguard pay for that. Someday soon he must visit Maiev and show her exactly how unhappy he was with her, too.

But he did not have time for any of this now. The fate of existence rested on his shoulders.

"Do what is necessary," Illidan told Gathios. He scattered the tokens on the map with a sweep of his claw. "Other matters demand my attention."

An appalled silence filled the council chamber. All gazes turned to him, expecting leadership. He had made a mistake. He still needed his people to have faith in him, to follow him to the final battle. Illidan leaned on the map table and looked at each one in turn—the demon hunter leaders, Akama, Gathios, the rest of his council, all of the others.

"We are fighting a war to preserve all existence from the fury of the Burning Legion," he said. "It does not matter whether we hold Outland for a few more years. Once the Legion regroups, it can bring overwhelming force against us. What happens here and now is no longer important save as it bears upon the true struggle."

The silence deepened. The demon hunters nodded. They had shared his vision. They knew what the Burning Legion truly was. They understood the magnitude of the threat it represented. The others looked unsure. Fury filled Illidan's heart. He wanted to lash out, to strike their uncomprehending faces.

He drew himself back from the brink, tried to look at things as they might. They saw only the fiefdoms they ruled, the power they held, slipping from their grasp. They feared for their lives, as if those lives could have any meaning in the face of the cosmic threat of the Legion. They did not understand that victory here on Outland merely preserved their lives for a few more months or years. The end was coming for them all, unless Kil'jaeden was defeated, unless the Burning Legion was destroyed.

It was not their fault that they saw only the smallest details of the overall picture. He had never really troubled himself to convince them otherwise. He had relied on their ambitions, their greed, the things he could offer them to keep them loyal. It was time he let the others know how things stood.

"We need to take the war to Kil'jaeden," he said.

"You have said this before, Lord," said Akama, "and of course we all agree." His tone and the looks of the advisers scattered around the room made it clear that they did anything but agree. "But surely we must keep our bases secure so that we can launch our great attack."

Illidan shook his head, and he knew he had their complete focused attention now. "We need keep our bases secure only so long as it takes to open the way to Argus."

Akama looked at him as if caught somewhere between horror and awe. "You are ready to reclaim the original home of my people?"

"I am. I wish to see the ones defiling it dead, finally and forever," Illidan said. "And I know how to do that."

"My people fled from there millennia ago. It fell to those who allied with Sargeras, to the followers of Archimonde and Kil'jaeden. It must lie a thousand worlds in the distance, through a thousand portals."

High Nethermancer Zerevor smirked as if he already knew the answer. Veras Darkshadow listened in silence. Illidan sensed growing excitement among his demon hunters.

"If we followed the paths along which the draenei fled, that would be true," said Illidan. "I propose a more direct route."

"You plan on opening a portal through the Twisting Nether all the way to Argus? Forgive me for saying so, Lord, but that is impossible."

"Not impossible, Akama, merely extremely difficult. I can open the way there. Anything is possible using magic when you have a sufficient concentration of power and knowledge."

Akama appeared to be doing a quick calculation in his head. "There is no such concentration of power except the sort you used to get to Nathreza."

Illidan nodded, encouraging Akama to continue with his line of thought.

Vandel surprised Illidan by speaking up. "Is it worth it, Lord? Can we truly end the Burning Legion's threat?"

Illidan glanced from face to face. The truth was that he did not know. He was only making a leap in the dark. Perhaps the Legion was invincible. Perhaps killing Kil'jaeden would make no difference. Of one thing he was certain, though.

"I have dwelled on that question for ten thousand years and more, Vandel," he said. "Since first I made contact with Sargeras, since the first time I truly understood what the Burning Legion was."

He paused for a moment, recollecting that. He had been shown the same vision he had shared with the demon hunters, only a hundred times more vividly. It had been meant to convince him that the Legion was invincible, that it was pointless to oppose the will of Sargeras, that the best and only thing he could do was join the Legion and have a say in the remaking of the universe.

His mind had not crumbled, though. He had remained who he was. He had taken what he had seen and used it to motivate himself through all the long centuries of opposition. He had had plenty of time to dwell on such things, he thought bitterly.

"I was imprisoned for ten thousand years. In those ten millennia I was not idle. I considered everything I had learned about the Legion. I ran through every possible way of opposing it. All the ways

anyone could oppose it. That was why I had joined the Legion. I sought to learn all that I could about it. I gave up everything for that knowledge. I know more about the Burning Legion than any living creature save perhaps its rulers, if you wish to count them among the living. I learned many things but they all boil down to one stark and terrible fact.

"I learned that there is no way that the Legion can be defeated by simply waiting for it to come to you.

"The Legion is too strong. If you turn it back once, it will return. If you turn it back a thousand times, it will return. And every time, it will be stronger. Its commanders will have learned from their mistakes. Its generals will be prepared for your strategies.

"They are immortal. Their souls cannot be destroyed in most places. They can be merely thrown back into the Twisting Nether. Eventually they are reborn there, with all the knowledge of thei previous lives. Imagine fighting a warrior who, every time you ki him, comes back. And this warrior remembers the trick you used t defeat him previously, and returns prepared for it. Eventually yc run out of tricks. You run out of luck. That is why the Legion ca not be beaten on Azeroth. The spirits of demons can only be d stroyed in the Twisting Nether, in places where it bleeds into t world of mortals, or in places utterly saturated with the demo energies of the Burning Legion. Nathreza was one such pla Argus is another.

"There have been those who thought they had defeated Burning Legion. Dreadlords stride through the ashes of t worlds. Infernals desecrate the tombs of their children. You ca beat the Legion by fighting it on its terms. In the end you can lose.

"There is only one way of winning: to assault the Burnin gion where it can be destroyed. It is a slim chance, but it is our one. We do not have a choice. All we can do is stand and wait t or we can take the war to Sargeras and his minions. We will d

the lieutenants who motivate the Legion's forces. We will slay Kil'jaeden, and Archimonde, too, if he has been reborn. Sargeras needs commanders to control his soldiers. Without them, the eredar will fall to fighting among one another, and piecemeal may be destroyed."

Akama and most of Illidan's other advisers stared, in horror and in wonder. The demon hunters merely nodded. "I will take this war to Argus. You!" Illidan swept his arm about the room, gesturing to the assembled tattooed fighters. "All of you claimed you wanted to take your vengeance on the Burning Legion. I am offering you the greatest chance anyone has ever had to do that. We will take demon lives as a reaper takes wheat, and we will kill their commanders in a place from which they cannot return. All of you have proved yourselves worthy to accompany me."

He let that sink in. He was not asking them to accompany him. He was telling them that they were worthy, and it was the truth. He saw them, one by one, nod their agreement.

"Go now. Tell the others. Prepare for the opening of the way to Argus."

"Where are you going?" Akama asked. His voice was little more than a hoarse whisper. He tugged at the tendrils on his chin, appalled.

"To a place where there are many souls waiting for dissolution. To Auchindoun."

"The mausoleum of the draenei, Lord? But it is sacred."

Illidan focused his attention on Akama. Had there been a note of rebelliousness in his voice? "Not to me, faithful Akama."

Akama lowered his head slowly. His shoulders slumped. Illidan knew he did not like what was going on, but for the sake of his own soul and those of his people, he would have to accept it. "As you say, Lord."

Illidan spread his arms and wings wide. "Go now, all of you. You will all have parts to play before the end."

———

VANDEL WATCHED THE OTHERS depart from the room. He took a last glance at the great map board with its counters representing scattered armies. It looked like a toy now, a child's puzzle that had nothing to do with the business they were undertaking.

As he followed the others out of the council chamber, he thought about Illidan's words and the vision Vandel had seen when he consumed the demon's flesh.

He did not for a moment doubt that what Illidan had said was true. The Burning Legion was invincible when opposed by any normal means. There was no defensive strategy that could defeat an army that had unlimited resources and immortal soldiers. The real question was whether Illidan's plan made any difference. For the past few months the Betrayer had seemed even less sane than ever. And now Vandel understood why. All his schemes were nearing a climax.

Illidan did not care about Outland. He did not care about Hellfire Citadel or Coilfang Reservoir. None of it meant anything to him. None of it ever had, save as a stepping-stone to his ultimate destination.

Vandel saw what many of the other advisers did not. Illidan had no plan beyond this point. He was standing on the edge of a great abyss, planning on a long leap into darkness. Everything that happened—the taking of citadels, the coming of the Alliance and the Horde—was a sideshow to him. Vandel knew that come what may, all of this was going to go to pieces within the next few months. None of them were going to live much longer. Whether they followed Illidan to Argus or remained here to fight against the Legion or the Alliance and the Horde, it made no difference. They were all going to die.

The question then became what gave their deaths the greatest meaning. If what Illidan had said was in the slightest true, there was only one thing to be done. Vandel touched the amulet he had made for Khariel so long ago. He had come here with a purpose in mind. To oppose the Burning Legion and take vengeance if he could. He would see that through to the bitter end.

He glanced around at the other demon hunters and saw that they had come to a similar conclusion. The blood elves, as always, looked as if they were thinking of some way to take advantage of the situation.

Vandel knew that whatever happened, he would follow Illidan. He glanced over his shoulder into the council chamber. The Betrayer was still there, shoulders slumped, wings wrapped forlornly around them. He paced nine steps and then turned. As if sensing he was watched, Illidan stood taller, flexed his wings, and crossed his arms upon his chest. As the doors slid silently shut, Vandel knew that even their leader was consumed by doubt.

ILLIDAN CONSIDERED THE SILENT war room. Emptiness made the giant chamber larger. The lack of living sounds turned the place dead. He walked over to the map table and considered the fallen fortresses of his Outland empire. Each of those overturned models and carved blocks represented thousands of deaths, lakes of blood spilled. The thought occurred to him that he had long ago ceased to care about such things. In the game he played, tens of thousands of lost lives were a negligible cost.

There had been a time, long ago, when those deaths would have troubled him. He knew that intellectually, but he no longer felt the emotion, could not even begin to remember what it would have been like, and that bothered him. He had spent so long armoring himself against doubt, forcing himself only to ask questions that were relevant to his struggle. Now, in this empty chamber, he could hear only the echoes of voices no longer speaking.

Both Vandel's doubts and Akama's were justified. It was possible he was wrong. It was possible that he was as insane as he had often been accused of being. He picked up one of the pieces—an orc warrior carved from clefthoof ivory—and turned it over and over in his fingers. How many fel orcs had he sent to their deaths without a second thought? He could calculate the number if he wished. His sorcerously trained mind was capable of remembering all of the orders of battle and supply lists. That was not the point.

He thought about the demon hunters. They were his own people. He shared a kinship with the elves that he shared with no others, but even that seemed a remote thing. He had walked paths that separated him from even them. He had spent ten thousand years in isolation, with only Maiev and her Watchers for company, and they were mostly distant presences. Ten thousand years alone, with nothing but his thoughts and his plans and his visions. Ten thousand years of dark dreams and testing bonds that could not be broken until finally Tyrande had freed him. He considered visiting Maiev and inflicting a fraction of the punishment she deserved. The chess piece crumbled in his grip.

He threw the fragments back down onto the map. There was no time to get distracted now. He had a war to win. Doubts rose to torment him. What if he was wrong? What if he had miscalculated? His visions were not infallible. Perhaps there was another way and he had not seen it. Perhaps he was blind to a possibility that might win this war without all the sacrifices. He had searched and searched for one and had not found it, but that did not mean it was not there.

Betrayer. That was what they called him. That was how they would remember him. If they were lucky enough to survive and remember anything, it would be because he had saved them, and they would never know. That thought gave him a moment of dour pleasure.

He squared his shoulders, flexed his wings, and strode from the chamber without looking back. It was time to go to Auchindoun and face the spirits of the restless dead.

AKAMA STOOD BESIDE MAIEV'S cage. He had dismissed the guards. She had listened to the tale of Akama's last encounter with Illidan, her face becoming ever paler. He was running an awful risk coming here at this time, but he needed to talk with someone who shared his burning hatred of Illidan.

Sick horror filled the Broken's heart. The Betrayer planned yet another desecration of a draenei holy place. There was nothing he would not do. Not even the greatest cemetery of Akama's people was safe from Illidan's towering madness. Whatever happened, at whatever cost, Illidan must be stopped. Akama knew that now, felt it with every fiber of his being. Even if it meant risking his soul, it was time to begin his last desperate plan.

"He is mad," Maiev said. "He has always been mad. But this is the most insane scheme I have ever heard of. Opening a way to Argus! Are you sure he does not mean to summon reinforcements from there to let him defeat the Alliance and the Horde?"

Akama shook his head. "You were not present. You did not hear him speak. He believes in what he says utterly. He plans on going ahead with this scheme. He no longer cares about anything else. For the past few weeks, he has neglected his realm and worked feverishly on this solitary goal, to create this gateway of his. He has woven spell after spell, created astromantic chart after astromantic chart. He has done nothing else, even as his empire crumbled."

"Perhaps he plans on using the gateway to escape," Maiev said. A note of worry appeared in her voice, as if she still seriously believed she had a chance of hunting down her prey unaided. "Perhaps he hopes to open a way to some refuge far from here. You should understand that. Your own people did the same."

"Illidan is not the sort to flee. I believe he really and truthfully plans to seek out Kil'jaeden and fight him to the death."

Maiev's mocking laughter rang out. "He will lose. And all his efforts will go for naught. All your efforts will go for naught as well. Your precious temple will fall to the Alliance or the Horde. Free me. At least if the temple falls to the Alliance, I will be able to intercede for you and see that it is returned to your people."

Akama looked at her and smiled. "There is no need for you to worry on that score. I have made my own plans. All you need do is be patient."

"Is that why you have visited me so often, Broken one? Do you still think to use me in your schemes?"

"What if I do? What if I could release you from this place and set you on the path to vengeance?"

"You have made such promises before."

"Ah, but the time was not right then. It is now."

Akama walked away, enjoying the thoughtful silence as Maiev considered the implications of his words. In the distance the earth shook as the Hand of Gul'dan erupted. It had been doing that a lot of late. It was an evil omen.

CHAPTER TWENTY-SIX

The Last Month Before the Fall

ASH CRUNCHED BENEATH ILLIDAN'S HOOVES AS HE LANDED outside the broken gates of Auchindoun. Over him the walls of the mausoleum city towered. They were gray like the surrounding wastes. In the distance, a huge carrion-eating bonelasher flapped across the sky. A decrepit clefthoof, its massive strength all but gone, staggered through the waste. The chill wind stirred the dust, sending sandy rivulets trickling.

The city looked as if it had once been a massive dome, like the helmet of some titan, but it had been smashed to fragments, scattered across the dry, dead land behind him.

He sensed the distant pulse of magic thrumming between the spirit towers that loomed over the Bone Wastes. What purpose did they serve? He was not quite certain, and that disturbed him. He had spent a long lifetime mastering magic, and there were still gaps in his knowledge.

Even the fel orcs of the Shadowmoon clan, normally the most fearless and aggressive of creatures, shifted uneasily. There was something about this dead place that penetrated even their rage-filled minds and caused a feeling like dread. That in itself was disturbing, for of all the orcish clans in his service, the Shadowmoon was the most accustomed to necromancy and dark sorcery. Their captain, Grimbak Shadowrage, grunted encouragement at them, and they settled down to await his commands.

Illidan's mouth felt dry and his throat constricted. He tasted and smelled something odd, as if tiny particles of bone had infiltrated his nostrils and tickled his tongue. He felt as if bits of all the skeletons buried in the dust had found their way into the air. He ignored the sensation and studied the ruins.

Some dreadful disaster had struck the city. That much was clear. Huge gratings of tortured metal emerged from broken stonework, like ribs showing through the rotting flesh of a corpse.

According to Akama, this was a holy site where the bones of dead draenei had been interred. Something had gone wrong, though. There were many and conflicting rumors: that a dark ritual had unleashed the dead; that the orcs had tampered with something best left undisturbed and released forces of great evil; that the Burning Legion had tested some terrible weapon on the place, and the resulting evil energies had warped everything within it.

Illidan knew the truth. He had inherited it from Gul'dan's memories when he consumed the power in his skull. The old schemer had dispatched a group of warlocks to the city in search of artifacts buried there. The survivors had told him that something had gone wrong and they had summoned a strange entity. It had shattered Auchindoun, smashing the great dome, scattering the remains of countless dead across a huge area of the desert.

Illidan gave the signal to advance. The fel orcs roared a challenge and marched under the shadow of the dead city's gates. The heavy tread of their feet seemed like a desecration of the ancient quiet. In the shadows, old and hungry things watched and waited. It seemed as if a thousand eyes observed them unseen.

The dust crunched as they passed beneath a huge arch. It had piled up in drifts that made walking hard for the fel orcs, although he could move across the surface by keeping himself aloft with a simple beat of his wings.

The city had been built in concentric rings. Illidan's forces had no sooner passed through the arch than they found themselves confronted by the shattered remains of another wall. Stairs rose ahead. To both right and left, what once must have been a huge street curved away. In the outer walls were many openings that told of ways into the tombs and mausoleums within.

Everything had a tumbledown, forlorn look. The wind moaned as it caressed his skin and bulged his wings.

He led the fel orcs up worn stairs and passed under all that was left of a triumphal arch. Once through it, they looked down from the top of a wall as wide as a road into another ring of ruins within.

Like the rings within a tree, Illidan thought. From where he stood he had a fine view clear across the center of the dead metropolis. The city once must have been built on multiple levels, and this had been one of them. Perhaps it had all been one huge building with many chambers and halls. Now whole floors had tumbled in, to lie on the ground below. It was perplexing. This place had been built for unknowable reasons to please the alien sensibilities of the draenei. He wanted to reach the very center of the city, but there was going to be no easy way of doing so.

He could fly down to the lower level of the central area, but the fel orcs could not go with him, nor could the bearers of the huge casket containing the soul siphon. He pulled his wings tight around him like a cloak against the wind. It felt like a mistake to come here. Nothing good could come of this.

One of the scouts returned. A grin of triumph spread across his face. "We have found a way into the crypts, Lord!"

STRANGE BRAZIERS FLANKED THE archway, illuminating banners containing odd runes. A decomposed skeleton lay near. The air smelled of ancient incense and old bones. Everywhere hung the sick, sweet scents of putrefaction. The throat-tingling itch of corpse dust entered through Illidan's nostrils.

As he crossed the threshold of the underground vault, things immediately felt different, as if Illidan had gone through a barrier into some other dimension. The stone braziers glowed a fel green, and ahead the shimmering, near-translucent figure of a draenei spirit stalked forward, empty eyes gazing into oblivion. It looked more sad than frightening, and yet there was something about it that was deeply unsettling. The fel orcs growled threateningly but made no move to attack.

What are these ghosts, really? the sorcerer in Illidan wondered. Were they the disembodied spirits of the dead left to wander the world? If so, why did they not remember things and act under their own free will as his spirit did when it moved through the Twisting Nether?

The ghost moved backward and forward in a predictable pattern, like some mad, broken thing. Perhaps it was diseased or crazed or had lost something. Perhaps the magic that had turned the mausoleum city into a place of the restless dead had caused this, too. Such speculation would have to wait. It was time to move on.

Illidan's force pushed on deeper into a labyrinth of corridors and vaults. Auchindoun was vast and ancient, and the city below was many times larger than that which lay aboveground.

Cobwebs of spectral energy latticed the ceilings. More fel braziers illuminated piles of bones. They lay in great heaps, as if some insane collector had gathered them and tossed them into a jumble.

Here and there, shattered paving stones revealed pits in the rock beneath the crypts. In some, nuggets of raw adamantite gleamed. The only living things visible were the fist-sized spiders that scuttled from one shadow to another.

Illidan and his troops passed over strange bridges and by huge stone coffins. As they entered a massive chamber, lined by gigantic sarcophagi, Illidan sensed an eerie presence.

What had been only an empty archway contained a glowing form resembling that of a draenei. It radiated a cold, life-sucking force. Illidan unleashed a bolt of energy, and the thing disintegrated in the face of his power.

As if that were a signal, shimmering figures emerged from the shadows, suddenly just there. They fell upon the fel orcs and were cut to shimmers of ectoplasm by runic weapons and powerful spells.

A massive pile of bones sprang up as they passed, knitting themselves together into animated skeletons, their fleshless fingers clutching weapons that perhaps they had borne in life.

On ledges around the walls of the vault, robed draenei wove dark magic. Their power connected with unlife, but the ones tapping it were living. Their necromancy drew the dead to life. Illidan dispatched fel orcs to cut them down.

Slowly they fought their way into the center of the crypt. As they did so, the silvery, haunting call of horns rang out. It echoed away through the endless corridors. No doubt a warning was being spread. More defenders were being summoned.

Good, Illidan thought. *All the more to feed to the soul siphon.*

Illidan's forces continued fighting. Tides of strange spirits roared over them. More and more of the fel orcs went down.

It was a pity. Illidan had not yet had time to set up the soul siphon and make their deaths count in the great scheme of things.

Here was the place he wanted, though, deep below the city, beneath its endless halls of interred corpses.

The fel orcs drew up in ranks around the palanquin containing the soul siphon. It lay in an elf-sized sarcophagus of brass, fel iron, and truesilver. Illidan sprang into the air, felt a chill wind surge beneath his wings, and landed atop the container. He spoke a word of power and the casket sprang open, revealing the soul siphon.

Power pulsed through the fel iron piping, channeled by the runes inscribed in the artifact's side. He was proud of his sorcery. He had managed to re-create some of the magical effects of the ritual used to suck in the souls of the dead and the dying when he opened the portal to Nathreza. When activated, the siphon would sweep the restless spirits haunting Auchindoun into its vortex, disassemble them, and store their power. Three teardrop-like gems lay in the center of the device. Right now the gems were dull and black, but as the siphon filled, they would blaze. When all of them burned, he would have enough power to open the gateway to Argus.

He invoked the artifact's might, creating a psychic link between himself and the device. He felt the presence of it in his mind, a yawning abyss, a thing thirsty for power, hungry to devour whatever it encountered. The siphon held a fierce, primitive sentience. The moment he made contact, it began vampirically to drain the life from him.

He wove spells of protection and then mastery, binding the entity to his will as he would a demon.

More robed draenei arrived, heading companies of walking skeletons. They directed their forces to attack. The fel orcs formed up around Illidan.

"Hold them for a few minutes, and triumph will be ours."

The fel orcs closed ranks and raised their weapons. Wave after wave of the walking dead threw themselves forward. Individually they were no match for the fel orcs, but they came on in seemingly endless numbers. As they distracted the fel orcs, bolts of shadow magic flew from the necromancers.

Worst of all were the spirits. They slithered through unseen, their cold, spectral hands grasping fel orc bodies and sucking the life out of them, leaving chilled corpses to drop to the ground.

Illidan continued to wake the soul siphon to its full power. He forced himself to concentrate, knowing that he did not have much time. The fel orcs could not hold up under this pressure for long. Already a few of their corpses responded to sly necromantic sorcery and sprang up to attack their former comrades.

The siphon resisted him. Something about his surroundings aided it, lending power to that which fought against him. He gritted his teeth and howled the words of the spell. Skeletons disintegrated, particles of shadow flowing from them into the maw of the siphon. At first the fel orcs cheered, and then they were too busy fighting for their lives to notice that their spirits were also, upon death, consumed by the magical engine.

The tidal wave of oncoming ghosts was sucked in, like water gurgling into a sewer. The siphon exerted its tremendous power, its dark magical energy drawing souls to it like filings to a magnet.

The first of the gems on the siphon glowed bright as a demonic sun. A quick glance showed Illidan that almost half of his bodyguards were down. Without his magic to aid them, they were losing the battle. He wanted to join them but he could not; he needed to concentrate on the soul siphon lest it run out of control. If that happened, it might explode, killing them all.

He increased the rate of intake, hoping to destroy more of the spirits and gather their power swiftly enough that he could complete the ritual and turn the tide of the battle. Souls screamed into the siphon. The pain of holding the spell was agonizing.

Finally the necromancers realized what he was doing. They concentrated their attacks on him. A bolt of magical energy lanced into Illidan's side. Agony so intense that he almost lost control of the siphon smashed through him. He gritted his teeth and forced himself to hold the binding spell in place. The siphon fought against him again. Illidan felt part of his own spirit being drawn into the device.

Illidan forced his mind into a warding pattern, resisting the attack, slowing down the drain on his life force. As he did so, he felt his control over the siphon's binding spell begin to slip. The second gem glowed brightly now. Sparks of soul energy surrounded him like a blizzard of black snow. The power roared in, thick and fast. If he could only hold on for a few more moments.

His fel orcs were down to a third of their original number now. Grimbak Shadowrage roared encouragement at those remaining. He turned to Illidan, and just for a moment, hope, belief, and entreaty raced across his face before it became once more a snarling warlike mask for the benefit of his soldiers.

Illidan considered trying a counterspell against the necromancers but realized it was impossible. He could not hold the soul siphon, protect himself, and launch an attack at the same time. Even he was not so powerful a magician.

Illidan's legs felt rubbery and his head spun. Strength drained out of him faster and faster, and it was all he could do to restrain the growing power of the soul siphon.

He had not foreseen this. He had never imagined falling in this dark place. He was going to die here, and all his schemes would come to naught. The best thing to do was simply to release control of the spell restraining the soul siphon, and let its energies explode outward, killing everything around him. At least this way he would have vengeance on his killers.

No. He was not going to die. He still had work to do. His destiny must be fulfilled. The Burning Legion must be opposed. He drew on his last reserves of will to keep the soul siphon functioning. He fell to his knees as the life drained out of him. Slowly, the last gem filled.

Hold on. Hold on. Agony racked Illidan's body as bolts of dark energy lashed him. Grimbak Shadowrage tumbled to the ground beside him. A few of his bodyguards had made a fighting retreat alongside their captain and shielded him with their own bodies as the walking dead and their sorcerer masters closed in.

The final gem was full. Illidan spoke the words that tied off the flow of energy and imprisoned it. He raised himself slowly to his hooves as the last of the fel orcs went down. He gathered what strength was left in him and opened a portal back to the Black Temple. The last thing he heard was the enraged shouting of the necromancers as he and the soul siphon vanished.

Chest heaving, he settled himself on the cold stone of his sanctum. Sweat dripped down his brow. He could barely breathe. The room swirled around him and consciousness slipped away.

CHAPTER TWENTY-SEVEN

One Day Before the Fall

ILLIDAN SAT ON THE THRONE IN HIS COUNCIL CHAMBER. It had been weeks since his return from Auchindoun and still he was weak. His power had not returned to anything like what it had been before his use of the soul siphon.

Not for the first time, he considered dispatching an expedition to root out the necromancers. He could not waste the resources. He looked at the great map table. His armies were shattered. His empire, crumbling. Among them, the Alliance, the Horde, and the Burning Legion had riven his Outland realm. It was all his followers could do to hold together the last remaining outposts in Shadowmoon Valley. The reports from his captains, when he had felt well enough to listen, had been very far from encouraging.

He had only himself to blame. He had decided to go to Auchindoun accompanied only by his fel orc bodyguards. He had chosen to reserve the power of the demon hunters for the final confrontation, not understanding the very real danger that awaited him in the city of the dead. That overconfidence was going to cost him, and perhaps all who lived, dearly.

He pushed the thought aside. He could not afford to let himself think like that. There must be hope, some chance of victory. If he could not win the battle himself, perhaps his demon hunters could. They were powerful, and they had been trained for this fight. It might cost all of their lives, but victory could still be theirs.

Keep telling yourself that, and perhaps you might actually come to believe it. The sour thought crept into his mind no matter how much he tried to keep it out. Doubt was a demon against which he had no defense.

One by one, his blood elf advisers filtered into the chamber. He could tell by their expressions that the news was not going to be good. He rose from his throne, concealing the pain that hampered his movements as best he could, but all eyes followed him, measuring and judging. Those present were ruthless, ambitious, and unbound by any conventional ideas of morality.

They studied him as wolves might study the ailing leader of their pack. His empire might have shrunk, but it was still an empire, and many others no doubt thought themselves capable of ruling it and even reclaiming what was lost. Perhaps they were right about that.

It did not matter. Illidan resented being here, resented having to go through with this charade. Every minute spent placating his advisers was a minute not used finalizing his plans to end the threat of the Burning Legion. He forced himself to look around the room. Every one of those present had to meet the baleful power of his eyeless gaze.

High Nethermancer Zerevor spoke first. "The news from the Netherstorm is interesting. Tempest Keep and our treacherous former prince have fallen. Whether this is good or bad for us, I do not know . . ."

Illidan made an impatient gesture, cutting him off. Kael'thas had sided with Kil'jaeden, so he deserved whatever evil fate had befallen him. He was not worth any more of Illidan's time. He turned to Lady Malande. "And the news from the Blade's Edge Mountains?"

"Lord Illidan, Gruul the Dragonkiller has been overthrown. I can find other allies. All it will take is a little more time."

Malande was wrong. No allies would be coming from the mountains. Illidan nodded as if he believed her, though. The matter was irrelevant. He needed to get back to building the portal to Argus. He needed to perform the final ritual that would set up the terminus point.

"With all respect, Lord Illidan," said Gathios. "Time is just one of the resources we are running short of. We need to mount counterstrikes against both the Alliance and the Horde, teach them to fear us, regain our lost territories."

Gathios had been pushing for that for weeks, ever since the extent of the invaders' conquests had become clear. In purely military terms, he was correct. If Illidan's only concern were holding on to Outland, then he should be counterattacking. Although things had probably gone too far for that. They no longer had the forces to fight a war on three fronts.

Veras Darkshadow pointed that out, and added, "We could offer an alliance to one side or the other. Play them off against each other. It might buy us some time."

Veras clearly thought he knew what Illidan wanted to hear. It was also something that Zerevor and Malande would disagree with.

The blood elves fell to arguing. In his mind Illidan reviewed the plans for the portal to Argus. There was still too much work to do. He needed more truesilver for the inlays. He needed to reinforce the dampening spells that would feed power from the soul siphon to the portal itself. There would need to be ways of making sure that the flow of energy was even and swift, that the gate opened smoothly. He needed the visualization to be absolutely clear. Nothing could go wrong. There would only be one chance to get this right. At the moment, as things stood, he might be able to open the gateway, but it could not stay open without a guiding will to keep it stable. He needed to find a way to ensure that it would remain steady once they passed through it. There was so much to be done.

"What do you think, Lord?" Gathios asked. "What should we do?"

Suddenly he was tired of all this. He was tired of listening to this petty, pointless bickering over matters that were no longer of any concern to him. He was tired of the feeling of weakness and lassitude that filled him.

Time was running out and he had important work to do and this was a needless distraction.

Illidan dismissed them with a wave of his hand. "Get out of my sight," he said.

ILLIDAN LOOKED AROUND the great chamber of transference. Day by day, hour by hour, minute by minute, he had created the last and greatest portal spell he would ever weave. Every line had been etched in the floor by his own hand. He had boiled the alembics of truesilver himself and filled out line after line. He had inscribed the runes around the edges in demon ichor mixed with his own blood. Each wall was covered in intricate warding symbols based on his tattoos. At junctions in the pattern, he had placed the skulls of demons and sorcerers, each etched with miniature versions of their section of the pattern to help channel the flow of energy. These additions reflected the star beacons in the sky over Argus. At the center of the weave lay the Seal of Argus. It pulsed with power now, a direct link to the world of Kil'jaeden that would guide the unleashed energies of the portal.

Everything still had an unfinished, incomplete look to it. The spell engines that would feed power from the soul siphon into the pattern were untested. The generators, great machines of copper and brass and fel iron, intricate as gnomish engines, stood almost ready. The whole vast pattern was falling into place but too slowly. He had strengthened his weakened body with magic to give him the energy and concentration of a dozen lesser sorcerers, but it was still not enough. It would take many more moons to complete sorcery so vast and intricate, and he could feel the sands running through his life's hourglass far too quickly.

Now was not the time to allow himself to panic. Impatience led to mistakes, and in an undertaking as complex as this one, the slightest error could lead to catastrophe. He needed just to focus on the matter at hand, to do what must be done this day, this hour, this minute.

He needed to complete the link between Outland and Argus. He must set the terminal runes. He placed the incense and invoked the spell. One by one the magical engines sprang to life, filling the air with the stench of ozone and brimstone. Tiny trickles of energy, the slightest breath of power compared with the great roaring gale that would mark the portal's opening, leapt from the engines. The lines of truesilver shimmered. A mirror image of their pattern appeared in the air above them, projected from the Seal of Argus. He let his spirit exit his weary body.

It was easier to let go, as if using the soul siphon in Auchindoun had somehow weakened the link between his spirit and his flesh. He reached out and wove the flows of energy from the pattern into subtle threads, then gathered them to his spirit.

He followed the intricate pattern of runes out into the Twisting Nether. His spirit flashed through the void, and once again, Argus appeared beneath him. He looked down on the once glittering and beautiful world, then sent his spirit soaring downward into its glass canyons and diamond-edged mountains. He moved as cautiously as he could.

This time he sought to establish a terminal point for the portal. A web of magical energy linked him to Outland. He had done his best to conceal it, but a sufficiently adroit sorcerer—and this was a world full of them—might still detect him unless he was extremely careful.

The thought of the being he had encountered last time troubled him. It had seemingly aided him, but he knew how subtle and cunning the demons of the Burning Legion could be. Kil'jaeden was well named the Deceiver.

Illidan flew closer to the palace city where the demonic rulers of the Burning Legion dwelled. He feared that his comet trails of magic leading back to Outland might be spotted no matter how thin they were, no matter how well he had concealed them. He slowed his advance to a crawl.

A tingling of his spectral senses warned him that he was under observation. He tried to track whatever spied on him, but it eluded his perception. Alarm pulsed through his mind. The fact that it could elude his powers of observation even when he was alert spoke of tremendous sorcerous ability. The thing might attack him by surprise while he was most vulnerable, placing the points of resonance for the portal.

He waited for long moments, but nothing happened. Perhaps he was caught up in the backwash of some defensive spell designed to induce paranoia and doubt. Kil'jaeden was capable of such subtle magic. Every moment Illidan spent here was a moment wasted, one that increased his chances of being discovered. He needed to either proceed with his plan or retreat and wait for a more auspicious time.

It was now or never. He plunged toward Kil'jaeden's enormous crystalline palace, found the part he was looking for, and wove the spells. A small, temporary whirlwind of force appeared, a tiny echo of the vast pattern back in the Black Temple. Illidan glanced around, waiting for the hammer to fall. If he had been detected, now would be the time. No ward spell sprang to life. No alarm triggered. The vortex faded virtually to nonexistence, leaving behind a well-nigh undetectable residue of power.

As it did so, Illidan thought he was under observation once more. The sense of the watching presence returned, intensified. He felt as if something looked upon his action with immense curiosity, but when he sought out the source, he could not find it.

Wait. What was that? That faint aura of shimmering light. He focused on it, but even as he did so, it vanished from his perception—as if the owner had somehow withdrawn below the skin of the universe.

He needed to concentrate on the work at hand. He was distracted when he could least afford to be. He flitted through the crystalline palace to a new location, a vast chamber in which succubi danced for the amusement of demonic generals. He invoked the portal-anchoring spell once more, fixing it in place as swiftly as he could. He was closer to the throne room of Kil'jaeden now, and the danger of detection increased with that nearness.

He felt as if something vast and powerful loomed behind him, watching him work, studying the way he invoked the spell, observing how the anchor fell into place. He dared not interrupt the casting to try to catch it, otherwise the whole ritual would fail.

It was all he could do to focus on the work at hand when, at any moment, a blast of power might cast him into oblivion. He forced himself to concentrate on completing the anchoring spell, then swiftly attempted to bring his observer into view. Once again it eluded him.

Even in the reduced emotional state that came with being in spirit form, he was angry. He did not like being toyed with, and he felt that this was what was happening now. Kil'jaeden knew he was here and was playing with him. He was being allowed to get near the completion of his spell—and at the last moment his spirit would be captured and imprisoned.

He had only three more anchors to set, and one way or another the thing would be over. Part of him wanted to attempt an escape or draw his attacker out and get into battle, no matter how one-sided that conflict might prove to be.

The next two anchor points went down easily. Each time he felt himself observed, and he sensed the same deep curiosity about what he was doing radiating from the hidden watcher, but try as he might he could not find any way to make the creature reveal itself.

Now he moved cautiously closer to the great throne room. An enormous concentration of demonic power lay there. Kil'jaeden was in residence, and many of his generals were there, too. Illidan needed to be extraordinarily cautious now. In his spirit form, that assembled force could crush him as if he were an insect. All of them were, without a doubt, sorcerers capable enough to detect him unless he shielded himself with supreme skill and laid the anchoring spell with the utmost care.

He paused again, silently cursing his hidden observer, knowing that the attack would soon come, raging at the futility of what he was attempting but realizing he had no other choice. Perhaps another might be able to complete his great work even if he was captured here. It was the most forlorn of hopes. There were few sorcerers of sufficient skill in Azeroth or Outland, and they would be most unlikely to finish his work. What else could he do, though? He had come this far. He needed to continue.

He steeled himself and invoked the last anchor for the spell. This was the most dangerous moment. Instead of simply taking form and fading, this vortex sent out a pulse of force, leaping to the farthest anchor and then the next, forming a great pentacle and then filling in the complex web of runes until it had replicated the magical energy of the pattern in his sanctum in Outland.

The principle of harmonic resonance established a connection between the two great symbols. Despite his wariness, he felt a flush of triumph. The link between Argus and Outland was established.

The portal could be activated once the pattern was finished. He had but a heartbeat to enjoy his victory, and then the attack came.

The power of it was astonishing. His spirit form was swept up like an infant being snatched by an orc.

He was like a swimmer caught in an oceanic undertow. No matter how much he struggled, he could not break free. He stopped, determined to preserve his strength for when the worst came.

He emerged onto a plain of Light. Before him glittered a being of perfect geometric lines. They twisted in a way that made them seem to disappear and reappear a moment later in a completely different arrangement. It baffled his brain trying to follow the changes.

Illidan braced himself to unleash the most destructive spell he could in spirit form, but the creature did not attack. He realized he had seen its like before, in the Terrace of Light in Shattrath. If anything, this creature was possessed of even more power than A'dal and its followers.

"You are a naaru," Illidan said eventually, when he wearied of the silence.

"I am an elder naaru. Possibly the eldest now remaining in these universes."

"Why are you here? Do you serve Sargeras or Kil'jaeden?"

Gentle mirth emanated from the naaru. Sparkles of light shifted around its form, like the notes of laughter made visible. "I do not."

A faint sense of relief swept over Illidan. It might be a trick, though, meant to take him off guard. "Then what are you doing here?"

"Waiting for you."

"You knew I would come?"

"You or someone like you was bound to. The universe throws up champions in the face of those who would destroy it."

"It could perhaps have picked a better one." The words emerged from his mouth before he could stop them.

"I do not think so. You are what you are. All your days have forged you into that. A weapon aimed at the heart of a great demon."

"I would like to think I am somewhat more sentient than my warglaives."

"That is what makes you dangerous."

"So the universe has anointed me to slay Kil'jaeden." His tone was sardonic, but hope flickered inside Illidan. Perhaps, if what this naaru said was true, there was some chance of victory after all.

The swirl of lights indicated a negative. "No. Your enemy is far greater than Kil'jaeden. Greater even than Sargeras and his Burning Legion."

"Wonderful," Illidan said. "As if they were not strong enough."

The suspicion that this was all a subtle, mocking trap set by Kil'jaeden sidled once more into his mind. He fought down bitterness. It seemed as if all his sacrifices had gone for naught. If this was a trap, his struggle was ended. If it was not, then things were even worse than he had thought.

"The Void is a more potent foe by far than the Burning Legion. It is the ultimate opponent of the Light. It will take all the peoples of Azeroth and Outland united to oppose it." The naaru stopped pulsing. "You do not believe me? You lose faith and hope. Then know this."

Before Illidan could defend himself in any way, a bolt of pure Light blasted from the naaru. It struck his empty eye sockets and filled them with a golden glow. Illidan braced himself for a blast of agony that did not come. In the past such magic had always racked him with pain. It would normally have done the same to any user of fel magic. His vision shimmered and faded, and he found himself looking down on a terrible battlefield.

Amid mountains of corpses, a winged figure battled at the head of the legions of Light. A golden glow surrounded his warglaives. He cleft demons asunder with mighty blows. The soldiers surrounding him gazed up in awe and wonder at their leader. It took

Illidan a moment to realize that this being's features were his own, transformed, his eyes glowing fiercely. This avatar of the Light looked calm and strong and at peace. His face was filled with confidence, shorn of all suffering.

As Illidan watched, the winged figure rose above the battle, defying gigantic entities of darkness, creations of the evil of the Void. A halo played around his head. His body began to glow brighter than the sun, and from his outstretched arms, rays of Light emerged to strike down his foes.

There was a sense of rightness about this, as if he looked upon a vision of the unborn future. For a moment he could believe in it, but then his doubts rushed back. This could not be true. It was not any path he had ever set out on. It was not who he was. He was a fighter and a killer, as driven by darkness and his own desires as he was by any urge to do right.

"You will defy death," the naaru's voice said as the vision faded. "I have seen this. Whatever you were, whatever you are, a champion of Light is what you will be."

There was utter certainty in the naaru's voice, and it communicated itself to Illidan. For a moment, he felt the Light embrace him, and his heart was at rest. He had been given a vision of redemption beyond any he had hoped for. Peace filled him as he communed silently with the naaru. The moment lasted only a heartbeat, but when it ended, Illidan felt as if it might have been a lifetime.

"You will be a hero," said the naaru. "But there will be a price."

"There always is."

THE MOMENT ENDED. Illidan stood, suffused by a feeling of peace. The lattice of Light, the shimmering plain, faded, and Argus appeared around him and the naaru. It had always been there, he realized. The reality he had stood within with the being was entirely a product of its power, an illusion.

Sudden fear stabbed at him. He might have been detected. The minions of the Burning Legion could be closing in. Whether the naaru was friendly or not, it was placing both of them in danger.

"Farewell," the naaru said. A limb of Light flickered out of its body and touched Illidan on the forehead. He felt a sense of contact, as if another tattoo had been added to his flesh. It burned strangely, at war with the fel power contained within his other tattoos; then it merged with them and disappeared.

The contact was broken, and the naaru vanished from his sight as if it had never been. The image of himself transformed once again played through his mind. Could it be true? Was there really a path to redemption for him? He had never dared think such a thing was possible, and yet the naaru believed it would be so. It believed in him. Just for a moment, he let himself believe, too. Then he pushed the thought to one side, for future consideration. There was still work to be done.

Illidan studied the anchor points of the portal. He could just sense them, and he knew they were there. Hopefully they would remain hidden from any demon who sought them. It was time to go. He had been here too long.

He ended the spell of astral travel, and his spirit hurtled through the Twisting Nether and thundered back into his body. In front of his forehead, visible to his spectral senses, a rune floated. He knew its blaze mirrored the mark the naaru had left on him. Even as that realization hit him, the rune faded into invisibility, vanished as if the encounter had never happened.

He paused to recollect the meeting, using every trick of memory his sorcerer's mind possessed. It had been real, he felt certain, and the vision the naaru had given him felt true. Of course, that meant nothing if the creature was playing games with his mind. But if it was powerful enough to do that . . .

One could go mad thinking about such things.

As he adjusted to being corporeal once more, he heard the banging on the door, audible even through the spells of warding and protection he had set. He spoke the words that unlocked the sanctum, and the door slid open to reveal his advisers standing there.

"Lord Illidan," said High Nethermancer Zerevor. "You must come with us to see what is happening for yourself. The Black Temple is under attack."

There was an urgency in his voice that kept Illidan from dismissing him out of hand. Illidan rose from his posture of meditation and moved to accompany them. It was only then that it occurred to him that one of his advisers was missing.

Where was Akama?

CHAPTER TWENTY-EIGHT

One Day Before the Fall

MAIEV LOOKED UP TO SEE AKAMA STANDING IN THE doorway of her cage once more.

"Have you come to dangle vain promises before me again?" she asked. It was difficult to keep the bitterness from her voice. Akama limped closer, tilted his head to one side, and gazed up into her face. Such was his intensity that she grew uncomfortable, although she refused to show it.

"No," he said. His tone revealed both his weariness and his fear. "How are you feeling? Strong?"

"Let me out of this cage and I will show you." Maiev had spent the previous months conserving her strength. She was sure she had never been mightier, but still the spells binding her held.

"Do you remember how to hold a blade?" Akama asked. Maiev was about to pour scorn on his head, but something in his manner stopped her.

"That is not something I could ever forget."

"I hope so," said Akama.

"Why are you here?"

"The Horde and the Alliance besiege the Temple of Karabor.

They have made common cause with the Aldor and the Scryers. Even some of the naaru are present."

There was a sense of finality. "Has the Betrayer sent you to kill me? Does he lack the courage to do it himself?"

Akama raised a stubby finger to his lips. The Ashtongue leader considered his words and, just for a moment, allowed himself the tiniest of smiles. "You are not that important to him. Even as his empire descends into fire and ruin, he appears more concerned with other things. Fortunately for you and for me."

Maiev allowed herself to hope. She kept her features absolutely calm and cold. She did not want to give her enemies the satisfaction of seeing that they had gotten to her. "You think he will be brought down, then?"

"Who knows? Even now he is the mightiest being in Outland, surrounded by lieutenants of near-equal power. The temple is a fortress unparalleled in this world. He might hold out there for years. His enemies might fall out among themselves. I have known him for too long to think his downfall will be easy."

"And yet you think he might be overthrown."

"A small force of sufficient power could infiltrate the temple, if they were given the appropriate aid."

"And of course you are in a position to give such aid. Forgive me if I have some trouble believing you. I seem to have heard a story like this before. Last time this tale did not turn out so well for me or those with me. Or your people, either, if my memory serves me correctly."

Akama had the grace to look ashamed, but he still met her gaze. "This time, one way or another, there will be a different ending."

"I do not believe you."

"I can convince you."

"How?" Maiev put all the scorn she could muster into her voice, but she could not help but feel hope rising in her breast.

"Stand back," Akama said. He waited for her to do so and then invoked a powerful stream of magic. The locking spells fell away. Unable to quite believe what she was seeing, Maiev pushed the door of her cell. It swung open.

She was tempted to spring on Akama and wring his treacherous neck, but she was unarmed and he was still powerful. She did not doubt that he had bodyguards within call.

"If you are playing with me, ancient one, I will kill you." The words escaped her lips before she could stop them.

"You might find that difficult to do without weapons and armor," Akama said.

"I trust you are going to rectify that immediately."

"You trust correctly. This time."

MAIEV PULLED ON HER gauntlets, then raised her helm and placed it on her head as if it were a crown. A complex weave of protective magic sprang into being around her. She breathed a sigh of relief. She had power now, and she was not going to let herself be imprisoned again. This time, if it was a trap, she would force them to kill her.

Akama stood nearby in the guardroom, holding her umbra crescent. Maiev had noticed the demon corpses on the way. All that remained of her jailors were Ashtongue. The demons were dead. That was a pity. She would have liked to kill the abominations herself.

She held out her hand in an imperious gesture, demanding her weapon. Akama looked down at it, as if guessing what the first thing she would do when she got it in her hands would be.

"Are you frightened I am going to kill you?"

"I am frightened you are going to try."

"And why should I not?"

"Because you are not stupid. Let us not play games with each other, Maiev Shadowsong. You are free because I have set you free.

You can indulge a childish thirst for revenge or you can help me overthrow our true enemy."

"I can do both."

"No. You cannot. I alone can get you into the Temple of Karabor. I alone can guide you to the Betrayer. Decide now whom you wish to kill. Me or him. That is your choice."

"Why should I believe you this time?"

"Because I am risking more than my life to free you. I am risking my soul and my people. I have kept you alive for a purpose, Maiev Shadowsong. I have hoarded your life as if it were my greatest treasure. Follow me this day and you will face Illidan and perhaps conquer him. Kill me and you can walk free, but you may never get another chance to slay the Betrayer. Which is it going to be?"

Without saying another word, Akama thrust the blade into her hand. He stood watchful and ready. Maiev felt the weight of the weapon. She turned it over and over. If any spells booby-trapped it, she could not see them. She was tempted for a moment to stab Akama in his treacherous heart, but she restrained herself.

"You may have your life. I will have justice from Illidan."

"No," said Akama. "You will have vengeance on him. I think that will give you more satisfaction."

ILLIDAN LOOKED OUT FROM the battlements. A seething ocean of armored flesh broke against the walls of the Black Temple. Spells surged toward the defensive wards. Thousands of soldiers pressed forward to do battle with his demons.

He sensed the presence of more than just mortals down there. He discerned the pulsing of naaru. So much for the promises the elder naaru had made back on Argus. It looked as if only one of them had faith in his destiny. The beings down there were certainly against him.

Illidan shrugged his shoulders. His wings rose, emphasizing the gesture. "It matters not."

His councilors looked shocked. One or two of them smiled and tried to put a brave face on things, as if they believed that he had a plan that could save them. "We trust in your judgment, Lord," said Gathios the Shatterer.

"Trust in the walls of the Black Temple," Illidan replied, "and in your own spells and blades. Go below and prepare for battle. I do not think our new guests will be leaving anytime soon, and we should ready a proper reception for them."

Illidan considered ordering that Maiev be executed before she could be rescued. It would be a small morsel of vengeance, perhaps the only one he would get. Who would do it? Akama, perhaps. Where was the Broken? Illidan invoked the spell he had used upon the leader of the Ashtongue. It was still in place. The shade was bound and could be unleashed if it should prove necessary. There was a certain satisfaction to be had in knowing it was so. No. He would not kill Maiev yet, not while there was still a chance she could be made to suffer.

A group of draenei paladins in the tabard of the Alliance charged down the road toward the gates of the Black Temple. Of course, those sanctimonious oafs would be leading the charge. They believed in opposing evil wherever they found it, and he fit into their simple-minded view of what evil was. To them he even looked the part. A mass of his demonic guardians raced to meet them. Magical hammers clashed against fel weapons. It was difficult to see who had won amid the swirling melee; then the Alliance soldiers were thrown back.

A company of brutish-looking Horde trolls moved to reinforce the paladins. Among them flitted shadowy figures who struck with astonishing power and deadliness when the demons' backs were turned. Illidan could see the shimmer of spells concealing them. Apparently his demonic allies could not.

It looked as if the attackers would prevail—but then a shower of meteors crashed into the ground around the combat and broke asunder, revealing themselves to be infernals. One of the warlocks within the temple had taken a hand.

Illidan took stock of the situation. The temple was well supplied, and the sorcerers within it could summon demonic aid almost indefinitely. But there were magi out there among the attackers, and others who could counter his warlocks.

Plumes of dust in the distance announced the arrival of reinforcements for the attackers. They had the advantage of numbers, and that was only likely to keep growing. The Alliance and the Horde had the resources of a world to draw on, and armies that had been honed in endless battles. Their presence beyond his walls showed exactly how strong they had grown.

He studied his own defenses. In the training grounds, the Dragonmaw clan orcs had gathered. Overhead their dragons flew in formation. Their armies mustered in companies around the siege engines. At the entrance to the Sanctuary of Shadows, Supremus stood. The abyssal loomed over even the gigantic Illidari fearbringers who stalked through the courtyard, wings flapping, weapons held at the ready.

Any attacker who got beyond Supremus would have to enter the Sanctuary of Shadows and face more bound demons and sorcerers. And beyond them, layer after layer of defenses waited.

Illidan returned to contemplating the assaulting army. A huge disturbance loomed around the gates. Enormous battering rams rolled forward, propelled by sorcery. Wave after wave of Aldor and Scryer troops did battle with his demonic defenders.

It did not matter how strong his defenses were. Enough force was being brought to bear that the temple would eventually fall.

Deceiver, they called Kil'jaeden. It seemed he had deceived them all once again. He had not committed his own forces here because he knew he did not have to. His enemies could only be weakened by fighting each other. When this battle was over, the Legion would intervene and destroy them. By defending the temple strongly, Illidan was only doing Kil'jaeden's work for him.

But what else could he do? Surrender would serve no purpose. His enemies were sworn to slay him. He just needed to hold on until the portal was complete, and then . . .

Illidan had made a mistake, concentrating all his attention on the Burning Legion and the quest for Argus. His wings curled tightly around his form for a moment until he forced them to relax.

This was a sideshow. The Black Temple was the greatest fortress in Outland. He had time to complete the creation of the gateway to Argus. He needed to make a start now.

ILLIDAN RETURNED TO HIS casting chamber. His head ached. His body felt weak. Doubts assailed him from every side. Did he really have enough time to complete the gate? What if the forces besieging his citadel found a weak spot in the defenses? What if he had miscalculated even that? There was still the way in through the sewers. He should reinforce High Warlord Naj'entus with more naga and elementals.

He studied the half-complete pattern. It would have been his masterpiece. He picked up the Skull of Gul'dan and turned it over and over in his hands. *Is this how you felt at the end, old orc? Defeated before you could even start?*

He walked to the edge of the pattern, studied symbols inscribed in his own blood, read the messages of power there that were almost ready to spring to life and open a passage across the entire face of the universe.

He had thought he had factored everything into his plan. He had thought he had time. He turned the skull so that he looked into its empty eye sockets. Its death's-head grin mocked him.

He remembered the vision the naaru had given him. Was that a mockery, too? He tightened his grip on the skull, almost ready to crush it into tiny pieces.

This was not over. He would rally the defenses of the Black Temple. If need be, he could provide an anchor for the gateway himself. He could hold a way open by pure force of will if he had to. He was not going to fail now at this final hurdle.

He would strike at the heart of the Burning Legion, no matter what it cost.

CHAPTER TWENTY-NINE

The Day of the Fall

MAIEV INSPECTED THE IMMENSE WALLS OF THE BLACK Temple. The fortress loomed over them, radiating terrible strength. Huge stone spikes emerged from the walls like blades thrusting at the sky.

Akama looked upon the structure as one dying of thirst in the desert might gaze upon a fountain of sparkling water. Hope and desperation warred in his eyes. He completely ignored the sights and sounds of the battle going on nearby. He had eyes only for the holy place itself.

Maiev could not ignore the war raging all around her. Already the combined forces of the Aldor and the Scryers had begun the assault that would provide cover for Akama's attempt to infiltrate the Black Temple.

Bitterness ate at her heart as the naaru Xi'ri wove spells of protection around her, Akama, and his new allies from Azeroth. The Sha'tar had not consented to aid her when she had gone after Illidan. Things might have turned out differently on the Hand of Gul'dan if they had. Her companions might still be alive.

Maiev glanced at the Azerothian adventurers. She sensed their power and their nervousness. They had been secretly aiding Akama for weeks, acting as his agents to perform missions he could not. Now they were preparing to strike at Illidan himself. The prospect of infiltrating the Black Temple excited and scared them. Maiev herself could barely wait for the naaru to finish weaving its spells. The hour of her vengeance was almost at hand. This time the Betrayer would not escape.

Nearby she sensed the terrible presence of demons. Their brimstone scent filled the air, along with the stink of burning flesh and opened entrails. Something in it stirred her to the core. This was the scent of a battle worth fighting in, a war for the fate of worlds.

She shaded her eyes and watched a company of Aldor rush by the glittering form of a naaru on their way to engage a force of batwinged demons. Spells blazed through the air; enchanted weapons bit home. The Illidari were pushed back. Spectators jeered from the walls of the Black Temple.

Overhead, huge nether drakes circled. A wing of them hurtled in, breathing clouds of devastating arcane magic. She stood on the open ground and defied them to hurt her. In her armor, she was all but invulnerable to their attacks. She felt the naaru's power complete its weave around her, setting the air to shimmer.

The earth shook as another wave of meteorites smashed home and another wave of infernals clambered from the craters they made. Dust devils arose over the site of the battle. A troop of riders charged past to enter the fray.

Akama gestured to her. "Now is the time, Maiev! Unleash your wrath!"

Maiev smiled as she raced forward. Behind her rushed Akama and his Azerothian allies and a strong force of Aldor and Scryers. Ahead she could see the seething mass of demons that filled the killing fields before the walls of the temple. Satyrs, felguard, and worse things charged to meet her. Exultant, she shouted, "I've waited for this moment for years. Illidan and his lapdogs will be destroyed!"

Ahead winged dreadlords emerged from the murk of battle. They towered above her, filled with fel power. She aimed her umbra crescent at the nearest and slashed through his flesh, cleaving off part of a wing and then a leg. The demon crashed to the ground, and she leapt upon his back and drove her blade so far through his spine that the point was buried in the earth.

As the demon's life ebbed away, she pulled her weapon clear and blinked herself behind another, calling on Elune to aid her as she smote the creature.

The air crackled with magical energy as Akama and his other allies unleashed a torrent of spells. The dreadlords and their lesser demons fell before the savage onslaught, but more and more entered the fray. Fel magic pulsed in the air as a portal opened nearby. A huge nathrezim emerged from it. She recognized his massive crimson form. It was Vagath, one of the worst of the jailors Illidan had set for her. She remembered all his promises of torment. Somehow he had escaped the slaughter at her prison. She would ensure that he did not get away this time.

Akama bellowed, "Slay all who see us! Word must not get back to Illidan."

Maiev sprang forward, lashing out at the nathrezim. They exchanged blows. Vagath was strong but Maiev was stronger. She drove her blade through the heavy armor encasing the dreadlord's chest. "Meet your end, demon!"

Vagath looked down in disbelief. Akama limped over to Maiev's side. Vagath fixed his gaze on the Ashtongue leader and, with his dying breath, said, "You've sealed your fate, Akama. The master will learn of your betrayal!"

Akama shook his head. "Akama has no master, not anymore."

As the words left his mouth the portal pulsed once more. A tidal wave of demons surged forth. The sight of them filled Maiev with terrible wrath. She threw herself among them, striking left and right, cleaving through them like the prow of a ship through the waves of a bloody sea.

The enemy closed in all around her, seeking to drag her down into their midst. Felsteel axes glanced off her armor. Demonic claws bit into her chest plate. She unleashed the full fury of her blade, knowing she needed to close the portal through which the demons poured or her mission would fail before it began.

Behind her she thought she heard Akama give the order to enter the Black Temple. It seemed she was going to have to close the portal alone.

VANDEL LOOKED OUT THROUGH the murder hole deep within the walls of the Black Temple. He took a sip of the ethermead he had acquired from the blood elf revelers on the Grand Promenade. It tingled pleasantly on his tongue.

Another massive battle had erupted outside the gates. Glancing down, he saw a force of Scryers and Aldor charge into combat with the guardian demons.

Huge clouds of dust rose, obscuring the conflict. He caught glimpses of the battle through them. A blood elf warrior fell to a satyr. An Aldor priest blasted a felguard with the blinding power of the Light. There was something oddly thrilling about watching the fight, like having an arena seat for the end of the world.

He saw that the servants of the naaru appeared to be aiding a group of Broken—and could that be . . . Akama?

Rumor claimed that the old Broken had vanished, that he had gone over to the other side and was even now out there plotting the Black Temple's downfall with the leaders of the Aldor and the Scryers. It appeared that rumor was correct.

Small dribbles of rage erupted from the demon inside Vandel. Flickering memories of battles and kills came to him. He suppressed them easily enough.

Some anger remained when he watched the attacking forces gather. The fools. Did they not realize what was going on here? They thought they had come to attack the demon ruler of Outland. They had no clue.

Ah, but it was an easy enough mistake to make. Looking down at the bound demons defending the temple, Vandel could see how the invaders could think like that. Illidan had never taken any time to explain his purpose to anyone outside his immediate circle.

Not that it would have mattered. Most likely no one would have believed him if he had. They would simply have thought it was part of some cunning scheme. Perhaps it was. Even now, after all Vandel had seen, all he had done, and all he had been through, he was not sure of that.

Who really knew what went on in the Betrayer's mind? He took another sip of the ethermead and watched the pyrotechnic blast of spells claw away at the wards on the walls. How long would it be until the demon hunters were called upon to fight?

AKAMA LED HIS SMALL force toward the walls of the Temple of Karabor. In the distance Maiev battled to close the demonic portal. He prayed she was successful, at least for as long as it would take for him and his companions to enter the temple.

All around, demons made war with servants of the Light. Behind him, he sensed the heartbreaking presence of the naaru. It reminded him of all he had turned his back on when he had entered the Betrayer's service, all he had lost and hoped to regain.

He looked at the eager faces of his allies from Azeroth, the trusting expressions of his Broken bodyguards. He inspected the hollow places within himself where once fragments of his soul had been.

He had not felt whole for so long. He would rather die than continue this way.

Which was good, because that was exactly what would happen if things went wrong. In fact, that would be the best thing that would happen.

Still, these last few moons the lord of Outland had been distracted, caught up in his mad, grandiose plan. If plan it was. Even now, Akama was not sure whether the Betrayer was serious about opening a gateway to Argus, or whether it was all part of some great deception. Since Illidan had used the capture of Maiev to conceal the opening of the gateway to Nathreza, Akama was not inclined to take anything he said on faith. Akama remembered all the Broken and draenei slain in the opening of that gateway, their souls consumed, and all the draenei souls that met the same fate in Auchindoun. He would allow no chance for Illidan to repeat those abominations.

Felsteel bars and wards protected the sewer outflow. Those were the least of the defenses. Far worse lay beyond. Akama wove the spell that would open the way, and stepped through.

Ahead lay the sewers of the Black Temple. The path led up through a long rocky defile and then emerged into a chamber full of elementals and naga. Somewhere in the distance, he heard the naga champion High Warlord Naj'entus's roar.

He hoped his people were ready.

AS HIS SPIRIT HOVERED over the pattern, Illidan became aware of a banging on the door of the sanctum and a female voice screaming for his attention. They were audible through the ears of his body, which lay beneath him. He let his spirit drop back into his flesh and surveyed his surroundings. He spoke the words of opening, and the seal on the entrance was removed.

Lady Malande stood before him, looking at the vast shape of the pattern with something like wonder in her eyes. "Lord Illidan," she said. "An enemy force is within the gates. High Warlord Naj'entus has fallen at the entrance to the sewers. The enemy is on the move."

It took Illidan a few moments to register her words. Naj'entus had been set along with a small army to watch over the sealed entrance to the sewers. Illidan had sent reinforcements. The naga champion and his forces should have been able to fend off a legion. Something had gone very badly wrong. Treachery. The temple had been betrayed from within. Perhaps it was the blood elves or Akama's people.

It looked as if time had run out. Illidan picked up the Skull of Gul'dan. Its smile mocked him once more. There was only one thing left to do. He would need the power of the soul siphon. There was still a use he could put it to.

CHAPTER THIRTY

The Day of the Fall

MAIEV STOOD ATOP A MOUNTAIN OF DEMON CORPSES. Her breath thundered from her chest. The thrill of victory blazed within her heart. She had closed the portal and stopped the seemingly endless tide of demons. She only wished that there were more. She would have stacked their corpses as high as the walls and entered the temple that way instead of through the sewers as Akama had planned.

A huge surge of familiar energy pulsed deep within the temple.

No! She knew what that meant. She had felt its like before on the slopes of the Hand of Gul'dan. Somewhere within his fortress, Illidan was opening another portal, far greater than the one that Vagath had come through. Ominous energy filled the air as the rent in the fabric of reality widened. Perhaps the Betrayer was summoning some new demon from the depths of the Twisting Nether. Most likely he was planning on escape. She could not let that happen again. She needed to get inside the Black Temple now. She would end this thing today.

She used her power to blink swiftly across the battlefield and through the passageway into the sewers.

Illidan would not elude justice this time.

———

VANDEL WATCHED AS THE silver-armored figure completed the slaughter of an army of demons. He recognized her from the tales he had heard of the battle at the Hand of Gul'dan. Maiev Shadowsong was loose. That should not have been possible. She was bound in Warden's Cage, guarded by demons, rings of terrible warding spells woven around her. Akama must have freed her.

Come to me now, my demon hunters.

The voice echoed within Vandel's head. It was a summoning on a primal level. It vibrated through his tattoos and bored into his brain with a compulsion that was all but irresistible. Along with the summons came the knowledge of where he had to go, a place deep within the fortress, close to the council chamber.

He pulled himself away from the viewpoint in the wall and raced toward the distant stairwell.

All around him, he could see the signs of activity. Troops ran to defensive positions. Horns sounded and drums rumbled in the depths. These were warning signs. Somewhere the temple defenses had been breached.

He heard the sounds of combat in the distance. The demon urged him to race toward it, to take part in the killing, to reap souls.

Come to me now, my demon hunters.

Once again the command rang out. This time he felt it shivering through his very bones. Was this how a demon felt when it was summoned from the Twisting Nether? Drawn and compelled by forces it did not understand but struggled to resist?

Why was he even resisting? The voice was Illidan's and it contained such urgency that Vandel almost wept. Somewhere deep within the temple, potent energies stirred. Vandel recognized them. A gate was being opened, but to where, he could not tell.

Did Illidan plan an escape? Or was the opening created by his enemies? Perhaps traitors within the fortress were summoning aid from elsewhere. Perhaps Illidan himself had opened the portal. The energies of this gate felt very much like those of the one that had led to Nathreza. Had Illidan finally opened the path to Argus? There was only one way Vandel was going to find out.

Somewhere in the darkness, he sensed other demon hunters moving, felt the presence of their inner demons. He cursed. It seemed that his curiosity about the attack had put him the farthest away from their master. He leapt as he reached the top of the stairs.

Come to me now, my demon hunters. The voice boomed within his skull like the tolling of a great bell; then its echoes slowly died away, leaving him feeling alone. The sense of a summoning deep within the temple intensified. The way to somewhere else lay open, but he knew beyond a shadow of a doubt that it would soon close and that any chance of him reaching the portal would be gone.

He took the stairs ten at a time, bounding down them with the agility of a panther, tumbling headlong, rolling to his feet, taking advantage of the force of gravity to increase his velocity. Urgency burned within his brain, compelled him to rush. It was not just fear. Not just the sense that the temple was on the verge of falling. It was an overwhelming feeling that if he failed to answer the summons, he would regret it forever, that somehow he would not achieve his destiny.

He raced on toward the training grounds. Outside the doorway, he heard the gigantic, angry roar of Supremus, as if the abyssal was engaged in combat with some mighty foe.

Dragons flashed by overhead. Spells erupted. Demons moved toward the Sanctuary of Shadows, as if they were preparing to block the path of powerful intruders. All was confusion.

MAIEV EMERGED FROM THE sewers into the aftermath of a terrible battle.

She stood in a huge courtyard. The corpse of a nether drake lay on the ground near her, its tail still twitching as if the great reptile had not yet realized it was dead. Akama and his allies had carved their way through Illidan's defenses. Hundreds more corpses of Dragonmaw orcs and demons lay strewn across the ground. Potent magic had been unleashed here. Off to her right stood gigantic siege engines. Beyond them was a stairway fit for a titan. It led into the depths of the Black Temple.

Still she sensed the pulse of that great portal being opened. She glared around her, and her eyes caught sight of something startlingly strange. A demonic figure erupted from an archway in the wall on her left.

VANDEL RACED FROM THE stairwell into the training courtyard. The air stank of death and unleashed magic. Dead dragons and demons lay everywhere. The corpses of fel orcs lay piled in small hills. What had once seemed an invincible force had been defeated. Only one living thing moved in the aftermath of the awesome violence, a silver-armored night elf with a curved blade. Her entire body was shrouded by powerful magical armor. It was Maiev Shadowsong. Somehow she had managed to get into the temple as swiftly as he had gotten down from the walls. There was magic at work here.

Maiev stared at him and raised her blade as if ready to attack.

Vandel froze. He did not wish to fight a fellow night elf. He wanted only to get past her and answer Illidan's summons.

"Demon spawn, prepare to die," Maiev said. Suddenly she was no longer where she had been. Vandel sensed a disturbance behind him and threw himself forward, rolling as a blade cleft the air where his head had been. He tumbled to his feet, facing Maiev.

"I do not want to fight you," he said.

———

MAIEV CURSED. IT HAD been a long time since anyone had avoided one of her death strikes. It should not have been possible yet this foul monstrosity had done so. A mark of how potent he was.

Maiev studied the thing. He looked in some ways like Illidan, although less monstrous. He was tall, a whipcord-thin abomination that had once been a kaldorei. He had tattoos like his master. His skin was scaly. His eye sockets were empty except for the molten green light of fel magic. He lacked wings and hooves, but there was something undeniably demonic about him. He had once been an elf, but now he was something else, a dreadful hybrid of elf and demon, doubtless one of the army of horrors that Akama had spoken of.

Maiev aimed her blade at the monster. The demonically possessed elf leapt above the weapon. As she turned to strike at him again, he jumped to one side and once more eluded her.

"Stop. There is no need for this," he said.

She heard the grating anger in his voice, though, and was not about to fall for his trickery. She advanced upon him, her blade held at the ready. "I will have your life, monster."

THE TERRIBLE WEAPON SWEPT toward Vandel once more. He sprang over it, flipped himself clean over Maiev, and landed behind her. He had a clear shot with a spell at her back. He hesitated for a moment as she turned to face him.

"I am not your enemy," he said. Her umbra crescent licked out again. Sparks flickered as he parried it. "We are on the same side, you and I."

Maiev paused. Her cold laughter rang through the war-ravaged courtyard. "You serve Illidan. I mean to kill him. Of course we are not on the same side."

"I am here to fight the Burning Legion, not other night elves."

The point of the umbra crescent began to move from side to side, hypnotically. Vandel took a step back to give himself more room. "You have fallen for Illidan's old lie," Maiev said.

"It is not a lie. I have slaughtered demons by the hundred. I will slay more for as long as there is breath in me."

"That will not be for much longer." Maiev lunged, quick as a nightsaber. Vandel sprang clear and her blade passed through the spot where he had just stood. He fought down the urge to riposte. His demon urged him to attack. With an effort of will, he restrained himself.

"The Burning Legion seeks to destroy all who live. We need to stand united against it," he said.

"You will be united with your demon master in death." Maiev's strike was like a thunderbolt. Vandel hurled himself backward but it caught his cheek, slicing it open. Blood ran down over his lips. It tingled on his tongue.

Vandel had had enough. He had tried reasoning with Maiev. He could try running but he doubted he would get far with his back to her. She was too strong and too fast. He needed to face her.

You need to kill her, said the demonic voice in the back of his mind. *It is you or her. She will not let you live.*

Vandel would have liked to deny it, but he knew the demon was speaking the truth, and that lent its argument force. He summoned fel energy and sent a bolt racing toward the night elf. She parried, dissipating it effortlessly. Vandel doubted anyone save Illidan or his highest lieutenants could have managed that feat. He realized that the objective here was not going to be killing Maiev. It was going to be staying alive in the face of her fury.

MAIEV'S EYES NARROWED. SO the demon's true colors were revealed now. He had attempted to strike her down with his fel magic. For a moment she had almost believed the monster's protestations. He had sounded sincere and had made no attempt to harm her, only to defend himself.

In the distance the summoning reached a crescendo. Her prey was going to escape. It was time to end this. She launched a ferocious physical attack on the altered elf. Her blade flashed almost too fast for the eyes to follow. Her assailant raised his blades to parry.

VANDEL DANCED THROUGH A razor-edged whirlwind. It was all he could do to keep out of the way of Maiev's strikes. There was no chance of launching an attack of his own. She was simply too fast and too strong.

Already his muscles ached from parrying the fury of her assault. It felt as if his arms were going to be torn from their sockets simply from the effort of blocking her attacks. He could barely maintain the grip on his blades.

He backpedaled away from her as fast as he could. He was not worried about tripping over anything. His spectral senses allowed him to perceive everything around him. They also told him that he was running out of time. The demon within him howled its protests. It did not want to escape. It wanted to fight and kill. He allowed its power to flow into him. From the pores of his skin, darkness flowed, armoring his body with shadow. His arms grew stronger. His movements grew faster. He matched Maiev blow for blow, turning her blade with one of his, lashing out with the other. Metal shrieked as his weapon clawed its way along the vambrace of her armor.

He struck again and again, driving the warden back first one step and then another until he had regained all the ground he had lost to her initial attack. Maiev slashed at him and he leapt above her blade, bringing his dagger down on her helmet and knocking her off balance. As she fell, he aimed a bolt of fel energy at her. It ravened into her chest. The demon urged him on. *Kill her. Kill her.*

MAIEV TUMBLED TO THE GROUND. The impact of the Illidari's blow had surprised her more than hurt her, but the burst of fel energy was painful even through her armor. The shadow-encased demon loomed above her, an aura of power playing around his hands.

Maiev drew on the light of Elune and used her power to blink, vanishing from where she lay.

VANDEL WATCHED THE BOLT of yellow-green energy crash down into the ground where Maiev had been but an instant before. He felt the displacement of air behind him and turned a moment too late to block her strike.

Her blade scythed in from the right and cut his arm. Pain blazed through it. Blood flowed. He hurled himself back and realized then that the attack had been a feint. Her blade crunched into his skull. He rolled away even as it made contact, but agony lanced through him. Darkness encroached on his field of vision.

The last thing he saw was Khariel. A disappointed look was on his little boy's face. He was never going to be avenged now.

"Thus will your master fall, too," he heard Maiev say. Then the darkness took him.

AKAMA ENTERED THE REFECTORY. Racks made from the bones of monsters flanked the doorway. A massive altar stood upon a plinth at the rear of the room. The flickering light of eldritch energies sent shadows skittering across the floor of the desecrated space. His allies had already slaughtered most of the opposition within and now confronted the shade that Illidan had drawn from Akama's own spirit. It looked like the Broken's shadow, if his shadow had been granted form in three dimensions and evil life. It was perfect in its way, a miracle of dark magic, a testament to the evil genius of Illidan, its creator.

The massive form of the stolen part of his soul loomed over the adventurers from Azeroth. Sensing Akama's presence, it moved toward him, tendrils of dark energy lashing out from it, smashing into him. His allies attacked it head-on, hammering at it with spells, charging in with their swords. He wrestled with the pain, kept himself on his feet. He gritted his teeth, even though he wanted to scream. He studied the weave of the magic attacking him. It led all the way back to the shade.

The adventurers from Azeroth had done everything Akama had asked. They had opened the way into the refectory. They had slain the renegade Ashtongue forces guarding the place and then, one by one, had killed the channelers casting the spell that held the shard of his dark soul. Now the thing was free and it was coming for him. It intended to kill him if it could, to take possession of his body and, through him, all of the Ashtongue.

He gazed at it with something like wonder. How many in their lives got to look upon everything that was evil in themselves? How many confronted all the darkness within?

To anyone else, it looked merely like his evil shadow. He saw that it was made up of every bit of wickedness that had ever been in him. Every mean and petty deed, from the smallest to the largest. Looking at it, he could see when he was a child coveting his brother's toys. He saw himself gloating over the untimely death of a rival for the leadership of his people. He saw the shadow that lurked behind his every outward show of piety and goodness. He saw the vanity and the egoism and the lust and the greed for glory. He saw all his demons, all that had driven him to become what he was.

Illidan had freed him of that, in a way. He had taken part of his strength, too, for in that darkness had been many of the things that had driven him to master magic, forged him to become leader of his people. He had always thought of himself as humble, but looking on this monster, he saw that humility had been a mask he wore, all the better to fool those who had followed him.

He wanted to tell himself that these visions were part of the shade's attack on him, that it was attempting to undermine his will, to drive him to his knees, to force the rest of his soul from his body so that it could take residence. He knew that such was not the case. This shadow was part of him. He needed to reclaim it, for it held a great part of his strength, and only when he had reintegrated it would he have the power to do what was needed.

The shade was weakening under the onslaught of its attackers, Akama's allies from Azeroth.

Akama understood the spell now and unraveled it. He drew its energies into himself. The vortex he created brought the spirit home. It fell into him. For a moment, he shuddered in dark ecstasy; then he put the chains in place around his own evil, binding it to him, integrating it into his being. He felt strength return. He felt power and pride and ambition flow into him. He was once more truly Akama.

It was done. He took a deep breath and allowed the strength to surge back into his body. A crowd of Ashtongue entered the refectory and gazed up at him.

"Hail Akama!" they shouted.

THE STEADY PULSE OF the portal-opening spell vanished.

Maiev sprang over her fallen foe. She had no more time to waste. Even now she might be too late. She needed to find Illidan before he fled forever. She rushed past the smoldering stone form of some gigantic dead infernal.

She raced into the enormous structure. Dead satyrs and other demons sprawled all around a massive hall. Ashtongue moved in groups. They stared at her. There was no menace in their gazes, but no warmth, either. They clearly knew who she was. She wondered whether they would dare attack her. There was only one way to find out.

She marched over to the nearest of them. "Where is Akama?" she demanded in her most commanding tone.

The Ashtongue looked at her. There was something different in his manner. In the past, the Broken had usually been obsequious. Even the ones guarding her would never meet her gaze. This one did, as did all his companions. They did not look at her as if they were afraid. They looked at her as if they were her equals.

"He is deeper within the temple. He seeks to put an end to the Betrayer."

"Good," she said. "I shall go and help him."

CHAPTER THIRTY-ONE

The Fall

WEARILY ILLIDAN EMERGED INTO HIS COUNCIL CHAMber. The demon hunters were away. He had done all he could. He wished he could have gone with them, but he had needed to remain behind as one mystical pole of the portal, to hold the way open.

Now it was only a matter of waiting. Holding open that portal had taken almost all his strength and all the power within the soul siphon.

Lady Malande looked at him. "The Ashtongue have betrayed us. Our servants have turned against us. The gates are open."

"They must have planned this all along," said Gathios the Shatterer.

Illidan reached out with his sorcerous senses. The binding spell he had maintained on Akama's shade was gone. Akama had freed himself and, in doing so, had freed his people. The old Broken had been more cunning than he thought. One more miscalculation. Illidan had been too busy with the portal to Argus and his demon hunters to pay attention to Akama. Still, he would find a way to make the leader of the Broken pay.

"I sensed a portal opening," said High Nethermancer Zerevor. "I thought you had escaped, oh lord."

His expression held a complex mix of emotions: gladness that his overlord was still there, puzzlement as to why. If he wanted an explanation, he was doomed to disappointment.

Illidan sensed events closing in all around him. Things were unwinding. He was trapped by fate, his plans half complete. He thought of the vision the naaru had shown him. He doubted now that the creature was of the Light. Perhaps it had been part of the trap Kil'jaeden set for him. It had lulled him into a false sense of security at a critical time. Everything he had worked for so long to achieve had come undone.

Perhaps his demon hunters would fail. Perhaps he had only sent them to their doom. He resigned himself to the fact that he would never know. All he could do now was stand his ground. He would not give his enemies the satisfaction of his surrender. He would never be imprisoned again.

He regarded his councilors. They still looked to him for leadership. "Defend this place," he said. "Guard the way into the summit of the temple. There is a spell I will cast. It may turn the battle our way. We will yet overthrow our enemies. We are not defeated yet."

AKAMA STEPPED OVER THE CORPSE of High Nethermancer Zerevor. Ahead of him loomed the sealed gateway to the summit of the temple. It had been a swift, hard-fought battle to get to this point. They had left a trail of broken bodies and shattered sentinels through the perfumed gardens and palatial apartments the blood elves occupied. Now ahead of him lay the great black door beyond which Illidan worked his evil magic. What new fiendish spell was he casting?

The adventurers from Azeroth waited to see what he would do.

Akama said, "This door is all that stands between us and the Betrayer. Stand aside, friends."

He studied the spell sealing the way to the summit. It was a thing of fantastic intricacy, composed over multiple interlocking weaves of force. It would take a sorcerer a lifetime to unravel it. Fortunately, he did not need to do so. He merely needed to shatter it.

He drew upon all his strength and launched it at the doorway. Somehow that fragile-looking structure resisted. He increased the amount of power, his spell rending and clawing at the seal with all the energies he commanded. It was still not enough. His shoulders slumped. He had come so far, risked so much.

"I cannot do this alone . . ." Frustration forced the words from Akama's lips.

He sensed the presence of others of his people. Powerful spirits, familiar and mighty ghosts, unleashed to stalk through the Temple of Karabor by the events of the day.

"You are not alone, Akama," said one of the spirits. It wore the form of his onetime companion, the seer Udalo.

"Your people will always be with you!" The other spirit had taken the shape of Seer Olum. Akama was struck with awe.

I had not thought to see you so soon, old friend. The seer had been one of Akama's closest allies, until Vashj's naga discovered that Olum was plotting to depose the Betrayer. Olum had asked Akama to slay him in order to keep up the appearance that the Ashtongue were loyal to Illidan. Akama had sadly complied.

The spirits added their strength to his own. Slowly at first, the binding spell began to come apart, shredded by the torrent of power thrown at it, power backed by the will of an entire people freed from chains.

The spell collapsed. The ghosts began to fade. Akama said, "I thank you for your aid, brothers. Our people will be redeemed!"

Had Akama the time to reflect, he would have wept with joy. Olum's sacrifice had allowed him to get to this door, and his spirit had returned to help him open it. It was a good omen. But triumph warred with dread within Akama's soul. Soon he and his allies would have to face the Betrayer. Even after all this time, all his scheming, and all his planning, Akama was not certain that he was prepared for that.

ILLIDAN FELT THE SEAL give way on the gateway to the Black Temple's summit. Akama had grown powerful indeed to tear it down so quickly. He had learned a great deal during his time within Illidan's service, including how to work counterspells against his master's magic. Illidan remained crouched down, wings wrapped around his body, taking these last few moments to draw what power he could to himself before the final conflict of his life was upon him.

FILLED WITH TREPIDATION, Akama entered the summit. Even now victory was far from certain. The Betrayer might find some way of turning things around even as Akama's people threw the gates of the temple open to welcome the Aldor and the Scryers and their allies.

Illidan crouched down on the far side of the summit. In the center was a great grill, shielding a central well that went all the way down into the heart of the Temple of Karabor. The Betrayer held a skull in his hands as if contemplating a reminder of his own mortality. He was utterly still, immobile as one dead. Surely he could not have taken his own life.

Akama studied the aura swirling around his former master. No. He yet lived. Titanic swells of energy rose within him. He was merely gathering his strength.

All around, Akama's allies checked their weapons nervously. Illidan seemed to be waiting for all his enemies to enter. It was as if he wanted them all in one place and had no fear of their superior numbers. Given the powers on which he could call, Akama thought his lack of concern might be justified.

Where are his mutated soldiers? Akama wondered. All through the battle in the temple, Akama had looked for the demon hunters to appear, but there was no sign of their presence. Nor was there any sign of the great portal Akama had sensed being opened. He had expected Illidan to flee through it. In truth he would have half welcomed it, because it would have averted this final, likely fatal confrontation.

It spoke volumes of the Betrayer's confidence that he gave the intruders time to prepare themselves. Akama pushed the thoughts aside and began to draw on his own powers.

ILLIDAN STUDIED THE FORCES arrayed against him. It felt strange to see so many enemies within the heart of the Black Temple. It was even stranger in its way to see Akama standing beside them. He still could not believe the old Broken had the nerve to do such a thing. He had eluded all the traps and escaped all the shackles Illidan had prepared for him. And now he was here, surrounded by these outsiders he had brought to fight for him.

Anger filled Illidan's heart. He stared hard at Akama, letting his contempt show on his face. "Akama. Your duplicity is hardly surprising. I should have slaughtered you and your malformed brethren long ago."

Akama recoiled from the venom in Illidan's voice. He took a moment to gather himself and said, "We have come to end your reign, Illidan. My people and all of Outland shall be free!"

"Boldly said. But I remain . . . unconvinced."

"The time has come! The moment is at hand!"

Illidan glared at the Broken and his pathetic allies. "You are not prepared."

A massive warrior emerged from the pack, garbed in heavy plate, protective spells woven around him. Illidan saw the network of defensive magic that connected him to the Azerothian casters.

Illidan leapt forward and struck a powerful blow with his warglaive. The warrior raised a shield to block it. Illidan took advantage of the opening to slash at his neck with the left-hand blade. Blood spurted from the warrior's throat, but healing magic surged in, drawing the blood back and knitting torn flesh and severed veins.

Illidan summoned a parasitic shadowfiend to him. The creature slithered out of the Twisting Nether and into reality, racing toward the spellcaster who had done the healing. Unless the shadowfiend was stopped, it would soon spawn more.

A hail of spells smashed into Illidan's defenses but did not overcome them. For mortals, these casters were potent, but he would show them they were no match for the lord of Outland.

Illidan spread his arms wide and summoned fire. A great swath of it blazed all around him, scorching his attackers. One of them screamed and fell, his skin blackened, his eyeballs popping from the heat. Illidan laughed. The sorcerers among his host of enemies frantically redirected their spells to protect themselves.

Illidan sensed a presence behind him, a shadow figure bearing two blades. The poison coating the swords made his nostrils twitch. He turned just as his assailant was about to drive the weapons into his back. With one hand he caught him by the throat. With a word of power, he ignited his foe's flesh with persistent fire and cast him aside to burn down to blackened bones.

An arrow flashed toward Illidan's head. He turned so it glanced off his horn. A gigantic hunting beast bounded right at him. He summoned a wall of shadows that began to drain away the life of the beast and all the attackers close by. Their energy flooded into him, fueling his spells. He blocked another thrust, chopped down his attacker.

Wild joy flowed through his veins. He exulted in every death he caused, feeding on it. Every fallen foe filled him with glee and an urge to scream his triumph to the skies. They had come to slay him, had they? Well, they would find out he did not die so easily.

IN BATTLE THE BETRAYER was awesome. Akama had to admit it. The Broken's allies were among the greatest fighters of Azeroth, and he was aiding them as best he could, but one by one they were going down. Attacking Illidan now was like attacking a wounded rabid wolf. It was clear that he intended to drag as many down into death with him as he could. Worse, his unrelenting savagery might yet lead to his victory. If he triumphed here, he might leave this place and rally the defenders of the Black Temple. Then things would look black indeed for Akama's people.

Where is Maiev? Akama wondered. Her presence at this juncture could turn the whole course of the battle.

"Come, my minions!" Illidan bellowed. "Deal with this traitor as he deserves!"

Akama sensed the approach of reinforcements loyal to the Betrayer. If they should arrive and flank Illidan's attackers . . .

Akama shouted, "I will deal with these mongrels! Strike now, friends! Strike at the Betrayer!"

He turned away from the fight to confront the onrushing sentries. His allies were on their own.

THE MASSIVE FORM OF the sentinel golem loomed over Maiev, reaching out for her with its enormous metal hands. Maiev dispatched the blood elven construct with a blow and glanced around. All through the vast area of the pleasure gardens, she had found signs of conflict. Dead concubines sprawled on the flowering swards, poisoned blades clutched in their hands. The severed limbs and heads of sin'dorei sorcerers lay beside them. Akama and his allies had left a trail of destruction that was easy to follow.

She raced up the stairs. Somewhere above her she sensed titanic energies being unleashed. She recognized them as being wielded by the Betrayer. It looked as if the final battle had started without her. She raced on toward the conflict, praying to Elune that she would not be too late to mete judgment.

THE PALADIN BROUGHT HER gleaming hammer crashing down. It hit the ground in front of Illidan, splintering the stonework. He leapt into the air, wings beating powerfully, and surveyed his attackers. He spread his arms wide and called once more upon the power of flames. A huge fireball blasted down in the midst of his enemies. A warrior raced from the firestorm, burning cloak blazing behind him like the tail of a comet.

Illidan focused his gaze on the ground before him, summoning blue demon fire. A druid rushed into it. It clung to her form, burning her even as she rolled on the floor in an attempt to extinguish the flames.

Lightning bolts smashed up at Illidan from the ground. The air turned cold as one particularly bold wizard attempted to draw on the strength of ice to neutralize his power. Illidan sent a barrage of shadowy bolts raining down on him. The mage howled as they ravaged his flesh.

Now it was time to show these fools the true meaning of power.

He tossed his warglaives to the ground and then called upon the power within them. "I will not be touched by rabble such as you! Behold the flames of Azzinoth."

Twin flame elementals leapt forth in answer to his call. A line of fire linked them. They swarmed toward his attackers, who moved into a defensive circle.

The Betrayer took advantage of this distraction to rest. Beneath him the invaders lashed at his summonings with enchanted weapons and a barrage of spells. Another pair fell before they could overcome the burning elementals.

Illidan marshaled the last of his strength, determined to slay as many of his foes as he could before death had a chance to claim him.

He plunged down amid his attackers, drawing once more upon his fel power. It encased his form, transforming him into something gigantic, demonic, unstoppable. He lashed out with bursts of flame, incinerating his foes, burning flesh and blood and spirit.

A warlock cloaked with spells of protection charged at him, staff raised high. Illidan struck at her, but the wards surrounding the warlock neutralized some of the power of his blow. More and more spells hammered at him. He felt corruption seeded within his flesh. It started to rot. He imbued the shadows surrounding his body with a fragment of his will and then separated them off to bedevil his attackers. He did this again and again as his opponents attacked.

He sent waves of hellish fire sweeping over them. It was getting harder to kill his foes, either because he was weaker than at the start of the fight or because all the easiest enemies to slay were down. The constant hammering of the magical bolts was draining his strength. The enemy attacks reached a crescendo as his foes desperately tried to bring him down.

Then came a moment of calm. He had ridden out the storm. He stood upright, glared at his opponents, and said, "Is this it, mortals? Is this all the fury you can muster?"

A cold, familiar voice echoed across the summit. "Their fury pales before mine, Illidan. We have some unsettled business between us."

Illidan turned his head. An all-too-familiar armored figure stood there, weapon at the ready. At first he wondered if it was an illusion, a specter summoned from the depths of his imagination by some spell. His spectral sight told him otherwise. The figure had weight and mass and presence. He knew that armor well. He knew that blade. He recognized the arrogant superiority of the voice and stance. No doubt about it. Warden Maiev was here.

Rage boiled within him. He struggled to speak. All this time, he had her within his grasp and had not killed her. Now she was here. Memories of his long imprisonment flooded back. "Maiev . . ." How was it even possible?

But he already knew the answer. Akama. He had been responsible for her imprisonment.

Akama's cohorts drew themselves up in a new battle line. They seemed to have gained strength and confidence from Maiev's presence and his discomfiture.

Illidan could almost see the cruel smile curving Maiev's lips beneath her helmet. "Ah, my long hunt is finally over," she said. "Today, justice will be done."

MAIEV LAUNCHED HERSELF FORWARD, blade swirling in her hand. Illidan tried to stop her. Evil shadows clawed at her. Waves of fire swept over her. Yet her armor protected her as she closed the distance. She lashed out at the Betrayer. He parried. They stood for a moment, breast-to-breast, close as lovers. She sensed the blazing fury in him, the pent-up hatred and energy.

She unleashed the spell she had brooded on during her months of imprisonment. The enchantment glittered on the ground before her and she stepped back from it. The Betrayer pounced, activating the spell. Bonds of energy lashed out from the trap, draining power from him. His face twisted as he realized what was happening.

Akama's allies rushed into the fray, weapons bared, spells glittering in the air. Weapons thundered home. Illidan slashed at them, twisting to avoid their blows, countering their spells, but he had lost some of his fury. He stumbled forward into another trap Maiev had unleashed. The Azerothians pursued him as he reeled under the impact of the magic.

Maiev had eyes only for her ancient enemy. She knew, as surely as he did, that this would be their final meeting. One of them was not going to walk away from this. She thought of Anyndra, Sarius, and all the others who had died along the road to this moment. She thought about her own imprisonment. It had sharpened her hunger for justice. Her entire life had been leading up to this.

Maiev's and Illidan's weapons flickered too fast for the eye to follow. Blade parried blade. Ward countered destructive spell. Whatever Illidan threw at her, she neutralized. Victory rode on her every stroke. She was going to win. She could tell from his expression that Illidan understood this, too.

More spells smashed into him. She wanted to tell the others to stop. She wished to defeat him one-on-one, to enjoy a solitary triumph, but it was too late for that. She would have to settle for seeing justice executed.

The ending came suddenly. A flicker of steel and spells blurred the air and her blade bit home, passing through ribs, biting into flesh, seeking the heart that still beat in Illidan's demonically mutated chest.

For a moment, he attempted to strike back. His lips twisted into an arrogant sneer. He looked as if he was about to utter another spell, but then the realization of what happened hit him, along with the pain, and he crumpled to his knees.

ILLIDAN LOOKED UP IN DISBELIEF. His gaze met Maiev's. Her eyes glared down coldly at him. Her stare belonged to a predator that had finally dragged down its prey. There was satisfaction there, and madness, and something else. She had killed him, but she did not realize what she had done.

"It is finished," she said. "You are beaten."

Feeling the pain exploding in his chest, he knew the truth of her words. His time had finally run out. All those long years of study, of fighting, of imprisonment were done. He looked at her and felt a fleeting moment of sympathy for her. She did not understand that it was over for her, too. He forced the words from his lips. "You have won . . . Maiev. But the huntress . . . is nothing without the hunt. You . . . are nothing . . . without me."

Blackness swept over him. Just for a moment he had a vision of a sigil, the same one the naaru had placed on his forehead. It blazed in lines of golden light for an instant, and then the universe went dark.

MAIEV STOOD OVER THE CORPSE of Illidan. Her eyes narrowed as she studied her prey to make sure he was dead.

She was not certain what exactly she was waiting for. The exultation of triumph. The pleasure of a victory long delayed. Nothing came.

His corpse looked merely shabby in death. All the power, all the magnificence, had drained out of it. Here lay just another monster who had proved fodder to her blade. Looking at Illidan's body, she thought, *This is what I spent all the long millennia of my life trying to achieve?* It did not seem to be enough for the expenditure of all those years and all those lives.

She thought about his words. Had there been a spell woven into them, a last curse from the fallen lord of Outland? She inspected the weave of defensive spells around her and found them intact. If Illidan had cursed her, it was with greater subtlety than any mage in history.

No. There was no magic in his words. Only truth. She had dedicated so much of her life to hunting the Betrayer that now she felt lost. She was hollow.

"He is right," she said softly. "I feel nothing. I am nothing." She looked at Akama's allies. Were they responsible for this? Had they robbed her of her triumph by their presence? In a moment of near madness, she considered attacking them, but she pushed the thought from her mind.

"Farewell, champions," she said. She barely glanced at the returning Akama as she swept from the summit.

AKAMA WATCHED MAIEV LEAVE. The Broken had driven off the Betrayer's reinforcements to give his allies time to slay Illidan, and slay him they had, with the help of the mighty night elf. He would have liked to thank her, but he was relieved she was gone. There was no telling what one so violent, impulsive, and powerful would do under these circumstances. She had reason to hate him. He was glad she had not tried to take vengeance on him as well.

Akama looked down on the body of his former master. It looked smaller now, and when he bent to lift it, it felt lighter than that of a child, as if all weight had left it with the spirit of its owner. There was still a mystery here. Where were the demon hunters? Why had they not entered the fray? He had sensed the portal Illidan had opened. If they had gone through it, where did it lead? Had they really gone to Argus? He pushed the thoughts aside. These were problems for another day. Now he must deal with the consequences of victory.

The summit looked as if demons had made war in it. Stone had melted and flowed like lava. Patches of shadow clung where no shadow should have been.

This place would need to be purified, he thought. Shrines would need to be built, services for the fallen to be held. There was a lot of work to be done here. But his people could do it. They were whole once more, and together there was nothing they could not achieve.

"The Light will fill these dismal halls once again," he said. "I swear it."

Then he turned and limped away from where the lord of Outland had fallen.

VANDEL WOKE, IF IT could be called waking. His arm was scarred where Maiev's blade had bit into it. His wounds had knit together, but he felt weak. His skull ached from a huge gash.

Glancing around, he saw that the training grounds were full of Aldor and Scryer fighters. They chanted victory songs, swigged from one another's canteens, slapped one another on the back. All the rivalries between the two factions seemed to be forgotten.

Among the soldiers were the Ashtongue. There was a new confidence about the Broken. They moved with purpose, not listlessness. They eyed their surroundings with the air of owners who had newly come into their heritage.

Vandel tested his limbs. They still worked. He crawled into a patch of shadow and willed himself invisible.

"The Betrayer is dead!" shouted a blood elf triumphantly. The announcement was greeted with cheers. He could hear them echo around the vast courtyard where once the Dragonmaw had gathered their mighty steeds and demons sworn to the service of Illidan had walked.

Could it be true? Looking at the aftermath of the carnage, Vandel could not see how it could not be. He thought about the threat of the Burning Legion. What would happen now that the only leader who had ever understood its true magnitude was gone? Where were Vandel's fellows?

He reached out with his senses, stretching them to the limits as he tried to find another demon hunter. They were all vanished, as if they had never been. Could they all be dead? Was he the last? Was Illidan's great war finished before it had even begun?

Black despair swept over him. In the midst of the songs of triumph, he felt like weeping. These would-be heroes had no understanding of the damage they had done.

All was lost. There was nothing more to do here. He could throw himself into their midst, striking right and left until he was cut down for certain this time. He looked at the amulet he had made for Khariel so long ago. There would be no vengeance. He rose to attack, drew on the fel energies that would let him slay and slay.

Then he heard it, Illidan's familiar voice, a whisper so faint that it might have come from the far edge of the universe or the other side of death, or from the deepest recesses of his memory.

You must be prepared.

He paused for a moment, restraining the urge to violence. The voice sounded too real to be a mere memory. It was as if the Betrayer was speaking to him as when he had summoned him for the final time. Was it possible that some remnant of his spirit survived?

There would be time to think about such things later. Now there was still work to be done. Demons to be slain. Revenge to be taken. Perhaps he could pass on the message, train others, try to be ready for the final days, when the Burning Legion reappeared seeking ultimate victory.

He drew upon his demon's energies, stepped deeper into shadow, and vanished into the night.

NOTES

The story you've just read is based in part on characters, situations, and locations from Blizzard Entertainment's computer game *World of Warcraft,* an online role-playing experience set in the award-winning Warcraft universe. In *World of Warcraft,* players create their own heroes and explore, adventure in, and quest across a vast world shared with thousands of other players. This rich and evolving game also allows them to interact with and fight against (or alongside) many of the powerful and intriguing characters featured in this novel.

Since launching in November 2004, *World of Warcraft* has become the world's most popular subscription-based massively multiplayer online role-playing game. The upcoming expansion, *Legion,* will show what happens next to Maiev and the Illidari demon hunters as they battle the Burning Legion's latest invasion of Azeroth. More information about *Legion* and the current expansion, *Warlords of Draenor,* can be found on WorldofWarcraft.com.

WILLIAM KING is the author of more than twenty novels, an Origins Award–winning game designer, and a husband, father, and player of MMOs. His short stories have appeared in *Interzone* and *Year's Best SF*. His Warhammer books have sold almost a million copies in English and been translated into eight languages. His novel *Blood of Aenarion* was shortlisted for the 2012 David Gemmell Legend Award.

A B O U T   T H E   T Y P E

This book was set in Bembo, a typeface based on an old-style Roman face that was used for Cardinal Pietro Bembo's tract *De Aetna* in 1495. Bembo was cut by Francesco Griffo (1450–1518) in the early sixteenth century for Italian Renaissance printer and publisher Aldus Manutius (1449–1515). The Lanston Monotype Company of Philadelphia brought the well-proportioned letterforms of Bembo to the United States in the 1930s.